THE
TRAITOR'S
GAME

JENNIFER A. NIELSEN

THE TRAITOR'S GAME

• BOOK ONE •

Library of Congress Cataloging-in-Publication Data

Names: Nielsen, Jennifer A., author.
Title: The traitor's game / Jennifer A. Nielsen.
Description: First edition. | New York : Scholastic Press, 2018. | Summary:
After three years in exile Kestra Dallisor has been summoned back to Antora by
her father, right-hand man of the seemingly immortal king, Lord Endrick, but she
is intercepted and kidnapped by the Coracks who want to use her to get the Olden
Blade, which they believe can be used to kill the despot—Simon, one of the rebels
with his own grudge against the Dallisors, is assigned to accompany her, but
Kestra has her own plans and she does not intend to let anyone get in her way.
Identifiers: LCCN 2017020257 | ISBN 9781338045376
Subjects: LCSH: Weapons—Juvenile fiction. | Conspiracies—Juvenile fiction. |
Kidnapping—Juvenile fiction. | Friendship—Juvenile fiction. | Adventure stories.
| CYAC: Weapons—Fiction. | Conspiracies—Fiction. | Kidnapping—Fiction. |
Friendship—Fiction. | Adventure and adventurers—Fiction. | GSAFD:
Adventure fiction. | LCGFT: Action and adventure fiction.
Classification: LCC PZ7.N5672 Tr 2018 | DDC 813.6 [Fic] —dc23
LC record available at https://lccn.loc.gov/2017020257

10 9 8 7 6 5 4 3 2 1   18 19 20 21 22

Printed in the U.S.A.   23
First edition, March 2018

Book design by Christopher Stengel

To Jeff,
Every dream for my life includes you.

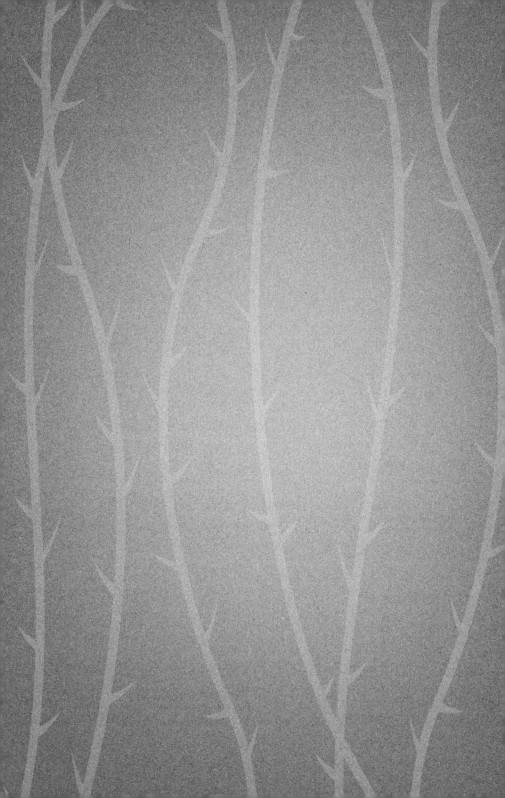

In a traitor's game, there are no winners.

Only those left standing at the end.

Cheat or be cheated.

Crush or be crushed.

Play . . . or be killed.

The next move is mine.

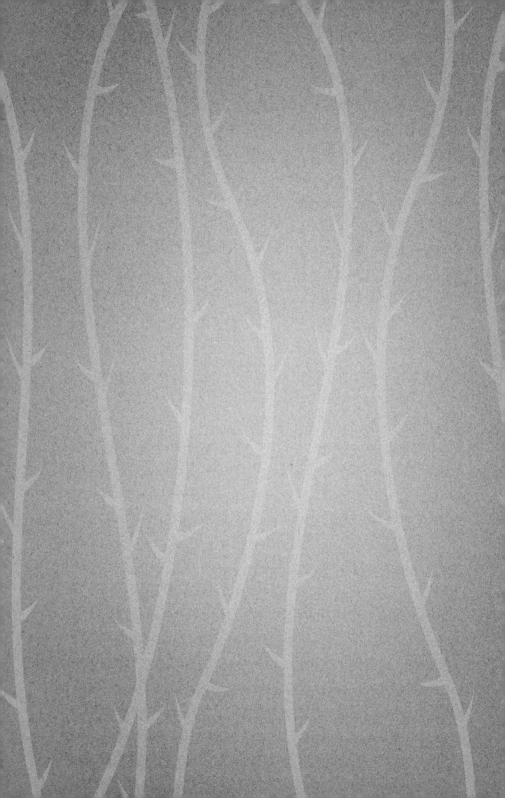

· ONE ·

KESTRA

The truth of where I'd been for the past three years wasn't
what anyone believed.

It wasn't exile, as my father claimed. The Lava
Fields were barren and unforgiving, and charming in the way that
discovering a thorn with one's bare foot might be charming. But I'd
gladly choose to live there before sacrificing my happiness for my
father's political demands.

Nor was I hiding, as most people in my country suspected.
While it was true that I'd been sent to the Fields on the same day I
escaped a kidnapping, I had Darrow to protect me now. Thanks to
him, I was stronger than before.

And I wasn't away learning to become a proper young lady. If
anything, the opposite was true. My handmaiden, Celia, had tried
her best, encouraging me to put down the swords and disk bows
Darrow liked to train me with and pick up a hairbrush or sewing
needle instead. But so far, I'd done more damage to my fingers with
the needles than had ever been done to me by the edge of a blade.

The truth about the Lava Fields was that very few people knew
my whereabouts, making it the first place I'd ever felt truly free. Free
to explore the knifelike maze of sharp, black rocks. Free to sit in the

stone cottage near Unknown Lake and eat at the rickety wooden table with Darrow, Cook, and Celia. Free to run and sing and let my hair tangle in the wind.

Free, that is, until last night, when a garrison of six Dominion soldiers had unexpectedly arrived with a summons from my father to return home to Woodcourt.

Why? Nothing on my end had changed, and he would certainly never back down. Yet here I was tonight, boxed inside a cramped security carriage, unable to block out the incessant noise of gravel grinding beneath our track wheels. I felt trapped.

No, I *was* trapped, a thought that choked my breath. Everything had been fine in the Lava Fields. Aside from the occasional rumblings of an ancient volcano and a relentless odor of sulfur, we'd enjoyed a simple life there, one with few rules and even fewer people to tell me how I'd disappointed them that day. Why should I have to go home?

"Are you all right, Kestra? You look worried." Sitting across from me in the carriage, Celia had spent the past hour knotting and unknotting her fingers. She was nervous, which was no great surprise. So was I. My first meeting with my father in three years could end poorly.

Celia was a wisp of cloud, a crocus flower in bloom, far too delicate for a life in my service. Her hair was much lighter than mine, and naturally curly, which gave me a fierce amount of jealousy, though because I belonged to the Dallisor family, I could never admit to feeling inferior.

"I'm fine," I told Celia. "I just want this ride to end." How long had we been stuck inside this carriage? Hours at least, though it wouldn't surprise me if the world had shifted into a new century since we'd left the cottage. Cook was probably an old woman by now. Or an *older* woman.

"Another hour, and we'll reach the inn." Celia seemed to believe if she always spoke with patience, the trait would inevitably rub off on me. I doubted that.

To her credit, although she was only two years older, Celia had been patient with me for a year, a record for any lady in my service. My former lady-in-waiting, Ibbi, had lasted less than three months. Ibbi had been prone to "frantic episodes" that Darrow insisted were brought on by the suffocating Lava Fields, and not by my difficult behavior. I rather doubted that too. Her last episode came on after I stitched her into her bed one night as she slept. It wasn't my fault. I was bored.

That was nothing compared to my boredom now, and an aching restlessness to escape this coffin on wheels. As a protection against attacks, security carriages had metal sides, a single narrow window with thick glass, and steel track wheels that could crush anything in its path, preferably the attacker. A clearstone hung in one corner of our carriage, though if I warmed it with my hands to freshen the glow, I'd only be reminded again of how tight our space was.

This carriage was also a symbol for what my life might become now. Maybe everything I knew and wanted—everything I *was*— would soon be compacted into some safe, proper world.

Unbearable.

Darrow would understand.

With a grin my poor handmaiden had too often seen before, I sat forward, unbolted the door, and reached for the handle.

"My lady, the carriage is moving." No details escaped Celia's sharp attention.

"Then I'd better not fall." I pushed open the heavy metal door and a crisp evening wind awakened my senses. It smelled like rain, though the dirt road beneath us was dry. A half-moon did little to cut through the dark night, but tall trees lined the road, and I thought I heard a river nearby. That could put us practically anywhere between the edge of the Lava Fields and the outskirts of Highwyn.

Celia put a hand on my arm. "The garrison won't like this—"

"Well, I don't like them either." The garrison served Endrick, our Lord of the Dominion, because even the title of king was not grand enough for him. Part of service to Lord Endrick required that a piece of the soldier's heart be replaced with a magical ball of iron that Endrick could control when necessary. Hence our nickname for them: Ironhearts. Never a compliment.

Before Celia could protest again, which she undoubtedly would, I found a solid grip on the carriage frame and put a foot on the step.

"Darrow!" I called up toward the driver's box.

Darrow was almost thirty years my senior, but had the energy and spirit of a person half his age. He had dark hair that was rarely combed, a beard always in need of a trim, and, I believed, an infatuation with Cook. It wasn't fair that she had been dismissed upon my leaving the Lava Fields.

He shook his head when he saw me. "You're in a security carriage for a reason, Kestra!"

"I'm not in it now for other reasons. Give me a hand up!"

He chuckled, then shifted the reins into one hand and scooted across the bench toward me. "You have to get higher than the wheels, or you'll be caught in them."

Darrow used to discourage me from such risky behaviors, but as soon as he understood I was going to do them anyway, he'd changed tactics. Now he taught me how to survive the risks I took.

I checked my grip on the rail, then took my first step forward, blinking hard against the brisk evening air. This wasn't a good idea. Which was the very reason to do it. If nothing else, it might be my only chance to study Lord Endrick's newest creation up close: the oropod. These creatures pulling my carriage fascinated me. Oropods were slightly larger than horses but had the muscle structure of a snowy lizard, with leathery, green-patterned skin and two powerful hind legs. Before we left the Fields, the garrison leader had explained how their front claws could be used for fighting or climbing, and showed us their fanged teeth. I'd asked to ride one back in the Fields, just to see if I could, but was told that an oropod had to know its rider's scent, or it'd eat the rider. Hence the reason Lord Endrick was fond of them.

Celia opened the carriage window. "This is reckless, my lady. If your father finds even a scratch on you, he'll kill me."

I glanced back, expecting to laugh off her comment. But Celia sounded upset, and for good reason.

I was thirteen when I'd been sent from my father's home, still young enough to excuse his flaws as my own failures of understanding. I'd been young enough then to love him despite his coldness, and to pretend that he cared for me too. After three years, I wondered if any love remained in his heart at all. It was still beating, so there had to be some humanity left. Yet it would take a special talent for cruelty to become the chief counsel to Lord Endrick. I couldn't imagine the terrible things my father must have done in Endrick's name.

After one more plea from Celia, I called to Darrow that I'd go back inside the carriage after all. It meant delaying our talk, but I couldn't risk her getting into trouble because of me.

Before I took my first step, a *whoosh* came from the woods on both sides of the road. At first I thought it must be a swarm of bats flying from behind the trees, but then I heard the cries from the garrison. These were disks, dozens of them.

"Get back inside!" Darrow yelled as he pulled up on the reins.

Four Dominion soldiers were leading our carriage. Three of these men were immediately cut down by the disks' sharp edges, and the fourth didn't get far before he was hit too. The two riders behind our carriage shouted for me to duck, but I was too terrified to move. Seconds later, they were struck as well, tumbling off the backs of their oropods.

Fear flooded into me, so forcefully I couldn't hold my thoughts together.

My garrison was dead. All of them. Dead, and in mere seconds. Who could have done this? And why?

"Kestra, get down!" Darrow ordered.

This time, I obeyed, bending my knees low, my hands clinging to the frame of the carriage. Darrow steered sharply around the riderless oropods, so I couldn't open the heavy door, but if another disk attack came, I'd be vulnerable. Two oropods still pulled our carriage. If they fell, we'd be trapped here.

Trapped by whom?

The clan of the Banished, who'd kidnapped me three years ago, were enemies of my family and had been exiled from the Dominion. After four days in their captivity, during which they'd somehow failed to kill me, Darrow had come to my rescue, and remained in my service ever since, in case the Banished returned.

Except this didn't feel like the Banished. They weren't known for precision attacks.

The Coracks were. This thought chilled me to my bones.

The reason *why* I'd been missing for three years didn't matter. What did matter was that no one was supposed to know *where* I'd been, or that I was headed home tonight.

But whoever was hiding in the woods knew. And whatever they wanted with me, they were obviously willing to kill to get it.

I was in serious trouble.

· TWO ·

KESTRA

Darrow had been hurrying our carriage forward, but now it slowed. Not a good sign. I peeked out from the side of the carriage, as much as I dared. On the road far ahead were several riders on horseback, their faces shadowed against the rising moonlight. Whoever they were, we were heavily outnumbered.

My hands shook, but I tried to steady them. I could do this. I had to do this. Tucked into a garter around my thigh was a knife, which was there for this very reason. Celia was useless with a blade, but Darrow was well armed, and I could do my share of damage. It would have to be enough.

Darrow checked my position again. "I'll steer the carriage sideways and slow it for you to jump."

"What about Celia—"

"It's the Coracks. They're here for you."

I cursed, something that in ordinary circumstances would make Darrow laugh, and would've made my father collapse a lung. But if ever there were a proper time for a curse word, this was it.

The battle for control of Antora raged between two bloodlines: the Dallisor family and the Halderian clan, now generally known as the Banished. Until the most recent war, the Dallisors had become numerous, powerful, and occupied the throne more often than not. Now we were simply powerful. All Dallisors served Lord Endrick, with my father at their head, and together with our armies and all those loyal to Endrick, we were known as the Dominion. What we lacked in love from the citizenry was compensated by our demands for respect and the fact that the Dominion was never going away. At least, not because of the Banished. Since the war, their clan was far too weak and scattered to mount any significant challenge.

But the Corack rebels were a significant worry. These common citizens resented the Dominion, and were tired of waiting for the Banished to organize again. In seven years of the Corack rebellion's existence, the Dominion had failed to wipe out their numbers. The Coracks were ripping apart our country from within. I couldn't help but wonder if they had similar plans for me.

"Kestra, it's time to run!" Darrow hissed.

A flash of terror sliced through my heart. Darrow had taught me what to do in circumstances like this—I knew he had, and yet all of that vanished from my mind. A part of me still felt like that weak girl from three years ago, the one who'd cowered in fear, waiting to be killed.

No, I knew what to do. *Jump. Hide. Run and don't look back.* That's what Darrow wanted.

"Go, Kestra. Now!" Darrow's urgent tone forced me into motion.

I leapt to the ground, attempting to roll with the fall. My shoulder slammed hard against the dirt, and my knee skidded into a rock. But I hurried to my feet, stayed low, and bolted for the side of the road. It was a short run to the nearest stand of trees, but I could make it.

Almost immediately, a voice shouted out for Darrow to stop, which he did. Celia had closed the carriage door, but I pictured her huddled into a corner of one seat, frozen with fear. Darrow held his hands in the air.

He said, "We haven't got much money, but you're welcome to it."

A voice called back, "We don't want money tonight. Coracks only steal what we need." A beat passed. "Or who we want."

Run.

The word screamed into my brain, somehow becoming louder than the pounding of my heart, or the pulse in my ears. With a little cleverness, I could evade the rebels inside the thick woods just off the road. But what would happen to Darrow and Celia after I ran? I'd heard plenty about Corack brutality, of their willingness to kill. Could I abandon my servants if I was the intended target?

I lifted my skirt enough to withdraw the knife, then stayed low while I crept to a better vantage point. In the moonlight, eight horses were visible, though some of their riders were standing on the road with disk bows in their hands. Theirs were larger than those of the Dominion, designed to fire horizontally, unlike our vertical bows. Moreover, their disks slid automatically from a pocket directly onto the string, which explained how relatively few rebels had launched such a comprehensive attack.

"Everyone inside the carriage, come out!" I couldn't see the man who was shouting, except to note that he was still astride his horse in the center of the road.

Celia didn't have to obey. If she sealed the window and bolted the door, they'd have a hard time getting her out.

But the carriage door opened anyway, and Celia emerged with her hands raised. "Please don't hurt me. I'm alone now."

Now? I could have groaned out loud. Celia had served me well, but not always with the full function of her brain.

A girl in riding crops and a fitted tunic dismounted and grabbed Celia, pulling her forward and forcing her to her knees directly in front of the oropods. Under my breath, I swore again. They didn't know her scent. If she was too close, they might try to bite her.

They didn't know the scent of the Coracks either. If I could release them from their harnesses, how much damage could they do? But what about Celia?

A second rebel made a quick search of the carriage, commenting on the value its metal frame would offer the Coracks if they kept it. A third opened my trunk and tossed out the clothes packed inside. Because that would've been a brilliant place to hide someone, apparently—smothered in a sealed iron trunk between layers of clothes.

"She must have jumped out," the man on the horse shouted. "Everyone, start searching!" He raised his voice further. "For your own sake, Kestra Dallisor, surrender!"

They knew my name? I'd spent the past three years wondering if my father remembered it, but the rebels clearly did. Why me? There were other Dallisor families they might have targeted, other daughters who surely had more value to the Dominion. My life could not possibly matter to a Corack.

Another reason to worry.

As the rebels spread out to search, I tucked myself between two beech trees, hoping their thick branches would shield me from the moonlight. The knife was firm in my grip, ready. Willing.

Two Coracks passed by me, so close that I caught a whiff of their rebel stink. One was a man about Darrow's age with unnaturally white hair and, in his right hand, a lever blade longer than my arm. These weapons were illegal for all but Dominion soldiers. Its bearer would stab the victim, then click a lever to spread apart two halves of the blade. I couldn't imagine the pain it caused before death.

Following distantly behind him was the second man, a little younger, but much shorter and with half the build. He moved with halting steps, every crack of a twig beneath his feet requiring a pause to catch his breath. He was my target.

As soon as he passed me, I stepped out from the trees and grabbed one arm, then held the knife against his shoulder, pressing downward.

"Let us go!" I shouted. "Or I will kill your man!"

"There you are, my lady." The man speaking for the Coracks dipped his head at me. "I believe your problem is that you have only one of my people to kill, and I have two of yours. Do the math."

Darrow had a bow hidden near his feet with a black disk already loaded against the string. He used the distraction to slowly reach for it, but before he could straighten up, a rebel's silver disk sliced Darrow deep across his gut. He crumpled and fell to the ground, blood spilling from his wound.

I screamed and stabbed the man in my grip, though my aim hadn't been as lethal as I'd wanted. I ran forward, determined to go down fighting if they attacked me too. Then Darrow's suffering cry echoed in the darkness and I stopped. We had cauterizing powder in the carriage. I had a chance to save Darrow, and to rescue Celia. But not by fighting.

"Drop that knife!" someone yelled at me. "Or we will kill this one too!" He held a blade near Celia's throat. The whites of her eyes had widened with horror.

"Release her, and let me save my driver," I countered. "Then I will drop the knife!"

Someone grabbed me from behind, and a blade pressed against my neck. "No," a voice hissed. "You're no longer giving the orders, Princess. Drop your knife."

It was enough effort just to keep myself standing. For three years in the Lava Fields, I had longed for more adventure, for any excitement beyond what Cook made for dinner or what Celia bought at market. Now that I had it, all I wanted was to return to that place and be forgotten once more.

I dropped the knife and closed my eyes.

Three years of Darrow's training, and a missed opportunity to escape. This was my own fault. I had just become a captive of the Corack rebellion.

· THREE ·

KESTRA

Corack was the name of a weed that grew plentifully throughout Antora. It was brambly and dense and nearly impossible to get rid of except by fire. Thus the reason the rebels had adopted the name.

They are weeds, I told myself as the rebel at my back pushed me toward the man on the horse, the obvious leader. *He's only a weed.*

"Get her on her knees," the leader ordered.

"No!" I shouted. "First you must help my driver, Darrow. There's some cauterizing powder inside the carriage. If he dies, you might as well kill me too, because I won't cooperate." Darrow was somewhere behind me in the darkness, groaning with pain. I couldn't bear to hear it.

"We also have your other servant, the girl." The leader leaned forward in his saddle. "Does she matter?"

"Please do what I ask." I'd beg if he required that of me. "Darrow will die if you don't help him."

With a flick of the leader's head, a girl with dark hair ducked inside my carriage and came out a minute later with the sack of powder. I wasn't sure if she'd know how to use it. The powder was only available to loyalists to the Dominion. As soon as she knelt beside

Darrow to begin attending to the wound, the leader dismounted. He was shorter than most of the men around him and of lean build, but every part of him exuded strength. He must have lost his right leg below the knee at some point, because it was now replaced with a gold-toned mechanical leg fitted with gears and tubes for fluid movement. With keen eyes, a closely trimmed graying beard, and faded scars on his neck and across one cheek, it was clear this man was not to be toyed with.

The rebel standing at my rear pinned my arms behind my back, forcing me to hunch over a little. I still stood as tall as I could, hoping to intimidate these people, and knowing it likely wouldn't work.

"My name is Captain Grey Tenger. I am the leader of the Coracks." His voice was calm, dispassionate. It gave me little to work with. "And you are Kestra Dallisor."

"If you want a ransom, I'm the worst possible target. My father would pay more for you to keep me away." That's exactly what he'd already done to my servants in the Lava Fields. Paid them to keep me as far from home as possible.

"We're not here for a ransom," Tenger said. "But it's helpful to know that you and your father are not on the best of terms."

That was an understatement. "Anything you want from me, your threats to Darrow are enough to get it. There's no need to hold my handmaiden too."

"Everyone you care about is useful to me." Tenger took a lock of my hair that had come loose and raised his knife, slicing off the end of it.

"Troll," I breathed out.

"Murderer," he replied.

"I'm nothing of the sort, you foul-smelling pig!"

"Just like a Dallisor. Always wanting the last word." He tucked the lock of my hair into a pocket of his vest. "We know the kind of person you are, my lady. We're not stupid."

I smirked. "Aren't you? If Lord Endrick was eager to mop the earth with your blood before, what will he do if you kill the daughter of a Dallisor?"

He gestured to his golden leg. "Probably finish what the Dominion started here." If that was supposed to be humor, it was crass, and his smile was wolfish. "Besides, Lord Endrick won't know this conversation has happened, not until it's too late." When I remained silent, he added, "Your father is Henry Dallisor, enforcer of Dominion crimes, murderer of innocents, and chief footstool for the tyrant, Lord Endrick."

"Don't you say another word about my father!" I could think whatever I wanted about him, but I'd defend him to his enemies with my final breath.

However, I couldn't, and wouldn't, defend Lord Endrick. The darkness surrounding him was tangible, and terrible. Endrick had taken power shortly before my birth and to do so, he had all but destroyed the Banished and everyone who stood with them. The Scarlet Throne of Antora, once a symbol of honor and nobility, had become the blood throne of Lord Endrick, who wielded an iron fist against anyone who defied him. Most Antorans believed he was immortal, or close to it. To serve such a man, my father had to prove himself equally strong. He did not tolerate weakness in his servants.

Or his daughter. I had to be strong, now more than ever before.

Celia was still on her knees near me. The oropod closest to her was craning its leathery green head toward her scent, but if she remained in place, she'd be safe. Farther off, the Coracks were preparing to carry Darrow away. A silver line had raised along his wound, so at least they had figured out how to use the powder. But if these rebels weren't careful, the wound would tear again.

"Let me talk to my driver," I begged. "Please."

Tenger gestured his permission and I quickly ran to Darrow's side, kneeling beside him on the cold ground. I touched my hand to his cheek, brushing away the dirt that was bound to the skin with his sweat and tears. Panic began to overtake me. What if he died? There was so much more blood than I'd thought.

"You're going to be all right." He'd know I was only saying that to make him feel better, but maybe I needed to hear the lie more than he did.

"I'm fine." He drew in a sharp gasp. "It's not as bad as it looks."

Now he was lying. I didn't know what to do. Fear swelled in my chest, choking off my breathing.

He touched my arm. "Listen to me. You will get through this, Kestra. Be smart. Be strong."

"No, I can't—"

"They'll say terrible things about you. Don't listen. And whatever they want . . . do not help them."

Tears filled my eyes, blurring Darrow in my vision, which was the last thing I wanted. I needed to see his face, needed to remember him more clearly than this. "If I don't, they'll kill you and Celia!"

"A small price . . . to save Antora." His breaths were shallow and obviously came with great pain. "I loved you as Henry Dallisor should have done. I'm so sorry . . ." His consciousness was fading, which terrified me, and though his chest still rose and fell, I felt his life fading too. He tried to continue, but the rebel who had held me before pulled me back to my feet with an unforgiving grip. Or, rather, it was a grip I would never forgive. What if Darrow died? What if that was my last moment with him and these monsters couldn't even let him finish his sentence?

To the men surrounding Darrow, Tenger said, "Put him in the back of our wagon. Take her servant girl too."

"Kestra!" Celia cried out as the rebels took her by the arms and pulled her deeper into the darkness. "Kestra, help me!"

I opened my mouth to respond, but nothing came out. Within seconds, they had dragged Celia from my sight, though I still heard her muffled sobs, each cry ripping at my heart. Darrow was lifted by his legs and arms, a cruel way to treat a man with injuries such as his. They didn't care. They had me alone now.

Tenger said to the rebel behind me, "Simon, search her for any weapons, and hurry."

"No!" I tried wrenching free, but this rebel—Simon—and his knife were uncompromising. "How dare you do this?"

"How dare I?" Tenger pointed at the man whom I had stabbed. The girl who had treated Darrow was using the last of the cauterizing powder on his wound. *My* powder, which should have been saved in case Darrow needed more. "That's my man, Pell, and until you put a knife in his shoulder, he was a vital part of tonight's plan. You're no better than we are, my lady. Search her."

Simon ordered me to turn around and face him. When I did, I was surprised to find that he wasn't much older than me, maybe seventeen or eighteen. His hair was a darker shade of brown than mine, and closely cropped on the sides, but longer on top with a fringe of hair near his forehead that I suspected was often out of place. If he were a higher form of life than a Corack, his strong, square jawline might have been considered attractive. His brown eyes were striking, with thick lashes that gave them prominence, I'd give him that much. Something was familiar about those eyes, though I couldn't place the memory. But I would, eventually.

He raised a hand, clearly hesitant to conduct the search, and I made certain to glare directly at him, hoping to shame him. He started where it was easiest, with a leather band around my wrist that crossed the back of my hand with cording, and was held in place by rings on three of my fingers.

"What's this?" he asked.

"Jewelry, nothing more." Since that was one of the larger lies I would probably have to tell tonight, I had to be convincing. This glove had been a gift from Darrow when he was first teaching me to use a sword. It had been his own glove before that, though he'd never explained how he had come to possess one. Grip gloves were rare, powered through the grace of Lord Endrick's magic, and considered valuable since wearing it gave its bearer extra strength in the hand. I hoped Simon didn't know that.

He grunted. "Only a Dallisor would consider a grip glove an item of jewelry."

So he did know. I cursed under my breath while he pulled the lacing, loosening the glove and then removing it from my wrist. He passed it to Tenger, who immediately began fastening it on his own hand.

Simon continued with my hair, possibly checking for hidden

pins that might be sharpened to a fine point. I had none, but once this was over, I planned to have some made. Next, he pushed back my cloak, his rough hands grazing my skin. In this dress, my shoulders were bare except for two straps of my shift. He ignored them, instead running hands down my sleeves. He also avoided my back and sides. The tight fabric of my corset would make hiding a weapon nearly impossible.

"Enjoying this?" My tone was as bitter as I felt.

"I'd rather search a bear."

"I wish you would. If I'd known this was coming, I'd have brought one along."

"But you didn't know, because we outsmarted you." For the first time, he looked directly at me. His smile was triumphant. Arrogant. It wouldn't look that way during his execution. He pointed to my boots. "Remove them."

"You do it." All the easier to kick him if he got into the right position.

And that's when the memory nagged at me again. There had been a Simon years ago, when I was a child. That boy lived at Woodcourt as a servant, and had been one of the rare children near my own age I ever saw. We hadn't been friends, my father never would have allowed that. But we were . . . something like friends. It didn't matter anyway. This couldn't be that scraggly boy. That was impossible. Wasn't it?

He frowned and knelt before me, unlacing each boot until he could fit his fingers inside to check for any weapons. I clenched my jaw, determined to endure this last part with some shred of dignity. He reached up over the top of my skirts to feel for my legs, running his hands down the left first, and then the right. On my right thigh, he paused.

"What's that?"

"It's not a weapon."

"But it could hold one. Give it to me."

"That's indecent."

"You can fetch it, or I will. Your choice, Princess."

My choice? Like, did I prefer to die by hanging or beheading? Did I prefer the taste of hemlock or mandrake? Were my feelings about Coracks closer to loathing or hatred?

I turned away from the rebels, lifting my skirts only as much as was necessary to roll the garter down my leg and over my boot. I handed it to Simon with a glare that could have melted iron. I was still afraid—it'd be foolish not to be—but I was far more angry.

Simon stood and passed the garter to Tenger with a report that I had no weapons with me. Maybe I didn't now, but I'd get one as soon as possible.

And when I did, I already knew my first target.

The boy my father had somehow failed to kill when he'd had the chance.

· F O U R ·

———

KESTRA

Satisfied that I was unarmed, Tenger put my garter in his vest pocket, then gestured toward my carriage. "Perhaps you and I can continue this conversation in private."

Alone? My stomach twisted. "I won't go in there with you."

"You will, my lady."

Simon took my arm, but I twisted against his grip and got one hand free, which I used to swing at his face. I sideswiped his jaw, an indirect hit that didn't do nearly as much damage as I'd hoped. In the process, I tripped over my unlaced boots and fell to the ground, causing every rebel in the group to burst out with laughter.

Feeling the heat of embarrassment, I kept my head down and started to lace up my right boot. Simon was ordered beside me to lace up the left.

"Do you know me?" I asked him.

Without offering a shred of recognition, he returned the question. "Do you know *me*?"

"Simon . . ." His full name clicked into my mind. "Hatch." He looked up, startled. "You're supposed to be dead. My father ordered your hanging."

"Your father ordered an eleven-year-old boy to be hanged." He made no effort to hide his bitterness. "I was eleven. Let that sink in, Princess."

I was no princess, and he knew it. If he meant to demean me with such a word, it was unnecessary. I was already humiliated enough.

Once my boots were laced, Simon offered me a hand up but I refused it, testing to see what would happen if I ignored their orders.

"You'll walk to the carriage, or I'll drag you there," he said. "I don't care which it is."

I looked again for Celia and Darrow, but both had been removed from my sight. To Tenger, I said, "Guarantee my servants' lives."

He casually waved off that demand. "We'll treat your driver's wound, or dump him by the side of the road, as we please. If you resist, your maid will be next to suffer. Do not try to trick us."

I wouldn't *try* to trick them, I had to succeed at it. But not enough to endanger Celia's and Darrow's lives. I got to my feet, then we walked past the area where Darrow had fallen. The cloying scent of his blood overpowered me and I retched.

I should've run before. If I had, maybe they'd have left Darrow and Celia alone and only gone after me.

Or maybe they'd have killed them both first. My servants were alive and needed to remain that way. I had to remember that.

Tenger entered my carriage first, then offered a hand to help me inside. I brushed it aside and climbed in on my own. Simon began to close the door behind us, but Tenger said, "No, I want you in here."

Simon groaned softly, then climbed in after me. I took a seat opposite Tenger, who was in the center of his bench, the same spots Celia and I had occupied only minutes ago. Simon sat beside me, gripping my arm again.

I shook it free. "Where will I run in here, you imbecile?"

Meanwhile, Tenger brushed his hands over the clearstone, warming the gem enough to raise its light. The clearstone's glow did little more than set his and Simon's faces into sharp, menacing shadows. I took the opposite tack, giving the impression of the least threatening girl in Antora, slouching so low in my seat that every governess from my past would have simultaneously shuddered in horror. But underplaying the moment would be Darrow's recommendation.

Tenger clasped his hands together. I hoped that with the grip glove on, he'd accidentally squeeze his left hand off. No such luck there. Instead, he leaned forward, resting his elbows on his legs. "It's been three years since you were in Highwyn. Why were you sent away?"

My mouth opened, long enough to consider hurling an insult at him. But in the end, I figured that even if it made me feel better, it wouldn't improve my situation.

"Surely you know," I said. "I was kidnapped by the Banished."

"They are the Halderians."

My jaw tightened. "They are the Banished. They lost the war and lost the right to their name."

"You will refer to them as Halderians or I will have your heart banished from your chest."

"I'd prefer to keep my heart where it is, thanks." I drew in a slow breath to cool my temper, then said, "After escaping from the *Halderians*, I was sent away for my own protection."

In appearance, there was little to distinguish the Halderian clan from my family, or from other Antorans, though Darrow used to claim he could "just tell." Most Dallisors believed the Halderians were soft and feckless. The Halderians accused my family of brutality and paranoia. I figured the truth was somewhere in the middle. The Dallisors were cruel because Lord Endrick required it. And the Halderians were hardly weak. I knew that firsthand.

My kidnapping was their first major strike against the Dallisors since the War of Devastation, so called because of its utter brutality. Months into the war, the Halderians, led by King Gareth, seemed certain to win. As a final effort to reclaim the throne, the Dallisors chose the unthinkable, to unite with the Endreans, a people who'd rarely emerged from the Watchman Mountains before then. The Endreans were few in number but had something that would change the course of the war: magic. Most powerful among them was Endrick, who, unbeknownst to everyone, planned to do more than help the Dallisors win the war. By the time the war ended, he intended to rule all of Antora, my family included. Once the Endreans joined the fight, the Halderians were crushed, their King Gareth disappeared, and his few surviving subjects were scattered across the land or lived in exile in the farthest reaches of Antora, hence their name, the Banished. To be a Halderian now was a death sentence. Or, at least, that was the price paid by those who had kidnapped me three years ago. My father made sure of that.

"Why did they target you?" Tenger's question was an absurd waste of time.

And it deserved an equally ridiculous answer. "The pleasure of my company. I'm a lot of fun at parties."

"No doubt." Tenger's smile reeked of insincerity. Or maybe Tenger just reeked. "Perhaps that's why we're here as well."

"It's after the party that people regret kidnapping me. Forty Halderians were executed for the crime."

"Forty *people* were executed," Simon said. "Some of them were Halderians, some were rebels or rebel sympathizers. Some were innocent citizens who happened to be in the wrong place at the wrong time."

"There were no innocents," I insisted. "That's a Corack lie."

"How do you know?"

"My father told me—"

"How do you *know*?" Simon raised his voice. "Did you gaze into the faces of those who hung from the gallows? Did you hear their stories, their defenses? You know nothing about it, because by the time the executions happened, you had already disappeared."

I lowered my eyes. That much was true.

The kidnapping had happened in the days after my mother's death, at her wake, during which hundreds of people had filtered through Woodcourt Manor to gaze upon her body. After I escaped from the Banished, my father barely looked at me. He blamed me for the disruption to her mourning rites and told me I'd have to leave Woodcourt immediately. The deaths of those forty people would be my fault, since I had been "careless enough to be taken."

My father also claimed the reason I was sent to the Lava Fields was for protection from any remaining Halderians, or from rebels who would view the kidnapping as a sign of Dallisor weakness. But I knew it wasn't that. He wanted me out of his home. For my mother's sake, he'd always tolerated my presence, but little more. Now he resented me for surviving a kidnapping when my mother hadn't even survived a winter flu.

Tenger continued, "Why is your father bringing you home again now?"

"He misses me." Which wasn't even close to the truth, but if what I suspected was true, then the real reason was worse. Marriage. A marriage of alliance, undoubtedly to some scaly old man, all to improve my father's standing in the kingdom. What could be more repulsive than that?

My words brought on a bitter chuckle from Simon, who said, "I told you she wouldn't cooperate."

"She will." Tenger leaned forward. "She's going to do everything we want."

"And what is it you want?" I asked. "Because one day you'll be discovered, and then Lord Endrick will crush you just as he has thousands of others in this land. Once we destroy all of you Coracks, we'll finally have peace again."

"Crushing a people into submission is not peace, my lady." Tenger's nostrils flared. "Lord Endrick's days upon the Scarlet Throne are numbered."

I snorted. Like everyone in Antora, I feared Lord Endrick, but I'd be a fool not to respect his power. Lord Endrick could not be defeated. He could not be killed or even wounded, certainly not by the Coracks. At best, they were like fleas to him, a persistent irritation, but a pestilence he would eventually crush between his fingers. Sooner than later, I hoped.

Unless the Coracks wanted a prize that was bigger than me. If they asked for that, I couldn't agree. Darrow had begged me not to. But if I didn't cooperate, he and Celia would die.

The best I could do was convince them not to ask. "Endrick is no ordinary man. Bring an army of a hundred thousand against him if you want. It will do you no good."

"Not yet, my lady. That's where you come in."

Almost unwittingly, I sat up straight, shaking my head as fiercely as possible. "What you want cannot be done."

Tenger leaned in to me. "It will be done, and you will do it. The Coracks have not yet decided who will replace Endrick as ruler of the Scarlet Throne, but he will be replaced."

"You will hang for this." I tilted my head toward Simon, to be sure the message was clear. "All of you."

"So you've said." Tenger had probably heard that threat as often as the church bells chimed. "You'll attend our hanging, I assume."

"I'll give the executioner his orders, gladly." My voice became ice. It frightened me to hear it, to realize I was capable of such words. Maybe I was more of a Dallisor than I wanted to believe, because I truly meant everything I'd just said.

Tenger smiled at my threat. "If you fail us, with similar enthusiasm we will execute your servant girl and driver. Only our methods are far more painful, I can promise you that. Now, what do you know about the Olden Blade?"

My gut twisted, but I tried not to let my worry show. If the Coracks knew about that dagger, then they needed my help to complete their wicked plans. They intended to make a traitor of me too. If I was not careful, I would hang with them.

· FIVE ·

SIMON

Kestra wasn't supposed to remember me. I'd changed too much in the last six years.

As a young boy, I'd served the Dallisor family, and been paid in misery, mistreatment, and starvation wages. I'd been a scrawny thing back then, able to worm up the fireplaces and clean them out between burnings. When I started to grow, they underfed me, hoping to keep me small.

For most of my years of service, I had believed that Kestra was different. I used to enjoy watching her scramble through the halls of Woodcourt like a wild pup, straightening up only when her governess scolded her or when her father approached. She kept a collection of odd-shaped rocks hidden in her bedroom, even showed me her favorite once, a dark yellow rock shaped like a crescent moon. Her smile was so bright that some days . . . on the worst days, it was all I lived for. Privately, I thought of her as my friend.

How wrong I'd been.

Until tonight, the last I'd seen of Kestra was when I'd been dragged off to her father's dungeons. She was my accuser and never blinked once as I protested my innocence. She'd wanted to please her father, and it seemed I was the price for his approval.

Somehow, I had survived the dungeons, and against even greater odds, escaped them. But I left with a bitterness that still burned in my chest, hot enough to endure these next few minutes at her side.

Tenger repeated his question about the Olden Blade two more times, but all he got in return from Kestra was a blank stare, as if he'd never spoken at all. This was a game to her, one I used to see her play in defiance of her father. But tonight's game would not end with a simple missed meal or a rod to her hand.

At Tenger's signal, I pressed on her arm as a warning. The captain wouldn't tolerate silence, and nobody wanted the consequences if she refused to cooperate. Especially her.

"The Olden Blade is a myth," Kestra finally said. "I'd believe in flying oxen before I put faith in some magical dagger."

A vein at the side of Tenger's neck pulsed, something I'd seen before. Most Dallisors wrapped themselves in arrogance the way others might wear a winter cloak, and no one detested that more than the captain. We'd never captured a Dallisor family member before, but we'd certainly cured many Dominion soldiers of their arrogance, usually with a slit to the throat.

I pressed on her arm again, harder this time, but she yanked it away. Fine. If she insisted on doing things the hard way, we would.

"The dagger is real," Tenger countered. "In the War of Devastation, the Halderians had the numbers, but the Dallisors had the Endrean magic. Hoping to ensure victory, Endrick retreated into the Blue Caves, the source of Endrean power. He used the darkest magic there to pour his soul into a dagger made of Dirilium, an Endrean metal harder than diamonds. In doing so, he became like the Dirilium itself: unbreakable, immortal. So powerful that the only thing able to destroy him is himself."

"Or the dagger," I added. "Endrick intended to keep the Olden Blade by his side at all times—"

"But it was stolen by Risha Halderian, I know the story." Kestra sighed as if we were a mere nuisance, like a fly buzzing too near her ear. "And that's all it is, a story. She had no dagger at her execution, which I can attest to because my father was there. If such a weapon ever existed, Endrick's soldiers would have found it by now."

I arched a brow. "If it never existed, then why have his soldiers been looking for it?"

She flinched and quickly recovered, but she knew I'd noticed. That would bother her, hopefully throw off her edge. "What if it is real?" she asked. "Let's assume the story is true, that it is the one weapon capable of killing Lord Endrick. He designed it so that anyone who attempts to wield the blade will die. That's what happened when it was stolen from Lord Endrick seventeen years ago. Risha Halderian died for her theft."

Tenger's eyes lit. "That isn't what happened. Risha stole the Olden Blade and wielded it. She could have defeated Lord Endrick had she not been captured by Dominion armies first, and then killed."

Kestra smirked at him. "So she . . . *died*. Isn't that what I said?"

She'd be lucky if Tenger allowed her to ever leave this carriage.

Hoping to calm things between them, I picked up the story. "If Risha was able to wield the dagger, then we believe another Halderian can claim it too. Risha's heir."

"You *believe*?" Kestra sat up straight. "You half-wits captured me over some mindless *belief*?"

"It's more than that." Tenger cast a well-deserved glare at me. "After Risha stole the blade, others tried to use it in her place, but merely touching it left them burned or seriously injured. Once we have the Olden Blade, somewhere within the Halderian clan, we'll find the next Infidante, the challenger." A satisfied grin tugged at the corner of his mouth. "The Infidante will go on to kill Lord Endrick."

Her lips pursed in anger. "Then it's simple. All you must do is find some mythical dagger that's been missing for almost seventeen years, locate Risha's heir in a country of dead Halderians, and get this Infidante past the Dominion army to fight an immortal, all-powerful Lord Endrick to the death. Brilliant plan, Tenger. It can't possibly fail."

Tenger's smile darkened. "Before her death, Risha Halderian was imprisoned in your father's dungeons. With her was an Endrean servant named Anaya. Risha and Anaya entered the dungeons with the Blade, but it was gone when they were executed. Risha hid it there, somewhere. Your job is to get a few of us inside those dungeons."

"I'm happy to put you in the Woodcourt dungeons, but I will slam the door shut behind you. I will not help you find that dagger."

Tenger leaned farther forward, grabbing Kestra's knee with the grip glove I had taken from her, and squeezing. The glove would directly trigger the nerves, with far more strength than an ordinary hand could achieve. She bent forward in immediate pain, obviously fighting the urge to cry out. She tried to pry his fingers away, but she couldn't do it.

Tenger said, "Is that true, my lady? You will not help us?"

"Let go of me." She could barely breathe, but his fingers only pressed tighter.

I looked away, wishing that I could be nearly anywhere else. Why didn't Kestra just cooperate? She could make this stop at any time. But she only cursed at us and then cried out as Tenger pinched deeper again.

"Two minutes of this, and you will lose the leg," Tenger said. "Would the Dallisors tolerate a cripple amongst them? I rather doubt it."

"Please let go!"

She would beg, and cry, and curse out her anger, but she would not give in. I knew this. I'd once watched her stand barefoot in the snow for an hour after refusing to tell her father the name of the servant who'd tracked mud through the great hall. Her mother had finally rescued her.

But she'd never told him my name. *That* time.

I laid my hand over Tenger's. "You're hurting her."

Tenger's eyes flashed, but I wouldn't remove my hand until he did. Tenger was the captain and I was sworn to obey his orders, but Tenger was only angry because she wasn't cowering the way he'd expected, and that wounded his pride. We'd get her cooperation, but not like this.

I hoped.

Finally, Tenger let go and she began to breathe normally again.

"The Olden Blade," Tenger said.

"It doesn't exist." She was still out of breath, still reeling from pain. "What you ask is impossible."

"Nothing is impossible." Tenger brushed his gloved fingers

together, a clear reminder that he could hurt her again. "Bring me the Olden Blade. In exchange, I will return your servants and set you all free."

"Even if you find the dagger, you can't do anything with it."

He gave her a wink. "Perhaps I'm a Halderian."

"If you were, I don't imagine you're stupid enough to admit it. Anyone who crosses the Dallisors, as you've done tonight, will be killed for it. But if a Halderian does it, we'll kill you twice."

That was true, but hardly a good enough threat to worry a Corack. None of us were likely to survive this rebellion. Just sitting in this carriage probably cut my chances of survival in half.

Tenger smiled. "And what do you think we'll do to you if you ignore my orders?"

"To steal the most valuable weapon in Antoran history, and betray the Lord of the Dominion? Do whatever you want to me. I'm no filthy traitor, like you."

And now she had crossed the line.

Tenger opened the carriage door enough to put out a hand and snap his fingers. Instantly, we heard the cry of Kestra's servant, the handmaiden. It was a bloodcurdling scream that nearly made me sick, so I couldn't imagine what it did to Kestra. Her face drained of color and she started from her seat, but Tenger slammed her back into it, keeping his hands on her arms.

"Help me!" the handmaiden screamed again.

Tears streamed down Kestra's cheeks, leaving behind long lines that glistened in the clearstone glow. She closed her eyes as if that would block out the screaming, but didn't try to pull her arms free to cover her ears, like I would have expected. Her muscles had become taut though, and her breathing more irregular than before.

With another scream, Kestra cried, "What are they doing to her?"

"Bring me that dagger," Tenger said.

The handmaiden screamed again, sharp enough to awaken the dead. I wondered if the other servant was dead, the driver.

"Are you monsters?" Kestra yelled. "What you're doing here proves everything we believe about the Coracks is true."

"It *is* all true. Trust me on that." Tenger leaned forward. "We'll do whatever it takes until you cooperate."

Could I say the same thing? I couldn't help but wonder if we'd crossed a line of our own tonight, becoming the very thing we were fighting against. Kestra's hands were clenched in white-knuckled fists and were visibly shaking. Was this any different than the fear created by Dominion soldiers when they rounded up innocent civilians for half-crimes and demonstrations of Endrick's power?

But Kestra was not an innocent. I had to remember that. She was a tool in a plan. Nothing more.

Kestra's tone went lower, commanding. "Stop this, *now.*"

Tenger stuck out his hand again and the screaming stopped, though the girl's sobs continued, almost as loud. Then his hand returned to Kestra's knee. "You have four days to find the Olden Blade."

"There is no Blade—"

He ignored her. "To get it, I don't care who you lie to, cheat, or harm—in fact, it'd do some good if you caused a little trouble in Highwyn." He smiled at that. She did not. "After the Blade is in my hands, you will be free."

"Free? I'll be killed for betraying Lord Endrick this way."

He didn't even blink. "Well, you can always join the rebellion."

"I'd only do that if it got me closer to a knife and your throat."

Tenger chuckled at that. "You were a child when you left Highwyn. Perhaps after you have a chance to see the Dallisors for who they really are, you will come to the rebellion more willingly. Now do you agree to our plans"—he stuck his hand out the carriage door again—"or shall I let them continue?"

"I'll do what you ask." She lowered her eyes so they wouldn't reveal too much of her thoughts.

Despite the meekness of her voice, I noticed the set of her jaw. Couldn't Tenger see that she was absolutely going to betray us, or worse? I wouldn't say anything in front of her, but Tenger needed to know that she was lying to us.

And scheming. Looking at Tenger, she asked, "In four days, we'll meet here?"

She wanted to know where to send her father's soldiers in four days.

Tenger wasn't that naïve. "Not here, my lady. You'll be told where to go once you have the item I want."

"By whom?"

"You were traveling with a handmaiden and a guard. Since we have robbed you of their services, we will replace them." This time he leaned out the door, calling, "Trina, please join us."

Something twisted in my chest, though I didn't let it show. Trina was . . . difficult, but in an entirely different way than Kestra seemed to be. Trina had offered Tenger valuable information about this plan a year ago, which was the only reason he had let her join the

Coracks. No one else knew what she'd told him, but I'd never cared to find out. My role in this mission was nearly completed.

Thank the heavens for that. I'd joined the Coracks to fight the Dominion, not to threaten and terrify their daughters. Even *this* daughter.

Trina entered the carriage, having changed from riding breeches into the skirts of a lady, probably one of Kestra's skirts from the trunk at the rear of her carriage. One glance at Kestra and I knew my guess was right. Her cheeks were aflame with anger at seeing her fine skirt on a Corack.

Trina's hair was black and worn loose down her shoulders, unlike Kestra, whose brown hair had been woven into complicated plaits around her head, except for the lock Tenger had cut off as his usual token of victory. Both girls were about the same size, though Kestra's dresses had been fitted perfectly to her curves, and hung a little loose on Trina's straighter frame.

What I noticed most was the difference in their eyes. Trina's were like disks, narrow and sharp, and eager to do damage. There was an intelligence behind Kestra's green eyes, and determination. This wouldn't be nearly as simple as Tenger had thought.

Trina returned Kestra's glare and sat beside Tenger, directly across from me. She gave me a wink but I pretended not to see it. Trina was nearly impossible to figure out. Her emotions could shift within a single breath, and I'd seen her lash out in violence over the smallest of issues. It was easier to avoid her. Most Coracks did.

After a careful appraisal of Kestra, Trina said, "Let's be clear about one thing. I'm not your servant and I have no loyalty to you. Unless we're in public, I will not do anything for you, not for any reason. My orders are to find the Olden Blade, or to kill you if you try to betray us."

Kestra rolled her eyes, making sure Trina saw it. "That was five things, not one. If you can't count any better than that, it doesn't seem I have much to worry about."

Trina's face reddened, but Tenger put out an arm to keep her in her seat. Then his attention shifted to me. "You will go as her guard. Act as her protector through this."

"What? No!"

I'd rather have been ordered to jump from a cliff. Coracks were forbidden from contradicting Tenger's orders in front of the enemy, but hadn't he also taught that our missions must be carried out with pure emotional detachment? I wouldn't dare attach the Coracks' fate to a girl I so passionately loathed.

Before Tenger could speak, in a humbler tone I added, "Pell was assigned to Woodcourt, not me."

Tenger spoke between clenched teeth. "Pell would have gone, if Kestra had not left a stab wound in his shoulder. You're the only other Corack who knows the layout of her home. It must be you."

No, it must be anyone else. I shook my head. "I'm too young to be a guard. And what if I'm recognized?"

Tenger shrugged that off. "Kestra will make sure you're not."

"Sir, you don't understand." I licked my lips, trying not to say anything more than was necessary, especially since she could hear every word. "I don't want to guard *her*."

"That's irrelevant." Tenger's tone sharpened. "You will carry out my orders."

In frustration, I dug a fist into my thigh, the most I dared do in front of the captain. This order could prove to be a grave mistake. Why couldn't he see that?

"Then we all have our jobs." Tenger gave Kestra's knee a final twist. "I'll see you in four days, my lady. Don't let me down."

She glared a warning back at him, with flushed cheeks and a determined set of her jaw. I could almost read her thoughts.

She had no intention of disappointing Tenger. No, she would do worse than that.

In four days, Kestra intended to destroy the rebellion. Tenger may have finally picked the one target that would hand him a fatal loss.

· SIX ·

KESTRA

Tenger had forced my agreement to get the Olden Blade, but that agreement came with consequences he might not have anticipated.

He left me with his final threat, after kissing my hand, a mockery that nearly made me sick, and then departed the carriage. I suspected he didn't want his rebels out in the open any longer than necessary. They were rodents, and by morning they'd all have to scurry back into their holes.

Once the carriage door was shut, Simon took the seat where Tenger had been, allowing him to face me directly. A leather satchel hung crossways over his shoulder. It was tightly fastened and knotted at the top, sparking my curiosity about its contents. A sword was sheathed at his side with a handle tightly wrapped in worn fabric, perhaps for the comfort of his hand. Most people considered swords outdated, which made the fact that he openly carried one interesting. The knife in his hands was simpler, a hand-forged blade with a worn wooden handle. I wondered where my knife had gone, which scum rebel was holding it. I briefly considered asking Simon how he'd survived the dungeons, then decided it was pointless. Whatever friendship we used to have belonged to the past. We were enemies now.

There was something about his eyes though that grasped my attention and wouldn't let go. They had an intensity that he seemed to wield like a weapon, cutting, or bruising, or boring into me. What I didn't understand was *why* they made me uncomfortable, as if I were the criminal here, not him. I had no doubt that he believed his fight was just.

Which made him all the more dangerous.

His eyes were on fire now, communicating his anger at being assigned as my protector or whatever fraudulent title he'd been given. Did he really expect me to ever ask him for help, or to depend on him for protection, pretending I didn't know his real purpose? Did he think I'd care that this attack was inconvenient for him?

He said, "A lot of lives depend on you, Princess, including your own. If anything goes wrong at your father's home, our orders are to kill you immediately. And if all three of us do not return in four days, then your servants will die."

He could fill his voice with weight and authority, as though this had been the plan all along, but we both knew the truth. Simon had never expected to be in this carriage and he was making things up as he went along.

Of course, so was I.

By now, my heart was in knots and my mind was spinning, but I couldn't let them see that. Cocking my head, as if I'd been in this situation a thousand times, I said, "I've already promised to return."

And when I did, all the rebels would die, not Celia or Darrow— or me.

"You'll find the Olden Blade," Trina put in.

"Did you just figure that out?" As often as possible, I intended to remind her that I had more respect for a common stinkbug than for her. "Let's get this over with."

Simon handed Trina his knife, then left without looking back, something I understood perfectly. If he could avoid thinking of me as a real person, then I was only a tool for the rebellion, little different from any other weapon. I'd be used for as long as I could help their cause, then tossed aside.

When I'd protested to Tenger that I would be killed if caught stealing the Olden Blade, Tenger had seemed both unsurprised and unimpressed. The reason, of course, was perfectly clear. After I led him to the dagger, Tenger had no intention of letting me walk away from the Coracks. He'd lied about that. Even if I was allowed to leave, after such a betrayal of my family, where could I possibly go?

With Simon up in the driver's box, my carriage started back on the road again, and Trina breathed easier once it did. She kept one hand firmly wrapped around her knife, and smoothed over the folds of her skirt with her other hand. *My* skirt, that is.

Personally, I preferred trousers, but they were frowned upon for women in general society and my father would consider them intolerable. So if I had to wear skirts, then they had better be beautiful enough to compensate for the inconvenience of wearing them. Trina had chosen one of my favorite gowns. I'd have to burn it now. Whether she was still using it or not.

"What kind of fabric is this?" she asked. "I'll bet it's expensive."

"You think wearing the gown of a lady makes you one?"

Trina leaned forward. "It's worked for you. Your hair is perfumed and styled, you casually wear jewels that would feed my people for a month, and you have servants to wait on you at all times. But your heart is as black as Lord Endrick's. When the Coracks heard you were returning to Highwyn, my vote was simply to kill you on this road. Antora would be better off with one less Dallisor."

"I've done nothing to you," I whispered, struck by the potency of her hatred, and its focus on me.

She snorted and turned sideways to prop her feet on the cushioned bench of the carriage, clearly communicating her disrespect, her lack of honor.

A thousand years ago, the first recorded Dallisor, Gridwyn Dallisor, took control of Antora from its founder, a Halderian king. Gridwyn built the Scarlet Throne and made his children vow that a Dallisor would always occupy the throne, or make war until they did. If Lord Endrick had not claimed rule over the land, then my father would sit upon the throne now. He wasn't the original heir, but the War of Devastation had severely diminished our numbers. Five pure-blooded Dallisor families remained. Among them, an aunt who governed the Watchman Mountains region, my father's cousin who was an emissary to Tarbush, and three other cousins who dwelt in Highwyn. Every grandfather in our history had served as a military commander. If I had been a son rather than a daughter, that would have been my fate too. As much as I would have loathed standing at the head of an Ironheart garrison, at least it might have earned my father's attention.

For most of my life, I'd longed for a relationship with my father. I didn't need his warmth or approval or even his love. But it would've been nice to see him look at me just once without that hollow regret in his eyes. If he found out what I'd just agreed to do . . . *when* he found out, I could well imagine his expression then.

Trina wouldn't understand that. If anything, knowing she came between me and my father would only bring her a twisted sort of joy.

So I wouldn't think of my father now, wouldn't think of anything but the job that had to be done. If I was careful, and smart, and held my ragged emotions together, there was a chance to defeat them, save Darrow and Celia, and redeem myself in my father's eyes.

It would begin by putting Trina in her place. I nodded at her boots. "Those are impossibly ugly." They were dusty and scuffed, and seemed more appropriate for a man. "No one who sees them will believe you're my lady-in-waiting."

She looked down as if she'd never seen them before. "I'll keep them covered with the skirts."

"Brilliant plan. Really, I'm already impressed by your attention to detail. But when your identity is discovered a whole three minutes after we enter Woodcourt, remember that it wasn't my fault. I warned you about the boots."

She lowered her feet to the floor and smoothed out her skirts again. Because that would help.

"You're expected to stay at the inn near Grimlowe tonight, yes?"

I frowned at Trina's question. "How do you know that? How did you know I'd be on this road tonight?"

"We know more than you think."

"The rebels might. I doubt you know much at all."

"Tell me what I'll be expected to do when we reach the inn."

Drown yourself. There was a pond near the inn and I'd gladly show her the way if she was interested. But Celia was too much on my mind. Remembering the terror of her screams sent a cold shudder through me. I couldn't imagine what she was going through now, or how they were treating her. What of Darrow? Was he still alive? Would they care for him and try to heal his wound, or would he be left to his own fate?

Four days. I just needed them to survive that long. More importantly, I needed a plan to get them back.

But in answer to her question, I only said, "The innkeeper was warned that we'd arrive late. We'll rest there for a few hours and be on the road again before everyone is awake."

She gave a wide yawn. "When do I get to sleep?"

"You don't. Nor will Simon." She did a double take at that, which gave me a little pleasure. "He'll greet the innkeeper and pay him for the night. I hope he's prepared for that, because Darrow carried my money." This wasn't true at all. I had plenty of money in a satchel inside my trunk, but if they were going to kidnap me, then they could do it with their own coins. "Simon will carry in the trunk and secure my room while you prepare a bath for me and serve me a meal."

"When do we eat?" She was all but drooling with hunger.

I hardly cared about that. "You eat when you can pay for it. But if you don't arrange for my meals first, it will arouse the innkeeper's suspicions. After my bath, you'll dress me for bed, and if you were a normal servant, you'd sleep on the floor beside me, like any good dog. However, I assume you and Simon will want to stay awake to guard me and be sure I don't run."

Trina shook her head. "Run, and we'll kill your servants."

I leaned forward, scrunching my face into the cruelest look I could muster. "What makes you think that I care about them? Maybe the death of some silly handmaiden and an aging driver are the least of my concerns. Maybe I'm luring you and Simon into a trap from which you'll never escape, and the last words we torture out of you before your horrible deaths will be a full confession of everything Lord Endrick wants to know about the rebellion. I'll gladly sacrifice my servants for that."

Trina reached out and slapped me hard across my cheek. I drew back, but she caught my other hand with hers and let the knife lay upon my wrist, blade down. When I tried to pull away, the knife sliced—not deep, but enough to draw blood. Trina smiled when she saw it. She wanted more.

I slowly shook my head at her, because as a general rule, I always tried to calm anyone who was about to kill me. "Whatever you think I am, if you do this, you'll be just as bad."

Her eyes narrowed. "Nothing I am compares to you." Her knife pressed deeper into my wrist, widening the cut. "Sit back and don't say another word until we arrive at the inn. Or I'll tell Tenger you attacked me and I had no other choice."

When she released me, I leaned back, pretending my wrist wasn't stinging fiercely. "I only wanted to warn you that at the inn— oh, sorry, I won't say another word."

That made Trina curious. "Warn me about what?"

I shrugged and motioned that my mouth was shut. She knew I was mocking her, that there wasn't anything to warn her about before our arrival at the inn. She knew that . . . but still it bothered her. And that alone gave me enough pleasure to sit back in my seat, keeping one hand tightly wrapped over the cut, and relax.

· S E V E N ·

SIMON

I'd heard the fight inside the carriage. Heard it, and wondered how the rest of Antora had somehow slept through it. It was quiet now, which possibly meant one of the girls had killed the other. Trina was plenty dangerous, but my bet was on Kestra. From what I remembered, her father had never allowed her to train with weapons, but she had stabbed Pell, so she wasn't entirely helpless. I had no doubt she'd figure out how to punch back if she wanted to.

Yet another reason to be glad I was up here driving. I'd rather face a hundred unharnessed oropods than get between those two below.

Either of them could have started the fight. Trina hated Kestra in a way that Kestra couldn't possibly understand. And Kestra had good reasons to defend herself. She saw what had happened to Darrow, and heard Celia's screaming. She had to be thinking of her own safety too. Things would worsen as she began to grasp the full consequences of agreeing to help us. If she failed to find the Olden Blade, I would have to kill her. Those were Tenger's orders. If she was successful, she would become a traitor to Antora, a target for Lord Endrick's vengeance. Sooner or later, Endrick would find her, and her death would be awful. But this was a rebellion, not a tea party. Sacrifices had to be made for the Coracks to succeed.

Tonight, Kestra was that sacrifice.

I'd learned about sacrifices the hard way. On one of my earliest missions with the Coracks, I'd been on a team ordered to stop several supply wagons from reaching the Dominion barracks. My assignment was to locate an abandoned home where the team could hide at the end of its mission. If none were available, I was to clear a home, by the occupants' choice—or by their deaths.

Shortly before ten bells, when the team was expected to arrive, I finally found a home that was a perfect choice, except for two elderly women huddling in a back room, faces cast in shadows and trembling with fear. They were too sick to leave, one of the women claimed. The other promised if I left them alive, they would remain in hiding. Captain Tenger didn't have to know they were there. It would be an act of mercy, a favor they promised to repay one day.

Naïve, and eager to avoid unnecessary killing, I'd agreed.

Within minutes, I welcomed my team into the home, jubilant from a successful mission. They'd barely sat down to rest when the elderly women charged into the room, armed with lever blades that cut through three rebels before anyone had time to react. These were no elderly women but two Dominion soldiers in disguise, ordered to lie in wait for an expected Corack arrival.

I'd led my team into a trap, and thanks to Tenger, was an undeserving survivor. Tenger poured oil into the lit fireplace, creating a diversion for the few surviving Coracks to escape. Then he pushed me out a window, saving me from the fire, though he lost his leg in the process.

Back at camp, my punishment was the cruelest possible. I was assigned to visit the family of each dead team member and deliver the terrible news. To hold every wife and mother who collapsed from sorrow, comfort every weeping child who asked when their father would come home. I faced them all, each visit instilling in me a deeper vow to never again ignore Tenger's orders. Orders that had brought me here, now.

The inn came into sight about an hour later. It sat on the northwestern border of All Spirits Forest, a place so desolate that even the birds wouldn't fly overhead. The inn itself was small and in great need of repair. The main floor was mostly stone and brick, but a half upper story was made of dry and cracked wood. I wondered why a Dallisor would choose to stay in such a crumbling place. Maybe because the finer establishments didn't allow swine for guests?

I was particularly glad to see the inn, for two reasons. The first was that if both Kestra and Trina were still alive, then their truce wouldn't last long. Separating them was a survival decision.

The second reason was more significant. My gut told me we were being followed. That was impossible, of course. No one knew our plans to take Kestra, and no one other than Kestra's father and her two servants should have known she was headed back to Highwyn tonight. So why did this feeling nag at me? Obviously, I was on edge. I'd never planned to do this job, and knew I wasn't prepared for it.

Almost as soon as I alighted from the driver's seat, the innkeeper ran outside to greet us. He was a large man with hunched shoulders, a bulging waist, and a scalp that was clinging to its final few hairs. Yet he was all but bouncing on his heels in anticipation of our arrival.

"This is young Lady Dallisor's carriage?" he asked.

Yes, and I was her driver now, and her protector. The irony of this whole situation would've made me laugh if it weren't vital that the innkeeper accept us. This inn proudly displayed its green and black Dominion colors. No sane Corack would come within a mile of this place.

"My . . . lady is inside this carriage." I nearly choked on having to refer to Kestra so politely.

"Wasn't a garrison assigned to accompany her home?"

"Those plans changed." The simplest lies were usually the most believable. Then I added, "The lady is tired and hopes her room is ready."

"It is, of course." The innkeeper coughed and held out his hand. He expected payment.

I had a few silver coins in my satchel, but not enough for a room, and I wouldn't empty my pockets anyway to provide a Dallisor with a soft pillow for the night. How had she planned to pay? Did she have the money, or did Darrow carry it? With the innkeeper directly in front of me, I couldn't just open the door and ask her.

But the carriage door did open. Trina leaned out with a necklace in her hand that Kestra had been wearing. The ribbon was cut, but it held a gemstone that would be worth a month's lodging.

"The lady wishes to pay with this," Trina said. "It should cover her room and provide generous meals for all of us."

I passed it from her to the innkeeper and wondered how the man could have missed Kestra's horrified expression, or the way her chest heaved in anger. Maybe because he only had eyes for the precious gem.

"You'll want a separate room, I assume?" the innkeeper asked me.

I shook my head. "I'll stay with the lady. For her protection."

"Sir, I can assure you, my inn is very safe. If it's the rebels you fear, we keep them far away."

Somehow, my smile hid my true feelings, and my identity. All I said was, "I have no fear of the Coracks. But I'll protect my lady in her room."

The innkeeper snorted, but with that gemstone clutched in his palm, he was hardly going to argue the matter. I held out a hand for Kestra. Her expression could freeze fire, which made me nervous. This was the first big test. She could tell the innkeeper who Trina and I really were. She only had to say the words and the innkeeper would call for help. My other hand shifted to my sword. The innkeeper would die first, and anyone who came to his assistance. Then I would have to kill Kestra. She'd get no second chances.

I hated this. Hated that the determination of whether I was about to use my sword rested in the hands of a girl who had so little respect for life. If the innkeeper had to die, Kestra probably wouldn't care. I did. I killed when I had to, when there was no other choice, and it made me sick every single time. Dallisors killed for pleasure, and power, and to gain favor from Lord Endrick.

Kestra hadn't even wanted that much. She'd sent me to my death for little more than a pat on the head from her father. How disappointed she must be to see me still alive.

Luckily, she accepted my hand and somehow managed a smile at the innkeeper as she exited the carriage.

He bowed low to her. "The daughter of Sir Henry Dallisor comes to us. It is an honor to receive you. If you will dine with me, I have kept a meal warm."

"My lady is not hungry," I said. Under no circumstances could she have an hour of privacy with this man. "And she should get out of this cool night air."

"Of course. I meant no offense in inviting her."

"And my servant means no offense in speaking so boldly." Her gaze flicked upward. "My apologies for his lack of manners. If you wish to give the boy a good whipping, I won't object."

I would. Thanks to her, I'd already been whipped once. That was enough.

The innkeeper only bowed again and then led us into the inn. The interior was nicer than I had expected, based on what I'd seen from the outside. We first entered a dining area, which seemed reasonably clean and had a lingering smell of roast that made my mouth water. Behind that was a narrow hallway that probably led to other rooms. I wasn't sure how many other guests were here tonight, or who they might be. The way my night was going, each room was probably stuffed with soldiers.

Kestra was offered the upstairs room, where the innkeeper assured her she would have absolute privacy for as long as she wished to stay.

"We'll be gone first thing in the morning." I was too tired and nervous to care about manners. How did Dallisors endure such suffocating hospitality?

"But meals can be delivered to our room." Trina exchanged a glare with Kestra as she spoke. Maybe that was what they had fought about. We'd had to leave camp early to get into place before Kestra's carriage arrived on that road. Neither of us had eaten for hours.

"We require no meals," Kestra said to the innkeeper. "As you were informed, I am not hungry and my lazy servants deserve no food."

Pretending not to hear Trina's muttering scowl, the innkeeper kept his eyes on Kestra. I'd expected that. We were only servants.

52

Our room was waiting at the top of a narrow flight of stairs. I went in first, assuring that no surprises were waiting. Everything seemed fine, so maybe I'd just been spooked on the road before. The room was simple, with a single four-poster bed, a stand with hooks for a traveling cloak, and a table with two chairs. A window offered a view to the side of the inn, though it was mostly blocked by a massive oak tree. The bedding was thick and warm, made for someone of her status. Had Kestra ever spent a night on the cold, hard earth, or gone without a meal? Had she ever gotten her hands dirty? What a joke to think such a thing. Of course she hadn't.

The innkeeper entered the room right behind me. "May I show you—"

No, he may not. "My lady is tired," I said. "She hopes you understand."

"Of course!" The innkeeper dipped his head at her. "May I say again, my lady—"

"Good night." I practically pushed him from the room, hoping the door didn't bang on his bowed balding head in the process. "She thanks you for your service."

Technically speaking, Kestra's thanks would likely come in the shape of a fist. Not to the innkeeper, but to me. And to Trina. Her current expression was murderous.

Let her be angry, then. She had made a promise, and my job was to ensure she kept it, nothing more. Four days. All I had to do was outlast this girl for the next four days.

Only one of us could win.

It had to be me.

· EIGHT ·

———

SIMON

Kestra might've been angry, but Trina's fury created a charge in the air that bristled against my skin. The instant the door closed, I stepped between the girls, holding Trina back.

"I'm starving!" Trina said. "She knows that. She did that on purpose."

"It can't be changed," I said, ignoring my own hunger pangs. "The innkeeper will be suspicious."

"He's already suspicious." Kestra's face was flush with color. She started with me first. "What was all that 'my lady' talk? You're my guard, not my chaperone. I'm old enough to speak for myself, you fool." To Trina, she added, "And every gesture you make reeks of irritation, like you're hoping for a fight. Do you think a Dallisor would employ any lady's maid with your attitude? Both of you listen carefully. Sometime tomorrow, we'll arrive at my father's home, where mistakes like these will get you killed, and may get me killed if my father thinks I'm helping you by choice. You will stop with this stupidity, for all our sakes!"

My head was down and I kicked at the floor, keenly aware of how silent the room had become. Much as I hated to admit it, Kestra was right. I had overplayed my role, Trina had trumpeted her anger, and if anyone became suspicious about Kestra, a lot of people would have to die. Including the three of us, no doubt.

I finally looked up, feeling the weight of Kestra's frustrations. I expected to face another challenge from her, but instead, tears had welled in her eyes. She was struggling to fight them back, but one had already spilled onto her cheek. When Trina saw, she would mock Kestra brutally over this. There would be another fight.

I turned to Trina. "Go find the innkeeper and tell him your lady has changed her mind and desires a supper, in private. Wait for it and bring it back here yourself. After our generous payment for this room, he'll prepare a nice meal."

Trina practically danced from the room. As soon as she had gone, Kestra said, "You paid for it with the one gift I had from my mother. All I had left of her."

The hurt that caused her creased every word. I considered apologizing, but then when she turned away to brush at her tears, her attention fell on the window, remaining there far too long. I grimaced, feeling a pressure building in the back of my head. She was assessing her chances of escape. It would be a long night ahead.

A moment later, Kestra turned back to me, speaking so quickly that she clearly had planned this speech. "Your captain's plan won't work. This idea of a dagger choosing some Infidante to assassinate Lord Endrick is preposterous. It's a myth, a story the Banished hold on to because it's their sole hope of regaining power. Even if it's true, there are no clues to the whereabouts of the missing dagger. Don't you think those dungeons have been searched a thousand times already? And even if we do find something, the Woodcourt gates will not open for me to leave after only four days. It usually takes at least five before my father is fed up with me."

"It'll work. You'll find a way." I sounded more confident than I felt. If anything, I agreed with her. Tenger's plan was insane, and probably based on hope more than reality. It wasn't like the captain to be this careless.

But she wasn't finished. "As you know, Henry Dallisor is not a man of affection." I snorted at her words, but she quickly added, "If he cares for me, I've seen little evidence of it. You must understand that if he suspects me of betraying Lord Endrick, he will dispose of me as quickly as he would any other traitor. Henry Dallisor serves Endrick first, and remembers his daughter last."

"Lord Endrick protects the Dallisors."

"He protects those who serve him. If I'm discovered, nothing I tell him will matter."

Silence fell between us. Fear registered in her eyes and deepened the lines between her furrowed brows. Her family served Lord Endrick, but she was just as afraid of him as most other Antorans. Maybe more.

I stepped closer to her, testing to see how she'd react. "You obviously know how evil Lord Endrick is. How can you support such a man?"

She moved away, obviously uncomfortable. "He's strict, not evil, and he's forced to be so by scum like you." She pressed her lips together in a tight line before adding, "If there were no uprisings, there would be no need for him to respond to regain order."

My jaw clenched. I'd heard these lies many times before, just never from such a beautiful mouth. "Endrick's idea of order is total control, and he'll destroy anything necessary to have that. As an immortal, life has become meaningless to him."

"Your lives are worse than meaningless. You spread fear and chaos, inciting uprisings and violence in your wake, and then you claim it's the Dominion's fault for making you do it."

"The Dominion is crushing this country!"

"You are bees that sting and then complain when Lord Endrick slaps you down. The Corack rebellion and everyone who supports you are destructive. All of you should be hanged!"

I had to contain my temper, or I'd bring that ridiculous innkeeper back here to check on us, but my muscles had tensed and I spoke through gritted teeth. "If you truly believe that, then you are no better than Endrick. Think back, Princess. When did you first decide that some lives were more important than others?"

She blinked hard at that, registering pain from my words. So she could feel. Who knew?

Kestra stepped back farther, trying to recover. "It's irrelevant what you think of me. My point is that you must understand the flaws in your plan. I'm begging you to send word to your people to release my servants. If the Olden Blade does exist, then I'll keep my end of the bargain, but if I fail, they shouldn't be held responsible."

My bitter laugh mocked her, which was my exact intention. "You care for your servants now? Since when?"

"I care about these two. I remember when you served my family, Simon. I remember that day—"

No, we weren't going to talk about *that day*. If Tenger knew the details of it, he'd never have assigned me to this job. I marched forward, forcing Kestra back until she was against the wall. "Everything you say is a lie! Do you think I'm stupid?"

She smirked. "Stupid is the least of your problems."

Kestra stopped there, unwilling to back down, so neither would I. The anger between us was like fire, and the next one to speak would likely pour oil on it.

How foolish I'd been. I never should've cared if Tenger hurt her knee, or if she was afraid, or if this mission destroyed her life. I'd been wrong before. She didn't feel, no more than any of Endrick's puppets.

We both turned as Trina entered the room, carrying a tray covered by a cloth. She looked from Kestra to me and smiled. "It feels like war in here. And they say I'm the hotheaded one."

I closed the door while Trina set the tray on the small table in the room. Kestra's eyes immediately found the bowl, filled with a thick venison stew. But I knew she wouldn't say anything, no matter how hungry she was.

"What should we do about her while we eat?" Trina asked.

My temper had cooled enough to think rationally again. We couldn't bring her into Woodcourt half-starved. I motioned Kestra over to the table. "Come eat."

"After Trina has breathed on it? I'd rather eat off the floor."

Cursing loudly, Trina scooted back the chair she'd already been sitting in. She leapt toward Kestra, who waited until the last second before sidestepping, leaving a foot in her path. As quickly as Trina was moving, her sprawl onto the floor went wide. Trina's hand caught the edge of the meal tray, sending the stew to the floor, its inviting scent rising in the room. None of us would eat now.

I withdrew my sword from its sheath and held it out toward Kestra. But she casually waved it away.

"Don't pretend you'll use that." She scowled. "You have your orders."

It had never been about using the sword. It was a distraction for Trina, who pounced on Kestra from behind, bringing her to the floor. She locked Kestra's arms behind her back, shoving her face down.

"Get me some rope, Simon!"

I hesitated. Everyone just needed to calm down and get through the night, but Kestra was clearly determined to cause problems. Tying her up would be our only chance to keep the situation under control.

I dug into my satchel for a ball of twine and handed it to Trina. She wound it around Kestra's wrists, more times than was necessary and probably tighter than it had to be. But Kestra didn't complain, either because the knots weren't bothering her or, more likely, because she didn't want us to think they were. While Trina pulled her to her feet and tied her to a post of the bed, Kestra glowered at us as if already plotting her revenge.

I knew I should intervene, but I didn't. After what she'd just done, Kestra deserved to be tied up. Besides, I still had scars on my wrists from when I'd been bound up *that day*. A part of me wanted Kestra to know how that had felt.

Trina stood back to admire her handiwork. I noticed Kestra was already twisting her wrists, trying to loosen the knots. I'd give her a few minutes with them, then loosen the knots myself.

"What do we have for a gag?" Trina asked.

Kestra's head shot up. "Don't gag me. I won't scream."

"Look at her eyes!" Trina squealed, enjoying this moment far too much. "She's afraid!"

Yes, she was, though I didn't know why and knew she'd never offer the information. Maybe this had something to do with her kidnapping a few years ago. I'd heard rumors about what happened to her then, why she vanished from her home the same night she returned from the Halderians. But that's all they were, rumors.

Use that knowledge against her. Tenger's voice echoed in my head, his unspoken order. It's what the Dominion would do to us, turning information into torture. But we weren't the Dominion.

Trina wasn't ready to let anything go though. She picked up a roll that had fallen to the floor in their scuffle and held the warm bread beneath Kestra's nose. "Can you smell this? Wish you could eat it?"

"All I smell is you," Kestra countered. "Did you bathe in horse manure?"

"Enough." I only wanted the night to end. "Trina, enough! Help me clean up."

"Make her do it. It's her fault."

"Yes, but you're the servants, not me." Even in bindings, Kestra still believed she was the mistress here.

Trina checked her knots again, tightening them out of spite rather than necessity. Then she knelt on the floor beside me, using one of Kestra's fine skirts from her trunk as a rag for the stew.

When we had finished, Kestra said, "You both hate me. Not the idea of me, as a Dallisor or a lady of the Dominion. You hate *me.* Why?"

Trina started to answer, but I shook my head. "Don't."

"It's her fault that you—"

"Don't."

Kestra's face softened. "Do you mean when you were sent to the dungeons? We have to talk about that."

"No, we don't."

"I remember—"

Trina cut in. "Do you remember kicking him in the head?"

My hands clenched into fists. Of course Kestra would remember that. She had stormed into the servants' quarters, ten years old but thinking herself twice that age. I'd been asleep in a corner of the room. She had kicked me awake.

"You kicked hard for a ten-year-old," I said.

"I kick harder now. Besides, you took my mother's ring—you deserved it."

"I never did." Our eyes connected. "Nor did my friend John, whom you also accused to your father. You lied, Princess. You lied and got an innocent man executed."

Silence fell heavy in the room. For six years, I had waited to say that to her, but now that I had, I simply felt empty, as if the anger that had fueled me all this time had suddenly dried up. I should have expected this. No words between us would change *that day*.

John and I had each received ten snaps of a whip against our backs. Then we were thrown into Henry Dallisor's dungeons, bound with ropes that had cut into my wrists just like the twine was no doubt cutting into hers right now. Thanks to a sharp edge on the rocks of my cell, I'd escaped the ropes. Escaping the dungeons themselves was a matter of dumb luck, nothing more. John got no such favors from the fates.

Kestra's lashes fluttered, as if I'd care about her regrets. "I was ten."

"And we were friends! Or was that also a lie?"

Her voice was barely above a whisper now. "We were friends, Simon."

"You had a strange way of showing it." We all fell silent, until I said, "That's why I know you're lying about wanting to save your servants. I don't know your reasons for agreeing to Tenger's plan, but it's not about saving anyone. And when I figure out why you're really helping us, I'll do everything I can to stop you."

A tear finally escaped, landing on Kestra's cheek. But her voice was firm. "Try your best to stop me. But you will both end up in those dungeons again, where you belong. And this time, I will not have any regrets."

Despite the advantage of our situation, something in the tone of her voice set me on edge. I knew Kestra meant every word she just said.

· N I N E ·

KESTRA

During my first few months in the Lava Fields, sleep always brought on nightmares of the kidnapping that jolted me awake, but with lingering memories that threatened to suffocate me. On the worst nights, my handmaidens learned to fetch Darrow, the only one who knew how to soothe the fears away. He'd distract me with stories of his youth or sing playful tunes, despite the fact that under Endrick, music was illegal. Darrow was a terrible singer, the worst, but I never told him so.

Around that time, Darrow began training me to defend myself, and to think like a survivor. He filled my days with swords and disk bows, and our evenings planning battle strategies, making my poor lady-in-waiting and Cook stand in as our presumed enemy. If I survived this, it'd be thanks to him. How I wished he were here.

I wasn't anywhere near asleep, but I did let my body slump over as if I were. It was uncomfortable, and Trina made several comments about my unladylike slouch. But neither of them suggested releasing me.

After enough time passed, they seemed to think I was truly asleep and began talking more freely. Their voices remained low, barely more than whispers, but it was a quiet room and my ears were tuned to nothing except their conversation.

"She thinks Tenger's plan is going to fail," Simon said.

"She was only telling you that to make you doubt our mission," Trina responded.

"Maybe, but it echoed my own doubts. I served in that home. I've been in those dungeons, made of rock walls and wooden cell doors. There's nowhere to hide a weapon. Even if the dagger exists, are we certain the mythology of the Blade is true? Only a Halderian can hold it? Only the Infidante can kill Lord Endrick with it?"

"We have to trust the people who are certain," Trina said. "The Blade does exist, Simon, and it's somewhere in her home. And when we find it and the Infidante is chosen, we'll be heroes."

"Or martyrs." Simon lowered his voice. "After this is over, we'll become the two most hunted Coracks in history. Let's hope it's for a good reason."

It wasn't. I knew for a fact that Lord Endrick had ordered the kingdom to be turned inside out in search of the Olden Blade. Nothing had come of it. When his search failed to produce any results, he had declared the dagger a myth, and asserted that his immortal status could never be challenged.

But there was a problem with Endrick's story. Simon was right about that much. If it was a myth, then why had Endrick himself made a search for it? As much as Simon worried that the Olden Blade's existence was false, I worried that it was real.

"Let's try to sleep," Simon finally suggested. "We only have a few hours before we ought to be on the road again."

"What if she escapes?"

There was a pause and someone, probably Simon, got to his feet. He walked close behind me, studying the knots around my wrists, I assumed. My breaths weren't calm enough or as even as they should have been. He should've realized I was awake, yet his attention went to something else.

"Her wrists are raw from the rope."

"Good." The answer had come so quickly that Trina either knew and didn't care, or else she hadn't bothered to notice. Before pretending to fall asleep, I'd tried to work my hands free of the knots, gently twisting them until they hurt too much to continue. This hunched-over position I was in had only made the sores worse.

"This isn't us, Trina. This isn't what we do."

"She deserves it. I also cut her wrist while we were in the carriage."

Simon crossed back to her, his voice still low. "Listen, I understand how you feel about Kestra, but we need her to succeed. This assignment requires you to put away your personal feelings."

"Have you?" A chair scooted across the floor. Trina standing up, perhaps? "I've seen the way you look at her. Maybe she's got a pretty face, but that's all. This girl is part of the Dominion! Don't let her get to you."

Get to Simon? The whole idea of that was a joke. He hated me, and I wasn't exactly planning parties for him. Not unless we were celebrating in my father's dungeons.

"She won't get to me. Anything beautiful about her faded as soon as she began defending Lord Endrick." Simon scowled. "I'm here to carry out the plan. Nothing more."

"I'm too tired to care." To prove her point, Trina yawned. "Can we discuss this tomorrow?"

Irritation filled Simon's sigh. If he preferred never to discuss me again, I had equal hopes of never having to hear it. He said, "You take the bed. I'll sleep on the floor."

If I'd really been asleep, Trina's rough entry into the bed surely would've awoken me, but I only pretended to stir and let my head fall forward again. The last thing I needed was for them to figure out I'd been listening to their conversation.

I wasn't sure exactly where Simon decided to sleep, but it wasn't long before they had both gone quiet and their breathing became even. Only now did I dare relax, but I couldn't do it, certainly not while standing up.

I twisted my hands again, working at the knots. It wasn't about getting free—I wouldn't go anywhere—but I did want these two Coracks to know they'd have to do better than this to control me.

The problem was, they *were* in control of me. They had me physically bound to this room, had extracted my agreement to betray the Lord of the Dominion and my family. They even controlled my emotions with every foul word or icy expression cast my way.

And I couldn't escape the knots. The cut from Trina had opened again and blood ran down my palm. The flesh beneath the ropes was hot and swelling. Worst of all, Simon was right. At home, I would have to come up with an excuse for my wounds. Nothing else could've caused these sores other than my being tied up.

Could these injuries be my proof that the rebels were forcing me to find the Blade? Wouldn't it become obvious that I was acting against my will? I finally relaxed with that thought, smiling at how they had surely doomed themselves and saved my life.

If I fell asleep, then it wasn't for long, when the sound of horses outside awoke me. At any other time of day, that wouldn't have deserved my attention, but this late at night, and in my present situation, everything seemed important.

I strained my neck, hoping for a glance out the window, but I wasn't close enough to see anything beyond dark trees silhouetted against the moonlight. There were noises from several horses though, and their riders were dismounting in front of the inn rather than taking them around back to the stables for the night. These people had not come for lodging.

Both Simon and Trina were still soundly asleep and I debated whether it was a good idea to wake them up. I should at least have them check who had come.

"Simon!" I hissed.

"Hush, Princess, or we'll gag you," he mumbled.

"Simon!"

He sat up as the riders entered the inn, loudly demanding to see the innkeeper. He leapt from the floor, tossing the blanket he'd been sleeping with back onto the bed. That startled Trina awake.

"Get her out of those ropes." Simon pointed at me, then reached for his boots.

"Why?" Trina asked.

He rushed to the window, and when he turned back to Trina, eyes wide and alert, she immediately understood.

"Blue-and-brown hats." Simon's voice tightened. "Halderians."

"Here?" Trina checked the window too. "Wearing their colors in the open?"

"They've come for me." Certain of my suspicions, a rushing sound filled my ears. "You can't fight them all. Give me a weapon."

"No chance." The way Trina sliced through the cords on my wrists showed her confidence. She wanted this fight.

"We're not fighting anyone." Simon was digging into his satchel. "Wait, don't—" He sighed. "You cut the ropes?"

Trina gathered the pieces from off the floor while I tried to regain some balance on my numb legs. "You said to get her out!"

"The rope could've gotten us out the window to escape."

"The window is sealed shut. I checked it earlier."

I started toward the window, but Simon pulled me back. "Don't let them see you."

"They obviously know I'm here." Though I wasn't sure how. Did *everyone* in the kingdom know where I was?

Without knocking, the innkeeper opened the door and shut it behind him. In any other circumstances, this would've been inexcusable, so his invasion signaled how serious the situation was. His focus went directly to me. "My lady, you must hide. Hurry."

He crossed past me and pressed on a panel of the bedroom wall, which swung open like a thin door when he released it. A small window was high above us, opened to allow air inside and a beam of moonlight by which to see. "This is why the Dallisor family chooses my inn," he whispered. "You are not the first to need it."

Was he joking? That tiny window couldn't possibly bring in enough air. Everything was stale in this hidden cupboard, and far too narrow. After he shut the door, the space would close in on me, my personal oubliette. I shook my head. "Find something else. I can't go in there."

"My lady . . ."

"I won't . . ." The panic began with numbing in the tips of my fingers, and moved into my heart, which was already racing wildly. My thoughts flew apart. All I knew was that I could not go into that tiny space. "I don't like—"

Simon pushed me inside, then motioned for Trina to join me. It would fit two people if we pressed close enough together, but not all three of us. Someone would have to remain in the room.

"Delay them," Simon said to the innkeeper. Once he had gone, Simon turned to Trina. "If they get this far, I'll stop them."

"You can't." Trina took a step back. "Kestra's trunk has women's clothes. When those men come, they'll expect to find a girl in this room. Besides, if she's missing, they'll expect her guard to be missing too, not her handmaiden."

"All right, but don't resist their search," Simon said as Trina returned his knife, something a handmaiden would never be expected to carry. Also his satchel, the only other item we had brought in from the carriage. "You can do this."

"Whatever happens, it's better than being stuffed in that wall with her," Trina said.

I didn't want to hide in here with Trina either. More accurately, I didn't want to hide inside this wall at all. I couldn't.

I started to push my way out, but Simon forced me back in, then flashed the knife at me. Did he think that would help? That he'd solve my growing panic with a threat? He seemed to recognize that and put his knife away. That didn't help either, because the knife was never the problem.

My shallow breathing got worse when the panel closed behind us. Simon faced me, our bodies now pressed together in a sort of harmony. He clasped my right hand in his, holding it between us. Even through my panic, I felt the strength of his grip.

With a grim smile, he whispered, "Do you remember when I was nine and got stuck in your chimney? It was smaller than this. The butler threatened to burn me out, but you tied a rope to my foot and pulled me down."

I didn't remember that. I didn't care. I barely heard him over the beat of my heart. How could it pound so loudly without him hearing it too?

"Look at me," Simon whispered. "Kestra, keep your eyes on me. I won't let those people take you again, I promise."

He couldn't make such a promise, nor did I need it. What I needed was to escape this thimble-sized space. And once I did, I needed a weapon of my own, such as that knife, sheathed again at his waist, opposite his sword. With my free hand, I felt for the knife's handle, but he moved before I could take it.

The Banished burst into my room with loud, angry voices. I didn't know how many there were but the bedroom seemed to shake under their combined weight. I must've dug my nails into Simon's hand, because he flinched until I loosened my grip.

"We've come for Kestra Dallisor," one of the men said. "Where is she?"

I knew that voice. His name was Tor, Torn . . . or Thorne.

Thorne. When I was taken from Woodcourt three years ago, he was the one who had grabbed me. I still remembered his rough hand over my mouth. The small box where he'd hidden me. The fear.

Simon's hand shifted to my back, and I realized I was shaking. His fingers were confident, each tip sending a pulse up my spine, trying to communicate that if I remained still, everything would be all right.

Everything would be all right. He seemed to believe that.

And somehow I believed it too. I believed *him*. How strange that feeling was.

In some ways, Simon was very different from the boy I remembered from so long ago, stronger, and with an air of confidence he never used to have. But now he was gentle, even kind, as he always was when we were children. I knew he was only doing this to protect Tenger's plan. But I wanted to believe a part of him was doing this to protect . . . me.

I had to win against the Coracks, obviously. But I regretted the consequences to Simon, who would have to lose.

Beginning with losing his knife. I still planned to get it. The problem was the commotion happening just outside this tiny room.

"Lady Kestra has been missing from Antora for years. She isn't here." The innkeeper was a worse liar than me, if that was possible.

"Are you sure?" I could hear the smile in Thorne's voice. "Give the lady up, or as the heavens are my witness, you will die."

· TEN ·

SIMON

I should've made Trina come into this space with Kestra. Not me. Not with our history. Not a breath away from me. This was too close.

Kestra's heart pounded against mine, and with every breath, I inhaled the cinnamon scent of her hair. A thin line of moonlight teased at the angle of her jaw and highlighted her dark lashes.

If I didn't know who she was, I would . . . but I did know. I knew her far too well.

Kestra's breaths were still shallow and too fast, too panicked. My hand moved to her face, my fingers brushing against her cheek. It wasn't a gesture of affection, but it did seem to calm her.

It did the very opposite to me.

As she relaxed, her body began molding to mine, impossibly becoming closer than before. Every shift of her position left me increasingly unsettled and distracted, a dangerous combination.

In the outer room, Trina was in far more danger. If I could've stayed in the room to help her, I would have. But if I had, they'd know Kestra was here too.

"I'll ask you again," one of the men said. "Where is Kestra?"

The innkeeper seemed to be at a loss for words, but Trina

quickly filled in. "I'm Lady Kestra's handmaiden. She was here until about two hours ago. Then she heard of an approaching threat—you, I assume—and rode on with her guard for Highwyn. They'll be there by morning."

"Her carriage is still outside," a man said.

"They left by oropod, naturally. It's faster."

"Oropods." The man snorted. "Evil creatures born of dark magic. Kestra agreed to travel on one?"

Trina's voice rose in pitch. "I'm telling you the truth, sir. If my lady were here, do you think I'd have been allowed in this bed?"

"We have a . . . *gift* for her in this sack. Something Darrow wanted."

Kestra's attention was immediately drawn to the mention of her servant's name. When she realized I had noticed, she looked away, but her breaths became harsher than before.

"What is the gift?" Trina asked. "Give it to me, and I'll see that my lady gets it."

"Tell me where Kestra really is, and I'll give it to her myself." When Trina remained silent, he said to the other Halderians with him, "Search this inn, every room. Kill anyone who stands in your way."

Kestra tried to push past me, obviously wanting to surrender herself, but I pressed her back to the wall. This was not negotiable. I felt the same ache for the guests here as she did, but her promise to find the Olden Blade was bigger than this one moment, and ultimately would save more lives than might be lost tonight.

Footsteps pounded into the hallway, though it sounded as if at least one man had remained in the bedroom. He seemed to be making a cursory search, though with such spare furnishings, he shouldn't be out there for long.

Kestra touched my cheek to get my attention. If only she knew how much she already had it. She motioned again that she wanted to leave this passage. I gave her hand a firm squeeze, then pressed it flat against my chest, where she could feel my heartbeat. A heartbeat was life, and all that mattered now was to remind her she was alive, and would remain so if she stayed quiet. It seemed to calm her a bit, so I left it there. Would she notice the quickening of its pace, the way each beat seemed to beg her to come closer?

Kestra began breathing more evenly again, and her eyes closed as if she was deep in thought. I took the chance to steal another look at her. To ask myself who she really was.

A cipher. A lockbox.

A girl who'd obviously learned long ago how to keep her guard up. She wasn't always this way, I remembered that.

Then she opened her eyes, letting them drift to mine like a rising dawn. Her stare was heat, melting away my defenses, exposing more than I'd ever intended for her to see: the real me, flawed and too often foolish, and funneled into a life of rebellion. Certain of nothing but the weight of her hand on my chest. Aware of nothing but the softening of her expression, the parting of her lips. Her other hand wrapped around my waist, though I noticed a slight tremble of her fingers, nervous, anticipating. I was nervous too.

Something about her had gotten beneath my skin, like an itch that couldn't be scratched. And that was hard enough when she was across the room or out of my sight, but here, now, the itch was unbearable.

Every instinct within me shouted to turn away from her. To keep her out of my mind, and certainly nowhere near my heart.

I knew exactly who and what she was, and I had some idea of Tenger's ultimate plans for her. Only a fool would pretend that she was any kind of heroine, or that her past crimes should be forgiven.

Yet she wasn't a villain either. She seemed genuinely concerned for her servants, and had just tried to sacrifice herself rather than put anyone else at risk. On my darkest days at Woodcourt, she used to smile for me.

And the way she was looking at me now. Drawing me in, a willing moth to the flame.

This was the girl who'd nearly gotten me killed six years ago. The girl who surely had been making plans to try again since the first second of her capture. She could not be trusted. I knew that.

Just as I knew I should not be leaning in to her.

Kissing her was the last thing on my mind.

But there it was . . . on my mind.

Something in the bedroom made a sudden crashing sound. We startled apart, the moment severed between us.

"I know you, girl," the Halderian in the room said. "Don't I?"

Trina murmured something inaudible and laughed nervously, but Kestra caught my unguarded reaction. There shouldn't be any reason for a Halderian to recognize Trina.

A new man entered the room, reporting, "She's not here. Maybe she did leave."

"Is Kestra hiding somewhere?" This was the first man speaking again, more sharply now. "This is your last chance to answer."

It wasn't clear whether that question was addressed to the

innkeeper or to Trina, but the innkeeper made a high-pitched gasp. "I serve the Dallisor family as they serve the Lord of the Dominion." His denial was followed by a sharp cry.

Just as before, Kestra tried to push forward, but I held her back. She shook her head, her eyes filling with tears. She pushed at me again, but I cupped my hand around the back of her neck and drew her to me. Her head turned sideways against my chest, and the desperate clutch of her hand on my arm soothed some of the anger within me. I held her tighter as her body trembled with sorrow, but she remained quiet.

"Don't kill me." The innkeeper's pained voice pled for mercy. "If you have any message for Lady Kestra, tell it to me. I will be sure she hears it."

"The Halderians are organizing, and we're coming for her again," a man said. "To anyone who stands between us, that is the message."

Trina cried out as the innkeeper grunted and a body fell to the floor. Had they killed him?

Kestra pulled away from me, her expression one of horror. As much as she wanted to get out of this hiding place, surely those men had made it clear how deadly serious they were about finding her.

She had the same seriousness about her as well. She raised a knife—my knife, in fact, stolen from the sheath at my waist. I scowled, knowing I'd been tricked. We'd deal with that issue later, because I guaranteed there'd be a fight about this. But for now, I grabbed her arm and pressed it against the back wall, which instantly cracked. The brittle wood was older than I'd thought.

Kestra's eyes sparked. She wouldn't dare.

"No," I quietly warned.

But she did. She raised a leg and kicked it backward against the same panel. The wood didn't break entirely, but it splintered enough to let a wisp of air through.

"What was that?" the first man asked. "You all, stay here and find out where that sound came from. I'll go outside!" He must've been talking to the other Halderians in the room.

I grabbed Kestra's shoulders, hoping to stop her from breaking through to the outside wall, but her expression was fully defiant. When she kicked backward again, a small hole opened. Behind it, the trunk of the oak tree could be seen.

The Halderians began pounding on the right side of the wall, trying to break in. They'd eventually find the door.

Kestra kicked yet again, widening the hole.

"There'll be more of them outside," I hissed. "You'll fall right into their arms!"

"Come out!" a new man ordered, addressing me. "I have your girl!"

Trina gasped, so I knew the threat was real. "I can't open the panel!" she shrieked. "I don't know how it's done!"

Furious at Kestra, who was still bent on widening the hole she'd made, I shoved open the secret door, drew the sword that had been at my side, and charged into the room.

The man closest to me was wiry in build, carrying a horseman's axe that most Halderians favored. He raised his weapon, still coated in the innkeeper's blood. So far, Trina appeared to be safe. I took the aggressor's stance and locked blades with him.

From the corner of my eye, I saw Trina lunge toward the secret cupboard, but Kestra was already climbing through the hole, which was barely wide enough to squeeze through.

I didn't know if Kestra could make the jump between the hole and the tree, but it was clear she intended to try. While I finished this fight, Trina would have to follow Kestra.

"You're insane!" Trina scowled.

"I'll survive." Kestra's words were clearly a taunt. "Not sure if you will."

"Kestra?" Getting his first good look at her, my opponent seemed to forget about everyone else in the room. "You must come with us!"

I used the distraction to thrust my blade into the man's gut, feeling his pain for myself, as I always did. He fell, but other footsteps pounded up the stairs. More Halderians. My only option was the hole Kestra had made. She must've made a successful jump, because Trina immediately followed. Through the hole in the wall, I heard Trina say, "I hate you, Kestra. I really do."

By the time I got to the hole, Kestra had already shinnied to the ground and was wrangling one of the Halderian's horses. Trina was shouting at her to hurry, that more Halderians were coming.

There was no time to think, or even to beg the heavens' forgiveness before I jumped. The first tree branch I grabbed quaked beneath my weight, then broke almost immediately. I fell past three or four other branches, failing to slow myself down, then landed on a thicker branch below it and from there, simply dropped to the ground. The bruising in my feet tomorrow would be brutal.

To get into the saddle, Kestra had used my knife to lengthen an existing tear in her skirt halfway up her leg. The fact that she knew how to ride astride was surprising. Girls of her status all rode sidesaddle, if they rode at all. But Kestra knew exactly what she was doing.

Another problem I'd have to deal with after we escaped. *If we escaped.*

Meanwhile, Trina had taken the reins of another horse into her hands and shooed the rest of the horses away. She was making it impossible for the men to follow.

Which they would try to do. I already heard yelling that we were outside.

I scrambled to my feet, and although Kestra tried to maneuver her horse away from me, I got hold of one rein and yanked the horse toward me. I swung into the saddle behind her and rapped the horse's side with my heels.

"I can handle this horse just fine!" she scowled. "Why don't you get your own?"

"Because I know you can handle this horse just fine. Were you escaping with us, or from us?" I sped up the horse enough to discourage her from attempting to slide off, then called to Trina. "Let's get off the road!"

Trina checked the skies. "The moon will go behind the clouds soon. We'll have the darkness on our side."

We left the road and headed into a patch of weeds, which would openly expose us, but if we weren't spotted, we'd soon be in the trees, where it would be much easier to hide. Trina was keeping up behind us, though she was hissing at Kestra the whole time.

"You never should've kicked through that wall! You gave away your hiding place!"

"I had to, based on the stellar way you were handling things!" Kestra snapped.

We angled back toward the inn. Trina cursed my decision until she understood my intention: The building would mask us. The men would likely split up to search the area, but I doubted they'd think to look behind the inn itself.

It would have been better to enter All Spirits Forest, on the opposite side of the road. Magic was said to exist there, both for good and for evil. For that reason, the Halderians wouldn't be stupid enough to follow us in. But I wasn't stupid either.

As soon as we were deep enough into the woods behind the inn, I growled at Kestra. "Kicking out that panel could've gotten us all killed, including you!"

"Well, maybe you should've threatened someone else!" she replied with equal force. "I'm sorry this kidnapping isn't going the way you wanted! Did you also want to thank me for saving your lives back there, or are you angry about that too?"

"I'm definitely angry," I said, and I meant it. Despite that, I smiled. "But maybe one day, I'll return the favor and save your life."

She frowned back. "Coming from someone who's currently threatening my life, you'll forgive me for doubting you."

For a moment, I'd forgotten that we were on opposite sides of this rebellion, and yes, that if anything went wrong with the plan, I had my orders from Tenger. But the first night with Kestra wasn't over, and I'd already begun to wonder if I could fulfill those orders.

· ELEVEN ·

KESTRA

Simon led us over a small hill where the brush became too thick to continue. We moved slower now, which helped to soothe everyone's ragged nerves. By the time Simon stopped, both he and Trina seemed as tired as I felt, too weary to argue anymore.

"They won't find us here," Simon said. "I think we're safe to rest and wait out the night." Hopefully he was right.

I ignored Trina's complaints about how she hadn't slept for even an hour back at the inn. Did she think I'd have sympathy, or that I'd care? Thanks to her, I'd barely slept at all. The exhaustion was making me dizzy.

Simon dismounted, and this time I did accept his steadying hands at my waist. That was better than falling onto the ground, which I might've done. But rather than releasing me, his grip tightened. "Give me that knife."

I didn't want to. "A knife is the most basic of weapons," Darrow once taught me. "Learn it first and learn it well."

I pulled my hand free from Simon's and backed away. "What if they come again?"

Neither of them had an answer for that. "No one knows we're here," Trina finally said. "They came to the inn because your servant told them you'd be there. Darrow betrayed you."

"He wouldn't. There must be another explanation."

"He betrayed you, Princess." Simon had begun tying up the horses and barely looked at me as he spoke. "Get used to that. There's nobody you can trust."

"Including you two?"

Trina snorted. "If you ever try a trick like that again, trust me to make your kidnapping seem like a birthday party."

Simon walked up to me, the curl of his lip a clear signal of how little patience he had left. I raised the knife to defend myself, but he grabbed my forearm, pinching until he forced the weapon's release. "Get some sleep, Princess."

"Stop calling me that—you know I'm nothing of the sort." I sat down against a tree and stifled a yawn. "The Lord of the Dominion rules alone."

"As long as you act like a spoiled princess, that's what I'll call you," he said.

I swallowed every retort that would have started yet another fight, then turned away from them both, hoping when I woke up, all of this would have been a dream. Burying myself into the folds of my cloak, I realized this was nothing so simple as dreaming. My life had become a nightmare.

———◆———

Simon shook me awake before dawn. Instinctively, I flung out a fist, catching his shoulder hard enough to knock him backward. He chuckled as he rolled back to his feet. "Not a morning person, I see."

I reclined again, eager for even a minute or two more of sleep. "Go away."

"It's a five-hour ride to Highwyn. Stand up, or I'll pull you to your feet."

"I've got to figure out an excuse for the slit in my gown and wounds on my wrists. If my father sees me this way, I'll be in serious trouble. Come back in an hour."

He grabbed my hand and pulled me to a sitting position. I opened my eyes, more irritated than awake. At least he looked as tired as I felt. Trina came into focus behind him, in a yellow dress trimmed with a beaded blue sash. *My* dress, *my* sash, both of which had been left behind at the inn. That got my attention, and I stood, pointing at her. "Where did you get that?"

She pointed to a clump of bushes nearby. A blue dress with a patterned skirt and cropped vest had been laid over it, kept off the damp morning ground.

"You went back for these?" I asked.

"Simon did during the night. This blue dress has very long sleeves. We think they'll cover your wrists."

Simon reached into a pocket of his trousers and pulled out a handful of gold coins. "I also found these in your trunk. My payment for having to deal with you."

"The sack that Thorne—one of the Banished—brought to the inn, did you get that too?"

His gaze remained steady. "There was nothing in it of value. Only a lure to draw you out from your hiding place."

"What was it?"

He shook his head. "I already told you. Nothing of value. Get dressed. I'll go water the horses."

After he'd left, Trina tossed the blue dress at me. I thrust it back at her. "You're my lady-in-waiting. You dress me."

She threw it at me again. "I'm not your maid. Dress yourself."

"If you want anyone to believe you're a maid, you'd better know how to do it."

"Maybe you're the one who doesn't know!" Trina's smile became smug. "That's the truth, isn't it? You don't know how to dress yourself."

I knew *how* to do it, obviously. I'd just never had to do it. But it was irrelevant. I didn't see how the ability to dress oneself mattered. If Trina was my superior, then how had she failed to notice the leaves in the back of her hair from where she'd slept?

I tossed the dress onto another bush and started walking away. "When we arrive at Woodcourt, I'm going to blame you for my appearance. I assume you know what happens to lazy servants of the Dallisors."

Trina muttered a string of curse words, all of them aimed at me, and then grabbed the blue dress. This one was more complicated to put on than most, with crossed ribbons on the front that needed to be laced at the back. A row of buttons also ran up the spine, tiny enough to frustrate even the most patient servant. I wouldn't be surprised if Trina quit before she finished dressing me. Celia had threatened to do just that the last time I'd chosen to wear this dress.

Celia. I wondered what was happening to her right now. Her screams still haunted me.

"Before we leave, we should talk about your first task once you're home," Trina said. "Somewhere inside your father's home is a diary that I need to read."

"Whose diary?"

"I can only say what it looks like."

I rolled my eyes. "By chance will it look like a book?" If this was a sample of what it would be like to work with Trina, I would soon die from prolonged exposure to idiocy.

Trina's impatience took the form of an extra-hard pull on the ribbons of my dress. "It will be covered in pink satin with flowers hand-sewn into the fabric."

"A woman's diary, then," I mused. "Risha Halderian's?"

"Perhaps. Or Anaya's, her servant, who went into the dungeons with her. Anaya was Endrean, just like Endrick. Maybe her magic allowed her to hide the diary."

"Her magic could save a diary, but not her mistress's life?" I chuckled, communicating how ridiculous I thought this entire notion was. "If you're right and Risha brought a diary into the Woodcourt dungeons, what do you suppose happened to it? Do you think she was given an ink and quill, and perhaps a comfortable sofa where she could recline as she wrote out her plan to kill Lord Endrick?"

She said, "Just find that book. It will lead us to the Olden Blade."

Trina tugged at another ribbon, cursing me for owning such a complicated gown, as if I'd care that she was irritated. If anything, I was disappointed in myself for not having been awful enough to make her abandon this plan, just to get away from me. It wasn't for lack of trying.

She added, "The diary might have belonged to someone else too.

All I can tell you is that it's vital to our plan. We find it, and we find the Olden Blade."

I sighed again, louder this time. "Let's pretend you're right—because there has to be a first time for everything—and there's some special diary at Woodcourt containing the secret to all the mysteries of life. If it's just there to be read, then it's been studied a thousand times, searched for any clues about the location of the Olden Blade. But you, who probably can't read your own name, think you will find something new in those pages?"

"I will." Trina was all business, just as she was all heart. By then, Trina was working on my hair, pulling at it so roughly that I fully expected to be bald before she finished. When she had formed it into a clumsy sort of plait, she said, "Beauty hides your ugly heart."

I swerved on her. "Is this about those forty people my father executed? Because if so—"

"If I listed all the reasons I hate you, we'd be here until sundown. Let's go find Simon."

At least that meant we were leaving. I'd choose a torture rack over spending another minute alone with Trina.

Simon was saddling the horses as we arrived. I assumed our travel would take place as it had last night, with Trina on one horse, and Simon and I on the other. That way he could keep control of me. Or believe that he was.

"I have questions," I began. "Are the Banished still in the area? Do they know you're after the Blade?"

"It's more important to focus on what happens when we get to Highwyn." He barely looked at me as he spoke. "Your story will be that thieves attempted a robbery of the inn. Darrow was killed but I rescued you and your handmaiden here. Don't say anything more specific than that."

I huffed. "I was being entirely honest before, Simon. This plan, to get the dagger, will fail. We can't just walk into the dungeons and ask to search them, and even if we do, we won't find it because it's not there. Please go back to Tenger and release my servants. It might be the only chance any of us has to survive."

"Get on the horse or we'll drag you behind it," Simon said. "We're not giving up."

He didn't know it yet, but those words were about to become his biggest problem. Because I wasn't giving up either. Not even close.

· TWELVE ·

SIMON

Kestra rode sidesaddle in front of me, with Trina on the mount behind us. I held my arms away from her as I managed the reins, a necessary inconvenience. Foolishly, I'd lowered my guard with her last night, which could've gotten us killed. I wasn't about to let that happen again.

We rode in silence, with thick woods on one side and a vast stretch of farmland on the other, probably owned by loyalists who were granted use of the land in exchange for the donation of soldiers to the Dominion. Lower-class Antorans could farm, but before they pulled their first crop from the ground, half of the land's yield would go to the Dominion. Some of it would end up on Kestra's supper table without her asking once where it had come from.

She turned back to me with a mischievous smile. "You're afraid of me, I can tell."

No, I wasn't going to play. "I'm not afraid of you, Princess."

"Yes, you are."

I grimaced. "Why do you think that?"

"It's obvious by the way your arms hover around me, as if touching me is dangerous."

"It is. I learned that last night."

Her smile darkened. "That was nothing. End this now, while you still can."

If only I could.

The horses were keeping up a brisk, constant pace, and every step closer to Highwyn quickened the pounding of my heart. Despite what Trina had said last night, I couldn't shake the worry that Kestra might be right about the Olden Blade. Tenger's entire plan was built on the premise that we would find it. What if it couldn't be found? What would happen then? The fact that the Halderians also knew Kestra was returning to Highwyn only complicated an already precarious mission.

The Halderian clan and the Coracks had similar goals—to remove Lord Endrick from power. But the Halderians mistrusted us, thinking that all we wanted was a back door to the throne, and maybe Tenger did. He had resisted any effort for the two groups to unite, saying he would not sacrifice his men to put a Halderian on the throne.

"If we find the Blade, then we can choose the Infidante," Tenger had said in his final speech to us before we launched this mission. "And the Infidante will choose the next king. Why shouldn't Antora kneel before a Corack?" I'd cheered along with everyone else at the time, with no idea then how I'd be drawn deeper into Tenger's plan.

And now I had to complete this mission. It required me to separate Kestra entirely from my feelings. Maybe in time, I could forget my anger or forgive her naïve view of the world, but how could I ignore the emotions she had stirred in me last night, feelings that only intensified the more I tried to shake them off?

With the same mischievous smile as before, Kestra turned to me and asked, "Why do you always stare at me?"

I shifted my eyes to the road ahead. "I don't."

"You were just now. Tell me why."

"You remind me of a girl I once hated, that's all."

Her smile fell. "Did you really hate me back then?"

If anything, I'd liked her more than someone of my station ever should have dared. I recalled one summer's day when she was nine, and I'd seen her dancing alone in the gardens. Her dress had twisted in a perfect circle as she swirled around, the beads on her scarf reflecting pops of light. The head servant caught me looking and I lost a full day's meals. Kestra probably never knew I'd been there.

"I never hated you," I mumbled. "Until—"

"Until that day." Now Kestra became serious, and lowered her voice to a near whisper. "How do the Banished know Trina?"

"Can you use their names, please? The Halderians."

"How do they know her, Simon? Thorne told Trina he knew her."

"Trina denied it."

"No, she laughed at him. That's different."

I pinched the bridge of my nose. What had started as a headache back at the inn was quickly becoming a thunderstorm inside my head. "What's your point?"

"My point is that she's working with them!"

"If she was, then why would he have to say that he knew her? He'd know her and she'd know him—he wouldn't have to say it."

"Forget that," she scowled. "*How* does he know her?"

"How does he know Darrow?" I countered. "Why did Darrow arrange with the Halderians to meet you at that inn? He obviously didn't share that detail."

She bit down on her lip and looked away. Clearly, that bothered her, a vulnerability I would absolutely use to my advantage.

I continued, "Darrow apologized to you last night. Why?"

"Maybe for failing to protect me from you."

"Maybe for turning you over to the Halderians."

She fell silent, and stubbornly faced forward without saying another word. Good. I needed the break.

After another hour of riding, we passed through a dismal market that looked like the center of what had been a nice town once, probably before the war. A grand fountain had dried up and filled with leaves, its foundation cracked. A church in the distance had been looted down to its frame and steeple. The few homes that remained had disintegrated into little more than dried mud and bundled-reed shacks. The coming winter rains would destroy what was left of them.

A fair number of people were here, so it was likely the only market within miles. I heard a passerby call this place Pitwill. A sad name for an even sadder place.

I leaned toward Kestra to whisper in her ear, "Keep your head down. A Dallisor shouldn't be alone in a group like this."

"I'm not alone, I have you and Trina." She tilted her head. "Oh, I see what you mean. I *might as well* be alone."

She could mock me if she wanted, but I'd been trying to help. "What I mean is that nearly everyone here is trying to survive beneath the might of Lord Endrick's immortal fist. They know the Dallisors enforce his cruelty, and nobody here would lose any sleep if they showed you what being crushed feels like."

"They wouldn't dare."

I hoped her show of arrogance was a mask to soothe her nerves. If it wasn't, this simple ride through town could go badly. I tried again. "Stop looking around. And cover your dress with your cloak. It's too elegant for these parts."

"You chose it. I'd be better off in the ripped one from last night."

"I hardly think a skirt ripped halfway up your thigh would keep people from noticing you." I followed that with a chuckle that sounded fake and forced. Which it was.

We rode deeper into the market, passing vendors selling cloth and bonnets that a lot of women were staring at but nobody was buying, and fat cuts of meat that practically made the men drool. Disk bows were laid out on another counter, but they were cheaply made with blunt-edged disks that wouldn't cut through a summer breeze. No one had money for luxuries here, although payment wasn't always made in coins. To avoid the heavy taxes, a lot of under-the-table bargaining happened in places like this. Kestra probably had no idea of any of it. In her world, she ordered what she wanted from a servant and never saw the faces of those who were slowly starving to death.

Proof of that was in her next question. "Why are the people so poor here?"

"Here?" Trina, riding near us, scoffed. "Get five minutes of distance from Highwyn, and you'll see it's like this everywhere. Last year, Endrick demanded three-quarters of everything the people produced. When they protested, he came in and took all of it. There was a lot of starvation over the winter, and a lot of deaths. Simon and I both lost friends."

"Fewer rebels in Antora? Good." But as she spoke, Kestra's

shoulders slumped a little. I knew firsthand how winters passed in the Dallisor households. No family member ever suffered a hungry or cold night. If they lacked something, they sent soldiers to pilfer it from the defenseless. If Kestra had never wondered where all her niceties came from, then it was about time for her to find out. There was a reason the only line in this market was for the cheapest item available: bread.

The girl selling it couldn't have been older than eleven or twelve, and I overheard as she introduced herself as Rosalie to a customer in line. The hems of her skirt were frayed and dirty, but she was clean otherwise. Not that it mattered. I smelled her bread from here, and even if she were covered in dung, I'd still have wanted a loaf. I'd eaten worse before.

At the moment, Rosalie was being pestered by a woman who insisted she should get a better price because she bought bread every day.

"I can't," Rosalie protested. "I don't set the price."

The woman got louder and Rosalie more anxious, enough that she didn't see a young boy sneaking up on the back of the stall. He took one loaf, and when he got away with that, he put three more loaves under his arm and scampered away.

Kestra had been observing him too. I asked, "Is he a criminal? Or is he simply hungry?"

"I suspect he's both." Then with a humbler tone, she added, "But I see your point. He should be fed, not arrested."

"Rosalie, you stupid girl!" A man appeared from a small tent behind us, putrid enough to offend the common pig. "We just had more bread stolen! I warned you last time." He shoved her to the ground, yelling, "You'll pay for that!"

"No, she won't," Kestra mumbled. Before I realized her intentions, she slipped beneath my arms and jumped off the horse.

The man hadn't yet noticed Kestra. Instead, he picked up a stick from the ground and raised it against Rosalie. From behind, Kestra grabbed his upraised arm and locked it with hers while with the other arm she put a knife against his throat.

I felt for my sheath and cursed. When did she take my knife . . . again?

That had been a masterful move on Kestra's part. More reason to worry about exactly who we had captured. Kestra was naïve, but she was also dangerous.

"Run," Kestra said to Rosalie, who merely stood there, frozen with fear.

I slid off the horse, one hand on my sword, approaching Kestra like I would a frightened child. "Let this man go. Dominion soldiers will be here. Let's not call their attention to us."

"You will be arrested for this," the man said. "Rosalie is my property to deal with in my own way!"

"She's no one's property," Kestra said. "And no longer your concern."

Rosalie probably was his property, something else Kestra had yet to learn about her country. Indenturement wasn't exactly legal, but the Dominion always overlooked it.

At my continued urging, Kestra released the man and he turned to face her, then laughed, revealing several missing teeth. "Well, you ain't more than a child yourself. A wealthy one too, I can tell. Pay me enough, and you can take Rosalie with you."

The knife twisted in Kestra's hand. "How dare you demand payment? I just told her she's free to go."

His beady eyes narrowed further. "Oh, *you* told her, like you're something special? If she tries to leave, she'll pay for it."

Kestra turned to Rosalie. "Run. I'll take care of this!" And this time, Rosalie left, though she only crossed the square and crouched beside a small wooden fence, huddled, waiting to see what would happen next.

The man immediately cried out, "Thieves! Arrest these two!"

I grabbed Kestra's hand, trying to pull her back toward our horse. But she shook it free, and instead landed a fist on the man's fleshy jaw.

As he reeled backward, she said, "We cannot steal what cannot be owned."

"Stop!" Two Dominion soldiers ran forward, wearing black uniforms with a green stripe across the shoulders. Endrick's colors.

I'd already noticed their eyes. Glazed over, looking but not truly seeing. These were Ironhearts. Through those eyes, Endrick might not be aware of everything happening here, but then again, he might. Either way, this was a disaster.

One soldier grabbed Kestra, but she twisted around and with a steady voice said, "My name is Kestra Dallisor. You will release me at once!"

Her voice was firm as she spoke. Dallisors never hesitated to say their name, especially to inferiors, which they figured everyone was. Except Lord Endrick, of course.

"Daughter of Sir Henry Dallisor?" The soldier who spoke

immediately dipped his head at Kestra and let her go. "We heard your father was bringing you home. Our apologies."

She nodded at Rosalie, still crouched near the fence. "You will not threaten that girl, on my orders."

"No, my lady, of course not. If you are headed to Highwyn, it would be our honor to escort you there."

It would also be their honor to arrest me and Trina and escort us to Highwyn as their trophies. I didn't know these men, or, at least, I didn't think I did. But I'd offended plenty of soldiers before. It was possible they knew me.

Kestra gestured at me. "I've already got a protector. He'll take me home."

I straightened up in a lame attempt to look confident, but based on my rigid smile, the soldiers had to be wondering if I had thorns inside my boots. If only my life were that simple.

"Your young protector was unable to keep you out of trouble here," the second soldier said dismissively. "We'll get our oropods and meet you back on the main road."

Kestra agreed, far too readily, and my temper warmed. As soon as they were gone, I marched over to her. "This is perfect! Are you going to have Trina and me arrested now, or wait until we're closer to your father's dungeons?"

"I did us a favor," she hissed. "If they accept you two as my servants, nobody in Highwyn will question it. I just got you both inside Woodcourt's gates!"

"Escorted by guards whose careers will be made if they figure out who Trina and I are. All you do is make things worse!" I pointed to Rosalie. "Do you think you helped her? Where will she work tomorrow, and the day after that? You've doomed her, and probably her entire family!"

Kestra's cheeks reddened before she shoved past me and crossed over to Rosalie. She removed her cloak and wrapped it around Rosalie's shoulders, then knelt in front of her. "Your family needs to find another place to live. Far enough away that you don't have to work in this market."

Rosalie's lower lip quivered. "We have no money to leave."

"You do now." Kestra held out a hand to me, but I was already on my way with her bag of coins. I gave them to Kestra, who passed them to Rosalie.

"I'm so sorry," Kestra said. "I was trying to help."

Rosalie nodded back, as if to acknowledge that Kestra hadn't intended any of this. It didn't matter. Kestra looked wounded, stripped of her Dallisor superiority. I almost pitied her.

When she stood again, I took her arm. "Our escorts will be waiting." My tone was gentle. After what had just happened, Kestra would scold herself far worse than I ever could.

This time she went with me. Every face in the market watched her leave, none of them in a friendly way, and I knew she felt it. One hand was on my sword, but nobody would try anything. Not with Dominion soldiers nearby.

Trina was still on her horse, holding the reins for the mount we had been riding. Her face was nearly purple with anger.

Before climbing on the horse, Kestra paused to say, "I didn't know places like this existed."

And I didn't know how to respond to words filled with such sadness. I finally said, "Dallisors do not live in the same world as the rest of us."

She gave a halfhearted shrug. "That's why everyone thinks Dallisors are horrible people, right? Because we support a ruler who allows such a country as this? Maybe we are horrible. Maybe I am, and I never knew it."

Maybe. Or, there was a thought that bothered me more. Maybe she wasn't horrible at all. Despite my efforts to pretend otherwise, she had gotten into my head, stirring up emotions that kept my breath lodged in my throat whenever I looked at her. I could tell myself this was only the energy between rivals, or the stress of the mission we were about to undertake, but that'd be a lie. Whatever I felt, it was real and growing stronger. I'd sooner divide the sun from its light than separate Kestra Dallisor from my feelings.

· THIRTEEN ·

KESTRA

As awful as I felt upon leaving Pitwill, what remained of the ride into Highwyn only worsened my mood. The poverty we saw on our journey was rampant, with empty shops, abandoned or neglected homes, and children in overgrown fields foraging for scraps to eat. This was good land. Where were the people who used to tend it?

Meanwhile, I was headed home to a manor of brick and stone with deep woven carpets and plush bedding. At each meal, we'd be offered more food than we could possibly consume, and every day, I'd have my choice of new dresses to wear. I was utterly ashamed of myself. How could I not know these realities of life outside of Highwyn?

Behind me, Simon barely said a word for the entire ride, if his occasional mumbles could be considered that much. Trina kept quiet too, which was a relief. If we weren't being escorted, they'd have had plenty to say. About what a terrible person I was, how I'd ruined Rosalie's life, perhaps a comparison of me and the average rabid skunk.

Trina could say any of that and it would roll off me without leaving a scratch. But I didn't want to hear it from Simon. I'd spent much of this ride replaying in my head the way he'd looked at me last night, while we hid inside the wall. His hands on my face and back, the warmth of his expression.

Him.

It was all a game to distract me from the trouble outside while I was distracting him from his knife—I knew that. Nothing that had happened there was real. But I wondered what it would be like to see that gentleness in his eyes again . . . when he meant it.

From there, my thoughts descended to dangerous levels.

Lord Endrick was not a tolerant man. That was something I'd always understood, even when very young. Before she died, my mother had been afraid of him and taught me to be afraid too. She'd kept me hidden every time he came to our home. She whispered about the violence of his magic, and the casual cruelty of his heart. I accidentally encountered him once when he'd come for a supper, and remembered him saying that he'd forgotten Henry Dallisor even had a daughter. Then he'd ordered me away, claiming that I had the look of trouble in my eyes. I'd gone to a looking glass from there, searching my face for what he might have meant. It was years before I understood it, and before I saw that same look too.

The official Dominion explanation for Endrick's harsh rule was that it was forced upon Antora by the uncooperative masses, by the Corack rebels who terrorized the countryside, and by the occasional appearance of a Halderian, which always caused unrest as people wondered if they would bring back another war. Nobody wanted that, certainly not me. Even if things were bad, maybe it was best to let everything remain as it was. Trying to help only made lives worse. Rosalie proved that.

But what if Tenger was right? What if the Olden Blade was real, and the Infidante could be found among the Banished to claim it? If that was true, then I was playing a role in Endrick's downfall.

And my own family's downfall.

And possibly the collapse of Antora itself.

A wave of nausea rose in me, forcing my hands into fists to fight it back. I had always loved my country, but what if I only loved the idea of it, of what Antora could have been if anyone else were on that throne? Maybe I'd spent a lifetime staring at a glossy painting of Antora, beautiful and rich in color, but which was actually rotting beneath the surface.

If that was true, then there were other questions I had to ask, with answers that could earn my execution. What if saving Antora required Lord Endrick's destruction? What if the Coracks were right?

Simon touched my arm, and I jumped. "Are you all right? You seem nervous."

Nervous? No, I was unnerved, and completely unsure of what I was meant to do next. I just had to get home, back to what was familiar, and center myself again. Then everything would be all right.

"I'm fine," I said to Simon. It was a lie, but I made myself believe it, at least until the worst of the nausea passed.

Crossing into the capital city of Highwyn required us to pass between the Sentries, two blue granite statues so enormous that on horseback, we were barely taller than the toe of a Sentry's foot. The one to our right stood as a warning to all who came, his sword outstretched and body in a fighting posture. The one to the left faced toward the city, its sword sheathed and arm outstretched, an invitation to leave in peace. The Sentries had been built by the Dallisors during our family's earliest days in power. My mother once told me that Endrick hated them, felt dwarfed by them, but had never destroyed them for fear of losing our family's support.

Immediately after crossing the Sentries' Gate, the hills of Highwyn rose before us. The capital city was grand and regal, its streets clean and in good repair. Buildings were close together and stood tall. Each new layer upon the city became increasingly elegant as Highwyn's height grew along with its wealth. Numerous suspended bridges overhead connected the various buildings, leaving the narrow streets for animals and carriages. My father often described postwar Antora as an empire in eternal blossom, reflecting the immortality of its Lord. But if that were true, how would he explain what I'd seen in the countryside, in Pitwill? The Lord of the Dominion's green and black colors waved in flags hung over most building entrances. The streets remained busy for most hours of the day, populated by loyalists or those who wanted Dominion favors. And the deeper we went into the city, the tighter Simon's hand gripped his sword and the more ashen Trina's face became. I figured I was still more nervous than the two of them combined. They were risking their lives for this mission, but so was I. If they succeeded in obtaining the Olden Blade, I would also lose my honor, what was left of my family, and any future I might have otherwise had. But with soldiers as our escorts, none of us could go back now.

In the center of town, an ancient Halderian monument dedicated to the citizens of Antora was gradually being replaced with a grand statue of Lord Endrick. I'd been told it would be completed by spring and then the entire country would celebrate it together. After what I'd seen earlier today, I knew people would stand in the streets when commanded to do so, with smiles on their faces and cursing us under their breaths.

The higher we climbed the hills of Highwyn, the more Dallisor family homes could be seen. They were easily identified by the Dallisor crest on the gates, a shield with the upper half depicting the conquering sword of Gridwyn Dallisor, and the lower half a solid red, representing the Scarlet Throne of Antora. It was a source of family pride and, I assumed, of pain as well. The throne belonged to Lord Endrick now.

Of all the houses on the hill, my home, Woodcourt, stood highest among them all. That was because of my father's position in the kingdom. Lord Endrick's coziest lapdog.

The Dominion Palace sat highest on the hills of Highwyn, almost as if Woodcourt itself bowed to Lord Endrick, which I supposed was accurate enough. I'd never been allowed inside, nor had I ever asked to enter. Despite its glistening marble walls, the palace felt dark to me. A tomb for an immortal Lord.

Up here, near the palace walls, it wasn't hard to know when Endrick's condors were near. Their screeches carried for almost a mile and always left my ears ringing.

Endrick had created his own breed of the bird, born of magic and his unquenchable thirst for death. Each was large enough to carry a grown man and had talons that could rip flesh. At the palace, they were caged and fed live animals by their riders to keep them both loyal and bloodthirsty. They flew higher than any opposing weapon could reach, and their trained riders carried shoulder cannons with leaden fire pellets that exploded anything and anyone they landed on. Nothing in Antora had yet withstood their attack.

"What is making those sounds?" Trina hissed over at Simon.

He said nothing. He knew, which meant he had probably seen them in action.

I never had, and I never wanted to. It was a relief when our road bent away from the palace, toward my home.

Woodcourt was L-shaped with a circular tower at its center. Gray granite blocks made up most of the exterior, along with white-shuttered windows and a gabled roof. There were several entrances into Woodcourt: the main doors in the tower for guests and members of the household, another for servants, one for the vast gardens that extended to the rear of the home, and another one set just outside the gates for prisoners to be escorted directly into the dungeons, unseen and unsmelled. One word from me and these soldiers would use that entrance for Simon and Trina. The temptation of it was difficult to shake from my mind.

The soldiers left us at the main gate into Woodcourt with polite bows. I thanked them for their service. Simon and Trina didn't even acknowledge them, which was both rude and foolish. Real servants would have expressed gratitude for their protection.

The three of us slid off our mounts, and Simon walked the two horses through the main gates. Trina almost immediately recoiled, then pointed forward, saying, "What is that?"

When I saw who she was looking at, I hissed back at Trina to shut her mouth. Celia had already warned me about my father's household manager, so at least one of us here wouldn't behave like an idiot. He was of medium height, with a plump body, bald head. And blue skin. Or grayish blue, to be more specific.

He must have seen Trina's reaction, but he ignored it and turned to me. We exchanged polite bows, then he said, "My name is Gerald Bones. I am the manager of Woodcourt. Are you Miss Dallisor? Your father expected your arrival today."

"I am." My formal tone matched his. "With me is a guard, Simon, and my handmaiden, Trina."

Gerald raised a hairless brow when he noticed them. "Your handmaiden is supposed to be Celia. I chose her for you myself."

"You chose a stupid and lazy girl. I released her and selected my own handmaiden."

It was a question I'd anticipated, so my answer was ready. But it felt like a betrayal to describe Celia so cruelly, after her months of patience with me. It was also a ridiculous excuse, considering that Trina was still staring at him as if she'd forgotten how to blink.

"I have a condition," Gerald said at last, uncomfortable beneath her gawking. "I'm as human as you, only—"

"Blue." This was the word Trina used to shake herself from her trance?

"Speak so rudely again, and you'll go to work in the laundry!" I scolded, then returned my attention to Gerald. "Forgive my handmaiden, sir. Clearly she's even less intelligent than Celia was."

Gerald grunted and turned toward Simon, who had made himself busy with our horses that needed no attending whatsoever. "We expected a man named Darrow to bring you back . . . in a security carriage. And with a garrison accompanying you."

"They're all dead." Simon spoke stiffly, clearly uncomfortable. "Lady Kestra's carriage was attacked at the inn where she stayed last night. I rescued her and came on as her protector."

Thinking of the soldiers and why they died, I clenched my

teeth, an angry retort at the tip of my tongue. But not in front of Gerald. Not in front of any servant of my father.

Instead, I offered Gerald a wry smile. "These two aren't much, but I intend to keep them . . . for now."

Gerald dipped his head at me. "Very well, my lady. Your protector can attend to the horses while your handmaiden prepares your bath for a special supper tonight. Your father asked to see you as soon as you arrive."

Simon and Trina exchanged a wary look—one so obvious I would have to discuss it with them later. Neither of them seemed to like the idea of being separated from me this soon, but what had they expected? It would never be tolerated for servants to follow me around Woodcourt.

After Gerald moved out of earshot, I whispered to Simon, "Either you trust me or you don't."

His gaze on me was steady. "I don't."

For some reason, that made me smile. I took his words as a challenge to a game I fully intended to win. He should already know how comfortable I was with cheating.

He didn't like seeing me smile, and certainly didn't return it, which only made me enjoy the moment more. I said to him, "Nor should you trust me. Now go attend to those horses." Then I called to Trina. "Draw a hot bath for me, and have some food waiting in my room. If you do a good job, you can have my scraps."

I felt rage rising in her, which gave me a particularly satisfied smile. I swerved on my heel to follow Gerald into Woodcourt, never looking back.

Why would I? They were only servants.

· FOURTEEN ·

KESTRA

I t was strange to be here again after three years. The house itself looked exactly as it always had, yet it wasn't the same at all. It wasn't the house, of course. I had changed. The first thirteen years of my life had been spent here, existing under my father's rules, where one did not speak until spoken to first, where an accidental cough at dinner was considered unpardonable, and where, aside from Lord Endrick alone, my father ruled his world. Even the cut flowers seemed to bow to him when he walked the halls. Since going to the Lava Fields, I'd eaten beside my servants because it was preferable to eating alone. Darrow had taught me to ride astride, and Cook showed me how to gut the fish Darrow and I used to catch from Unknown Lake. At best, rules were a suggestion, and no one cared when I broke them. Except my handmaidens, of course, but none of them lasted long enough to re-civilize me.

As Gerald led me into the east wing of Woodcourt, he said, "You've been away for a long time, my lady. Do you feel you are coming back a stranger?"

No, I was coming back a traitor, which was much worse. And I'd always felt like a stranger here.

That was true today, more than ever before. I was seeing my

home like a forgotten memory, unknown and familiar at the same time. Most rooms bore dark wood-paneled walls, and tiled floors with thick rugs that I used to roll myself in as a child. On the plastered walls in the grand entry, artists had painted scenes of Dallisor family history, though I wondered how many of those were exaggerated in my family's favor to earn the artist extra gold for his work. Surely not all of us were as bold or as handsome as the paintings made us appear. I knew for a fact that before her death, my Grandmother Dallisor had more closely resembled a walrus than the painting in front of me depicted.

Since I hadn't answered Gerald's last question, he changed the topic. "Your father is waiting for you in the library. Did you know he's read every book the library holds? A brilliant man, your father."

"Hmmm." That was the most energy I could muster for this conversation.

When he was home, my father spent most of his time in the library, perhaps because its civilization stood in such stark contrast to Endrick's torture chambers, the other place my father frequented. The library was two stories tall, filled floor to ceiling with books. If a satin-covered diary was still here in Woodcourt, then it was probably somewhere in this room.

Gerald knocked to announce our presence, then opened the door. "Sir Henry, your daughter is here."

I was given permission to enter, and saw my father seated at his desk, reading from a thick marble slab known as a tablet. All Dallisor families had one, as would most loyalists and traders. It was one method by which Endrick sent his orders throughout the country, as messages or images would appear on the tablet at his pleasure. Whatever my father was reading now was obviously more interesting than the daughter he'd not seen for three years.

My father hadn't changed much in that time. He did appear older than he should have—he was near Darrow's age, yet had the face of an elder. He also looked harder than I remembered, any warmth in his expression deadened since our last meeting. The lines around his mouth were creased with sadness, making me sad too. Despite who I knew him to be, no daughter wishes to see so much regret in her father's eyes.

Was it too late for him? Or for us? I drew a deep breath and held it, unsure of whether I wanted those questions answered.

Finally, he glanced up, appraising me with all the generosity of a miser on his last coin. "You look well, though a little untidy."

If he wouldn't show any affection, then neither would I. "I've been traveling since early yesterday morning."

"Yes, but then you were never one to fuss with your appearance. That must change now, Kestra. You are not a child anymore."

"My travels here were an adventure, thank you for asking. But the past three years of my life went well, if you were wondering."

He frowned. "Of course they did. I'd have heard if anything was wrong."

Such as a small garrison of his men having been killed? No doubt Gerald would give him the report later today. I shifted my weight to the other foot, hoping it wouldn't be perceived as my growing impatience with this conversation, although that was exactly the problem. "Why did you bring me home again? All I got was a message demanding that I return by today."

He leaned back in his seat, touching a finger to his lips. "My reasons should have been obvious. You finally agreed to my terms."

"To a marriage of alliance? I'm not seventeen yet. Is this a joke?"

He grunted. "You did agree, Kestra. You sent a letter through your handmaiden, telling me you'd had enough of the Lava Fields and would agree to wed the person of my choice."

My hands curled into fists. "I sent no such letter! Does it sound like me to have made such a stupid concession?"

He stood, thrusting his chair back with enough force to leave a crack in the plaster of his library wall. "It sounded like you had finally grown up, that you were willing to accept your duty as a Dallisor!"

"Agreeing to marry someone I may not like—a person I don't even know—is not a sign I've grown up. The fact that I've grown up is evidenced in the fact that I don't have to subjugate my happiness to your desire for power. I will not do this."

My father marched around his desk and grabbed my arm, hard enough that I suspected it would leave a bruise. Then he all but threw me out of his library, where Gerald was waiting in the hall. No doubt he had heard every word of our fight.

"Tell her maid to dress her like a proper lady, and to have her at supper tonight, where she will meet Sir Basil of Reddengrad and charm him if she knows what's good for her. She will not eat until then. If she does not attend, she will never eat again."

Gerald bowed and then waved a hand to motion me ahead of him down the corridor. I didn't look back at either him or the library as I walked, and not from defiance or conceit. It's only that I didn't want anyone to see the tears so thick in my eyes they nearly blinded me. Simon and Trina could talk all they wanted about the privileges of being a Dallisor, of how I was so much better off than they were. They had no idea what they were talking about. A true privileged life had nothing to do with the softness of bedsheets or the spread of food on a table. It would have meant I still had a mother to welcome me home, and a father who cared more for my happiness than for his personal ambitions.

My room was on the upper floor at the end of the west wing, literally as far from my father's apartments as he could place me without requiring me to sleep on a perch outside. Trina had a hot bath waiting for me there, and was putting the finishing touches of a warm meal on a table in my old room. It would've been easier to accept my punishment if that food had all the aroma of a barn floor, but sadly it didn't. Woodcourt cooks were second only to those who served Endrick and could spin delicacies from straw, if necessary. Trina curtsied to Gerald when he entered, like a proper handmaiden would, and when he acknowledged it, he said, "The lady's father has ordered that she is not to eat until she agrees to attend a supper with him tonight. You will enforce those orders with absolute strictness."

"Of course." A wicked smile crossed Trina's face. "It's a pity to see this lovely meal go to waste. I could eat it, I suppose. My lady hasn't fed me as well as she should have."

I exhaled a stiff breath, loud enough that if I were convicted of treason one day, at least Gerald would know I'd already been sufficiently punished.

"You may eat it, this once," Gerald said. "But remember she is your mistress, not the other way around."

In any other circumstance, Trina would've argued that. But

now, she immediately sat down, attacking the food like it was her first meal in months. She must have been hungry, for most people outside the Dominion didn't like the spicy way we prepared our food, or the expense of the spices, perhaps. Gerald remained in the room long enough to assure himself that she wasn't going to share with me. If only he knew how unnecessary his concern was. Trina would lick the plate before letting me have a crumb.

I didn't care. Or, at least, I tried not to care. I spent most of the time pretending I couldn't hear the smack of her mouth as she ate, instead reacquainting myself with my old room. The walls had once been lined with golden fabrics, though I'd heard that Lord Endrick banned the use of gold cloth for anyone but himself. My other furnishings were still here: a bed, a writing desk, a reclining sofa—yet the things I'd cared most about were gone. On a shelf in the corner, the rock collection I'd spent years gathering had disappeared. An autumn leaf, plucked from a tree the day my mother died, was nowhere to be found. Whatever clothes I'd left behind when my father rushed me away were gone too, though that was understandable. I'd grown taller in the last three years. I'd grown up.

"The water will be cold by the time you get around to bathing me," I told Trina, who was finishing the last of the boiled meat on her plate.

"Probably."

"Let's do it now."

"Do it yourself, brat. I'm not your servant."

"Here at Woodcourt, you are."

She tossed her head upward, hard enough that I wondered if she'd cracked her neck. "I am superior to you, Kestra Dallisor, in ways you cannot imagine. I should be the one having a bath, not you."

"As you wish." I marched over to the large basin that had been placed in the center of my room. It was nearly full of water, and the soaps and rinse-water buckets were set out on a nearby stool.

I put a leg up on the edge of the basin, aware of Trina's eyes on me. By the time she realized what I intended to do, it was too late.

"Don't you dare!" she cried, leaping to her feet.

I pressed my foot down and with it came the entire basin. An avalanche of water splashed into the room, soaking everything on the floor and probably already leaking through the floorboards into the servants' quarters below.

"You are so clumsy today," I told Trina as I opened the door to my room, spilling even more water into the hallway. "Since you're my servant, why don't you clean up this mess and draw me a new bath? I'm going for a walk."

There would be consequences for what I'd done, no doubt. But whatever they were, as far as I was concerned, it was entirely worth it.

· FIFTEEN ·

SIMON

After a fair amount of searching, I finally found Kestra in the gardens behind Woodcourt, about the farthest she could run without leaving the gates. She was lucky it took so long to find her. Even a minute sooner, and I would've stormed in loud enough for the whole estate to hear.

She turned to see me, then folded her arms and faced away, suddenly fascinated by a nearby rosebush. She could try her best to ignore me, but it wouldn't work.

"It took every servant in the household to get that cleaned up!" I wasn't yelling, but my tone was just as harsh. "All that, because Trina wouldn't help you bathe?"

"Go away." She started to walk deeper into the gardens.

I crossed in front of her, refusing to let her escape so easily. "You arc spoiled and selfish to the core. How dare you compromise our plan?"

"It's *your* plan!" She spat the words out, suddenly as angry as I was. "Not mine! None of this is what I want! I shouldn't be here."

"Well, you are, and you know the consequences if you try to betray us."

She snorted out a laugh. "The consequences to Darrow, who

arranged a meeting for me with the Banished last night? Or the consequences to Celia? Tell me this. When did Celia first betray me?"

I stopped, unsure of how to answer. Kestra was not supposed to
have figured this out.

In the face of my silence, she continued, "Celia sent a letter here,
agreeing on my behalf to accept a marriage of alliance. That's why I
was summoned back home. Not because anyone missed me, or cared
about my well-being, or whether filthy Corack rebels abducted me on
the way home to force me into treason!"

"Hush!" I did a quick survey of the area, then stepped closer.

"You knew I'd be on that road last night, and at what time.
Celia arranged all of it, didn't she?"

There was nothing to be gained by lying. I said, "Six months
ago, Celia was in town shopping for fabric, probably because you
wanted a fancy new dress, right? She struck up a conversation with
the clerk, not realizing he was a Corack. The clerk figured out who
Celia must have been working for and contacted Tenger. It took some
persuasion, but she finally agreed to our plans."

"Persuasion? Was that in the form of a threat, or a reward?"

There was no good way to answer that. "Both, I suppose."

She took a breath, hesitating on her question. "Last night, when
Tenger was forcing me to agree to his terms, were her screams real? Or
was she only pretending to be hurt so that I'd agree?"

Celia didn't have a scratch on her and was a better actress than
we could have hoped for. But Kestra didn't have to know that, nor
was she in control of this conversation. "Celia doesn't matter. What
do you suppose will happen if your father discovers you've brought
two Coracks inside the walls of his home?"

"Not by choice!"

"But you still did it. He won't protect you. He doesn't care for you. I understand now why your father sent you away in the first place."

I instantly regretted my words. They had come out colder than I'd intended and hit her deep. Her lower lip quivered before she pushed past me and began marching out of the gardens. I followed close behind, calling her name and getting nothing in response. At the entrance, she nearly collided with Gerald. That was no coincidence. Obviously, he was there for Kestra, and didn't seem at all happy to be the one sent to fetch her.

Cautiously, he said, "My lady, your father requests that you return to his library at once."

She folded her arms again. "Nothing has changed since our conversation an hour ago."

"Your handmaiden claims it was you who overturned the bath, that it was not her fault. Your father believes she is only saying that to save herself from a whipping. He wants to hear your answer."

Kestra released a deep breath, then followed Gerald back into the manor house. I continued to follow them, hoping no one would stop me. And hoping even more that if they did, Kestra would cover for me. After my final words to her, I had my doubts.

I was the last to enter the library and stood in the doorway, eyes down. When I served here, I'd never taken orders directly from Sir Henry, but he would have seen me in the home. As much as possible, I'd have to avoid him.

Trina was farther inside, her hands bound in front of her with rough cording and her yellow dress ripped at the shoulder. A guard standing beside her had a stiff rod in his hands, ready to deliver a brutal punishment. Trina had gone so pale that I wondered if she was about to faint.

When she saw Kestra, she cried, "Talk to your father. Tell him the truth, please!"

Sir Henry was standing in the center of the library, arms folded and with a face the approximate color of a ripened plum. Not good.

Kestra crossed her arms and stared off at the shelves. It obviously wasn't the first time she and her father had faced each other this way.

He finally erupted, at a volume high enough that the northern territories could surely hear him. "Water seeped beneath the floorboards, Kestra! It wouldn't surprise me if it all must be torn out and replaced!"

I'd seen the damage myself. It was worse than that. Some of the furniture was spoiled, heirloom pieces that had probably been there for ages. A couple of rugs were ruined too. Kestra barely reacted and only kept her eyes grazing along the shelves. Was this about the diary that Trina had told her to find? If so, then Kestra's timing was awful.

"Look at me!" Sir Henry ordered, and Kestra did. "Your servant claims you overturned the bath, that you did it out of spite and anger. I told her that Dallisors have enough dignity to never do such a thing. Tell me she is lying, Kestra. Surely you have matured enough that you would not willfully cause damage to my home." His voice sharpened to a fine point, making sure she understood his full meaning. "Be bold enough to assign blame onto your servant, and perhaps I will let you miss tonight's supper with Sir Basil."

Trina mumbled Kestra's name, her voice quivering with fear,

but Kestra's attention had returned to the shelves. Most books in this library were very old, some of them probably dating back to the times when books were largely unknown in the world. Trina had described the diary we were seeking as being covered in pink satin, but nothing I saw came close to fitting that description. I doubted it was as important as Trina had made it out to be anyway. Who'd be foolish enough to write down the secret location of the Olden Blade, risking discovery by Lord Endrick?

With Kestra's silence, the guard reached for Trina's damaged sleeve, preparing to bare her back.

Kestra sighed, as if she'd grown tired of the conversation. "Stop this, Father. You know I'm the one who did it."

"That's irrelevant!" He stepped closer until he towered over her. "Do Dallisors let harm come to themselves, or do we bring it to others?"

"Maybe if Dallisors were less concerned with bringing harm to others, Antora would be a better place to live. The people hate us!"

"Are you more concerned with what the people think?" His tone darkened. "Or what I think of you?"

Remembering what I had said to her in the gardens, my eyes shifted to Kestra. Her breaths became shallow, and her lashes fluttered as she tried to hold her stare at her father. No wonder my words had hurt her. She wanted his love. He wanted her respect. Neither of them would be the first to budge.

Finally, Kestra took Trina's arm and walked her over to Gerald. "Take her to my room and help her draw another bath. I have a supper to attend tonight."

"My lady—" he began.

"What happened was my fault." Kestra's tone was commanding. "Get her out of here, Gerald. *Now.*"

Trina glanced at me as Gerald led her out, leaning heavily on his arm. I'd known she was afraid of that rod, but not the full depth of her fear.

As soon as she was gone, Kestra faced her father, as defiant as before. He didn't appreciate his daughter taking responsibility for the bathwater, but once she did, he wasn't likely to punish Trina. Kestra might not be so lucky.

"May I go?" she asked.

Sir Henry's eyes narrowed. "You chose a servant over your own father. There are consequences for your disrespect. Put out your hand." A flick of his head brought his guard forward with the rod.

Instinctively, I gripped my knife, but as soon as the guard noticed, I released the handle. I had to. If Kestra took notice of the exchange, she didn't acknowledge it. She walked up to her father and held out her hand, using the same indifferent attitude she had attempted with Tenger in the carriage.

Sir Henry took it, drawing back the sleeve enough to ensure she would fully feel the sting on her palm. In doing so, he saw the sores on her wrists, still red and swollen. His brows pressed together. "Where did these come from?"

From the same girl he had wanted to punish, ironically. If he would whip Trina for overturning the bath, I could easily imagine what would happen if she were exposed for tying Kestra up last night. That was my fault as well. I hadn't tied Kestra's wrists, but I'd allowed it, wanting her to know what it felt like. How selfish that had been, how cruel.

Kestra only shrugged. "We were attacked at the inn last night, on our way here."

"Who did this?"

"Do you care?" She licked her lips. "I mean, do you care . . . for me?"

"I care about any attack on a Dallisor. Was it Coracks? What did they want?"

He missed Kestra's meaning, deliberately, I thought. Sir Henry would rather discuss anything but his feelings for his daughter. *If* he had any feelings for her.

I'd had two fathers in my life, the one I was born to, the other who took me in and adopted me. Both were great men whose lives had ended too soon. In half the lifetime of Sir Henry, they had felt ten times the love a father should have for his child.

Kestra ignored her father's question, instead retorting with "Most people out there think that being a Dallisor is enough reason to attack us! Why is that? Can we have that conversation, Father, about the real reasons people hate us?"

He studied the sores again, noting with his finger the difference between the cut from Trina's knife and the sores gouged into the skin from the rope. Finally, he released his daughter's hand as if it had burned him. "Cover these for the supper tonight with Sir Basil, and have your handmaiden apply healing creams to them. That will be enough punishment for the bathwater. I won't have you meeting your future husband with your palms bandaged too. Agreed?"

Kestra pressed her lips tightly together. It was obvious that all her strength was going into containing her temper. "Agreed."

· SIXTEEN ·

KESTRA

Trina was alone in my room when I entered. Simon was probably itching to be here to see how these next few minutes unfolded, but, of course, his presence in a lady's bedroom would never be tolerated.

The large basin for my bath was upright again and filled with steaming water that beckoned me closer. I paused, trying to figure out what Trina meant by all of this. Was it a show for Gerald, expecting he would accompany me here? Was she going to tempt me toward the water, and then use the bath herself instead?

Trina stood when I entered. The ropes around her wrists were gone and she had been given a new dress with a handmaiden's apron, much humbler than the yellow one of mine she had been wearing. She looked more the part of a servant now, and seemed to feel the difference, which must have been humiliating. She had joined the Coracks to fight and find glory in disrupting the peace. Not to help bathe an arrogant and spoiled Dallisor daughter. That much about me was true.

I said nothing to her, and she remained silent too. She only shut the door, then crossed behind me to unlace my dress. Once I was in the bath, I closed my eyes and let the worst of the day wash away from me. Not even on the coldest winter night had warm waters given me such comfort. Trina undid my braids and let the hair fall outside the tub, then brushed it out, all in silence.

I mumbled that I would wash my own hair and reached for the soaps before she could say anything, if she would have. When I'd finished and dried myself off, I realized for the first time that all of my gowns had been left behind at the inn, except the blue one, which was dirty and smelled of our travels.

Trina's eyes were cast down when she said, "Your father had a new gown waiting up here, in anticipation of your supper tonight. I'll get it."

The gown had a black shift with narrow sleeves that widened at the wrists, an off-the-shoulder green corset that laced up the back, and a long green sash that tied at the waist. Endrick's colors. Considering that my father could not have known how much I'd grown in the last few years, once Trina helped me into it, the dress fit remarkably well. Maybe Celia had sent him my measurements. She was certainly telling people everything else about me.

"Gerald's blue . . . condition," I said. "You can't stare at it like you did before. You're a servant and he is your superior here at Woodcourt."

"I know that. I just wasn't expecting . . ."

"He probably used to live near the silver mines, or worked in them as a young man. The silver dust affects the skin, that's all. Don't stare anymore. Don't stare at anything here."

We cut off the conversation when a knock came to my door.

Trina answered it, returning a moment later with something wrapped in cloth.

From it, she offered me an apple. It wasn't much, but I hadn't eaten anything for a full day and dove at the fruit like it was the last of its kind.

"Thank you!" Simon must've brought this, an unexpected kindness. Even more unexpected was the flutter within me. Was that for him?

I ate it, every bit of the fruit that I could get. While I did, Trina worked at my hair, piling it on my head and using curling tongs for the loose ends. If she got it too hot and burned my hair, I'd have a second reason to see her hanged.

"What do you know about Sir Basil?" she asked.

I'd have ignored her, except that we needed something to talk about while she did my hair. Basil seemed like a safer topic than most others. "He's from Reddengrad. Lord Endrick ordered a marriage between us years ago, but my mother protested because both of us were still too young. After she died, I told Lord Endrick I refused to go along with his plans. That's the real reason I was sent away. It never had anything to do with the kidnapping."

"So your father thinks you've agreed to the marriage?"

"It doesn't matter what he thinks." I shrugged with indifference. "In three more days, I'll have betrayed my kingdom. After that, I'll never be able to come back home. Basil wouldn't marry me then, even if I begged him to."

She finished pressing another curl, letting it fall against my cheek. "You could've let me take that whipping earlier. If our positions were reversed, that's what I would've done. I know he's your father, so you won't want to hear what I have to say, but it's the truth: He's evil, Kestra, as bad as Lord Endrick."

"Don't say that."

Not because it was a lie, but because I feared it might be true. Now that I was home, the evidence of her words surrounded me.

"I understand how you feel," Trina said. "More than you might think."

"No, you don't."

"You don't fit in here. We haven't been at Woodcourt for a day yet and I can see that."

"Please stop talking." I couldn't listen to her any longer.

"I never belonged anywhere either. Not until I joined the Coracks."

Rather than answer her, which would have implied that I cared, I closed my eyes as she finished with my hair and the final details on my dress. It was still early for the supper, so I said, "Leave me alone now."

"Either Simon or I must be with you at all times."

"That's not possible and you know it," I snapped. "Besides, you need to give Simon a message. You're expected to present yourselves to Gerald and give an accounting of any weapons you've brought into Woodcourt. If you delay any longer, it will arouse suspicions. But you might be searched, so don't bring anything else."

Such as his satchel.

That seemed to make sense to Trina, who hurried out the door. What I had said was true enough—Gerald would eventually ask for an accounting from these new servants. And that fact was very convenient for me.

Immediately after she left, I dug into a chest of stockings, tying one around my right thigh as another garter. I didn't have a weapon for it yet, but I would, soon.

Shortly after that, I left my room, following in the direction Trina would have gone. From a hiding place behind one of the carved stone pillars of Woodcourt, I spotted her talking to Simon in the stables. He grabbed his satchel, but she put her hand over his and said something, likely my warning about him being searched. He set it down again, surveyed the area, and then walked with her directly toward the spot where I was hidden. I had to counter their movements around the wide pillar, which was a trick because I didn't want my skirts to rustle or to flare out from behind the pillar, but it worked. They didn't see me.

"I don't trust this Gerald Bones," Simon muttered to Trina as they walked past. "He looks at me with suspicion."

"He serves the Dallisors, and they serve Endrick," Trina said. "Of course we don't trust him."

Then they were past. I made certain they had gone, and hurried over to Simon's satchel. There wasn't much time.

He had left his sword here with his horse, covered with a saddle blanket. Gerald would have noticed it when we arrived. He would wonder why Simon had neglected to bring it for inspection, especially if he was supposed to be a protector. But Simon would have to explain that. I couldn't do it for him.

I dug inside the satchel. Simon had a few silver coins that might buy him a day or two's worth of meals, a heavy gold ring he'd probably stolen, and a roll of fabric that could be used for bandages, or to bind hands, or for the gag Trina had wanted to use on me. He was also carrying a bound sketchbook and a lead pencil. A quick scan of his drawings impressed me, though most were only abstracts of an eye or hand, nothing to tell me who had inspired the sketches. They were beautiful, though, a part of Simon I had not expected. In a different life, he might have been an artist, not an insurgent. I found nothing in the pages or in the satchel to identify him as a Corack, nor any means of contacting Tenger. Since I knew Trina carried nothing of her own, this was all they would have brought with them. It was true, their lives were entirely dependent upon me keeping my agreement, just as Celia's and Darrow's were.

But none of this was what I'd come to search for. That item was at the very bottom of Simon's satchel. It was the sack the Banished had brought to the inn, an item so small that I'd have missed it unless I'd been deliberately hunting for it. Inside the pouch was a silver key, too delicate for a door or even the lock on a set of manacles. I knew Woodcourt well and couldn't think of a single thing this key might be used for. More importantly, I couldn't think of any reason the Banished would want me to have it.

I briefly recalled Thorne's words to Trina last night, that the Halderians were coming for me again. Let them try. I was not the cowering little girl I'd been three years ago. If I could turn the tables on the Coracks, I could hold my own against the Banished too. And I would begin by figuring out the purpose for this key.

I folded the key and its sack inside my skirts as I hurried back to my room. There I deposited them behind a loose wall panel in one corner. That cavity used to hide personal treasures and candies, relatively innocent things I didn't want to explain to my parents. Now it hid something that I suspected people had risked their lives to protect.

I wasn't alone much longer before Trina returned to my room. Her smile was so fake it might have been painted on. "Were you here the whole time I was gone?"

If there was ever a time to play innocent, this was it. "Where else would I go?"

"Did you go to the stables?"

I bit down on my tongue, checking any expression of triumph. After seeing Gerald, she and Simon had gone back there together. He had searched his bag and realized the key was missing. He must be furious right now, or, at least, I hoped he was.

"I'd get filthy in the stables." I brushed off her accusation with a casual wave of my hand. "Mess up all the work you did for tonight. Why do you ask?"

It was a question she couldn't answer. Simon had told me that the sack from the Halderians contained nothing of importance, and if she asked me specifically about it, that would suggest it was important.

She replied the only way she could. "No reason. Someone mentioned they had seen you there, that's all."

Nobody had seen me there. I wasn't foolish enough to allow that.

She took time to fix a few loose curls of my hair, and it was far too soon before a knock came at my door. Was it time for the supper already? Hungry as I was, no food could taste good enough to counteract the bitterness of meeting someone I'd soon be forced to marry.

You won't be here by then. That thought was poor comfort, but it was all I had.

I had expected Gerald would escort me, but Simon poked his head inside. His attention instantly fixed on me and a small smile escaped his lips before he corrected it. "Gerald is attending to your father. I'll take you to the supper."

Well, wouldn't he like that? Three minutes longer that he could keep an eye on me, lecture me. I walked beside him while we passed a couple of maids, but once we started down the steps, Simon paused on a landing and touched my arm, asking me to stop too.

"I know the plan!" I hissed. "Honestly—"

"That's not it." He glanced around, ensuring we were alone. "I just wanted to say . . . about Trina . . . well, that was a decent thing you did."

I wasn't sure how to respond. Was this an attempt at kindness? Maybe he was confusing me with someone else, someone he didn't hate.

Finally, I shrugged. "I caused the problem. I couldn't let her take the blame."

"Six years ago, you let John and me take the blame for that missing ring. Maybe I judged you too harshly, and if I have, then I'm sorry." A beat passed. "I'm sorry things have to happen this way."

He stopped there, searching my eyes with his. What was he hoping to find in me? Goodness? Proof that he was right to apologize? Because if he was looking for anything redeemable, he'd be disappointed. I did accuse him and John *that day*, I was never going to put the Olden Blade in his hands, and I was part of the Dallisor world, not his. None of that would ever change.

Unless it could change . . . back. We had been friends once, in our way. If I had not set a torch to that friendship, things might have been very different now.

If he had stayed on in our household, if we had grown up as friends . . . perhaps as something more than friends, maybe I'd be used to him looking at me with this intensity. Like he was memorizing the details of my face, and at the same time, scrambling my thoughts, softening the shell I'd built around me.

If he was testing my courage, then I couldn't be the first to lower my eyes. He couldn't think, or suspect, or *know* how his gaze unnerved me, disarmed me. The depth in his eyes emptied me of my defenses, protection I absolutely needed if I was going to survive this. If he was strong, then I had to be stronger. I held his gaze, determined to hide my every weakness. Or to discover his.

Our standoff only lasted a few seconds, though it felt much longer, and Simon was the first to blink. I started back down the steps, saying, "We can't be late."

He had been about to say something, probably to ask if I'd stolen anything from him recently. But with bustling noises below from the servants, we no longer had the privacy of the landing for such a conversation.

He held out his arm for me to walk at his side. I also knew what that was—a polite excuse to keep me close enough for us to speak quietly.

"You clean up well," he said. "Your . . . er, hair."

The compliment was awkward, but sincere. The fact that he had anything nice to say surprised me. "Trina does better work than I'd have expected."

"She's not as stupid as you've made her out to be." He sighed. "Trina's had a difficult life, rejected nearly everywhere she's gone."

I snorted. "Shocking news."

He tried again. "All she wants is to do something important. You can understand how humiliating this must be."

"Yes, constantly threatening my life must be awful for her. Maybe you're offended because you like her."

He paused, taken aback. "That's not true."

"Isn't it? Then why are you ignoring her connection to the Banished?"

He stopped and released my arm, pulling me into an alcove near the main vestibule. A marble bust of Lord Endrick gazed down on us here. How appropriate.

Simon said, "In the first place, I'm not ignoring anything! I just don't feel the need to share my deepest thoughts with the girl I'm—"

"Kidnapping? Whose life you're destroying?"

His eyes flashed, an honest reaction before he steadied himself again. "The girl who gave her word to cooperate with us. And in the second place, Trina is loyal to the Coracks and so am I. There is nothing more between us."

I stared back at him. "She might be loyal to the Coracks, but not in the same way you are. As someone who is in the process of lying to nearly every face I see, trust me when I say that I can recognize it in someone else. Find out the truth about her, or she could put both our lives at risk."

He licked his lips, then held out his arm again. "Worry about your own traitors, not mine. You were right before. I shouldn't make you late for that supper."

· SEVENTEEN ·

KESTRA

Formal suppers were usually served in the great hall of Woodcourt. However, Gerald met us there and, with a polite bow, said, "Your father was unexpectedly called away by Lord Endrick. He sends his apologies and has ordered me to sit in on the supper in his place. We'll be in the small dining room."

"So it's just the three of us?" I asked. "You, me, and this Basil person?"

"This *person* is Prince Basil the Fifth of Reddengrad, son of King Albert and heir to the throne of Reddengrad."

I grimaced. "Can I just call him Basil?"

"Sir Basil is eager to meet you. Your father has told him all about you."

"If he truly had, then *Sir* Basil wouldn't be at all eager to meet me. I'm sure everything he's been told is an exaggeration, at best. Either that, or he's been forced here tonight, as I have."

"That's not the case, Lady Kestra, I assure you." Gerald signaled to Simon, who bowed to dismiss himself. "As Kestra's protector, you're expected to stand watch at the supper." He eyed me. "Unless the lady doesn't want you there."

I didn't.

"It's not necessary for him to come," I told Gerald. "There won't be any trouble, I'm sure."

"I'll come anyway," Simon offered, ever vigilant. "We can't take any risks involving you . . . my lady."

If Gerald had not been here, those words would've been the start of a glorious fight. As it was, I only took Gerald's arm, letting Simon trail behind us.

"I remember you from your earliest years," Gerald said as we walked.

"That cannot be true. No offense, Gerald, but if I had seen you before today, I would remember."

He smiled. "No offense is taken. I know how I look. But I have worked here for many years. Most of that time was belowground, where you'd never have seen me."

Belowground meant the dungeons, I was sure. Nothing else at Woodcourt fit that description. I stole a glance at Simon, warning him not to walk so close. If Gerald were to recognize him from six years ago, that would be a disaster.

Or it might make Gerald useful to the Corack plan. If he could be trusted, he might have some idea of where Risha's dagger was.

I quickly dismissed that thought. Gerald would surely have been questioned, probably by Lord Endrick himself. And nobody could be trusted. Nobody.

"What I meant to say, my lady, is that you have grown into an impressive young woman. If you ever need help, for any reason, then you can ask me."

I was in desperate need of help, but not from anyone who bowed to my father. Even if he meant well, Gerald's help could only sink me further into trouble.

Whatever I had expected Sir Basil to be, it was not who I saw as I entered the intimate dining room. He stood when I entered, giving me a low bow, which I returned with a halfhearted curtsy. Like most people raised in the softer climes to the south, his hair was light blond and hung in loose tousles from his head. He was tall and lean, near my age, and, as far as I could tell, made entirely of fluff.

He took my hand and gave it a kiss, though I quickly pulled away. He drew back, offended, but my sleeve was riding up on my wrist and I didn't want him to notice the wounds there. Hoping to cover, I said, "You make me blush, Sir Basil."

What a stupid thing to say! I didn't blush, and it was simply fine manners for him to have kissed my hand. It was fortunate that I didn't care what he thought of me, because otherwise, I'd have cared deeply that I had just taken on the role of a simpering ninny. That was almost worse than being a traitor.

"You are more beautiful than your father described," Basil said.

Maybe that was because my father hadn't seen me for three years, and probably couldn't even remember what I looked like.

"She is beautiful indeed," Gerald said. "Such striking eyes, wouldn't you agree?"

I'd always wished to have my mother's eyes rather than my own. Hers were kind and loving, eyes that radiated peace. Instead, my eyes had the look of trouble. Wasn't that what Lord Endrick had said?

"Shall we eat?" Gerald politely gestured to our seats.

The table in this room was small, though it was larger than the three of us needed and certainly more elaborate than I'd been accustomed to for some time. Gerald took a seat at the head of the table, then Basil pulled out a chair for me at the far end and chose the chair nearest to it for himself. As a protector would be expected to do, Simon stood against the wall directly behind me. Basil never gave him more than a passing glance, but as I turned back, I noticed Simon's full attention was fixed on Basil, much like a wolf observes a sheep.

Plates were brought in piled high with candied plums, goat cheese, and rye bread. I was ravenously hungry and wanted more than anything to dive face-first into the food. Darrow's training from the past three years echoed in my mind, however.

"Patience brings victory," he often said. "Do not be in a rush."

He might have had different advice if he'd known I was starving, but as it was, all I could do was remember his words and know that I had the whole evening to eat as much as I wanted.

"Can we begin by agreeing this is awkward?" Basil reached for my hand. "We've just met, but it's already settled that we will be married."

I smiled insincerely and pulled my hand away to stuff a cube of cheese into my mouth. If he noticed, it didn't stop him from talking.

"We'll make our home in Reddengrad, of course, though allowances will be made for you to visit your father as often as you might want."

"I haven't been here for three years," I said. "I didn't miss this place even once."

"Ah." Well, *now* it was awkward.

"What sorts of activities do you enjoy?" Basil asked. "Sewing? Dancing?"

Sword fighting. Riding horses. Occasionally shooting disks into hay bales dressed like anyone who had annoyed me that week, if I was in a bad enough mood.

Of course, I didn't say any of that. I only nodded and ate another cube of cheese.

He broke some bread and, while eating pieces from it, said, "Let me tell you about myself, then. I'm good with a staff—"

I'd choose a sword over a staff any day. I preferred weapons with a pointy end. Darrow used to joke about that.

Used to . . . I wondered if Darrow was still alive. If Celia had been rewarded for her treachery, or if the Coracks had decided she was no longer useful to them. It was increasingly difficult to tell the difference between innocents and enemies.

Basil was still talking. I'd probably missed a few things on his list. "I have a great deal of family money—"

As did I. Which was merely luck on both our parts, not a character trait. Unless he did consider that a character trait, which would be another strike against him.

"—and I'm kind." He leaned forward. "I'll be kind to you, Kestra. Always."

Behind me, Simon coughed, probably one he'd faked. He mumbled an apology, but it wasn't at all sincere.

After the first course, a spiced pea soup was brought in. To his credit, Basil had excellent manners, a reminder of how relaxed Darrow had been with the proper training I should have received while he was teaching me to drop from a tree onto a moving horse instead. No wonder I had driven Celia to betrayal. It was a miracle she hadn't done worse to me.

As we ate, Basil told me all about his estate, our future home, which had been given to him by his father, the king of Reddengrad. Basil would inherit the throne one day, though he anticipated that was many years away. His father was in excellent health and expected to live a long life, or something like that. I'd mostly quit listening by then.

Midway through his monologue, I turned to Gerald. "When do you think my father will be finished with his business for Lord Endrick?"

Gerald seemed surprised to have been remembered and looked up from his soup. "My lady, I don't know."

"Another hour? All evening? Until tomorrow?" In other words, if I got rid of Basil, would I have time to search the library?

"With the Lord of the Dominion, anything is possible," Gerald said.

Then my attention went to Basil. "What is your opinion of Lord Endrick?"

I suspected Sir Basil would've filled his cheeks with cheese cubes if it would've helped him get out of this change in the conversation. But the cheese tray was gone, and filling one's cheeks with soup didn't work in the same way.

"I . . . er, admire him greatly, of course," he finally sputtered.

"Of course. And when you're on the throne of Reddengrad, do you hope to be like him? Is that the reason for our marriage, for you to gain favor with Lord Endrick?"

"Kestra—" Gerald started.

"It's a fair question!" I turned to Basil again. "Why did you agree to this marriage?"

Basil leaned forward. "Why did you, my lady?"

We stared at each other for a moment and then we began to laugh. Nothing forced or fake, but a real laugh, both of us conceding that we were only here because someone else had made it so. With that, the awkwardness dropped away and we enjoyed the rest of our meal with ease.

In fact, the only time it became uncomfortable after that was when I caught a glimpse of Simon from the corner of my eye. He wasn't enjoying this meal at all. He was furious.

Good.

· EIGHTEEN ·

SIMON

I t's hard to know how long the supper went, but based on my growing impatience to finish the evening, I figured that I'd stood against the wall, watching Basil and Kestra flirt, for approximately nine hundred hours.

When Gerald finally suggested they end the evening, I pulled Kestra's seat back before he'd even finished his sentence.

"Your protector is anxious for his own night's sleep, I see," Basil said, laughing at me.

He could laugh all he wanted. I wasn't letting go of Kestra's chair.

"He knows I'm tired," Kestra said. "We arrived this morning from a difficult journey, and as you say, he's my protector. Whether I like it or not."

Basil stood when she did. This time, I noticed her hands deliberately clasped behind her back. With no hand to kiss, Basil gave Kestra a low bow, meeting her eyes when he rose again. A smile spread across his face as he surveyed her, top to bottom. Briefly, I considered the consequences if I smacked that eager expression off his face. What was he doing? Appraising her as his future queen? As his wife? Basil didn't know her, not after just one supper and not when she was hiding so much. He had no right to look at her that way.

I shifted my position to stand directly behind Kestra, making sure Basil saw me. I couldn't make Kestra leave, but the instant she took her first step, I would gladly escort her out the door.

"I'm staying here in Highwyn for a few days," Basil said. "Perhaps I can see you again before I return home?"

"Perhaps."

Was that a flirtation, a way of teasing him into another visit? Or was she politely avoiding any further connection to him? I couldn't tell, which frustrated me to no end, but I hoped it was the latter. She was already being forced to commit treason against Antora. Her schedule was full.

She curtsied to Basil and Gerald, then took my arm to walk out to the corridor. When I pulled her in another direction, away from her room, she huffed like a spoiled child. That was too bad. We needed to talk.

"You're being ridiculous," she muttered.

"*You* were ridiculous!" I hissed. "Why didn't we bring in a priest and marry the two of you right there?"

"You know why not! It's because in three days, he won't have me for a scullery maid, much less a wife."

"I thought you didn't want anything to do with him!"

"I don't, but if I were going to be forced into marriage, I could do worse than him. At least he's kind! A word, I'm sure, that has never entered your vocabulary!"

I was plenty kind. Just not to Dallisors. She would understand that, if she were anyone else.

But she wasn't. And it was becoming far too easy to forget that.

We paused for a couple of passing servants and then I led her deep into the gardens, still blooming with late-season lilies and dogbane that added a whiff of perfume to the evening air, a sweet contrast to the fight that was clearly coming. This late at night, nobody else should be out here. Still, we kept our voices low.

I started, "The person you met tonight is a fraud—tell me you saw that too!" I couldn't place exactly what was wrong with Basil, but something definitely was wrong. Was he too eager? Too friendly? Too irritating as he tried in every possible way to get close to Kestra? "The real Basil is . . . different. You cannot trust him."

"I don't! Just as I don't trust Trina, or Gerald, or Celia . . . or you."

"You don't have to like me, but you can trust me." I wanted to be clear on this point. "Keep your word to the Coracks and I'll do everything I can to help you get through this."

I'd meant well, but her cheeks turned to flame. "Is this your idea of kindness? What I'm doing could destroy my family! Perhaps the whole Dominion."

"The Dominion must be destroyed. You've seen the effects of their rule for yourself."

"Not this way. This is wrong."

I gestured toward the center of Highwyn. "No, what is happening out there is wrong! You are not the victim here."

"Nor are you. For those years you worked here, we fed and clothed you, put a roof over your head, and paid you for your work."

"I only worked here because my father had died and the rest of my family was starving. I needed the money."

"Which my father provided. But somehow we deserve this?"

"Did I deserve *this*?" I turned away from her, lifting my tunic just enough for her to see the scars on my back from where I'd been whipped. On the darkest nights, I could still hear the whip's crack against my flesh, the way I'd screamed for mercy until I realized begging only made the next hit harder. With the cold air bristling over my back now, I remembered the sting as if I were there again. It had been worse for my friend John.

She drew in a sharp breath, then immediately fell silent. I lowered my tunic and turned back to her. The arrogance had faded from her expression, her shoulders had hunched, and she had become hauntingly still.

Finally, she said, "You were the last one in my mother's room that day, and John supervised you there. I thought it had to be one of you." When she looked up, something was different. This wasn't a challenge, or a trick. Her eyes had become windows, clear and unfiltered. This was the real Kestra.

She continued, "It makes no difference, I know, but I've thought about that day a thousand times since then, wishing I could go back. My mother's ring was found a week later in the cushions of her chair. By then, it was too late for John, and for you as well, I thought. I am so terribly sorry."

I stepped closer and was surprised that she didn't move away. "John and I were sent to the dungeons, to be executed at the end of the week. I was in the lowest cell beneath Woodcourt, where all the sewage eventually collects, making the ground muddy. They warned me not to go toward the back of my cell because if I slipped, I'd fall into an endless pit."

"The Pit of Eternal Consequence." I must've looked confused, because Kestra added, "When I was young, that's what my governess called it. She described a pit beneath Woodcourt where the spirits of all who had died in the dungeons roamed, eager to grab anyone who tried peeking over the edge. She threatened to toss me in if I didn't finish my lessons."

The corner of my mouth lifted. "Well, I haven't heard it called by that name, but the guards told me the story too, and I think some of them believed it, based on the smell alone. For three days, I stayed as far from the pit as I could. But then I saw a rat headed toward the ledge. I followed it, intending to catch and eat it. The rat slipped into the pit, and I fell with it. Had I been less scrawny then, and on my feet instead of crawling, I probably would've died in the fall. Instead, I slid on my back, quite a long way down. My ankle was sprained, but I was alive."

"So there is a bottom to the pit?"

I thought back. "Of course. It was awful, littered with bones, and waste, and other odds and ends I'd wager prisoners threw down there so they couldn't be used as evidence against them."

"How'd you get out?"

"I followed the same rat into a tunnel, almost impossible to find unless you already knew it was there. I don't know how long I crawled, and I don't want to think about what I crawled through, but it felt like hours. Gradually, the tunnel went uphill again, to an exit far beyond Woodcourt's gates." I rapped a fist against my thigh, suddenly uncomfortable. Tenger and several other Coracks knew my history, but I'd never spoken this next part to anyone. "I abandoned John, who was in a nearby cell. Every night for months afterward, I pictured him calling to me, wondering where I'd gone, and finally figuring out I'd left him behind."

Kestra hadn't visibly breathed for some time. Finally, she said, "Your leaving didn't cause his death. I—" She stopped abruptly. We both knew how that sentence should end.

We exchanged another look then, something softer, gentler. My hand brushed against hers, and hers against mine. Her fingertips were cool in the evening air.

"John used to say it was a pity you're a Dallisor, because you might've turned out all right otherwise." My forefinger circled hers. "Sometimes you left little gifts on my bed."

She sighed. "They weren't gifts, Simon. They were leftovers, scraps that might've been given to the dogs if I hadn't snuck them to you."

"They were gifts."

Her thumb brushed over mine, sending a shiver up my spine. "I remember when you came," she said. "You were the first friend I'd ever had. What I did—"

"—was awful." I drew in a deep breath. "But in the long run, it probably saved my life."

I'd never intended to tell her so much. It had nothing to do with finding the Olden Blade, or helping her understand the importance of destroying Lord Endrick. At the moment, all I wanted was for her to understand . . . me.

"Soon after my escape, I was attacked by some passing thieves who beat me when they discovered I had nothing they could steal. A kind old gentleman named Garr rescued me. He said if I worked for him, he would feed me and, more importantly, train me with a sword so that I'd never have to endure such a beating again."

Even now, I had a perfect memory of when he'd found me on the roadside, the pity and compassion he'd shown. "Three years later, he was collected by Dominion armies, one of forty people your father claimed were Halderians responsible for kidnapping you. Garr was no friend of the Dominion, but he had nothing to do with your kidnapping. At those executions, Lord Endrick publicly announced that the deaths were in your honor. If Antora didn't know your name before those executions, they did afterward, and not for anything good."

She stepped back, but kept her eyes low as she said, "I never asked for those executions. I didn't want them."

I only nodded. It wasn't the same as saying I believed her, because I wasn't sure if I did. But I wanted to. For now, that was enough.

I continued, "Garr adopted me as his own son. When he died, he left everything to me, far more than I deserved. I gave Garr's house and what money he had to my family. They live there still. All I kept was a ring and his sword." That was the weapon at my side now and the ring was in my satchel. "I joined the rebellion to honor him. And, more importantly, I joined to bring down the Dominion. Endrick is our target, but I won't pretend bringing down your father in his wake hasn't crossed my mind."

She stepped back, repulsed. "And you're equally comfortable with destroying me?"

That was an accusation, not a question, but it deserved an honest answer. "I'm never comfortable with what I have to do for the Coracks, and I don't want to be. But you've said it yourself, Princess— by the time we're finished here, the Dallisors will never take you back. If I can separate you from them, I'll consider that the greatest act of service I could offer you."

She shook her head. "This is no service."

"It's no curse either." I checked around us again, keeping my voice at a safe whisper. "I'm a good person, Kestra. So are you. One of us is on the wrong side of this fight."

"I saved Trina from a serious whipping today, and covered for your mistakes here, risking my own life each time. I am doing everything you've required of me. Will Darrow be killed if I fail to find the Olden Blade? Celia? Will you kill me too?"

I opened my mouth to respond, but this time, no answer came. My silence became my conviction.

With a sharper tone, she said, "I think we know who's on the wrong side. You are stealing away everything that's important to me."

"Speaking of stealing . . ." I needed to ask if she'd gotten into my satchel. She must have, though I wasn't sure how or when.

But I wasn't able to finish my question before Basil emerged from the home into the gardens and called her name. When he saw Kestra, his whole face lit up, like a giant mole rat approaching its next meal. If there was a better analogy for Basil, I couldn't think of it.

"I was told you'd come out here," Basil said. "Perhaps you weren't really tired before. Perhaps you were only tired of me."

Her grin was coy. "My protector was tired."

"Sick . . . and tired," I mumbled.

"Ah." Basil smiled back at her, forgetting me almost instantly. "Then maybe you should dismiss your protector for the night and take a stroll through the gardens with me? I promise to see you safely back to your room."

"Her maid is expecting her—" I said.

"My maid works for me and not the other way around," Kestra

snapped. Then to Basil, she added, "However, the air outside has chilled. If you'd like, I can show you around Woodcourt. I think you'd love my father's library."

Basil smiled and offered Kestra his arm. This time she took it, pressing closer to him than was necessary for an escort. I wasn't sure what she thought about Basil, or about me, or what tricks she was still plotting. But one thing was certain. She knew I didn't like her walking off with Basil, and that there was nothing I could do or say to stop her. And that was exactly the way she wanted it.

· N I N E T E E N ·

KESTRA

I pointed out to Basil the various features of Woodcourt as we walked through the home, but cared little for my own words. Basil seemed to sense my nervousness.

"Will your father object to us going in there?"

"It's his library, not his confessional," I said. "There can't be anything too private here."

Except maybe a pink satin diary. And if he kept it here, then what else was he willing to hide? Maybe the elusive Olden Blade itself, buried beneath some loose floorboard? Probably not. Concealing a diary from Lord Endrick was one thing. He'd never deliberately keep the Olden Blade from his master.

Once inside the library, I shut the door tight and began scanning the books, making casual conversation about the various titles. However, I barely listened to my own chatter, much less Basil's. I had a vague notion that he was trying to show how intelligent he was, by claiming to have read many of these books himself. I figured if he was particularly intelligent, he'd have already sensed that I wasn't listening to a single dreary word he said.

At one point, I saw on an upper shelf a book with a faded fabric binding that might have been pink once. I reached for it, and failed, so Basil came beside me and lifted the book down. It was a treatise on seedlings, which I'm sure would be an instant cure for insomnia. But it wasn't Risha's diary.

"What happened to your wrists?" Basil took my upraised hand in his and pulled back my sleeve. "Kestra?"

I pushed the sleeve down again. "It's nothing. We had some trouble getting here last night."

"Trouble? From the Coracks?" Basil's face tightened. "Your father explained to me how much trouble they cause here in Antora. After we're married, my father will send in his armies to help destroy the Coracks for good."

I pressed my brows together. "Why would your father do that, risk his own soldiers to quash our rebellion? Sir Basil, what benefit is our marriage to you or your family?"

His expression became somber, and suddenly he seemed much older than he had before. "Lord Endrick's power extends beyond the Antoran border. If we do not join with him, we face destruction. Reddengrad is a strong country and we could hold out for a long time. But if Endrick is immortal, in the end, he will always win."

I tried to smile that away, but could not. "So the reward for marriage is preservation of your country."

"Those are the terms of our marriage, but the reward is you." He released my wrist but took hold of my hands instead. The flesh of his palms was softer than mine, like holding on to flower petals. It was odd, and not the least bit attractive.

My pulse quickened as I tried to figure out how we had suddenly gone from a bland discussion of books to a moment that had nothing whatsoever to do with being in this library. All I could think about was Simon's warning, that Basil was not who he appeared to be.

Simon clearly didn't like Basil, but I wondered if that was because Basil clearly liked me. Was Simon jealous? Had his feelings for me changed?

Had mine changed? I hadn't truly hated Simon for several hours, despite a sincere effort to do so. Twice during supper, I had thought about the unruly lock of hair that had fallen to his forehead. My father would hate it, which somehow made it even more appealing. Then, in the gardens, when Simon had stepped closer, and his fingers brushed against mine, I could feel his nearness tugging at me, sending warm shivers through my belly. Had he reached for my hand deliberately? I wondered. I hoped.

When had all this changed?

Basil whispered, "May I kiss you, Kestra?"

He was still here? And he wanted to kiss me? I was supposed to be looking for a diary. Also, I had no intention of marrying Basil, so it was unfair to allow him to think otherwise.

Unfair, but necessary.

I forced a smile to my face and lifted my chin. He pressed his lips to mine with all the romance of kissing a clam. When he pulled away, he took my hand and kissed it too, as if a second touch to my lips might be too much to expect.

"I will make you happy, Kestra," he said.

That was nice, but I'd be happier if a book covered in pink satin spontaneously ejected itself onto the floor.

"I'd like to ask your father to move up the wedding date," he continued. "It's supposed to be another year away, but I don't see why we should wait."

Would we wait longer than three days from now? If so, what did I care when the date would be?

"Please do," I said.

He smiled and went in for another kiss, but by then, I had returned to studying the shelves. He missed, and sort of got my ear, then pretended he had meant to do that.

A knock came to the door, which startled us apart, but before either of us could reply, Simon poked his head in. Of course he did. He wouldn't have been far away. He gave a quick look from Basil to me, surely noticing how close we were standing to each other, but all he said was "Sir Henry has just arrived. I suggest you both leave."

Basil must've seen the worry in my eyes, for he immediately agreed, and hurried us out of the library. He bowed to me in the hall, saying, "I'll speak to your father about the new wedding date."

"I'll go to my room," I said. "I'm tired now." Which was true, but hardly the reason I was leaving so quickly.

Simon fell in beside me, escorting me toward the stairs up to my room. Once we got a safe distance away, we slowed down. With a terse edge to his voice, he asked, "Any luck?"

"No."

"Maybe the diary isn't in there."

"But it's the place to start. I'll try again in the morning. I only had the chance to examine a few of the shelves tonight."

"In all the time you were in there? What else were you doing?"

I stopped and released his arm. "Turning cartwheels, of course!" He squared his body to mine and his eyes sparked with anger. So this *was* jealousy, and a ridiculous jealousy at that. Basil was as significant as a pincushion, a sea sponge. A bluster of wind, nothing more. Yet, although it bothered me to realize that Simon cared what had happened, even worse was the realization that *I* cared what he thought might have happened.

Well, let him wonder. I said, "You have no right to ask me about anything other than what is necessary to get that dagger. Remember that, Simon."

"Everything affects whether you'll find that dagger! I'll ask you whatever I want."

"And I'll refuse to answer." I strode forward, determined to outpace him. "I can find my own way to my room. I don't want to see you anymore tonight."

I knew he was still following, though at a greater distance. I entered my room and slammed the door shut behind me. It startled Trina, who was on her knees in a corner of the room. Only one purpose would place her there. She was searching for secret hideaways in my room. It was no longer safe to hide the silver key behind the wall panel. Sooner or later, she would find it.

She stood, forcing an expression of innocence on her face so laughable that a child would see her guilt. "You're later than I expected. How was the supper?"

No, we weren't going to chat, or pretend to get along, and we both knew I'd just caught her invading what little privacy I still had. "Can you help me into my nightclothes? I'd do it myself, if I could. But this dress—"

"It buttons up the back." She smiled and walked over to me. "I'll help you, but as a friend, not as a servant."

"You're going to kill me if I don't do what you want. We're not friends, Trina."

That stopped her in her tracks, though she recovered quickly enough. Her mouth pinched into a tight line as she walked forward again to unbutton my dress.

I knew it was unkind, the way I had just spoken to her. But between her and Simon, I was having a hard time finding air of my own to breathe.

When she finished, she backed up, cocking her head away from me. "Do the rest yourself, then. I'm going to sleep here in the room with you. And since I have the only weapon, I'm taking the bed."

"Fine." She'd sleep more comfortably there, more deeply. As soon as I was certain she was asleep for the night, I was sneaking out.

· TWENTY ·

KESTRA

The biggest trick of the evening was silently changing from my nightclothes into a tunic and trousers. Fortunately, they had been a little large on me three years ago, so although they were tight now, I could still move in them better than I would in a nightdress. Or in any dress, for that matter. They were also dark in color, so I could blend into the walls.

Trina had stirred while I changed, but she was undoubtedly exhausted from the previous couple of days, an advantage I was happy to exploit. I removed the silver key from its hiding place behind the loose panel, and tucked it in a pocket of my trousers. Then I entered the corridor with caution, expecting Simon to be watching the door, but he wasn't there. That was a surprise, and a relief.

I had two purposes for leaving. The first was to find a knife. I was used to having one hidden on me at all times, and I hadn't liked the feeling of its absence. This wasn't particularly difficult to do. Extra weapons were always kept hidden at Woodcourt in the event of an attack. The one I found was behind a hutch in the music room, at the bottom of the stairs from my room. Two knives were there, in fact. The first was longer and had an exquisite silver handle with inset quartz lines. But I didn't need a beautiful knife, I wanted a sharp one. So I took the second knife, ivory-handled with the Dallisor name carved into it, as most of our knives had. If I bothered to stab someone in the next several hours, I might as well do it right. After I returned to my room, the knife would go into the garter on my leg. For now, I tucked it in the waist at the back of my trousers. Darrow always kept his knives in the waistline of his trousers too. Not for the first time, I wished he was here.

From there, I crossed the vestibule into the east wing of the home, to the master apartments. My father's were to the left, and he was probably in there for the night. My mother's rooms were to the right, at the rear of the house. I listened for several minutes to be certain all was quiet. If I was caught, I had an excuse ready, but I didn't want to tell any more lies involving her. My mother wasn't like the other Dallisors. As it was for me, marriage had been planned for her, and I'd always felt a part of her resented that.

It was possible that after her death, my mother's things had been removed from her apartments. If so, then coming here was an unnecessary risk and a waste of time. Yet I couldn't sleep with so many unresolved questions in my mind. After my rescue from the Banished, everything had happened in a blur before I was sent away. And if I found the Olden Blade for Simon and Trina, I'd never be allowed back here. I'd lose every connection with my mother.

Lily Dallisor had been feminine, soft-spoken, and infinitely kind. For most of my life, I had never understood how she could have produced a child like me. Perhaps I took after my father, a thought that pierced my heart. Was that why he constantly rejected me, because he saw the worst of himself in my eyes? If I had been anything like my mother, maybe he would have loved me more.

Loved me at all.

Coming back home from my kidnapping four days later, with a father who resented me and no mother to comfort me, had been devastating. It was a relief to be sent away to the Lava Fields. I wished I was still there.

At least when I entered the apartments, I noticed everything of hers was exactly as I remembered it, which was little surprise. For as poorly as my father thought of me, he'd always worshipped my mother, and this was her sanctuary, still holy to him. Proof of that was in the gold ribbon trim around her bedding. My father had defied Lord Endrick to preserve her memory. Beyond that, her gowns were still in her wardrobe, her bed had the same quilts piled on top, and near it, a silver tea set was at her writing desk, as if she might call for more tea at any time. The room smelled faintly of her, though that had to be my imagination. She wasn't here.

I swallowed that aching thought and set to work exploring the room, careful not to disturb anything and especially careful not to make noise. The more involved I got in the search, the more difficult my lie would be if I was caught. It was one thing to be in her room—I could always say I missed her and had just wanted to see it. But how would I explain why I had come here in trousers rather than my nightclothes? And why I was on my back beneath her bed, searching between the boards and mattress? The answer to that question would absolutely require a lie, one I had yet to invent.

What I was looking for was simple: a blanket she'd knitted in anticipation of my birth. However, what I really wanted was far more complicated.

Darrow and I had planned for this search from the moment I'd been summoned home. Or, rather, we had gotten into a fight about this search after he heard I intended to do it, with or without his help.

"Woodcourt is not a place where you should go about digging for secrets," he said. "There will be consequences for any answers you find."

"And what is the alternative?" I'd argued. "A lifetime of ignorance? I accept the consequences, whatever they are."

"You cannot possibly know what you are accepting. But if you insist on doing it, I'll be there with you, and answer whatever questions I can."

"The blanket will be there." I'd spoken forcefully, believing enough willpower might make my hopes true. "You'll see, Darrow, it's there."

But maybe it wasn't.

I searched as carefully as I could, tears welling in my eyes as it became increasingly obvious that no amount of wishing could make the blanket real. How many times had I begged to see it when I was younger, to see the gift her fingers had lovingly and carefully created for me? Hundreds of times, at least, but her answer was always the same.

"It's kept safe beneath my bed," she'd whisper. "Safe where our enemies will never find it."

Also, too difficult to access while she was in her elaborate gowns, she assured me. The problem was, she was always in those beautiful dresses. Words do not exist for how much I had wanted to see that blanket over the past three years. It was proof that I was hers and she was mine. Just once, I needed to see it, to imagine her holding it, holding me in her arms.

But the blanket was not here.

"What are you doing?"

I shot up so quickly that I banged my head on the panels propping up the mattress, loosening them with a clunking sound. Maybe the whole bed was about to collapse on me. It might be a blessing if it did. That was Gerald's voice.

"Come out and talk with me," he said. "I won't speak to the bottoms of your feet."

He sat on a stool beside my mother's vanity, waiting while I wormed my way out. Once I did, I sat cross-legged on the floor and waited for him to speak first. This wasn't polite, admittedly, but I had my reasons. The knife I'd taken was still in the back waistline of these trousers. I couldn't risk it being seen.

"I asked you a question." Gerald's patience was already wearing thin.

"You are my servant, and not the other way around." I hoped the force of my voice would intimidate him. "You have no right to question me."

"Do you wish your father to ask these questions?" He started to rise from his stool.

"I missed my mother, and wanted—"

"If you intend to lie, you can do better than that." At least he sat again.

I forced a smile. "If I could do better, I assure you, I would have."

He didn't enjoy the joke, and instead clasped his hands and leaned forward. "I suggest a game, my lady. You reveal a secret to me, and I will reveal one to you."

"I won't play that game."

"You are playing it already! Making guesses of who to trust, and who trusts you. Who knows what? Who is hiding behind which mask? You are playing the traitor's game, and no matter how well one wins, even the winner loses in the end." He sat up straight again. "Now, you will answer my question, then I'll answer yours. Do you believe that Lord Endrick has magic, that he is immortal?"

Endrick was Endrean, and all Endreans had magic beyond my understanding. Endrick had the power to acquire the magic from whomever he killed, and he used that power to increase his abilities by extinguishing his own people. I'd been told he could ignite fires with a snap of his fingers, heal himself, and track his soldiers with his mind, allowing him to amass armies in half the time an enemy could. I didn't understand his magic, but I'd seen some of his powers for myself. No sane person would test themselves against him.

"Lord Endrick is not immortal," I whispered. "But his magic would make him seem that way. Do you know of anything inside Woodcourt that could change that?"

"You mean the Olden Blade, of course. I know Woodcourt has been searched thoroughly. Officially, Lord Endrick has now claimed there is no Olden Blade and never was." Gerald tilted his head, more blue than usual in the moonlight. "But we both know differently."

I weighed my response carefully. The consequences of telling him too much were disastrous. "Do you know where the Olden Blade is?"

"It's my question, my lady. If you found the Olden Blade, what would you do with it?"

My heart skipped a beat. Several beats, actually, leaving a deep pain in my chest. Tracing my finger along a crack in the floor, I said, "Whoever finds it must use it for good, to help Antora." Now I looked up at him, adding, "Is there any difference between loyalty to my father and loyalty to Antora?"

"An interesting question." He hesitated long enough to weigh his own answer. "If there is any difference, I love my country first."

"I don't believe you are loyal to the Dominion." My breath lodged in my throat. "You're one of the Banished . . . I mean, the Halderians."

His eyes shifted for the briefest moment before they returned to me, a spark of worry in them now. "How do you know that?"

"When I was kidnapped, I overheard talk about a spy inside Woodcourt, a highly placed servant. I think it's you." Gerald lowered his head and nodded, acknowledging that I was right. But I wasn't finished. "Most of the Halderians wanted me dead, but not all. Whose side are you on?"

Now Gerald met my eyes. "I'm on Antora's side, my lady. I'm on Darrow's side. And if both of those describe you, then I'm on your side most of all. Who are these so-called servants you brought into Woodcourt?"

It was my turn to hesitate, longer than Gerald had. "Simon and Trina are . . . not on the same side as me."

"They are not on the same side as each other, Kestra!"

This was something I'd already guessed, though hearing it from Gerald worried me. "Are you going to tell my father that I was here tonight?"

"What I report to Sir Henry Dallisor depends on why you're here."

I shrugged again. "When I was with the Halderians, they told me to search this room for the truth about myself. I never had the chance to do it before I was sent away. Darrow promised to help me search after we came home. I think he knew what I would find here . . . or what I wouldn't. Can you help?"

He reached into his jacket and withdrew a small book with a silver lock around it. "This is what you came for."

I caught my breath in my throat. The binding was beautiful, covered in faded pink satin and sewn with maroon thread in the shape of roses.

"Risha's diary?" I breathed.

He arched a brow, curious. "As far as we know, Risha never kept a diary, nor her Endrean servant."

"Then whose is that?"

"See for yourself. It was hidden beneath Sir Henry's desk in the library, and unless you want both of us to follow in Risha's footsteps, you will return it there by morning." He held it out to me. "I am risking my life to give this to you, Kestra, in hopes that you are the person I believe you to be. Do not disappoint me."

"Who do you believe me to be?" I asked.

"It's not what I believe about you, it's what I know." He stood and gave me a deep bow. "My lady, you are the only one who can play the traitor's game, and win."

I shook my head. "I don't understand."

"I suspect you will, after you read that book. I am telling you again, this must be back in its place before anyone discovers its absence. Our lives depend on that."

I clutched the book to my chest while I waited for him to leave. Once he did, I studied it more carefully. The silver band extended entirely around the book, and an etching on the front noted that if the lock was broken, ink would leak into the book, destroying anything written there. A key was needed to open it.

I had that key, in my pocket. This was what the Halderians had tried to give me at the inn, what I had taken from Simon's satchel. But if this was not Risha's diary, whose was it?

I pulled the key from my pocket and stuck it into the lock. It was stiff, but it did turn, and then the lock separated. I was in.

I opened the pages of my mother's diary. Her name was printed in neat handwriting right on the first page. "Lily Dallisor."

Page one began this way: "This is the only place I will ever be able to tell the truth . . ."

· TWENTY-ONE ·

KESTRA

I didn't shut my eyes all night, except when I paused from my reading to sob silently into my hands.

"What I have done for Kestra will have eternal consequences," the diary had begun. "Just as a mother's love should."

A few pages farther. "If Henry knew the full truth about Kestra, he would not want her. The blue-faced guard from the dungeons recommended a man named Darrow to protect her, but I know nothing about him. Still, I fear for Kestra's life. She's all I have."

Then several pages more. "The older she becomes, the more Henry pushes her away. He wishes to marry her to some king's son in Reddengrad. She's still a child! But I wonder if leaving Antora would be better. Darrow asks to take her into hiding, but what of his bloodline? The Halderians know about her. They will try to find her. This terrifies me."

And on the final page of the book. "This sickness overwhelms me. I have begged for Kestra to come to my side, but they fear I will make her sick too. What does that matter? If I die, Henry will no longer protect her from Lord Endrick. My daughter is in danger."

I cried again, hot, bitter tears that did nothing but sting my eyes and envelop me in the darkness of the tower where I had read the diary by the light of a single candle. Each word of the diary had bored itself deeper into my heart, revealing lies that cut like knives, and truths I would have traded my soul to forget. It was cruel of Gerald to have given this to me.

Cruel, but necessary. I blew out the candle and was distressed to realize I no longer needed it. Dawn had come.

I wiped my eyes, wondering how red they were, how swollen. Anyone who gave me more than a passing glance would know I had been crying. I was still in the tunic and trousers, and certain that back in my room, Trina was already awake and aware of my absence. More importantly, I had to return the diary to the library. But dressed as I was, I could not be seen by any servants. They'd surely report me.

I rushed down the tower stairs, which deposited me in the entry vestibule. Servants were already bustling through the corridors and living areas, stoking fires from what had become ash overnight, delivering warm water where it was needed, and preparing Woodcourt for a new day. My timing had to be impeccable to miss them. Fortunately, this was not my first time sneaking around. The routines hadn't changed much, or, at least, I hoped they hadn't. If I could do this, Darrow would be proud of me.

Darrow. I desperately needed his advice, for the night had given me far more questions than answers. He had been shot more than a day and a half ago. More than ever, I was determined to find the Olden Blade and earn his life back.

I continued hurrying toward my room, barely missing an oncoming servant who was dusting or doing some other useless job. Time was running out!

A hand went around my mouth, and before I could scream into

it, Simon turned me around to face him, then shoved me into my room, shutting the door behind us. Beside him was Trina, and from the looks of them, their combined anger could ignite fire on rainwater.

"Thank the heavens you're back! We've been searching everywhere!" Trina began. "Where have you—"

"I need your dress," I said. "Give it to me."

"My dress? There's only a shift beneath this."

"Be grateful you have that much. I need it now."

"First tell me why."

"Shall I tell you over tea and scones, or in the seconds before my father has us all killed?"

Simon faced the wall while she undressed, though she muttered a string of curses that lasted the entire length of time it took to remove the dress and hand it to me. My tunic acted as a clumsy half-shift, and I left the trousers on beneath the skirts, with the ivory-handled knife tucked out of my reach. The key to the diary was safely in my shoe. The diary itself was hidden beneath my tunic, and when Trina wasn't looking, I set it into a deep pocket of the dress's apron. Trina pulled a quilt from off my bed and wrapped it around herself while asking what she was expected to wear now.

I didn't know. I didn't care.

"Where were you all night?" Simon asked.

"Are you my interrogator or protector?" I replied. "Come with me. We must hurry!"

He sighed and threw an apology back at Trina, who was still muttering threats at me, then we entered the corridor. I wanted to run, to push past every servant we saw and get into the library, but I couldn't draw that much attention to myself. So we walked. Quickly.

"Your eyes are red," he said.

"Yours are brown. What of it?"

"You know what I mean. You've been crying." His voice was gentle, but his timing was terrible. He could accuse me of practically anything right now, and I'd be guilty.

"If anyone asks, it's only tears of joy to be back at Woodcourt again."

"But it's not just anyone asking. It's me, Kestra."

I huffed. "And who are you, Simon, that I should trust you with an answer?"

At the base of the stairs, he stopped and took my arm, forcing me to look at him. "I'm your friend, or, at least, I'm trying to be." His brows were pressed low and he was studying my face as if deeply concerned.

Was he sincere? Because I desperately needed someone to talk to, someone to trust. I needed him to stay with me even after he knew everything, and to take my hand and promise that it would be all right.

But he wouldn't say that, not if he knew. We could never be friends. And now . . . anything more . . . was impossible.

I pushed away from him and continued walking. "Stand watch outside the library. If anyone tries to come in, make a noise to warn me and slow them down."

"Why? What are you doing in there?"

I entered the library without answering him and quietly shut the door. I pulled the diary out from the apron pocket, then crossed the room to the desk, where it had been hidden. My father's tablet was on top, with an image of the oropods in motion, and a description of them beneath the picture. I knelt beside the desk to peek underneath it. Gerald had not given any details as to where the diary had been hidden, so I'd assumed the placement would be obvious, but now that I was here, it was anything but.

The underbelly of the desk was a series of boards fitted tightly together. Nothing could be hidden here, certainly not a book! Was this Gerald's way of trapping me? No, I had to believe that he meant well by giving me the diary, though at the moment, it seemed just the opposite.

I pressed on the boards, hoping to find one that was loose or that might be a false bottom, furious with myself for not asking how to hide this again.

"Sir Henry, good morning." That was Simon's voice!

"What are you doing here, boy?"

"Looking for your daughter, sir." He was speaking loud enough to warn me, but risked giving away that this was a signal. "She hoped to have breakfast with you this morning, to update you on last night's meeting with Sir Basil."

"Oh? You were there too, I assume. How did it go?"

"Very well," Simon said. "I think your daughter will soon find herself in love."

Was he talking about Basil? I'd sooner learn to love boiled intestines. Or was he just stalling, hoping to keep my father in the hallway as long as possible?

There was no time to continue searching for the diary's proper hiding place. All I could do was slip it between some books on a nearby shelf and hope it went unnoticed. I'd come back later this afternoon, or tonight, and try again.

For now, I needed a way out of the library—through a window perhaps? Did I have time?

"Lord Endrick." Simon's voice had changed. He wasn't talking *about* the Lord of the Dominion. He was speaking *to* him.

My heart crashed against my chest. This was the worst possible situation.

I'd known that I would have to face my father today, and that had worried me. But if Lord Endrick was here, all that remained within me was pure fear. I couldn't do this.

I had to do this.

I was terrified.

And I was going to do it anyway.

· TWENTY-TWO ·

KESTRA

No one is sure when the Endrean people came into being, or how. All that is known is they were first discovered in the Blue Caves of the Watchman Mountains, and that somewhere deep inside those caves was the source of their magic.

Because of the mystery surrounding their origins, and the mysteries of magic itself, most Antorans believed Endreans were naturally evil.

Darrow didn't believe that. He said we were a product of our choices, not our bloodlines. I agreed. Except Lord Endrick—he was never anything but evil.

When he spoke, his voice was a razor, each word a cut that would burn for hours. To Simon, he said, "Move aside, boy. We have business. Private business."

The door handle turned and I stood tall to see Lord Endrick enter the library first. An icy wind seemed to accompany him, and I'm sure he was pleased to see me shudder beneath his dark shadow.

It was said that Lord Endrick had once been exceptionally handsome, as all Endreans were supposed to be. Yet with every murder he committed against his own people, his skin had grayed and become etched with deep, creviced lines, particularly on the cheeks and around his eyes. His pupils had faded to a frosty blue and often darted around like he expected an attack. He wore a leather cap over his hairless head at all times, and when in public, he wore a golden mask to hide his grotesque appearance. Few Antorans had ever seen his true face. Unfortunately for me, a visit to Sir Henry Dallisor's home was not considered going out in public. Nor was it necessary to look at him to understand this man's dark nature. Even the most callous person could feel his emanating cruelty. I'd never been so close to him, though I wondered how I had not noticed all of this three years ago when I had seen him from a distance.

Lord Endrick had declared the heavens dead and himself the highest giver of mercy. Considering what I had to do now, I hoped he was wrong. I sent a silent prayer to the heavens for protection. It couldn't hurt to try.

"Who are you, girl?" Endrick said to me. "What is a servant girl doing here, Sir Henry?"

"My Lord, you remember Kestra, my daughter." He was clearly surprised to see me here, but not as angry as I would've expected. Probably because Simon had warned that I was looking for him.

"Dressed in a servant's clothes?"

I gave a low curtsy and kept my face down so he would not see the redness of my eyes, or the fear in them. "I've not had time to prepare a proper wardrobe yet."

As far as Lord Endrick was concerned, I was Dallisor property, so he felt no need to address me directly when he said, "Your daughter must fix that. She is an embarrassment to you."

"She is, my Lord."

"That won't be a problem much longer. Has a date been set for her wedding to Sir Basil?"

"We arranged it last night. They will marry in two weeks."

I looked up, despite myself. Two weeks? Then I reminded myself that it wouldn't matter. I would not be here in two weeks. I would not be here in two more days.

"Two weeks is too long," Endrick said. "Sir Basil is in Highwyn now. Why can he not marry the girl tomorrow?"

"What?" I spoke loudly, ignoring every instinct within me to stop. "No!"

"Kestra, remember yourself!"

I lowered my head again. "Lord Endrick, if I do not have a proper dress to greet you, how can you expect me to have a proper dress for marriage?"

He crossed toward me, his face pinched with anger. "You will, because I demand it. This is a marriage of one noble to another. You will marry when I say it is your duty to do so."

"Only if I agree to it. Tomorrow is too soon."

"Are you refusing your master?"

Fear flooded into me, drowning everything I needed to survive this. I had no more courage, no more determination, and certainly no idea what had gotten me here in the first place. Beyond my trembling hands and weak knees, all that remained was knowing I couldn't go back now anyway, even if I tried.

So I stared directly at the Lord of the Dominion, something I'd never before done, and summoned the last of my strength to straighten my shoulders and say, "I will not marry Sir Basil tomorrow."

"Go to your knees, girl!"

The instant he commanded it, my legs collapsed into a kneeling position, responding to his magic. I briefly wondered who he'd killed to have that power and whether it was possible to fight it. Then I folded my skirts behind me. The last thing I needed was to explain why I had trousers on. Or worse, why I was practically begging the Lord of the Dominion to punish me.

The weight of Endrick's attention fell upon me like a boulder. "Lower your head."

For the first time, I noticed a grip glove on the back of his right hand with attached rings on his fingers. It was similar in design to the one Simon had taken from me, but with a key difference: Endrick's was made of small bones that mimicked the bones of his own hand. This I had not seen before, which worried me even more.

I lowered my head, and he brushed my hair over one shoulder. I could barely breathe, and it hadn't even started. Whatever *it* was. I knew that when he used to require this of Dominion soldiers, my mother always whisked me from the courtyard before I had to see anything. I heard it though, no matter how far from the courtyard we ever hid. If Lord Endrick intended to cause a person pain, he could do it through mere touch. I hoped he would spare some mercy for me though. I was the daughter of his top counselor.

But maybe that was the very reason this would not go well.

Endrick brushed his leathery fingers along the back of my neck and a shiver rushed through my veins. He was finding the precise area of his target.

I wasn't strong enough for this. Or brave enough. I wasn't *enough* of anything to survive this.

But I was too late to stop it.

Using the power of his grip glove, he pressed directly on my spine with his thumb, like a knife drilling into my core. Every muscle of my body became rigid with pain and breathing was impossible. Then his thumb rotated on my neck and with it, my insides twisted. I screamed, the pain erupting like cannon fire exploding within me. If I were capable of collapsing, I would have, but I could only remain kneeling, acutely aware that whatever grace kept me alive was fading fast.

Sweat rose from every pore. I couldn't think, or remember my own name, if I even had one. Something like molten lava rushed through my veins, burning and hardening as it flowed. I cried out and tried to pull away, but couldn't do that either.

"My Lord, please—"

"I am dealing with your daughter, Sir Henry, if you won't." Endrick's full hand gripped my neck, and when he pressed down, my entire spine flooded with ice. I gasped as tears streamed down my cheeks.

I tried to speak, but my words were drowned out by my cries. He was killing me, and I felt from him his joy of doing it.

"Who are you to refuse my orders?" Endrick said.

Who was I? He could not have asked any more impossible a question.

"Look at me, girl."

Now I did. With a face marked by tears, any redness from earlier that morning would go unnoticed. It was a small consolation, but it was all I had.

"I beg you to stop this." My voice trembled as I spoke, and if he heard me, he ignored my pleas for mercy.

Endrick leaned down, though the awful pressure on my neck remained. "You will marry Sir Basil, because I want his father's kingdom. It is guarded by thick walls that I cannot penetrate without a substantial loss to my armies, and thanks to the trouble with the Coracks, I do not have any men to spare. After you are married, conquering Reddengrad will be a simple thing."

Despite my pain, through gritted teeth I said, "How?"

"The *how* is up to me," Endrick said. "Your role is to do as you are told. If you refuse, I will order your father to show you what happens to those who defy me."

Would my father carry out such a command? It was one thing to order the hangman's noose for those who stood in defiance of Lord Endrick, but—

Wasn't that exactly my crime?

"Well?" Endrick's patience had run out. "Will you obey my command or spend time in your father's dungeons?"

I lowered my head again and said nothing. I didn't trust myself with words.

"Have her guard escort her belowground," Endrick said, finally releasing me. "She can think about her answer from there."

Once his hand lifted, I fell to the floor, unable to draw a full breath and soaked with sweat. That was nothing compared to what he could have done; I had felt how much he was holding back. But still, that was far worse than I'd expected.

When he was called, Simon entered, though I only saw his boots through my blurred vision.

"Sir Henry's daughter will spend time in the dungeons," Endrick scowled. "She knows the one way to get herself out again."

"Yes, my Lord." I felt Simon's arms around me, lifting me, and almost entirely carrying me from the library. He had his satchel, and I tried to remember if there'd been anything in it before that could dull the kind of pain I was still experiencing. No, there wasn't, but at least the worst was over. It didn't matter where I was going next. Anywhere was better than here.

· TWENTY-THREE ·

SIMON

I didn't hear the smallest sigh from Kestra the entire time we walked down to the dungeons. Silence from her was almost always a bad thing—I'd certainly come to understand that. But this time, it was an entirely different kind of bad.

We had to walk through the servants' workstations to access the interior entrance, a place I remembered far too well. Those servants who saw Kestra stared and whispered about what she might have done, but she didn't seem to notice.

The dungeons were connected to Woodcourt by a thick wooden door with an even thicker lock. I knocked on the door, and it was opened by a guard who looked and sounded annoyed until I explained the lady of the house was to be their prisoner. The guard's eyes drifted to Kestra like a vulture's might, and I pulled her closer to my side. With a hungry smile, the guard said, "Down the stairs."

"Thank you," she whispered.

At first, I thought her words were directed to the guard, but she was looking at me, her face full of gratitude. Was she being genuine? Thanking anyone at all seemed unlike the Kestra I knew.

Maybe I still didn't know her. Maybe that was the point.

When the door widened, the stench hit me like a cannonball; a combination of decaying flesh, human waste, and mildewed walls all vomited from the bowels of the dungeons. I'd seen these soot-covered rock walls before, and the steepness of the stone steps that descended into near blackness. I'd been pushed down them after the whipping.

At the bottom of the stairs, Kestra's feet braced against a rock, as if she could not make them go any farther. I stopped with her, tightening my hold on her waist, a reminder that she was not alone. After a deep breath, she nodded, forcing herself onward.

"Careful." Despite my warning, she slipped on the damp soil. Her hand found mine and she gave it a quick squeeze. Was that more gratitude? Or confidence in me to help her through this? I wasn't sure, but it'd be a lie to suggest that her touch wasn't working its way inside me. Tenger had ordered me to pretend to be her protector, as part of the plan. But now it was different.

Now I *was* her protector.

We came to an open area where another two guards stood. Their faces were pale, and light from the torches on the walls cast their appearance in harsh, unfriendly angles. The stone floor was moist, where the groundwater beneath Woodcourt made its way inside. It would be worse below, down the slope where the dungeons themselves were.

"What is that smell?" Kestra dug her nails into my arm and her breathing became harsh again.

Kestra had obviously never been to the dungeons before, probably never even opened the door to them. The Corack in me was glad she was seeing them. Maybe she would finally ask herself about the hundreds of people who had come through here on their way to execution.

But every other part of me wished she had never seen this place. It would change her, create a memory in her that she could never erase.

"This is Sir Henry Dallisor's daughter," I said to the guards. "She won't be here for long, and you will give her the finest place to stay."

The taller one wrinkled his nose and laughed. "The finest place? Do you prefer the cell with the woven tapestries, or the one with the thickest rugs?"

Above the guards' mockery, Kestra mumbled, "Put me in cell number four."

My brows knitted as I looked at her. Lord Endrick had done something terrible to her in that library, something that was still causing her pain, but maybe more was happening than I had realized. Could she have *wanted* to be sent here?

I repeated her words. "Cell number four." When the guards hesitated, I added, "She's still a Dallisor. Give her what she wants."

"That's a horrible place," the shorter guard said. "I wouldn't put my worst enemy in there." But he led us there anyway, down the steep and muddy slope, where Kestra nearly slipped more than once.

The cells were randomly spaced apart on either side of the slope, built wherever a natural cavity existed in the rock. Any exposed sides were closed in with thick brick walls and a locked wooden door with a small carved hole to let in the tiniest amount of air and light.

Kestra seemed stronger now, not by much, but she could walk on her own, holding my arm for balance. Still, I sensed hesitation in her every step. The lower we went, the more toxic the stench became, the darker our surroundings. Torches were set into the walls, but their dim light only added to the gloom of these cells. No, not cells. These were tombs.

Soon we came to a door with four scratches on the front, like a claw had swiped down it. Cell number four.

Kestra stopped at the open door and dug her nails into my arm again. The room was large enough to fit three or four people, if everyone stood, but they wouldn't be able to stand to their full height, and the reeking air had no circulation.

"Don't make me go in there," she whispered. "Please, Simon."

I'd never expected any situation to come up in a thousand years where I'd have volunteered to stay in these dungeons. But now, I couldn't imagine being anywhere else. "I'll stay. I'll go in with you."

Tightening her grip on my arm, she closed her eyes to enter. It didn't matter if she did or not. The darkness was about the same either way.

Her shoulders began shaking as soon as she crossed the cell threshold. "She needs a blanket," I said to the guard behind us.

"This is a dungeon, not an inn."

My voice got louder. "If she becomes ill from this cold and dies, will Sir Henry take the blame, or assign it to you? Call for her handmaiden to bring a blanket and something warm to eat, and do it at once!"

"You don't have to stay." Kestra waited until the door had been shut and locked before slumping onto the hard ground. "I'd rather be alone anyway."

"No, you wouldn't." I sat beside her, wrapping my arm around her shoulders, and feeling surprised at how easily she allowed me to pull her close. I'd held her this way before, the night the Coracks stopped her carriage, though that had been anything but friendly. This was . . . different.

She shivered again and I brushed a hand down her arm, hoping to warm her. I'd never noticed before the softness of her skin, like a down feather that you'd protect against the wind or rain, just because you might never touch anything so delicate again.

Protect her. Those were my orders.

Then again, Tenger had also given me specific orders if Kestra failed to produce the Olden Blade. Was I supposed to protect Kestra . . . from myself?

When she began to relax, I said, "I heard what was happening through the library door. I'd have come in, but that would've made things worse."

I'd done more than just hear it. I'd fought every instinct within myself not to charge through the door and help. Every time she had screamed, or pled for mercy, or cried through the pain, it had echoed into the deepest part of me too. I should've found a way to help her.

Should have.

Couldn't have.

Should have anyway.

It would've been futile. If I had entered, I'd only have had my knife, which might have worked for Kestra's father, but I'd never have gotten as far as Lord Endrick. Only the Infidante could do that, if one was found.

"I knew you couldn't come in," she mumbled. "But I needed to get sent here, didn't I."

Another question that wasn't a question, another sharp prick of my conscience. The worst part was that she had clearly understood something I hadn't until now. Of course, she couldn't have simply walked down here on her own, demanding to inspect the cells. She had to be sent here. Which meant she had to do something awful enough to deserve it. She deliberately incited Lord Endrick's anger against her, because Trina and I had forced her to do it.

How had Kestra described the Coracks before? As scum? That seemed about right.

Kestra's shaking had stopped but her skin was like ice. I shifted until I was directly behind her, letting her recline against my chest, and folding her into my arms for warmth. It was the best I could offer for an apology. "Are you hurting?"

"My neck feels awful. I don't know what he did to it."

"Lean forward." When she did, I ran my thumb across the back of her neck, barely pressing in until she flinched and I stopped. It was swollen in one spot but had a hard center. I couldn't explain it. "Maybe a bruise is forming."

"I'll be lucky if that's the worst he did." Her eyes were growing heavy, which was no surprise. I doubted she had slept at all last night, and very little the night before. All I could do was bring her back into my arms, where she nestled in with her cheek against my chest. With great effort, I kept my breath steady enough that I wouldn't disturb her, but there was nothing I could do about the pounding of my heart, fully aware of her nearness.

She sighed, then her muscles trembled as another shiver ran through her. I tightened my arms to comfort her until she relaxed again, and I was sure she murmured my name. I wished I knew why.

This was not the arrogant girl from the inn, or the girl who had firmly resolved to hate me. This time, Kestra needed me here. I almost dared to believe that she wanted me here.

Just as much as I wanted to be here, holding her, breathing her in. I wasn't sure *when* my feelings had changed, only that somewhere between stepping into that carriage and this moment, she had turned my heart inside out.

More importantly, she seemed to be changing too. I saw it in her eyes, the way she occasionally lowered her guard, or in those few seconds in the gardens when her fingers had touched mine. But it never lasted long before she would catch herself and back away, every single time. Being this close to her was an entirely new form of torture, a constant twist on my emotions, but still a thousand times better than being apart.

"It's all right," I whispered. "You're safe with me."

She let out a gentle breath. "I wish I were back in the Lava Fields," she murmured. "I barely remember them."

"That was only a few days ago."

"It was a lifetime ago." A minute later, her breathing became regular. She was asleep.

And with her this close, I had never been more awake.

· TWENTY-FOUR ·

SIMON

At least Kestra was resting comfortably. For my part, I should've found a better place to sit than against a sharp rock wall with nowhere to recline my head. A half hour ago, a thick blanket had been sent into the cell, and when I wrapped it around Kestra, she settled lower onto the ground, using my leg for a pillow. The guards also gave me a thick slice of bread, wrapped in a thin cloth napkin. I briefly wondered what to do with it. Anywhere out in the open would call in the rats, so I set it inside my satchel and hoped the rats wouldn't be hungry enough to sniff it out.

I kept the satchel with me as often as possible now. Someone had searched through it once and taken the key, probably Kestra, but I couldn't allow a search to happen again. Nothing in it tied me to the Coracks, but Garr's old ring was in the bottom and I'd promised to keep it safe. On casual observation, it wasn't the kind of ring that would draw much attention, just a gold band with an inner inscription. It had meant everything to Garr, and since his death, it meant everything to me.

For the past half hour, I'd been rubbing my thumb along the ring, thinking of the kind of person Garr had expected me to become one day, and how far from that I was.

Garr would never have supported me joining the Coracks. He didn't trust their motives, or their techniques. He never would have supported this mission I was on, the hard things we'd put Kestra through.

Now that I was with the Coracks, I was disappointing them too, or I would soon. A few months ago, Tenger had hinted that I might one day take a leadership role, become his second-in-command.

What a joke that was. Tenger was as wrong about me as Garr had been—this mission proved that. It was pointless to pretend anymore that I was indifferent to Kestra, not when she constantly occupied my thoughts. And the more certain I became of my feelings toward her, the more I'd begun to doubt everything else, myself most of all. Cursing under my breath, I dropped the ring back into the satchel, where it belonged, and where it would remain.

Then I waited, occasionally brushing the tips of my fingers against Kestra's cheek. She seemed warmer now and was in a deep sleep. One hand rested just below my knee and every so often she gave a soft cry, squeezed my leg, and then released it. Probably nightmares. I hoped I wasn't in them.

Tenger's plan had been easy enough to accept when I hated Kestra and knew she hated me. Now I didn't know what to do. The only way to complete this mission was to stay near her, but the closer we became, the more I doubted that I could see this through to the end.

Nearly two hours passed before she awoke, and she did so slowly, as if she had forgotten—or hadn't wanted to remember—where she was. When she did remember, she sat up suddenly, as if slapped back into reality.

With some relief, I shook out my leg, which had long ago gone numb. She noticed it and wrapped the blanket more tightly around herself, staring at me like I should have made some profound discovery about the Blade while she slept. One of us had to say something.

Then I remembered the bread and pulled it from my satchel. "Not the best place to keep food, but I doubted you'd want to share with the rats."

She took a nibble from the bread, then hesitated. "Have you eaten anything?"

"I'm fine, Princess." I thought she was beginning to tolerate my nickname for her, but maybe not. Her face scrunched up the same as always.

"You still think I'm treated like a princess, after seeing me in here?" She broke the bread in half and held it out to me. "I can share with one rat, I suppose."

At least she smiled as she spoke. She must have been feeling better.

"You need it," I said. "You're imprisoned here. I can leave at any time."

She offered the bread again. "You can, but you won't."

"No, I won't leave." I took the bread, keenly aware of the way her fingers brushed over mine. Did she know how even these small moments dissected me? With some effort, I collected my thoughts again. "Was this Risha's cell?"

"It was her servant's. A woman named Anaya."

I snorted dismissively. "The Coracks believe Anaya betrayed Risha. That she was Endrick's spy among the Halderians, and the reason Risha ended up here."

"Anaya was executed, same as her mistress."

"And Anaya had magic, same as Lord Endrick. Magic is a corruption. Even for those with good intentions, eventually magic will corrupt. After what Lord Endrick just did to you, how can you doubt that?"

"Yes, Endrick is evil. But that doesn't mean Anaya was. That doesn't mean all Endreans are."

I took her hand, letting my fingers dance with hers. "My father was a good man. Soon after the war, he took in an Endrean woman who had escaped from Endrick and was begging for protection. She had the ability to infuse objects with magic, so you can imagine how Endrick desired that power. Over the next few weeks, her temperament worsened, her magic sometimes sparked out of control, and her skin began to gray." I hesitated. Despite how young I'd been then, I remembered everything, and even now, it was hard to talk about. "At the end of a month, she killed my father and claimed it as a victory for Endrick. Up until the night before that happened, she had claimed to be one of the good ones."

I waited for her to say something, anything. When she didn't, I continued, "Maybe you never saw what Endrean magic did to this land during the war, but I have. They destroyed whole cities, a single curse sterilizing vast acres of land. They killed innocents without a blink of mercy, all of them following Endrick's orders right up to the day he killed them too. If Anaya was good, then she was the only good Endrean . . . ever."

Kestra kept her eyes on the ground. "Did Endrick really kill all of his own people?"

"He didn't just kill them, Kestra. It was a planned annihilation, taking their magic in the order he needed it most."

"What if there are more in hiding, just like the Halderians?"

"The Coracks won't let them live." I folded my hand around hers. "We can't go to all this trouble to destroy Endrick and then risk another Endrean rising to power."

I knew how cold my words must have sounded, but there were reasons for the order. Nothing in Antoran history suggested magic was anything but evil.

Kestra didn't seem convinced, but rather than argue, she said, "Endrick would've searched Risha's cell, but might not have considered her servant's. We need to start our search here."

I began at the end deepest into the cell while she was nearer the door. With so little light, we traced our fingers along the rock, feeling for any patterns or gaps. The rock creased and jutted and cut on its sharpest tips, but there was nothing unusual.

That is, until several minutes later when Kestra whispered, "This is writing, Simon, I'm sure of it!"

I scrambled over to her and ran my hands along the rock. She was right—the etchings I felt were carved into the wall, but it was too dark to read them.

Then her expression fell. "In seventeen years, we wouldn't be the first to see this. Whatever is written here has been seen a thousand times already."

"Soon, it will have been seen a thousand and one times. Move back." I grabbed the napkin that had wrapped the bread and twisted it tight. Then I withdrew a piece of fire steel from my satchel. The napkin would burn fast. We'd read faster. I scraped the metal against the rock wall until it sparked enough to light the napkin on fire. Once it did, I held it close to the carving. Kestra leaned in beside me to see what was written there.

We only had a few seconds, but it was enough to read.

One to Vanquish
One to Rule
One to Fall
But All to Fool

I ground out the last of the embers from the napkin and leaned against the rock wall. "*One to Vanquish*. That must be the Infidante, meant to kill Endrick."

Beside me, Kestra mumbled, "*One to Rule*. Because the Infidante will choose the next ruler of the Scarlet Throne."

"*One to Fall*," I continued. "That's Lord Endrick, I assume. What of the fourth line, *But All to Fool*?" I pushed my hair back with my fingers, out of frustration more than anything else. "It's irrelevant anyway. Nothing in the carving tells us where the dagger is hidden."

Kestra's attention seemed to have shifted in another direction. "The carving is too clean to have been done by hand. Anaya must've used magic. I'd always heard her powers were depleted when she came here. Maybe they weren't."

I sat up taller. "What if the fourth line, *But All to Fool*, is about Risha? We know she brought the Blade into the dungeons. But somewhere between her arrest and execution, it disappeared. Somehow, she fooled everyone."

Kestra nodded. "Wherever Risha hid the Blade, she would've made sure someone knew how to find it. Maybe Gerald?"

"Gerald?" My face scrunched up in confusion. "Is he—" When she nodded, I added, "Then he's proof that the Halderians don't know where the Blade is. If they did, they'd have had Gerald retrieve it by now."

"But someone knows." Kestra touched my arm. "Why did Thorne Halderian recognize Trina at the inn? Why was she chosen for this mission, above other girls with more experience, or frankly, more stability? Trina knows more than she's saying."

Suddenly, I groaned. "Trina brought Tenger new information about the Blade. That's the only reason he allowed her to join us." I stood and banged on the door until a guard came down the slope. "Lady Kestra must prepare to see her father again. Call for her handmaiden to bring her a clean dress." After the guard left, I turned back to her. "Then we'll find out everything."

Kestra nodded, but already seemed lost in another maze of thoughts, secrets she guarded well. Yet more and more, it felt as if we were on the same side. In time, I would find out all her secrets.

Or worse. She would find out mine.

· TWENTY-FIVE ·

KESTRA

It took another hour before Trina came, and she did so with an apology, explaining that every maid in Woodcourt who could work a needle had been ordered to make dresses for me, in preparation for my coming wedding.

"Is that really happening tomorrow night?" Trina settled into the cramped corner of our cell, making it seem smaller, though I tried to hide the panic on my face. "Everything can still work out though. If we get the Olden Blade by then, we can leave tomorrow, before the wedding."

When neither Simon nor I replied, she held out the dress she had brought with her, a light blue gown with a high collar of white lace, something that might've been perfect if I were nearing the age of eighty, and blind. "It's the best I could do in so little time. It's only one dress, Kestra. Why are you so quiet?"

"You didn't sew that dress," Simon said flatly. "You don't sew."

"I didn't, until I had to pretend to know how three hours ago!" Trina's face wrinkled. "What is the matter with you two?"

"You're keeping a secret from us." I hoped my bold tone would intimidate her. "Now is the time to confess."

Trina's eyes darted. "There is something, but it would only matter if you marry Basil." Now our eyes met. "You won't do that, right?"

"What are you talking about?" I asked.

"Obviously, you want to know why Basil is really marrying you. Why he wanted to move your wedding date forward." Trina shrugged. "Isn't that what we're talking about?"

"No." Simon's brows pressed together. "We're talking about—"

"That's what we're talking about." I looked back to Trina. "Why is Basil marrying me?"

Trina paled. "When I was on my way down here earlier, with the blanket and the bread, I passed your father's library. He was in there, along with Endrick and Sir Basil. Basil was crying, I'm sure of it."

I sat taller, trying to ignore how much this cell closed in on me when I did. "What did you hear?"

"Endrick wants you dead—he said exactly those words. But he's worried that if he executes a Dallisor without cause, the other Dallisors will revolt. He reminded Basil that they had made a bargain. Basil is supposed to kill you, after your wedding. In exchange, Endrick will offer Reddengrad protection."

By the time she'd finished speaking, my hands were shaking. "My father was in the room for this meeting? Are you sure?"

Trina's eyes softened. "I'm sorry, Kestra. Yes, I'm sure."

"Endrick is lying!" Simon scowled. "He'll use Kestra's death as justification to invade Reddengrad. Basil might think he's protecting his country, but it will be the reason his country is destroyed!"

"None of this matters," Trina said. "We'll get Kestra out of

Woodcourt first. Obviously, we won't let her go through with this marriage."

"Basil was crying, the coward?" Simon kicked at the wall. "As if he should be pitied! What about Kestra's safety?"

"Listen to yourselves!" I shouted, then lowered my voice. "Do you have any idea how absurd this conversation is? Who are either of you to judge Basil?"

Simon and Trina fell silent. It obviously hadn't occurred to them that the three of us were not on the same side.

Simon spoke first. "Kestra, maybe things have changed since we came here."

"Or maybe things were never what we thought." I turned to Trina. "Are you a spy for the Halderians?"

Trina's eyes widened, to the point that even in this darkness I saw how suddenly large they had become. Silence followed my question, long enough and uncomfortable enough that I suspected she was working on swallowing her stomach again. Surely it had lurched into her throat.

Finally, she squeaked out, "I'm here for the Coracks! For Tenger!"

"Then explain how the Halderians know you," Simon said.

"Because of what that man said to me at the inn? I don't know him. But he did know Kestra. Why don't you ask *her* what he wanted?"

"We all know what he wanted with Kestra. To finish what he started the first time she was kidnapped, probably to kill her. When it came time to hide in the wall, you offered to stay out in the room. Why? Had you arranged for that meeting?"

Trina's laugh came from deep within her throat, and carried nothing but disgust. "I am not working for the Halderians!" Still addressing Simon, she pointed to me. "Whatever she's telling you, it's a lie! I promised Tenger that I would find the Blade for him, nothing more."

"For *him*?" I leaned forward. "Does Tenger want to be the Infidante?"

"Or the king?" Simon added. "Everyone knows Tenger wants more power."

Trina flinched and I asked her, "What do you get out of it? What did Tenger promise you?"

Trina shook her head. "I only want a place where I can belong, which both of you should understand. My father was loyal to the Dominion. In the War of Devastation, he fought for the Dallisors—fought for *your* father, Kestra—and ended up working here in the dungeons until he died of fever. I was never on the side of the Dominion. But still, his reputation has haunted me. I couldn't even get a meeting with Tenger, not at first. Then a year ago, I discovered my father's journals, which revealed the secrets of these dungeons. I brought them to Tenger, and he let me join the Coracks. We've been planning this mission ever since."

My gaze on her remained steady. "What were your father's secrets?"

She nodded toward the dark wall. "What you've obviously just discovered. He's the one who first found the carving in this cell. We believe the engraving is Risha's prophecy."

I arched a brow. "We?"

"Captain Tenger and I. We've studied every line, every word."

Simon folded his arms, obviously still skeptical. "How nice that you and Tenger had these conversations without me."

"You weren't supposed to be here, Simon! When could we have told you all of this?"

He shrugged. "Oh, I don't know. Maybe anytime today, or yesterday, or the day before that. Maybe five minutes before we had to drag this information out of you!"

"How do you interpret the lines?" I asked, hoping the question would avert the fight Trina and Simon were otherwise on the verge of having.

She sighed, obviously grateful for the distraction. "The first three lines mention the people who will be involved in Endrick's death: The Infidante, the new ruler of Antora, and Endrick himself." Which was roughly the same interpretation Simon and I had.

Trina continued, "Our best guess for the final line is that all three people have someone to fool. Maybe the whole country. Maybe a single friend." Her eyes roamed from me to Simon. "Or more than a friend, perhaps."

I wasn't taking the bait. Instead, I asked, "What's your role in the prophecy?" Trina opened her mouth to protest, and with an irritated sigh, I added, "Obviously, you believe you have a role."

Trina hesitated, then said, "My role is to find the Olden Blade, to set the prophecy into motion."

Her motives couldn't be that simple, or that pure. "For Tenger? So does he want to be the Infidante, or the king?"

"Tenger never reveals all of his plans to us." Trina looked over at Simon. "Tell Kestra that. He shares the least amount of knowledge that he must, to limit our risk to any mission."

If Simon heard her, he didn't respond. Instead, he was digging at the rock with his boot, maybe giving himself something to do in this cramped space. Surely he was frustrated to realize Trina knew things about Tenger's plan that he did not. Or that Tenger clearly had trusted her more than him.

"I have to succeed," Trina said. "If I don't find the Blade, I will be nothing to the Coracks." And from her tone, I knew that much was perfectly true.

No wonder she seemed so desperate, so worried that all their efforts might end in failure—and mark her as the architect of that failure. She had bet everything on this mission succeeding, and I was the last hurdle in her way.

As clear as Simon's and Trina's emotions were, my own were a mystery. Too much had happened today, too much had changed.

Worst of all was my father's collaboration in a plot to kill me. I should have been angry about that, furious and vengeful, but I wasn't. Instead, I was simply . . . empty, as if the part of my heart that I had reserved for Henry Dallisor was dead.

My anger was instead targeted at Lord Endrick, who had never viewed me as anything but a pawn, a sacrifice he was glad to make to expand his power. And what of Basil, who had agreed to such a dark plan? My feelings for him weren't so much anger as they were a single-minded desire to introduce him to Antora's largest catapult.

From the corner of my eye, I caught a glimpse of Trina. What did I feel for her? Sympathy, perhaps? She had struggled to find a place with the Coracks because of her father, just as I had never found my place as a Dallisor. Even if I disliked her, I could at least understand her, pity her.

But I wouldn't help her. Twice now, she had carefully avoided the question of Tenger's true motivations for wanting the Olden Blade. The idea of him as either Infidante or king was unacceptable.

Before I could allow the Blade to fall into anyone's control, I had to know who would ultimately take it. Because as bad as Lord Endrick was, I would not help one tyrant replace another. I would not have that blood on my hands.

"Enough of these suspicions," Simon finally said. "Trina, you should have told me the truth before, but if this is it, then I can live with it. The only way we'll ever get the Blade, and get out of here alive, is if we trust each other. Can we agree on that?"

"Agreed," Trina whispered.

They stared at me.

Trust Trina? Was he serious? She still had not told us the full truth. Surely Simon knew that too.

Trust him. Did I trust him?

My feelings regarding Simon were more confusing. He was a Corack, had threatened my life, and still held Darrow's and Celia's lives in his hands. He wasn't here for my well-being or safety, only to do what was necessary to ensure I located the Olden Blade. Once he had it, he would leave.

But he had also spent the past few hours with me in this cell, knowing my fear of such a tight, dark space, pulling me into his arms and promising to keep me warm and safe. He had hated watching me eat dinner with Basil, and had seemed genuinely concerned when Endrick had worked his dark magic upon my neck. He'd brushed his fingers over my cheek when he thought I was asleep, as tenderly as he'd touch a rose petal.

I didn't know how I felt about that, because I no longer trusted anything I felt about him. Except one feeling, something coming from the deepest part of my heart, and creeping in on me despite my best attempts to pretend otherwise.

I was falling for Simon.

"All right," I said. "We'll agree to trust each other."

It was a lie. I no longer even trusted myself.

· TWENTY-SIX ·

KESTRA

Once the three of us began talking again, the question turned to the necessity of finding the Olden Blade as quickly as possible.

Simon began, "Even if the carving is a clue to the dagger, it isn't the dagger itself."

"If Risha's servant gave us this one clue, then she gave us others," Trina insisted. "We have to find them in the next two days before we meet Tenger."

"No, before tomorrow's wedding," Simon put in.

"One day might not be enough time," Trina said.

"She'll be killed if she goes through with that wedding!" Simon said.

"And Tenger will kill me if I don't give him the Olden Blade." I tilted my head at him. "Remind me again how Coracks are better than Dallisors?"

Simon glared at me, though it wasn't in anger this time. My words had stung him.

Trina either hadn't heard me, or she didn't care. "First, you need to get out of this dungeon. Send word up to your father, agreeing to the wedding tomorrow night. It's the only way he'll let you leave. That gives us one more day to find the Olden Blade."

Simon kicked at the ground again. "She's right," he muttered. "What choice do we have?"

He banged on the cell door until the guard released him to allow Trina some privacy with me. After he was gone, I began unlacing the servant's dress, eager to be out of it.

"I know what you believe," Trina said. "That I'm not important to this plan. That it would end the same whether Simon finds the Olden Blade, or you do."

"That's not my belief. It's just a fact." I turned away from the closed cell door. Somehow, without Simon here, the cell had become smaller than before. "What's the truth, then?"

She sat beside me, placing the new dress on her lap. "If I tell you, will you keep it a secret?"

"Of course." Unless I decided otherwise. That all depended on what she was about to say.

Trina cocked her head toward the wall. "My father had a theory, one he never shared except in his journals. He believed your mother knew what happened to the Olden Blade, but the focus was always on Risha, and then your mother died and any chance to find out what she knew died with her."

I slipped the servant's dress off my shoulders, grateful that Trina had also remembered to bring a shift, which she passed up to me. "Why would my mother have known about the Blade?"

"That's why we need her diary, to get answers. That's my secret, Kestra. I thought if I told you whose diary we wanted, you wouldn't help us find it."

No, I wouldn't. Especially not now that I had read it.

"Don't disturb my mother's memories," I said. "Don't bring her into this."

"I have to, Kestra. I wish I didn't, but it's my future at stake." She paused, biting on her lip, trying to hold something back, I thought. Finally, she gave up trying. "If I don't get the Olden Blade for Tenger, I promised to leave the Coracks."

Again, I glanced at her over my shoulder, somehow managing not to throw any insults when I did. "Where would you go then?"

Trina shrugged. "I have nowhere to go. You know as well as I do how much one's blood matters in Antora. With my father's past, no Antoran will ever trust me. The Coracks offer more than just a place to belong, they're my protection. But if I can get the Blade, all of that will change."

"You believe if you find the Blade, the people of Antora will accept you?"

Now she smiled, and even stood to begin helping me into the blue dress. "It's much more than that! Tenger has quietly sent word to the Halderians all throughout Antora to gather in the Hiplands, where they've been slowly rebuilding their numbers. When we find the Blade, Tenger and I will take it to them. They'll hold a ceremony and someone will step forward to claim the Blade. It will light up for the Infidante, binding the dagger and its master together for life. Then we'll go after Endrick, finally able to win!"

My laugh spilled out as coarse as the rock walls. "You believe every part of the mythology, then? I wouldn't have thought you were so naïve. It's an inanimate piece of sharp metal, nothing more."

Trina stiffened. "The Olden Blade is full of magic, and that magic lives and breathes. When a Halderian claims it again, the true revolution will begin."

"Fine. So you'll go to a ceremony, the Blade will become a lantern or something, because for some reason it cares who holds it, then that person will defeat Lord Endrick?"

"And the Coracks will have started it all, maybe even finished it."

"The Coracks?" My brows drew together, wondering if she had said more than she intended. "I thought only a Halderian could hold the blade."

She stumbled for the right words. "Well . . . yes, but—"

If I asked again about Tenger, I knew she'd dodge the question. So this time, I tried something more subtle. "Are there any Halderians among the Coracks?"

Trina shrugged. "If there are, none will admit it."

"Would any of them hope to become the Infidante?"

She stopped working on my dress long enough to say, "Whoever the Infidante is, the Coracks will follow that person into battle. So should you."

If we were discussing Tenger, she'd be disappointed by my response. I'd seen what he was like as a captain. I wouldn't follow Tenger into the finest pastry shop in Antora, much less into battle.

"We don't need your approval," she said, sensing my disgust. "Just find us the Blade, and the Coracks will worry about the rest." Putting the final ties on my dress, she added, "You could join us, Kestra. You won't have any other choice, really. I had to leave my family name behind. You will, too."

A statement that proved words were far more cruel than any

weapon. I turned to face her, signaling the end of that conversation. Instead, I asked, "Aren't you afraid of Lord Endrick, afraid of the things he can do?"

"Sooner or later, Lord Endrick will find all of us. Our best chance of survival is for the Infidante to find him first."

I gave Trina my used tunic and trousers, which she bundled inside the servant's dress I had worn. The knife that I had taken from the hutch the night before was still with me, though I hadn't been able to reach it with the dress on over my trousers.

"Where did you get that?" she asked.

I rolled my eyes. "Honestly, Trina, you seem surprised every time I get a weapon. Take this if you want. I'll only find another one."

"Are you going to use it on me?"

Now I smiled. "If that was my plan, I would've done it already."

"Then keep the knife."

I smiled and lowered my skirts over the knife, now secure in its garter. When that was done, Trina pulled out a brush from her apron pocket and began to work on my hair.

"This was an unpleasant task when we were in your room, but it's nothing compared to this tiny cell," she said.

"Then let's go." I hardly needed a reminder that these walls seemed to be closing in on me. "Leave my hair as it is."

"Stay still." She pulled at a tangle, then added, "When the Halderians kidnapped you, I heard they held you in a very small box. What did they want?"

"My death. Most of them did, anyway." I shivered, wondering if the cell walls were actually shrinking, or if I was imagining it. "I doubt they've changed their mind in three years."

"The Coracks will protect you." Trina moved to where she could see me directly. "I know how that sounds, given what we've done to you, but it's not personal. All we want is the dagger. If you don't try to stop me, I promise I will never harm you."

Which was a problem, because I absolutely planned to stop her. Unless I had no other choice, that dagger would never fall into Corack hands.

A few minutes later, Trina pronounced my hair "good enough," which was more than I cared about. I banged on the cell door until a guard came to open it. "Will you need an escort to your father?" he asked. "Your protector already left to tell him you were coming." The guard's eagerness to go aboveground was apparent. I doubted he ever saw much light.

"We don't need an escort," I said.

Still, he walked us up the slope to the main gathering area and then fumbled for his keys. Before we reached the stairs, another door opened behind us, one that would allow prisoners to enter the dungeons directly from outside Woodcourt's main gates. The daylight from the open door was bright enough that I had to shield my eyes. But the light was also accompanied by the sounds of people, several of them.

"Make way for prisoners!" someone called.

"I can't unlock the Woodcourt door until everyone is safely put into cells," the guard explained to me. "Wait on the stairs, out of their way, or you might accidentally be put back into the cells with them."

Trina grabbed my arm and pulled me up onto the stairs. Not that I needed any persuasion. I couldn't go down into the dungeons

again. I barely could tolerate being here on the stairs, which by comparison felt like a palace.

Five Dominion soldiers came in, accompanied by a line of
prisoners too beaten down to raise their heads, much less offer any
resistance.

"Why are these people here?" the dungeon guard asked.
"Another uprising?"

One of the soldiers had already noticed me and cocked his head.
"Kestra Dallisor? My lady, it's appropriate that you're here to welcome
this scum. Your father ordered these Coracks rounded up in revenge for
the attack on you at the inn. Dallisors always get the last word, no?"

"Kestra wasn't attacked!" Forgetting her role as a handmaiden,
Trina had stepped in front of me, nearly bursting with anger.

"The master described sores on his daughter's wrists, and a cut.
Someone tried to kill her. Sir Henry wants people to know what happens to those who attack his family."

Considering the reason I was in these dungeons in the first
place, that was a joke, and I would've told him so if a face had not
caught my attention in the crowd of new prisoners.

Rosalie.

The young girl whose bread was stolen from the market. It was
easy to spot her because she still wore the cloak I had given her yesterday. It was wrapped tightly around her like a shell she hoped would
protect her from whatever was coming next.

I hurried to the bottom of the stairs and pointed her out, saying
to the soldier, "That girl with the cloak, she's only a child. You know
she could not have been involved in the attack at that inn."

"Of course not, my lady. But that's a Dallisor cloak she wears, so she knows more than she's saying, and she'll hang with the others."

"This is ridiculous!" I snapped. "I gave her that cloak myself. She's done nothing wrong!"

"Tell that to your father," he said. "I have no authority to release the prisoners once they're here."

"Your father won't release them either," Trina whispered.

No, he wouldn't. He believed compassion was a weakness, and refused to admit a Dallisor could ever make a mistake—even in the arrest of a young girl. But I had to try.

I started up the stairs again when Trina grabbed my arm, pulling me back beside her and nodding in the direction she wanted me to look. One man had stopped directly on the dungeon slope, his eyes on us, seemingly unaware of the other prisoners around him. The way his gold metal leg glinted against the torchlight should have already caught my attention.

Captain Grey Tenger.

I wasn't sure whether he was staring at me or at Trina, and it probably didn't matter. His expression was like stone, a practiced indifference to what was happening around him. He was in the middle of the line, unchained and with a shiny black eye. If the soldiers had known who he was, a fist to his face would've been nothing. They'd have shot him on the road.

"Is there a problem, my lady?" the guard asked.

"No," I mumbled. Yet another lie.

Should I tell them about Tenger? He was responsible for the attack on me, for what was happening to Celia and Darrow, and for the fact that my life was in complete chaos. Only two days ago, I had quietly vowed to destroy the rebellion.

Now here was their leader, in the bowels of the Dallisor dungeons. All it would take was a few words from me and I could end the Corack rebellion where it stood. I didn't need to prove who Tenger was. My accusation was enough to guarantee his immediate death. Trina's too.

And Simon's.

Darrow's and Celia's deaths would follow, wherever they were.

And mine, eventually. The Coracks would see to that.

But this was no longer about my life, I understood that now. I'd just spent hours in a dungeon once occupied by two women who sacrificed everything in the hope of defeating Lord Endrick. The Coracks wanted to continue their quest, and had forced me into their battle. My only remaining question was, would I join that fight, even if I were not compelled?

The churning in my gut returned, worse than before. I didn't like Tenger, didn't trust him, and the idea of helping him achieve anything made my head spin. But he was on the right side of the battle. He would make me a traitor after all.

"Take us upstairs," I ordered the dungeon guard. "Now."

"Yes, my lady."

He escorted us up the stairs to unlock the door that would take us into Woodcourt, placing us back in the servants' area, which appeared to be empty. Even here, the contrast from the dungeons was so sudden, it almost took my breath away. How could such horror exist directly below the plush carpets and fine wooden floors that I had once trod upon so casually?

Before leaving us, the guard offered me a slithery smile. "No offense, my lady, but you're the prettiest prisoner we've had in the cells since I've been here."

Trina made a gagging noise and shut the door in his face. Then she shoved me against the wall with her forearm pressing at my throat. "Did you tell your father to arrest those people?"

I pushed her back. "If you want to fight, then I will win, *and* I'll make you fix my hair when it's over." Trina wiped her mouth with the back of her hand, her chest heaving in anger. "I didn't know about this, I swear it. Do you think I'd let them arrest Rosalie, after what I've already done to that girl's life?"

"Maybe you don't care," Trina said. "Just when I thought you were different from the Dallisors, this happens!"

"How many of those prisoners were Coracks?" I wasn't sure why that question mattered to me, but it did.

Trina shrugged. "There were what, twenty people brought in? Maybe more? I'd guess less than five were Coracks. What are you going to do?"

Did she think I could fix a problem on this scale? "You know what Lord Endrick has planned for me tomorrow—what power do I have to change this?" I leaned against the wall, fighting the urge to run until this nightmare faded into memory. Rosalie had stared directly at me, and if there had been any expression in her eyes beyond blame and disgust for ever having met me, I didn't see it. And then there was Tenger.

Trina's voice became venomous. "Listen carefully. If those prisoners don't go free before the end of this night, I will leave Woodcourt and order Darrow's death. The Coracks will blame you for these arrests. All our future attacks will be targeted on Woodcourt, and on you specifically."

"Nothing I say could possibly help them!"

"Then do something! I swear to you, Kestra, I will follow through on my threats. If Tenger is dead by morning, then so is Darrow."

"I'll take care of it," I said, pushing past her and walking toward the library.

"How?" She was following so close behind me that she practically stepped on my heels.

I didn't answer. Mostly because I had no idea how to fix this. But I would. Whatever the line was between loyalty and treason, I was surely about to cross it.

· TWENTY-SEVEN ·

KESTRA

Gerald met me on the way to the library, his brow creased with concern. Was that because of his fear for my safety, or for whether the diary had been returned to its hiding place? Other than Darrow, my greatest worries were focused on the diary. I didn't know whether I'd get the chance to move it from the library shelves and put it back under the desk again, especially now.

After a quick assessment of my appearance, Gerald offered me a polite bow. "My lady, I am relieved. You look none the worse after that visit to the dungeons."

"I'm no better either." My anger at Gerald wasn't fair, but I felt it anyway. "Did you know what was in the diary when you gave it to me?"

He shook his head. "The day Lady Dallisor died, I snuck that key away from here and sent it to my people. The key was not supposed to return to Woodcourt until it came in your hands. No one but Lady Dallisor has read that diary, not even her husband."

I wished I could discuss its contents with Gerald, though it probably didn't matter now, and this open hallway was no place for such a dangerous conversation. Two nearby maids surely heard me whisper to him the only thing I dared say: "I don't want to know the things I now know."

"Life doesn't give us what we want. It gives us what we need and asks what we will do with it."

"Don't speak in philosophies, Gerald. You should have warned me."

He gave a quick bow. "Yes, my lady. I assume you are here to see the master? That's why you were allowed to leave the dungeons?"

A sudden weight pressed on my shoulders, but through it, I asked, "Where is he? In his library?"

"Of course. I'll take you there."

I had half-expected to see Simon near the library. He would've come here to gain permission for my release, and should've known I wouldn't be far behind. Maybe he'd been sent on other errands. It would have helped to see him.

Gerald knocked on the door and we were allowed to enter. "Sir Henry," he said, with his customary bow, "your daughter is here." I said nothing, and certainly did not curtsy.

My father was standing near the library's window, gazing out on his land, the colors of his fields cooling along with the weather. "Wait in here, my blue friend." That was undoubtedly meant as an insult, reminding Gerald of his place.

"Yes, Sir Henry." Gerald offered me a weak smile before bowing his way over to the back wall. He made an excellent spy, one who was perfectly willing to humble himself before a man he surely hated, all to remain trusted. Lacking Gerald's humility—lacking any humility whatsoever, actually—I could never be so successful.

Now my father turned, furrowing his brow as he looked me over. Normally, I would have returned his stare, pretending to feel as indifferent as he always was, but this time, I found it hard to look at him at all.

He began, "How are you feeling, Kestra? Your neck?"

"Did it bother you to watch him do that to me?"

"Of course it did. Though it wouldn't have happened if you had been wiser."

"Well, I am much wiser now." In ways he could not anticipate.

My father had been walking a circle around me, surveying my appearance. But now he stopped in front of me. "It could have been worse. The Lord of the Dominion has always been powerful, but by the end of the war, he had the power of all Endreans. You know that he placed all that magic within the Olden Blade, made of a metal that could neither rust nor rot, and left him immortal. What most don't know is that this act weakened his remaining abilities, requiring constant replenishment in the Blue Caves. What power he does have left, he uses to its full effects, even on a Dallisor, if necessary."

The question I had in mind was risky, but it might be my only chance to ask him. "So there *is* an Olden Blade? It's not a myth?"

"Of course there is a Blade, though it's been lost for so long, I doubt it'll ever be found." He retreated to his desk. "All of Woodcourt has been searched for it, beyond even the places Risha Halderian had access to."

"What about her servant? The Endrean?"

"Whatever magic she might have had was depleted by the time she was arrested. When I executed her, it was a life that ended in a flash of nothingness, just as Risha's did." His nostrils flared. "I hope you understand that if you disobey Lord Endrick, he will order your death too."

My answer came before I could think better of it. "If I wanted to die, I could just get married. Isn't that right?"

He looked up, eyes widened, but he quickly pasted over any expression of guilt with the same sternness I used to see when he ordered me to finish my supper or to stop digging in the gardens. How could he feel so little for me? This was worse than indifference. This was . . .

The answer came to me like a stab wound in the heart. It was exactly what Trina had said. This was evil.

When he spoke, there was no emotion whatsoever. "You will agree to the marriage for tomorrow night, I trust?"

I swallowed the swell of pain within me, and said, "I will, on one condition."

The relief in his eyes was immediately replaced with disgust. "The Lord of the Dominion does not make bargains. He's ordered you to marry this boy and you will."

"I will, if *you* agree to my terms. Otherwise, I will stand up with that boy beneath the marriage arch and when I'm asked if I accept him, I will publicly denounce Lord Endrick, and you."

"You would betray us?"

"I would tell everyone the real reason for my marriage. If that's a betrayal, then so be it!"

"Hateful child!" he spat at me. "What your mother ever saw in you is a mystery. What are your terms?"

"Several prisoners were brought into the dungeons just now."

"A proper response to those who attacked you at the inn the other night."

"Not one of them is responsible for that. They are innocent." At least, of that particular crime. I couldn't claim anything more for Tenger's innocence.

"They are enemies of the Dallisors. That is enough. They will be executed at midnight."

I stepped forward. "Release them, as a wedding gift to me. It's the only thing I will ask of you before I'm married."

"I will not free them, Kestra, nor will it be the only thing you ask of me today."

Something in his tone worried me, but I held my voice steady. "Oh? What else do you think I'll ask?"

"Forgiveness." He reached into a drawer of his desk and withdrew my mother's diary, letting it drop on the desk with a harsh thud. "Because if I don't forgive you, then I must execute my own daughter. How dare you break into my library and steal this?"

My heart crashed against my chest, all pretenses of indifference gone. No doubt, behind me, Gerald had stopped breathing too.

"When I was in here this morning, it had fallen to the floor." He'd know I was lying, but this was the best I had. "I assumed it had fallen from the shelves, so I replaced it. The book is locked anyway."

"It's locked for me, perhaps. Do you know what's inside this book?"

"Do you?"

He pounded a fist on the desk and stomped toward me, angry enough that I immediately backed up. My knife was within reach, if necessary, but I knew I wouldn't use it. Nothing in me was capable of that.

"Have you read this diary?" he yelled.

"Sir Henry, the fault is mine," Gerald said, inching forward. "I was cleaning in here last night and accidentally found the book. I thought I replaced it, but I must not have done so."

"No, it wasn't like that." I couldn't let Gerald take the blame.

"It was like that." He stepped forward, placing himself ahead of me. "Your daughter probably didn't realize whose book this was, so of course she wouldn't have thought anything of putting it back on the shelves. I'm sorry I didn't report it to you, Sir Henry."

"You've disappointed me, Gerald."

Tears filled my eyes. I'd heard him say those words before. For Dallisors, the other end of disappointment was death. "Please don't harm Gerald," I said. "This is all my fault. Punish me if you will. Not him."

"It's all right, my lady." Gerald's voice was so calm it unnerved me further. "We each have our roles to fill. I know mine, and you know yours."

"Her role is to become the wife of Sir Basil of Reddengrad. Until that happens, Kestra, you will remain confined to your room. Gerald, you will report to the dungeons to pay for removing this book from my desk."

"That is no crime!" I yelled. "The book is sealed shut. Even if he found it, he could not have opened it. And I am the one who put it on the shelves, not him!"

"A Dallisor would never take the blame when it can be assigned to an inferior!" he shouted back. "Nor do we defy the orders of our superiors, as you take such pleasure in doing. You are no Dallisor!"

"And you are no father of mine!" I shot back, with greater fierceness. "I will always love my mother, because she loved me. But from this moment forward, you are only Henry Dallisor to me. I will never call you Father again."

"I never wanted you to call me Father to begin with." His

whole body was shaking with rage. "Report to your room. If you are found anywhere else until your marriage, I will have you killed where you stand."

"No, you won't. You would never disappoint Lord Endrick that way. I know his plans for me, *your* plans for me. And I will do everything in my power to stop them!"

Before Henry could reply, I swerved on my heel and marched from the room, slamming the door shut behind me. It took every bit of strength I had to stifle a scream for the hurt within me. Henry Dallisor had severed the final thread in our rags of a relationship, yet I was the one who felt the cut. But I couldn't let any of it show. Not here, and not now. Gerald was seconds behind me, on his way to the dungeons. I couldn't face him, not after failing at the one thing he had asked when he gave me that diary. I had promised to replace the book where it belonged. He would pay for my failure.

"My lady?" he called. "Please wait."

I stopped, but didn't turn around. *Could not* turn around.

"What more can I do for you?" he asked.

"Gerald, no. It's my fault—"

"A guard will be sent to your room soon to verify you are there. I have a few minutes before I must report below."

I licked my lips, wishing I had any choice but to ask more from this good man. "How much would you risk to help me?"

His answer came quickly. "Everything."

I hoped he was sincere, because that was exactly how much I needed. "Wait for me in the tower. I have something to give you, and a request I wish I didn't have to make."

"Yes, my lady." After a quick bow, he left, and only then did I realize my guilt with a harsh gasp that crushed whatever was left of my heart. Gerald had agreed to my request too quickly, without knowing the risk he was about to undertake. He had offered his life to me, and might yet lose it because of me, and for all that, there was one thing I dared not ask for: his forgiveness.

And that would torture me in a way that Lord Endrick never could.

· TWENTY-EIGHT ·

———

KESTRA

I hadn't intended to come back to Lily Dallisor's room, but the diary had required it of me.

How strange it was to enter her apartments again, more carefully this time, ensuring that no one had seen me. This was of utmost importance. Not only was I supposed to be confined to my own room, but now, I was here for the most dangerous of reasons. It wasn't to renew my memories of being held in my mother's arms, or dancing around the gardens with her, or our sneaking pastries together from the kitchen late at night. It was nothing so pleasant this time, though I suspected this memory would outlast any other of my lifetime.

In skirts, it was harder to slide under the bed than it had been in the trousers. Last night, I'd wanted to find a hidden blanket under here, and failed. I hoped that I wouldn't fail now. I couldn't fail.

The boards propping up the mattress had shifted last night. They shouldn't have. The weight of the mattress would hold the boards in place . . . unless there was a gap between the mattress and the boards. A false bottom perhaps?

I squirmed into place beneath the center of the bed and took a deep breath before raising my arms. To be sure, the consequences of failing here were grim.

But the consequences of success terrified me.

I pushed on the first board, which easily slid aside. Dustball tufts came down with the shift, falling on my face and no doubt dirtying my dress, but I brushed it all aside and pushed on the second board.

When this one separated, something fell on the floor behind me, landing with a heavy thud. Still on my back, I froze, certain all of Woodcourt must have heard it too. I had warmed a clearstone in the room, but beneath the bed there were only shadows. I did observe the fallen object was wrapped in a burlap sack and was about the length of my arm from elbow to fingertip.

The Olden Blade.

I already knew it was, but the absolute simplicity of having found it so easily astounded me. For seventeen years, the Dominion had been seeking this dagger, searching endlessly for any clues as to its whereabouts. They would have interviewed every person who came into the remotest contact with Risha and Anaya. They would have bored holes into the floors of the dungeons, carved into the rock walls, and sent servants to search every crevice on pain of death if they didn't come back with the Blade in their hands.

I'd merely crawled under my mother's bed and shifted around a few boards. It had taken me less than three minutes. Of course, I'd had an advantage: the diary. If the situation were not so serious, I would have laughed at the absurdity of it all.

If Trina were here, she'd probably faint with joy, wrap me in a hug, and pledge eternal friendship to me. Simon . . . I didn't know how he'd react. Nor would I ever find out, I supposed. Not if I stuck to my plans.

I lay there for longer than I should have, listening to the pounding of my heart and the sound of blood rushing past my ears. The consequences of any decision I made now would change everything. What was the right answer? What choice might keep me alive? Or free Darrow? What would save Antora?

I genuinely didn't know.

A cock crowed outside, warning me that time was passing too quickly, and that it couldn't be much longer before a guard would come to ensure I was in my room. If I was found here, everything would be lost. Starting with my life.

I dragged the burlap bundle out from beneath the bed and then sat up, leaving it on the floor directly in front of me. After a few deep breaths to find my courage, I carefully untied the twine that held it together, unfolding each layer of burlap until the Olden Blade revealed itself.

It wasn't nearly as exotic as I would have expected and, in fact, didn't look much different from the knife I'd left behind in the music room last night or any of a dozen others one could buy in the finer shops of Highwyn. It was longer than a regular knife, though now that it was unwrapped of all its layers, the Olden Blade was smaller than it had seemed to be before. The Blade was made of Dirilium, a metal often mistaken for steel but with the strength of diamonds. The handle was highly polished and caught the light from every angle at which I studied it, and it was dotted with violet amethysts that seemed to glow with the magic inside them.

This had been Lord Endrick's prime weapon, and remained the source of his immortality. Risha once threatened that immortality, but she was gone. Antora needed a new Infidante, someone to challenge Endrick. Risha Halderian's heir.

I didn't know who that would be, but the list of who I didn't want was long and growing.

None of the Halderians who had tried to kill me three years ago. That was unacceptable.

Nor any of the Halderians who had let it happen. They'd been cowards.

Not Tenger, if he belonged to their clan. A streak of cruelty ran through him that bothered me.

Not me.

Me.

I immediately brushed that thought aside, wondering how such an idea had even entered my mind. I was not a Halderian. I couldn't wield the Blade. I couldn't even touch it.

But I wanted to.

I stared at it, unable to look away as treasonous thoughts swirled in my head. Thoughts I should not dare to have. But that I did.

Lying before me, the Blade became a beacon, suddenly like air for the suffocating, or bread for the starving. It was the only thing I wanted to touch because it was the one thing I could not touch, should not touch. But the idea was filling my mind, this sudden obsession, this desperate question of *what if?*

What if I could?

A flush of heat swept over me. What if I returned to my room, holding the Olden Blade in my hand, announcing to Simon and

Trina that their search for the dagger had ended with me? What would they do? What would they say?

I smiled. Trina's head would probably split apart.

But then I'd be declared the Infidante, tasked with thrusting the Blade into Endrick's heart, killing him. The idea of such a quest horrified me. Even for the right reasons, I couldn't do that.

Yet, I knew that I was going to touch the Blade anyway. I had to test the truth about myself.

I had to know.

Almost not daring to breathe, I stretched out my right hand, hesitating only a moment before I wrapped it around the handle.

It wasn't cool to the touch, as I had expected. Instead, the metal was warm and seemed to pulse from deeper within. Endrick's magic. I *felt* it, I was part of it.

And then I was attacked by it.

The magic seized my whole arm, locking the joints of my fingers so that I couldn't release the handle, no matter how hard I tried. Pain burst from my palm, flared up my arm, and across my shoulders. I let out a gasp, though I could not let myself be heard, not here, not now. Especially not now.

Instinctively, I understood that if the magic reached my heart, I was finished. It was searing through every nerve, every vein, working its way through me.

Finally, I forced my left hand over the right and pried the fingers apart, fighting to let the dagger go. After an exhausting effort, it fell to the ground again, back onto the burlap, as quietly as if nothing had ever happened.

I pressed my injured hand to my chest, leaving it there until the worst of the pain passed and my breaths came more steadily. As awful as that had been, I was lucky it hadn't killed me. If I had continued to hold it, surely I would be dead by now.

I was not the Infidante.

But I was alive.

And at least I knew. Maybe that was a relief. Nothing in me wanted the Infidante's burden.

Maybe it was a disappointment too. Was I meant for no purpose greater than myself?

When I felt steadier, I folded the blade back into the burlap, though I couldn't use my injured hand to tie the twine. That had to be good enough. I would ask Gerald to tie it later.

It was the least I'd have to ask of him. Gerald was my last chance to get the Blade out of Woodcourt. While sitting in that security carriage with Tenger, I had made a plan. I had to stick to it.

By now, Gerald would have waited for me long enough. And with my understanding of how dangerous the Blade truly was, I hoped we were both up to the enormous task that still lay ahead.

· TWENTY-NINE ·

———

SIMON

My gut was in knots. Kestra's meeting with her father had gone on too long. After what she had done to get sent to the dungeons, I had expected it would take a while to get herself out. But too much time had passed. Had she angered her father again, or Lord Endrick? Or somehow gotten herself into worse trouble? She was perfectly capable of that.

My fears deepened when Gerald turned the corner without her. He was practically wringing his hands into shreds and his eyes fixed on me so suddenly, I realized this was no accidental meeting.

"Where is she?" I asked.

"Coming soon, I hope." Gerald glanced around us. "Until her father sends different orders, she must remain in her room."

"What did she do?"

Gerald frowned. "Dallisors always get the last word, and she's as bullheaded as the worst of them. Lady Kestra will not be allowed to defy Lord Endrick."

"Will you wait here too?" Maybe it wasn't wise to offer, but Gerald seemed to understand things about Kestra that I didn't. Things I was sure I ought to know.

"I cannot." Gerald's foot began tapping, as if he was anxious to leave. "But will you promise to take care of her? Kestra needs a protector now more than ever before."

I licked my lips. Why was he speaking in such coded terms? Why was he in such a hurry?

We waited for a servant to pass, then I gave Gerald my answer. "I swear on my life to protect her."

He stared back at me. At first I thought he doubted the sincerity of my promise, but then the corners of his eyes creased. He asked, "Do you love her?"

Such a simple question, yet it felt like a minefield, one I was hesitant to walk, and Kestra certainly wouldn't go there. Not yet.

By now, I'd stumbled too long for an answer. Gerald stepped closer, whispering, "I know what you're hiding, my boy. Protect her, but do not give her your heart. That is too dangerous for you both." Before I could object, he hurried away, back from the direction he had come.

If I'd been anxious before, Gerald's visit only made things worse. It took another fifteen agonizing minutes before Kestra finally came around the corner, her face grim and focused, her fists clenching her skirts tight enough to rip holes in the fabric. I didn't know whether to be angry with her or simply relieved, but I took her arm and pulled her against the wall. "What have you done? Why were you—"

"Ask Trina what I had to do," she replied with an equal amount of fire. "And then tell her it didn't work!"

Trina had already told me about Tenger's arrest, but little more. Had Trina threatened Kestra again?

"Let's talk where it's safer." I opened Kestra's door and walked into her room. Kestra stood in the passageway, refusing to budge. I hissed, "Do you know what they'll do if they catch you outside your room?"

She checked the passageway again. "Probably the same thing if you're caught inside it."

"There you are, finally!" Trina had obviously been pacing. I saw the line she had worn into the weave of the rug. "What about Tenger and the others?"

Now Kestra marched inside and shut the door behind us. "Our agreement must change. I will help Tenger escape, but you must promise to release Darrow and Celia."

Trina shook her head. "Our agreement is for the Olden Blade—"

"Forget the Olden Blade! After I help Tenger, I'll have to leave Woodcourt too. I won't be safe here after that."

"Then we have to find it first!" Trina was doing a good job of controlling her temper, I had to give her that much. "You are our only chance to find that dagger."

Kestra's response came quickly. "Tenger will be executed at midnight tonight. We're out of time!"

Trina wasn't giving up. "What if Simon sets him free? He's escaped before. If we lower the prisoners into the pit, he can find that tunnel again."

"The three of us came here together," Kestra replied. "Once they realize Simon betrayed the Dallisors, they'll question you next. And then me."

A Dallisor questioning. And Dallisors always got the last word.

Trina combed her fingers through her hair, clasping them behind her head in utter frustration. "No, we can still do this!

Risha had the dagger when she was brought to the dungeons. It must be there."

Maybe it was. But my attention was fixed on Kestra. Her fists were clenched, one tighter than the other, and her breaths were shallow and tense. She was upset, but in a different way than I'd seen her before. She said, "The dungeons have been searched. Unless there's some hidden corner only you know about."

Trina clasped her trembling hands together, hoping to steady them. "You trust Gerald. Would he know where to look for the Blade?"

That wasn't necessary. My voice was flat and left no room for doubt. "Kestra already knows where to look." She protested, but the desperate gleam in her eye proved my guess was right. "This morning, you were rushing to return something to your father's library. What else belongs there but a book?"

"It's not Risha's diary," she said, suddenly on the defense. "I swear it's not."

"No, but I'll bet my life it was a diary with a pink satin binding. And I'm equally sure it can only be unlocked with a small silver key."

"Like the one the Halderians brought to the inn the other night?" Trina asked.

I kept my eyes on Kestra, whose expression was stone, and said, "Which you stole from me."

"Which was meant for me, so technically, you're the thief."

Trina drew in a breath. "You found your mother's diary? You've read it?"

"She read it, which was why she'd been crying." Turning back to Kestra, I continued, "It told you where the Olden Blade is hidden, didn't it? Now you're using Tenger as a distraction, to force all of us out of Woodcourt without the dagger."

Trina's face reddened. "Is that true?"

Kestra backed up, shaking her head. "There is too much about the Olden Blade we don't know. Does it lend magic to the person who holds it? What happens if the wrong person tries to touch it? Was it the reason Risha Halderian was killed, or was that a coincidence? And if it can kill Lord Endrick, what will be the price?"

"The Coracks will answer those questions," Trina said. "They're not your concern."

Kestra's voice rose in pitch. "Yes, they are! If I help you get the dagger, then it's my responsibility to know."

"We have a bigger responsibility if you don't help us," Trina warned. "What to do with you."

Silently, I groaned. Kestra responded to threats by tightening up on her secrets. Trina should have learned that by now.

My approach was gentler. "There's no future for you here, whether you help us or not. But if you keep your promise and tell us where the Blade is, we'll keep our promises to you. We'll rescue everyone in the dungeons and ride out of Woodcourt tonight, together. You'll get Darrow back, and Celia if you want her. And then you're free."

Kestra met my eyes, and I felt her resolve weakening. If Trina sensed it, then she misinterpreted it in the worst possible way.

"She's playing you like a game, Simon!" Trina said. "Don't give in to her." She marched toward Kestra, yelling, "Tell us where the Blade is—or else!"

She raised a hand, and when Kestra raised hers in defense, I caught it. Her palm opened and I saw a cross burned into it, reddened and beginning to welt. Where had that come from?

"Is that a burn?"

Kestra squeezed her hand back into a fist. It would have stung fiercely to do that, so she must've wanted to hide it. "It's nothing."

"That wasn't there when we were in the dungeons." I forced her fingers open again and studied the burn. "What caused it?"

Kestra's brows pressed together, as if this was nothing of interest. "What causes any burn?"

She knew what I meant. "From what fire, Princess? It's the middle of the day."

Trina cut in. "Aboveground it is, not below." Her tone darkened. "Maybe you went into the dungeons, hoping to find the Blade."

"You're wrong—" Kestra started.

Trina continued, "You took one of the torches for light and burned yourself."

Her eyes filled with tears. "I tried—"

I stepped closer and lowered my voice. "So the Blade *is* in the dungeons?"

Now her first tear fell, one she had been trying to hold in for some time. "There was an entry in the diary where my mother mentioned having been in the dungeons during the war, and that what she did down there would have eternal consequences."

"The Pit of Eternal Consequence," I mused. "You told me that name before."

Kestra nodded. "If Risha Halderian's servant, Anaya, was held in cell number four, then wouldn't Risha have been kept somewhere worse?"

I instantly understood her meaning. The cell where they had placed me when I was eleven, the one at the lowest point of the dungeons, was the worst of them all. "Risha threw the dagger into the pit, thinking it was bottomless. And no one has searched down there because they fear the stories about the spirits that roam there."

"This was my idea too." Her breathing was becoming irregular again, just thinking of it. "But I can't go down into the pit. You know that."

"I'll go into the pit." Trina spoke more kindly than I'd have expected. "When the Halderians kidnapped you, they kept you in that box. That affected you—of course it did. We understand. You can't go into that pit, but I can."

"Do what you must." Kestra seemed calmer already. "I only want Darrow back. But we'll all leave Woodcourt together, because once we find the Blade, we can never come back."

The girls both looked at me. "We'll leave after dark," I said. "Free the prisoners, find the Blade, and all of us escape."

· THIRTY ·

KESTRA

S imon returned to the hallway to resume his guard duties, or
to pretend that his reasons for watching my door were about
keeping me in, rather than waiting for the right time to get
me out. I told Trina that I was exhausted, which was absolutely true,
and took to my bed for a nap. I assumed she went back to pacing, or,
at least, that's what she was doing when I awoke several hours later.

I sat up in the bed and felt my hair, which was a mess again.
Before she realized I was awake, I removed the pins myself and began
combing out my locks with my fingers. It wasn't as neat as her work,
but I had to learn to care for myself. After I left Woodcourt, I'd never
have servants again.

When she heard movement, Trina stared at me, breathless and
face flushed. "What if the Blade isn't in that pit? Once we get into
that cell, we'll never be able to come back."

"Pray we should never come back here," I said, wishing my
words could soothe her. "Besides, if we don't find it, we're no worse
off than before."

"I will be." Trina's eyes were empty, desperate for comfort, like
a lost child's. I actually felt sorry for her.

"Tenger won't hold you to that agreement," I said. "Surely you've proven your value to the Coracks."

She shrugged. "This mission is the only major thing I've done for them. If I return empty-handed, Tenger will accuse me of sabotaging it out of sympathy for the Dominion, like my father would've done. If the Coracks reject me, where will I go then?"

"Maybe wherever I go, after I leave Woodcourt."

Trina and I were very different, yet somehow the same. If there was anything we both understood, it was the unfairness of being judged by who our fathers were. Maybe for that reason, neither of us would ever be fully accepted in Antora. I'd always looked down on the world through diamond-studded windows. She'd looked up at the world through salt glass. Despite those differences, we were both looking in from the outside.

"Tell you what," I said, letting a mischievous smile tug at my mouth. "If we don't find the Olden Blade, I'll tell Tenger how much I hate you, how many times you threatened me and forced me to act against my will."

Trina's brow wrinkled, trying to figure out whether I was serious. Finally, she burst into a laugh. "You'd do that? Tell Tenger how awful I am?"

"I try to help where I can."

Our giggling stopped when a knock came at our door. When Trina answered it, Simon was on the other side. He entered and all but slammed the door behind him.

"What's wrong?" Trina asked.

He cast a dark eye toward me. "Sir Basil has returned to Woodcourt and requested time with you in the gardens. Your father gave his permission for you to leave your room, on condition a guard accompanies you."

Trina caught my expression and walked over to begin winding my loose hair into something more formal.

"Don't go." Simon stepped deeper into my room, his jaw determinedly set forward. "We know the truth about Basil now."

"And he knows that I've agreed to marry him tomorrow. What happens if I refuse to meet him tonight?"

"Nothing happens because you won't be here tomorrow!"

"She has to go," Trina said. "Simon, you're not thinking straight. She has to go."

Simon cursed under his breath, keeping his head down. When Trina pinned the last braid into place, I stood and she straightened my skirt.

"You can't let him suspect that you know about Endrick's threat," she warned. "It would lead him to think that you're planning an escape."

"Agreed." Nothing more needed to be said. Trina's advice was obvious. Simon's childishness was useless.

He held out his arm for me and led me from the room without the slightest glance in my direction. The muscles of his arm were so tense I doubted a hammer could loosen them. I snuck a peek at him. The clench of his jaw brought out a small dimple in his cheek. Why did he have to be so handsome? Why did just looking at him cause this flurry of nerves in my stomach?

"If Basil tries anything tonight, I'll be right there," he said. "I can stop him."

I gave him a half smile. "I can stop him too. But he won't harm me tonight. Lord Endrick wants to save that for after our marriage, once I'm in Reddengrad. That way he can declare it as an act of war and rally Antora behind him."

"Then why does Basil want to see you now?" Simon scowled.

"Why do you care?" I asked. "We're leaving tonight, and once we get into that pit, you'll find the Olden Blade. You'll have what you want."

"The Olden Blade? That's all you think I want? Why I'm upset?"

I groaned. "What is it now? Haven't you asked enough of me yet?"

We should have started down the stairs, but the laughter of servants below stopped us both. Simon rolled his eyes, then opened the door to the nearest room.

I followed him inside, then shut the door and leaned against it, arms folded, determined to outlast this tantrum. He was deeper in the room and did a quick survey to be sure we were alone before he turned back to me. For a full five seconds, he didn't so much as blink. Then he opened his mouth and proceeded to say nothing whatsoever.

"Well?" I didn't have time for these games.

He was studying me, endlessly searching for clues to decipher me. It wouldn't work. If I couldn't understand myself anymore, what chance did he have?

It wasn't nearly so hard to understand him. He felt everything with such intensity that his eyes betrayed his emotions every time. Such as why he didn't want me going to see Basil tonight. This wasn't about my physical safety. Simon was protecting my heart.

Or his.

Finally, he said, "After tonight, Woodcourt can no longer be your home."

Obviously not. I added, "Antora can no longer be my home."

"No, you could stay in Antora if . . ." His voice trailed off and he seemed to struggle for the right words to finish. He scraped his boot along the floor before stepping forward, close enough that my pulse shot into my fingertips. I understood what the focused look in his eyes meant, why he seemed so nervous. Yet it couldn't compare to the flutters his presence created in me, a symphony of confusion. "Would you consider joining the Coracks? I know it'd mean turning on your father, but hasn't he already turned on you? Let's fight on the same side of this battle."

He was asking too much. Couldn't he see that? The sudden exhaustion I felt went deeper than a thousand years of sleep could cure. I lowered my eyes, mumbling, "We're not on the same side. We'll never be."

"Why not? Let's fight together. Let's be together." He put a hand to my cheek and held it there. His touch was gentle, barely a whisper upon my skin, but as his fingers swept around the side of my neck, something stirred inside me, a beautiful chaos that started in my chest and spread throughout my body. Did he know the feelings that were exploding in me, the tremors his touch caused?

My arms unfolded, inviting him closer. I'd always been drawn to his eyes, but it was more than that. I liked the hint of curl in his hair, the strong line of his jaw, the flush of color in his cheeks when he was angry or smiling or . . . or whatever was happening to him now.

What was happening to *me*? This couldn't continue. Not with everything I knew. Not if he knew.

Simon's fingers slid down my neck, tracing trails of shivers, his thumb caressing my collarbone and flooding my senses with *him*. If I had any control of my legs, I would have backed away, but instead,

I wanted to be near him, to feel the touch of his lips. Would his kiss be gentle, like the caress of his hands? Or would it be as intense as his gaze? Was he feeling the same as me, dizzy and frightened and fully alive? I tried to push those thoughts away, all the while letting them swirl in my head. My feelings for him were already dangerous enough. I couldn't let things get worse. I shouldn't even dare to call him a friend. Because he wasn't, not to me.

He spoke in a near whisper. "Once we leave Woodcourt, Lord Endrick will put a target on your back. You'll fight against him, or fall victim to him. The Coracks might be your only defense. And I will still consider myself your protector. I always will. Come with me, Kes."

Kes. Not Kestra, or Princess. And words spoken with such warmth, such tenderness, they threatened my last remaining defenses. If my heart and my mind could not agree, how was I to know which to follow?

I'd follow him. I wanted to be in his world, in his life. In his heart.

His gaze shifted to my lips. My breath lodged in my throat. He leaned in.

And I heard the words, "This won't work."

The voice that pushed Simon away didn't seem like my own, though I knew I'd said it. I knew what he was offering, and the temptation of it was nearly overwhelming. But I had to reject his offer, reject him. Reject *us*. I blinked away the sting in my eyes. "If we find the Olden Blade in the pit tonight, then Tenger should keep his agreement to return my servants. That's all I want."

Simon's face fell. "Are you sure?"

I was no longer sure of anything, except that I had just ruined a moment I might never get back again. With more reluctance than I wanted to admit, I pushed his hand away and left the room, alone and aching with regret. He grunted in irritation, but followed, letting me stay ahead of him until we were in the gardens.

Sir Basil was near the entrance and smiled when he saw me coming. "My lady Kestra. My wife to be."

His manner was more reserved than it had been last evening, I noticed. Perhaps Endrick's reminder that he had agreed to kill me on our wedding night weighed on him. Poor thing.

"How lovely you are tonight," Basil continued. "I cannot imagine any possibility of you looking more beautiful, not even tomorrow, on our wedding day."

From behind us, Simon swatted at the branches of a bush to get past us, making sure we remembered he was there.

As if I could forget. Even at a distance, his presence was still making me as nervous as I'd felt alone with him in that room. Simon's hand was calloused from years of hard work and managing a sword, yet it had felt soft as a glove against my skin. I wished I had not stormed away from him. I wished that had not been necessary.

Somehow, my expression with Basil remained calm. "Lord Endrick wanted the wedding tomorrow night, and, as you know, we must obey his demands." That poured some ice on his fire.

"Yes, of course." He gestured at Simon. "Your protector can wait out here. We'll be safe in these gardens alone."

"I have orders to stay with her." Simon spoke through gritted teeth. "Lord Endrick's orders."

"You can stay here at the entrance," I said to Simon. "That will satisfy Lord Endrick." Then I smiled up at Basil. "I'm safe with you, I'm sure."

Simon's anger could be felt as we passed, but I didn't dare give him so much as a casual glance back. Even if Basil did try something, Darrow had taught me a few tricks wherein I could disable him for weeks, if necessary.

I took Basil's arm and he led me down a path of tall hedges, thick enough that Simon would not be able to spy on us or eavesdrop. If Basil had been more clever, I would have thought this was planned.

"When my father told me I'd be married to a Dallisor girl from Antora, I confessed that I was less than enthusiastic," he began. "Dallisor women are usually quite . . . sturdy."

"What type do you prefer?" The question sounded flirtatious, but I truly was curious. "Dainty girls?"

Dainty, weak little ladies who are unable to defend themselves against a spitting snow beetle, much less someone who had been ordered to kill his new wife? I didn't say that part.

"I prefer you, whatever type you are," he quickly said. "I genuinely do, Kestra. Now that we've met, I would have chosen you, even if you had not been chosen for me."

How nice for him.

"And that's also the reason why I cannot marry you." His tone changed. Nervously, he looked around and I realized he had deliberately chosen this quiet path. Perhaps he wasn't the cleverest person, but he wasn't stupid either. "More importantly, Kestra, you cannot marry me."

I leaned back, playing innocent yet again. "What are you talking about?"

"There are plans for you after we're married, dark plans of Lord Endrick's doing and even your father."

"He's not my father, not anymore."

"I understand, in ways I wish I didn't. I've come to beg you to leave Woodcourt tonight, in secret. Get as far from Antora as you can." He swallowed hard, forcing his words out. "As far away from me as you can. For your own safety, you must go. I'm so deeply sorry."

I studied his face, for the first time seeing him as an actual person. Simon had been right about him, but for the wrong reasons. There was more to Basil than a first meeting suggested. He had honor and a fair amount of courage.

I asked, "If I leave, what happens to you, to Reddengrad?"

His eyes darted away, which was probably my answer. "We have some time, I think. I will play the role of the abandoned groom, an innocent victim of your deception. Lord Endrick cannot punish me for that."

"You don't know Lord Endrick."

Basil shrugged. "I'll leave here immediately afterward, claiming a broken heart and embarrassment to my country. Then I'll hurry back home and warn my people of war. We'll prepare for it as best as we can until Lord Endrick invades."

"Why are you doing this for me?"

The corner of his mouth lifted. "Because there is a small chance of Reddengrad winning that war. If we do, I'm going to find you again, and ask you to consider marrying me out of choice, not because it's been forced upon you."

I shook my head. "You don't know me, Basil."

"I'll always hope for a day when I can know you better, and you can know me. But for now, I've left a horse in the copse of birch trees outside the gates of Woodcourt. Get to that horse tonight and leave as fast as it will carry you away. Then one day, perhaps you'll consider a future with me. After what I've had to agree to, that's all I dare ask of you."

I smiled at him. "Thank you, Basil."

He lifted my hand in his, kissed my fingers, and then stepped away as if an invisible force had pushed him back.

"Let me take you back to your protector," he said. "Night is soon approaching. You have much to do before dawn."

Yes, I did. More than he could possibly know.

· THIRTY-ONE ·

KESTRA

For most of the walk back to my room, Simon was so angry he was unable to speak. He did manage to spit out a few semi-coherent words about how he was my protector, but then I replied he was only pretending in that role until we escaped Woodcourt, and after that I was on my own. He didn't like that, but he had no response to it either.

Or, at least, not until we were on the landing of the stairs near my room. We stopped there, where he used his body to back me into the corner. "You really won't tell me what happened when you two were alone?"

"I don't see how it's your business. It has nothing to do with our agreement."

His eyes flashed, but his voice remained calm. "Are we friends, Kestra? Are we at least that much?"

"Are we?" I countered. "If it came down to saving me tonight, or finding the Olden Blade, which would you choose?"

"I could ask you a similar question. You need the Olden Blade to save Darrow. Would you sacrifice me to get it?"

"That's not the same thing!" I said. "You're asking me to choose between the lives of two people I care about!"

Despite the seriousness of our argument, a mischievous grin escaped him. "So you do care about me?"

"Stop it. This isn't a game."

Except maybe it was. Gerald had called it a traitor's game. He believed I was capable of winning it. How wrong he was.

"You're right, this isn't a game," Simon said. "Or it isn't supposed to be. The consequences of what we are doing here are far too real."

Without answering, I took his arm as we started to walk again, and then Simon said, "You have secrets, Kes, that's obvious. Can't you trust me with them?"

"Do you trust me?"

His eyes fixed on mine. "Yes, I do trust you."

We were at my door, a welcome barricade between us. I took the handle and twisted it. "I wish you wouldn't. You shouldn't."

Then I left him to enter the room, firmly shutting the door behind me. I leaned heavily against it and closed my eyes, trying to absorb all that had happened over the past hour. Trying to forget how it had felt to be near Simon, his hand caressing my face, my neck, chilling me and warming me in the same touch. Every step he came closer, the bands of energy connecting us had tightened; my heart had pounded, then stopped. If it started again, that was only because I wanted to live another minute in his arms, losing myself in his gaze, flush with the desire to feel his lips on mine. With him, I became alive as I'd never been before. In a different life, or even in another time and place, I would have fallen into his eyes and let myself drown there.

How things might be different now if I had not walked away

from him. I wondered if he was still on the opposite side of the door. And what if I opened it and told him my secrets, and that I knew his too, and could we just start there? Or start over? Or go back in that room where he had almost kissed me, because I was sure that if we could return to that moment, I wouldn't walk away.

Or would I open this door and he'd be gone?

"You're back earlier than I'd expected."

When I opened my eyes, past Trina's curious stare, I saw a dozen different dresses laid out on the bed. In the center of them was an elaborate silver dress with red beads and fabric rosettes. It was the finest dress I'd ever seen. A wedding dress, obviously.

"These were all sent up while you were gone." Trina brushed a single finger over the dress nearest to her, as if anything more might ruin it. "A strange dowry, considering your father must know you won't live long enough to wear all of them."

"Don't call him my father." I had no father.

On top of the dress lay a silver necklace with a small ruby dangling from it, one that coordinated perfectly with the gown.

"I was told that used to belong to—"

"My mother." Suddenly, that necklace was the only thing I saw in the room. One of my earliest memories was sitting on her lap, rolling the ruby around in my fingers until she worried I'd break the clasp. Then I'd leaned into her, watching the way the gem caught the light, casting red glimmering shadows wherever it reflected.

I picked up the necklace and held it out for her. "Would you help me?"

Trina smiled and went behind me to tie it on. "I loved my mother too. I wish I had something of hers."

"What was she like?" I asked.

Trina shrugged. "I barely knew her when she was alive. But I know she watches me from the heavens, and I hope to make her proud of me one day."

I smiled back at her as she finished with the necklace. "I'm sure you will."

With that finished, Trina pulled out the trousers and tunic I had worn the previous night. "I assume you'll want to wear these tonight, instead of the wedding dress. I wish you had a set for me."

"You wear them. They'll fit you better anyway."

She held the clothes up against her frame, then her smile quickly soured. "Is this a trap? Why are you being so cooperative?"

"This isn't cooperation. It's desperation. I just want to get out of here."

She didn't believe me. "Once we're in the pit, you're going to try to find the Blade first. Is that it?"

"What difference would that make? Even if I found it, I can't touch it."

"No, but maybe you know a Halderian who could. Do you think Gerald could become the Infidante?"

I laughed, and meant every snort of it. "Gerald? He's no warrior."

"True." Trina tilted her head as though in thought. "But there will be a new Infidante soon!" She began changing, obviously eager to be finished with servants' clothing, her expression brightening. Perhaps she was imagining holding the Olden Blade. "Surely you can feel a little excitement."

My feelings were anything else. "Are you serious? Everything

I've known and believed is changing. Tonight will be the most dangerous night of my life. Don't ask me to be excited about that."

"But can't you be excited to turn the tide against Endrick?" Trina continued, making it worse. "I'll tell the Coracks how important your help was. They won't accept you at first, maybe never, but I'll try to change their minds. Or do you only care about one specific Corack's feelings?" The corner of her lip curled. "Do you think helping us will make him love you?"

"Hardly. By the time this is over, he'll want nothing to do with me."

While Trina finished dressing, my attention turned again to the wedding dress, almost too beautiful for words. I'd never have married Basil, even without the threats of the Coracks hanging over me, but since our conversation in the gardens, my opinion of him had improved.

And then there was Simon, someone about whom I could not keep the same opinion for two hours together. Whatever he felt for me, or thought he felt, was bound to change too.

A maid came to the door with a meal for me. Trina scowled when she saw it on my writing table, asking where hers was.

"With the other servants, obviously," I said, then softened. "But we can split this."

I pulled the tray toward me and broke half the bread, which I gave to her. While she ate that, I ate exactly half of the fish and cheese, and nuts that would've been imported at prices high enough to feed Rosalie's entire family for a month. Then I ate my half of the bread while she finished the food on the tray. Neither of us was as full as we would have liked, but we weren't starving either.

After we finished, she leaned back in her chair, letting her attention wander around the room. It settled on the knife I'd had with the ivory handle. It marked me as a Dallisor, and would have to stay behind. After a pause, she asked, "When did you start carrying a knife? After the Halderians kidnapped you?"

"Darrow gave me one during the escape. I've never gone without one since."

She sat up straight. "They held you for four days. What happened during that time?"

Why did she keep asking about this? Did she revel in hearing how terrified I had been, how a part of me still felt as if I had never escaped? Or was she trying to help me finally leave the kidnapping in my past?

When it became clear she would wait indefinitely for my answer, I said, "They drugged me here at Woodcourt, bound and gagged me, and carried me out in a box that felt like a sort of coffin. Or, at least, that's where I woke up. A couple of air holes were drilled into it, but other than that, I couldn't see out. I only knew I was on a wagon and that no matter how loud I screamed into the gag or cried, nobody released me. At the end of that first day, a man named Thorne met the wagon."

"Thorne?" Trina asked. "The same man who was at the inn?"

"Yes. He ordered my release at once. Then he told the others that I was a guest and was to be treated with honor, but they wouldn't listen. That same night, a group of Halderians dragged me from my bed and stuffed me in a sack that they dumped in a river. Two women assigned as my protectors pulled me out, but by the second day, the Halderians had gotten to those women. I overheard their plans to kill me after dark, so the first time they turned their backs, I ran. It was a full day before they found me again, miles away, but they put me into the same box as before and sent word to Thorne that he had until dawn to explain why they should keep me alive. If they didn't like his reasons, they would burn the box. Shortly before sunrise, Darrow rescued me. I don't know if he did it on his own, or if Thorne helped me escape."

Trina had been frozen while I spoke, and it took several blinks to bring herself back to the moment. "I can't begin to imagine how terrified you must have felt." She pressed her brows together. "But why would Thorne help you if he was responsible for taking you in the first place?"

"You and Simon have been helping me. And your motives are far worse."

She took that in without emotion. "You're helping us too, Kestra. I know you never wanted to and that you're only doing it to save your servants, but I have to ask something: Do you feel the same about the rebellion as you did the first night?"

I didn't feel the same about anything as I did that first night. My whole world had turned upside down and seemed to be spinning faster by the minute, out of control.

But to answer, I shrugged and said, "I understand Lord Endrick for who he is, and I agree, he must be defeated. All I can do is hope that whoever ends up with the Blade will serve Antora well. If I can help them do it, then I will."

Trina's face softened, and she was about to speak when Simon knocked on the door, then ducked his head inside. "All the servants were called to a meeting with Sir Henry to coordinate their preparations for the wedding. Even the guards have been called up, in case you give them trouble. If we're going to escape, now might be our best chance."

Trina took a deep breath and looked at me. "Well?"

I brushed past Simon to enter the corridor. "I never want to see Woodcourt again. Let's say good-bye forever to this wretched place."

· THIRTY-TWO ·

SIMON

My biggest worry of the evening was getting Kestra through Woodcourt without being spotted. Even a chance encounter with a maid could be deadly. But Kestra brushed off those concerns. "I got caught out here a thousand times as a child before I figured out how to do it right."

"You used to sneak into the dungeons?" Trina asked.

"Of course not." Kestra smiled back at her. "But I knew exactly where Cook hid the leftover pastries. She thought it was mice."

I chuckled. "It appears that you've never been entirely loyal to your family."

Instantly, I regretted my words. They carried in the air like lead.

Kestra stopped walking. "I broke rules, yes. But I never betrayed them. Not like this."

By then, we had reached the door connecting Woodcourt to the dungeons. Trina tried the door, then gasped. "It's locked!"

I gave a key to Trina. "As Kestra's protector, I was given one in case she tried escaping from her room."

Trina smiled as she began unlocking the door. "The irony is priceless!"

I pulled a long length of rope from my satchel. It wasn't as thick as some of the other ropes I'd found out in the stables, but it had to fit in the satchel, so my options were limited.

I gave Trina my knife, and then offered Kestra the rope, saying, "Trina and I will disarm the guards. Stay here where they can't see you. When it's clear, can you get this rope tied off in my old cell?"

Her face twisted into a noticeable grimace, but she took the rope and nodded. She could do this. I hoped.

Once we were inside, Kestra remained high on the stairs. I followed Trina down them as quickly as we could go without slipping. The first guard was the younger one who had leered at Kestra earlier. His hand was raised in a friendly hello, but Trina whacked him broadside on the head and he immediately crumpled. I figured that wasn't too different from her usual technique for making friends.

I took on the second guard, the man who had been clever enough to remind me that the dungeons were not an inn. I hit him on the head with the flat side of my sword, a single hammer stroke that sent him to the ground.

The third man immediately dropped to his knees with his hands in the air. "My name is Bragh. I have no love for the Dominion!"

"Then you'll gladly help me drag these men into a cell." I tilted my head toward Trina. "Give her your keys."

He did, and while we dragged the first two guards away, Trina hurried ahead of us to unlock the first available cell door. When they were all inside, I swatted Bragh hard enough to make him sleepy for a few hours. It wasn't personal, at least on my part. Bragh might feel differently.

By the time I left the cell, Kestra was already padding past us, on her way to cell nine. In her hands was a set of keys that must have fallen from one of the guards' pockets. She did not acknowledge either Trina or me. It probably required her full attention just to force herself down the dark slope.

"I'll free the other prisoners," Trina said, holding Bragh's keys. "Show them where to go, and hurry! The executions begin at midnight."

She went to work, but I followed Kestra. She had stopped just outside cell nine, frozen in place, except for her fists, which were slowly clenching and unclenching. It would only be darker inside, colder, and more closed in. The torch beside her flickered from a nearby draft. I wondered how it could have given her a cross-shaped burn on her palm. That didn't make sense.

I started forward again, but a girl pushed past me, the girl with the bread—Rosalie?—and wrapped her arms around Kestra's waist.

"I told the others you'd free us!" Rosalie said to Kestra. "I knew you'd come."

"You shouldn't have been here in the first place," Kestra replied. "I had to fix this."

"You'll save all of Antora. I know you will."

Kestra smiled sadly, but pressed her lips together in determination. When we were alone, I'd ask her again about joining the Coracks. We needed her on our side.

More than that, I wanted her at my side.

My motives were undoubtedly selfish, yet I didn't know how to feel any other way. After Darrow was released, she would try to leave with him, probably leave Antora entirely. I understood her loyalties.

Darrow was her protector and friend. But surely there was enough room in her heart to care for me too—as something more than a protector, and certainly as more than a friend.

Finally, Kestra began unlocking the door to cell number nine. Gerald's voice called back to her. "My lady? Is it you?"

To have earned this cell, Gerald must have deeply offended Sir Henry. He'd only been here a few hours, yet he already bore signs of his stay. He was filthy, his bluish cheeks were sallow, and his eyes seemed offended by the light of the torch.

Kestra greeted Gerald with a quick apology, then handed him the rope. "I need a place to tie this." She lifted her foot to enter the cell, then set it down again.

"A lady like you shouldn't have to do this," Rosalie said. "I'll help him tie off the rope."

"No, I'll do it." Kestra nodded curtly, as if she was giving herself an order, then stepped inside.

By the time I joined them, Rosalie was holding the bulk of the rope while Kestra and Gerald tied the other end around a rock pillar in the center of the cell. With more than twenty people needing to escape, I wished the pillar was thicker. But it was our only option.

I took the rope from Rosalie and tossed it over the edge of the pit. Behind me, Tenger entered the cell. Without warning, he twisted Kestra around and slammed her into the stone wall.

Gerald had been on his knees in the mud and went to his feet, but before either of us could act, Trina ran into the cell and cried, "Captain, don't!"

"I don't know how your father found us, but I warned you of the consequences of betraying us!" Tenger's threat to Kestra echoed throughout the cell.

"It wasn't Kestra!" By then, I was close enough to press between her and Tenger, and force him back. "It's only a coincidence that they found you."

"How do you know that?" Tenger snarled.

"Because if I'd arranged for your arrest, I'd have also arranged for your execution, not your rescue." She kicked her foot out, connecting with the knee on Tenger's good leg.

Tenger started forward again, but this time Trina intervened. "It's true, sir. We think we know where the Olden Blade is. If it's here, then we must hurry."

Tenger's glare beamed through the dim light. I understood that he didn't trust Kestra, but I did.

Did I?

Should I? Kestra herself had warned me against trusting her.

I took a deep breath, desperate to center my thoughts again. I was here to get the Olden Blade. That was my mission. My only purpose for coming here.

But not my only reason for staying. Tenger never should have sent me, but for the exact opposite reason I had first believed. My mind was spinning with confusion, questions, with Kestra a player in my every thought.

"Someone has to test the rope." Kestra's voice bore an unmistakable waver of fear. "I can't be first."

"Let me do it, my lady." Without waiting for permission, Gerald picked up the rope and swung his weight over the side. A soft crack came from the pillar as it felt his weight, but the knots held. After a breathless few minutes, he called up, "I'm down safe. Send more!"

Trina and Tenger pushed past the prisoners to get down to the pit. Trina went first, then Tenger. "You said we'd find the dagger," Trina immediately called up. "Where is it?" Kestra looked back at me and shook her head, her eyes wider than ever.

"I'll go right after you," I said. "And Tenger and Trina are already there."

She groaned. "Because *that* should make me feel better?" With that, she took the rope, offered me a grim smile, then made the muddy descent into the pit. I followed.

It was farther down than I remembered, and darker. But in all other ways, it was exactly as I recalled, a knee-high cesspool of rot that gathered the worst of everything that passed through the dungeons. Mixed in with the sewage and mud were various belongings of former prisoners, and bones from the prisoners themselves who had gotten too close to the ledge and fallen, or jumped. The gates of hell would be flower fields compared to this. Making it more awful, the pit was small, hardly room enough for all the people who would collect down here.

"As they come down, send them into the tunnel," Tenger ordered me. "No one lingers, except those of us searching for the Blade."

Kestra and Gerald were already searching with Trina and Tenger for any sign of the Olden Blade. Another hundred searchers still wouldn't matter. A horse could hide in this muddy soup, never mind a small dagger.

Others were already descending the rope, a few of them Coracks I vaguely recognized from other camps. Most seemed to be ordinary

Antoran citizens who must have already questioned a thousand times how they came to be here.

As each person came down, I directed them toward the small tunnel I had used to escape. The entrance was covered in hanging moss and a slime that reeked of decomposing flesh, but I cut away as much of it as possible to urge people inside. Nobody smiled when I showed them where to go, but they all went. It was better than execution. Slightly.

Kestra would disagree. She seemed to be holding herself together out of willpower and a desire to find the Blade, but nothing more. At least once a minute, she stopped to steady her breathing and to wrap her arms around herself. This was nothing compared to the tunnel, which was so narrow and fragile it had terrified me to crawl through it. I couldn't envision Kestra escaping that way, even to save her own life.

"If the Blade has been buried in mud all this time, it'll be rusted through," Trina said.

"Any other weapon, but not the Olden Blade." Tenger shouted to the prisoners. "If you're waiting to enter the tunnel, then help us search for a dagger. It's probably wrapped in cloth, or in a sack, but maybe not. Try not to touch it."

The searching intensified, but rather than joining in, I kept my eye on Kestra. I knew what she was up to, but said nothing. Not yet, anyway. This was the very reason why the captain always warned us to separate our emotions from our assignments.

"Never trust your heart," Tenger would say. "Only your orders."

Earlier tonight, Gerald had also warned me about having feelings for Kestra, though his warning had come too late. I knew he was right. My judgment was clouding, a flaw that could prove fatal. But if there was a way to force these emotions out of my heart, I didn't know how to do it.

"The dagger isn't here." Trina looked over at Tenger, defeated. "This is a trick!" She leapt to her feet, so muddy it was hard to see any actual flesh.

Trina reached for Kestra, but a large crack suddenly thundered from above. The woman who had been on the rope fell to the ground, crying that she had hurt her leg. Some prisoners began lifting her from the mud, but Tenger and Kestra sloshed over to help me gather the fallen rope in my hands.

"The pillar must have collapsed." I was furious with myself. If my attention hadn't been fixed on Kestra, I'd have noticed there were too many people on the rope at once.

Eight escapees were still waiting to come down. From what I could tell, four were children, Rosalie included, three were women, and there was one remaining man, though he was too old to bear the weight of lowering the others, even if he had any rope to do it. Another mistake, letting the strongest come down first.

"We've got to help them!" Kestra cried.

"If we get the rope back up to you, where can you tie it off?" Tenger called.

A woman's panicked voice came from higher up. "Nowhere. We're trapped!"

I looked at the rope in my hands, dreading the decision that had to be made. Someone on top of the wall would have to hold the rope for the other prisoners. Nothing else would work.

"There's a pounding sound!" Rosalie cried. "The guards are breaking down their cell door!"

When I had been eleven and slipped into the pit, my first instinct had been to get back up on top, to return to the main part of the cell. Thin outcroppings of rock dotted the wall, muddy and slippery, but with workable holds if you could find them. I had tried making the climb until my injured foot failed.

But I wouldn't fail now.

I threw the rope over my shoulder, then put my hands on the first hold. "I can climb this and lower everyone down."

"Then you'll be stuck up there!" Kestra said.

"I'll slide down on my back, like I did before."

She shook her head. "Luck saved you that day, nothing more. And you still got hurt in the fall." She turned to Tenger. "Let me climb out. I can't stand being in this pit anyway, and I'm strong enough to lower the others down."

Trina shouted, "She knows where the dagger really is! She wants to take it and escape on her own!"

"I can escape—that's my point. Simon won't! The guards never saw me here. I can play innocent. With my family name, they'll have to believe me."

"No." I respected Kestra's courage, but not her impulsivity. "Even if you convince them, returning to Woodcourt is not an option."

"Help us!" a woman above us called. "The guards have nearly broken down their door."

Tenger pointed to the remaining prisoners. "Everyone, get into that tunnel!"

"I'll stay with Lady Kestra," Gerald offered.

But Kestra shook her head. "I want you to go."

"My lady—"

She leaned closer to him, her voice rising in intensity as she said, "Gerald, you have to go. You know what you have to do." He clearly wasn't happy about the order, but bowed his head and obeyed.

Next, Tenger said to Trina, "You and Kestra will stay down here until we find the Blade."

"No!" Kestra shouted. "You need Simon more than you need me. I'm going on top!"

Tenger rubbed his chin, considering her, then me. When his attention fixed on Kestra again, his expression softened. He was going to choose her. That was unacceptable.

Despite the fierce pounding of my heart, it was time to do the right thing. I hoped this was right. "We have to keep Kestra with us. If she escapes up there, everything she knows about the Olden Blade goes with her."

"How dare you—" Kestra started.

"She'll stay in this pit until she finds it." There was ice in Trina's voice. "Or stay in this pit forever."

"You will not keep me here!" Kestra backed away from us, targeting her anger at me. "This is what I get for trusting you?"

I wouldn't let her go on top, but I wouldn't give Trina a reason to threaten her either. Barely looking at Kestra, I whispered, "Give it to them."

"I don't know what you—"

"We both know. It's over."

Her chest was heaving with a combination of fear and anger, but her fight was gone. Cursing under her breath, Kestra crouched down, retrieving a burlap bag from beneath her foot that seemed to have held up remarkably well over the years. That alone attested to the magic inside that bag.

She thrust it at Tenger. "You have what you want. Now, release my servants. I am free too, and I am going back up that wall."

Tenger took the bag, opened it, and smiled before closing it up again. Kestra was already trying to find the best place to begin her climb, so she didn't see the rest of what Tenger was doing. I did.

He grabbed Kestra, and Trina immediately offered him her knife. "If you want your servants back, then you will come with me to get them. Simon, climb that wall and bring the rest of our people down. I expect you to get safely down too, so hurry."

Kestra tried to break free of Tenger's grip, but stopped when she felt the sharp edge of his knife. Instead, she darkened her glare at me. She knew I'd let Tenger take her and would hate me for it. Well, she could be angry all she wanted. She was not going back up that wall. For better or worse, that was my job.

No, this wouldn't be for better or worse. When I reached the top, it was only going to be worse.

· THIRTY-THREE ·

KESTRA

I barely breathed while Simon made the long climb back up the wall. Two or three times, I was certain he would not find a reliable hold, but every time he did, I paid attention to his route. For a good reason.

As soon as he rolled safely over the top, he immediately lowered the rope back down, sending the women and children first. Tenger had backed me into the shadows while Trina directed them into the tunnels. No one noticed us. Even if they did, I'd get no sympathy. Most of these prisoners would blame me for their arrests.

"You have the dagger," I said to Tenger. "Release me."

"Not until I'm certain it's the Olden Blade."

"Do you want it for yourself? Do you think you are the Infidante? Then shouldn't it have lit up for you when you opened that bag?"

"It won't light up until the ceremony. You know that, my lady." He pushed me toward the tunnel. "Let's go."

Suddenly panicked, I dug my heels into the mud, and they found purchase with a buried rock, so for the moment, we stopped. "I can't go into the tunnel, Tenger. You don't understand, but I really can't. Let me help Simon. He'll bring me back to the Coracks to retrieve my servants."

"Simon has completed his mission." Tenger angled the knife, ensuring I felt its edge. "But you have not."

The last of the prisoners to come down was the old man, who upon landing said to Trina, "The guards are out already. They're just not sure where all of us went."

They'd figure it out soon enough, and Simon was alone up there. He threw the rope down, making it nearly impossible for the guards to follow the escapees. Now all he had to do was remember how he had come down before. He had to, because we all knew what the guards would do to him if he didn't. But I dreaded seeing his body come over the edge. There was evidence of many others who had tried that very thing, and failed.

Trina sent the final escapee into the tunnels, then at Tenger's order, followed.

Tenger called up, "Simon?" When no answer came, he said, "Simon understands the rules of war as well as anyone. Sacrifices must be made."

"He sacrificed himself for all of us! And you won't help him!" With all the prisoners down, I'd finally had enough of this charade. I yanked Tenger's elbow down toward my chest, grabbing his hand with the knife as it came up. With a hard kick backward, I was released, and as I twisted around, it was an easy thing to bring my own elbow down on the back of his neck, sending him to the ground. I rose up with Tenger's knife in my own hands and aimed it toward him. One of the first defensive moves Darrow had taught me.

"Give me that bag," I said.

Rolling on the muddy ground, Tenger pulled it closer to him. "Fight me for it, or go save Simon. What will you choose?"

Out in the narrow passage above us, the guards were shouting at one another to come down to this cell. Simon was trapped.

I looked back at Tenger. "If the Olden Blade does choose you, know this—I will get it back."

"Whoever it chooses, it is theirs for life," Tenger said.

I glowered at him. "But not in death, Captain Tenger. Not in death."

Once I released him, Tenger hurried toward the tunnel. I used his knife to cut my skirts just below my knees, as high as I dared. Every governess from my past had probably gasped with horror just now, not knowing exactly what had caused them to shudder, but that somehow, I was responsible. It had to be done though. I'd never make it up this steep slope with muddy skirts dragging me down. Leaving the cut pieces behind, I put Tenger's knife between my teeth and began climbing, exactly as Simon had done.

I was less than halfway up when the guards entered the cell. I heard Simon trying to fight, but he didn't get far before he was shoved down hard upon the ground, followed by several kicks that sounded like boots connecting with stone, or worse, the bones of his body. His groans were sharp and slightly muted, so I guessed his face was down in the mud.

"There's no escape from that pit," the guard shouted. "Where did the prisoners go?"

"Stupid . . . question," Simon said. "Stupid guards."

They didn't like that, and whatever they did in response caused him to cry out with pain. I had to keep climbing, and figure out a way over the ledge without being noticed. I slipped twice, but refused to fall. From this height, a fall would be the end of me. Simon's death would follow.

"Lord Endrick will want to talk to him," a guard said.

One of his companions laughed. "Yes. *Talk* to him. Boy, you'll be made of pudding by the time he's done with you!"

"Finish up in here," the guard who had called himself Bragh said. "Remind him of the power of the Dallisors, but leave him alive. I'll report to the master."

Bragh left, and I shifted my position sideways so that instead of rolling over the ledge directly in front of them, I'd come up near the side, hopefully without drawing their attention.

I snuck up on the closest man and sunk Tenger's knife deep into the man's shoulder, then pushed him into the pit, losing the knife in the process. Before the second could react, I twisted his arm behind him. He struggled to get away from me and in doing so, lost his balance and slid into the pit. I heard the thud of their bodies on the thick mud floor far below. Silence followed.

My attention had already turned to Simon. When I knelt beside him, he mumbled, "You . . . are frightening."

"You have no idea."

I helped him roll over, checking for any life-threatening wounds. From what I could see through the filth that coated him, there was a little blood, but his internal injuries worried me most.

"Can you move?" I asked.

"Give me . . . one minute more."

"Why did you do this?"

His eyes were closed, but his face relaxed. "I made a promise, Kes."

"To Tenger? He sent you up here, then abandoned you. I don't think—"

"Not to Tenger. To Garr, the man who adopted me. If I could be half the person he was . . ."

His voice dropped off while he forced himself to breathe. I pushed Simon's muddy hair away from his face. "Well, you made a good start tonight. It was stupid, but noble. We need to get out of here."

"Not through the tunnel below," he said. "I can't. And you won't."

I dipped my hand in the stream water that ran through the cell and used it to wipe the dirt from his face. His left eye was swollen and one cheek was cut.

"Everything hurts," he mumbled.

I slid my hand up to his shoulders. "There'll be bruises here too. But I think you'll heal, eventually."

His good eye winked at me. "I can see you. That's enough." He fingered the ruby on my mother's necklace. "This is beautiful on you."

"I'm covered in mud, Simon."

"Are you? I didn't notice."

Smiling, I leaned toward him, wiping more mud from his face and letting my fingers linger there. His grin widened, realizing why I had bent down so close. He put a hand up behind my head to pull me in closer, but when it slid down to my neck, he drew back. "That bump I feel—is that from Lord Endrick this morning?"

"I don't know, I haven't—" I sat up and felt back there. It wasn't large, but something was definitely there. "What is that, Simon?"

He sat up too, though it came with a gasp of pain. "The Coracks have a surgeon who has some powerful Endrean medicines."

"I thought Coracks hate the Endreans."

"We do. But their medicines work. If Endrick did something to you with magic, then we may need Endrean medicine to fix it. Let's go."

With great effort, I helped him to his feet. He would limp out of these dungeons the same way I had limped into them not so many hours ago. What a pair we made.

He leaned on me to hobble up to the exterior door, the one that would put us directly outside the Woodcourt gates. The horse Basil promised to hide for me wouldn't be far away.

I withdrew Simon's knife from his sheath and placed it in his hands. "If anyone sees us, then I'm your hostage."

"They'll still follow us. We won't get far, Kes."

"Trust me." That is, if I could trust Basil.

I fit Simon's key into the door, but this lock was stickier than the less commonly used door into Woodcourt.

"It's got to work," Simon said.

"It'll work. I just—"

"Stop!" a voice ordered.

Simon instantly grabbed me and put the knife to my chest. I felt his weight lean into me when he moved so suddenly. He was probably dizzy, but I hoped he'd stay on his feet. It'd be hard to justify how someone unconscious on the ground was stealing me away.

A Dallisor solider had entered the dungeons with my father—no, with *Sir Henry Dallisor* right behind him. I had no father. Both were at the foot of the stairs from Woodcourt, a stone's toss away. The soldier held a lever blade ready for attack. Sir Henry had a cloth to his nose, masking the smell. I wondered about him then. What sort of man shrinks at the odor of death, yet embraces a rotted soul like Endrick's?

"That's my daughter," Sir Henry said to Simon. "How dare you threaten her?"

"Stay back." Simon tilted the blade enough to let it flash against the torchlight. If they were closer, they would have seen the blunt edge was against my skin. "She's coming with me."

"Are you Halderian or Corack? Tell me so that I will know which group to round up and execute tomorrow."

"You wanted me dead, so consider me dead," I said to him. "You should thank this boy for getting rid of me."

"Oh, he will feel the weight of my gratitude." Sir Henry's voice became venomous. "This night will not pass before he will know that I have had the last word."

"Get that door unlocked," Simon muttered to me.

Sir Henry was not finished. "And I will not stop there. After you die tonight—and you *are* going to die tonight—I will find your people. I will send hordes of armies on giant condors, armed with disk bows, and raining fire pellets down until every last insurgent is dead."

"You've never found us before," Simon said. "And you won't find us this time either. Not until we bring the revenge to you."

By then, I had turned the lock and pushed the door open, all the while making it appear that I was being forced to do it.

"Try to follow me and you'll find her body left behind on the trail." Simon spoke so menacingly that if I didn't know it was an idle threat, I'd have been worried.

He pushed me out the door, slamming it firmly behind him to reengage the lock. The instant we were alone, he gave me the knife and let me support his weight. I locked arms with him to help him toward the birch trees. I knew this place well. It was a thick copse that the Dallisors had preserved because of the Halderian hangings that had happened there in the early days of the War of Devastation. They were a monument, not a memorial.

A horse was waiting deep within the trees, as Basil had promised.

"How did you plan this?" Simon asked.

"You wouldn't like it if I told you. Come on!"

He grabbed the saddle horn and dragged his weight onto the horse. Then I swung into the saddle ahead of him, careful to keep my cut skirts in place, took the reins, and with a quick warning to Simon to hold on, we escaped at a full gallop.

· THIRTY-FOUR ·

KESTRA

Simon leaned against my back as we rode, to the point where he was wearing my own strength down, but whatever I felt, I knew he was worse. A few scattered stars offered what light they could, but the moon had not yet risen, our clothes were wet and muddy, and the temperature was rapidly falling. At least it was late enough at night that we made it past the Sentries' Gate without any trouble.

But sure as the rising of the sun, trouble was coming. Simon had spoken boldly during our escape, and Dallisors never made idle threats. It wasn't a question of *if* the condors were coming our way, only whether we'd find a safe place to hide before they did.

By comparison, my worst day in the Lava Fields was a treasure. My mind drifted back to a warm autumn day about eight months after the kidnapping, shortly after my fourteenth birthday. I had received a letter from home offering me passage to Reddengrad to continue growing up in the court of my betrothed, Sir Basil. I had taken the letter and run into the Lava Fields, until I fell on some razor-edged rock and badly cut my leg. Darrow found me there, healed the injury with his cauterizing powder, and then talked me out of sending my father a rejection letter rolled in horse dung.

"I wish he weren't my father," I'd said. "When I was with the Banished, they told me—"

Darrow's face immediately became stern, which it almost never was. "Don't say another word, Kestra. Those are dangerous thoughts."

"Why?" I asked. "Don't I have a right to the truth?"

"With truth comes responsibility, and you don't want that."

When I pressed further, he boomed back, "Never ask again. Never!" It was the only time Darrow had ever yelled at me. The questions remained though.

Until now.

Truth brought more than responsibility. It had thrust upon me impossible choices with terrible consequences, and a lump in the back of my throat that swelled with every new revelation. Darrow had been right before. I didn't want this.

Pushing down those thoughts yet again, I said to Simon, "We shouldn't go to your base. Sir Henry's threats—"

"We have to go there, to figure out what Endrick did to your neck. Head west, to Silven."

"Silven?" Why did that sound familiar? I'd paid attention to my past geography lessons only enough to know that the small town sat too high on the cliffs to serve as a fishing village or a trading port. Most of the town's income came from sheep farming. A certain smell came with that business, enough to keep Dominion soldiers at a distance. Which, I supposed, made it an ideal place for the rebels to hide.

Simon took a measured breath before continuing, "If we ride along the northern border of All Spirits Forest, we should be safe."

All Spirits Forest. The spirits of those who had died in the War of Desolation wandered there, amid blackened trees that had been destroyed by fire so hot the earth beneath it could not heal. If the spirits considered you an enemy, you would never leave. Simon might be safe, but I'd absolutely be considered an enemy.

"How are you feeling?" I asked.

"I've been worse."

I chuckled. "Not unless your limbs have been lopped off in past fights, you haven't." His right hand had been resting near my leg. I took his hand in mine and folded that arm around my waist instead. His fingers pressed into my side, maybe as a romantic hint, or maybe to keep his balance. I knew he was worse off than he would admit, and it'd take us all night to reach Silven.

"How are *you* feeling?" Simon asked.

I'd just severed ties with the only home I'd ever known, and still didn't know if it was the right decision. "I've been better. I'll never return to Woodcourt."

"Of course not. Nothing is there for you anymore."

"Nothing was ever there for me. I know that now."

"Not your father. But what about your mother? I remember you were always close with her and there was no one in the world she loved more than you."

His words stung, though he'd never have intended that. All I could do was bite on my lip and keep moving forward, hoping he couldn't see enough of my face to read my thoughts.

But he seemed to already know at least some of the truth. "Your mother's diary must have told you more than the location of the Olden Blade."

"It did." Thanks for asking. Could we move on?

"How did you find the book?"

"Gerald gave it to me."

Our horse stumbled over a loose rock on the road. Simon drew in a pained gasp, and it was several long seconds before I felt him breathe again. Finally, he mumbled, "Can you slow down?"

"We're still too close to Highwyn."

"Please, Kes. I need to go slower."

I slowed the horse, though it was frustrating to imagine the snails beneath us beating us to Silven. Which they would now.

When he was ready, Simon asked, "Why did Gerald give you that diary?"

His question was far more dangerous than he could have realized, nor was there any way to answer it without that familiar feeling of panic in my chest. Finally, the words spilled from my mouth, like a flood I could no longer contain. "Did you ever wonder how Risha Halderian was able to steal the Olden Blade?"

He hesitated, considering the question. "The Endrean servant must have helped Risha do it, though nobody knows how."

"Anaya had a power that Lord Endrick very much desired: the ability to make her presence unknown to others, to fade into any background. The power came at a high price to her strength, but it kept her alive when all other Endreans were being slaughtered. Eventually, Anaya decided that she could not hide herself forever, so she had only two choices. Wait until her strength failed her and she was found by Lord Endrick, or fight back."

"Anaya used her power to steal the Olden Blade," Simon mumbled.

I nodded. "Yes, though it cost her the last of her magic. Unable to protect herself any longer, the dagger passed to her closest friend, the woman who had hidden her since Lord Endrick took power, and a warrior she believed was capable of victory."

Simon let out a low whistle. "Risha Halderian. You learned all of this from the diary? Why would your mother write about the Infidante?"

This time, I could not force myself to speak. And maybe the silence became its own answer.

"Oh," he finally said. "Lily Dallisor was not your mother."

I closed my eyes, feeling the pain of hearing the words spoken aloud. The blanket I had wanted to find in Lily's room was never there, because she had never expected to be taking in a child. Darrow knew it wouldn't be there. For three years in the Lava Fields, Darrow had let me believe lies about myself.

Pushing down those thoughts, I said, "When Risha and Anaya were brought into the dungeons, despite their crimes against Lord Endrick, Lily saw that my mother was expecting a child, and took pity on her. Gerald was a guard in the dungeons then and did all he could to protect Lily's secret visits. After I was born, Lord Endrick issued the order for the executions. My mother begged Lily to save my life."

"Her decision with eternal consequences," Simon suggested.

"Yes. Lily brought me before Sir Henry and said that if he harmed me, she would leave Antora the very next day. Whatever else he is or does, Sir Henry loved Lily and agreed to take me in, though he never stopped resenting me for it. You and I have at least one thing in common, Simon. We both escaped those dungeons, only I did it from my birth."

An hour seemed to pass while Simon let that sink in. All I

could do was ride onward, keeping my eyes on the western horizon, pretending that my heart was not about to pound its way free of my chest.

Simon's hands had loosened around my waist. But no matter how hard it was for him to contemplate this, he didn't know the worst of it. Finally, his hands tightened again, as if trying to comfort me, to assure me that this revelation would change nothing between us.

How wrong he was.

"This is why you were crying yesterday morning," he said. "If Risha Halderian is your mother, then—"

"I never said that." Dangerous as that would be, at least my life would still make sense. "It's a good thing you're weak as I'm telling you this, because I already know how you'll respond. My mother is not Lily Dallisor. Nor is it Risha Halderian."

As expected, his hands released me entirely, and he sat up straight, pulling away from me so suddenly that I felt as if I had just been separated in half. Yet I could sense his internal battle, not wanting to accept the only possibility that remained, or the consequences of it. At last he said, "Your mother was Anaya. You are Endrean, just like Lord Endrick."

"You said that if Endrick hadn't killed every last Endrean, your orders were to finish the job. You are bound by oath to kill me."

· THIRTY-FIVE ·

SIMON

In my life, I'd made three oaths. The first to Garr, that I would carry on my adopted father's legacy, to the best of my ability.

The second to Tenger, that as a Corack, I would fight against the Dominion until Endrick's death.

And the third to the Coracks. That I would not allow anyone with Endrean blood to live.

These weren't passing fancies, or a flirtation with philosophy. These were commitments I had considered for some time, and for which I was willing to die. Never once had I violated those oaths, or ever questioned my belief that history would put me on Antora's side.

Never once.

Until now.

Kestra halted our horse, her entire body suddenly as rigid as a board. Without a word, she slid off the horse from one side and I dismounted from the other, though that was far too elegant a word for my sloppy half-fall to the ground. Open road stretched out in both directions, leaving us completely exposed. Above every other emotion currently twisting inside me, our open position made me nervous.

Kestra remained exactly where she was, forcing me to limp around the horse. She faced me with fisted hands on her hips, ready to run if necessary. As if, in my current state, I had any chance of catching her.

I was still at a distance from her when I stopped, and kept my hand far from my sword. "You lied to us—to me—about who you really are."

She didn't flinch. "You have orders regarding who I really am."

"I would never hurt you, Kes."

"Are you sure? Eventually, Tenger will find out the truth. What happens when he commands you to execute the Endrean girl? Me."

I'd already considered this possibility when she was a Dallisor. My answer wouldn't change now. "I would go to my death before causing yours."

"You said that all Endreans eventually go bad. What if it's only a matter of time before I become just like Endrick?"

Most Antorans believed this wasn't a question of "what if," but a question of "when." The Halderians had nearly been wiped out by the Endreans. They would never trust one again. The Coracks were so certain of the Endreans' corruption that our orders were uncompromising, unforgiving. I was left to stand across from a girl who made my heart race, wondering if one day she'd put a knife through it.

Anxious to find any way to save Kestra, I remembered a theory about the Endreans. We had no evidence to support it, but it was her best chance to survive. Probably her only chance. "You have no magic now, so let it be. Maybe the lure of power becomes too great, or magic depletes the soul. Or maybe the water in the Blue Caves somehow taints the magic. I don't know why, but it always corrupts."

She wasn't convinced. "And if I never obtain my magic, would you still trust me to join the Coracks, to fight at your side?"

Now I took a single step forward, ignoring the pinch in my lungs. "Kestra Dallisor earned my trust. Kestra the Endrean will not lose it."

She shifted away, putting more distance between us than before. "I doubt your captain will see things the same way."

He wouldn't, nor would most Coracks. Even if Tenger allowed her to join us, Kestra would charge into battle, never knowing if her greater enemy was ahead of her, or at her back.

My failure to answer seemed to deepen her sadness. It was thick in her voice when she said, "This is why I've said there's no future for us. Surely you understand that now."

"No, I don't understand! Forget what Tenger believes! I don't know your future, or mine. But I know who you are today, and how I feel about you. Whatever your name, or your past, or whoever you will be tomorrow, I still want to be . . . yours." With that, I stepped forward again, and this time she didn't back away.

Kestra's smile came slowly, but it was real and it was for me. She started to speak when a loud cry overhead rang through the night air.

She was the first to recognize it. "Condors." Kestra grabbed my arm, yanking me face-first to the ground. A shock of pain lit across my injured back and ribs, and flashes of light appeared in my vision.

Wind from the condors' wings rushed past us, their screeches boring through me like a drill. I covered my ears, still fighting the echoes of pain reverberating through my body. Kestra probably didn't realize how hard she had pulled me down.

"These condors don't have riders," she said. "That's better, but we have to stay low."

The horse we had used to escape bolted away upon hearing the next screech. Kestra called after it, but to no avail.

"Keep your head down," she told me. "These condors notice faces, and movement."

I probably couldn't have looked up anyway, and I certainly didn't feel like moving, or breathing for that matter. Had we crashed onto solid rock?

A tremulous, high-pitched *neigh* rang through the air, overpowered by the condors' screech. The powerful flap of wings rushed more wind over me, and then it was silent.

"I think they took the horse," Kestra mumbled. I opened my eyes to see her beside me, visibly trembling.

Tenger had once described to us being in a battle where condors had plucked grown men from the ground, flying them off to their doom or to the bowels of a dungeon to be tortured for information. But clearly they were strong enough to carry a horse as well. Hardly comforting news.

"Henry Dallisor reported us to Endrick, who sent his condors for us," she said. "Endrick expected we'd be on that horse."

"At least they're gone."

But her eyes only widened. "The Dominion doesn't give up, Simon."

Neither did I. Holding my breath against the pain, I forced myself to my knees. It was too dark to see much, but I already knew our options were spare. The road we were on cut across a slope. Below us was tired grassland and thin bushes. Farther uphill, where the slope began to flatten out, was All Spirits Forest. Kestra had seen it too.

"Don't you dare." I was firm on this. "If Dallisor blood would've gotten you killed in there, imagine what would happen to an Endrean."

"We're no better out here! By now, Endrick will realize we weren't on that horse. Something else is coming."

In answer to her warning, the road began vibrating beneath us, a low hum that was quickly growing louder. Coming closer.

Kestra turned sharply. "Oropods!"

Dust was kicking up on the road, though with the hills between us and Highwyn, I couldn't see anything yet. It amazed me how on only two legs an oropod managed to turn up more dust than a half dozen horses. I guessed at least six of the lizardlike creatures were headed our way, and each of their riders would be well armed. At the rate the dust was rising, I guessed we had less than five minutes.

Desperately, I looked uphill again. How many times had I been warned not to go into that forest? Tenger had even forbidden it to the Coracks, unless there was no other choice.

There was no other choice.

Kestra helped me to my feet, and together we began clambering up the slope, slipping on dewy grasses or tripping over embedded rocks. We weren't yet halfway up when the first oropod reached the road directly below us. Every rider had a revolver that shot off fire pellets. I'd seen them many times before in skirmishes with Dominion soldiers. When the pellets connected with metal, they exploded in seconds. But at night, when they carried a visible glow, the Coracks had a way of dealing with them. One I rather enjoyed.

"Keep running," I told Kestra, then pulled out my sword, angling it over one shoulder.

When the spray of pellets came close, I swung out my sword, hitting them back toward the rider, where they exploded on contact, killing him. His oropod started to run free, but its reins were caught by a second rider who had arrived. It must not have known this man, because the oropod immediately bit into his arm with fangs that punctured deep into the flesh. By then, five other riders had arrived and it took all of them to rescue their companion. That gave us time we desperately needed. I'd sacrificed my ribs for that swing. Breathing hurt. Running was torture.

Kestra ran back down to me, taking my sword in her hands. "Come on." After a short run, we were beyond the reach of fire pellets, but not the oropods.

The riders wouldn't want to enter the forest, any more than I did. The remaining five slid out of their saddles, briefly conferring. Then I heard the order to their oropods: "Kill."

Kestra redoubled her efforts to pull me uphill. I did what I could for myself, but remained on my feet more from sheer willpower than physical strength. My legs were no sturdier than saplings, and my lungs couldn't draw a full breath. Since swinging the sword, my vision had blurred, making me stumble with every step. Oropods were pursuing us with jaws open wide and eager fangs. So maybe it wasn't willpower moving me uphill, as much as it was an overwhelming desire to not be eaten.

"Keep going!" Kestra stopped and I turned long enough to see her swipe at an oropod, but I was too dizzy to see what she did next. Seconds later, I heard the animal's shriek of rage. When Kestra took my hand again, hers was wet. Blood? Her blood or the oropod's?

Then her arm went around my shoulders, bracing me and

pushing me uphill again, toward the fringes of the forest. With the rising moon ahead of us, long shadows fell at our feet, spiny gray fingers cast by the burned, blackened trees. They sent a chill through me every time I crossed through one, as if each shadow stole a piece of my soul for itself. It was impossible to believe that *this* was the safest of our options.

On its first brush through one of those shadows, an oropod that had been following us arched high onto its hind legs, pulling back its front claws as if burned. Spitting with anger, it stopped on the exact line of the shadow, refusing to cross through it. None of them would.

I suggested we stop at the shadows. If the oropods wouldn't enter, why should we? But Kestra was still pushing us into the trees and I knew why. The soldiers were not finished.

At least one had followed us up the slope. A fire pellet hit the blade of my knife. Before I could react, it exploded against my thigh, searing my nerves. I didn't know how close Kestra was, if she had been caught in the blast too. But there was no time to think of it. Spotty lights filled my vision, brighter and brighter until everything suddenly went dark.

My body crumpled to the ground.

· THIRTY-SIX ·

·SIMON·

I awoke to the impossible. If anything I remembered from before I passed out had been real, then how could I be free of pain now? My eye that had been nearly swollen shut felt normal. I was breathing easily, without effort or thought. I felt strong and perfectly warm.

Also, I was sitting in a pool of warm water.

Where was Kestra?

My head had been resting on a mound of dirt at the edge of the pool. I raised it to look around. It was shortly past dawn, and I was somewhere inside All Spirits Forest. That much was obvious. No place like this existed anywhere else in Antora, maybe nowhere in all the world.

The trees here were thick, or had been years ago. Now all that remained were branchless black logs that stayed upright only from a memory of their past glory. The ground was scorched too, the earth refusing to regrow even a single blade of grass.

When the tide turned against the Halderians during the War of Devastation, many of them had fled into these woods to hide. Ignoring their pleas for mercy, Endrick used magic to build invisible barriers, locking in all those who had come here to hide. Then he burned the entire forest, a final act of brutality before the Dominion claimed victory in the war.

Since the war's end, nothing had changed here, nor would it ever. The spirits of those who had died still roamed the woods, forever unable to leave their borders, but eager for vengeance upon anyone with the enemy's blood, should they dare to enter the realm.

I sat fully up, alarmed. Maybe I was accepted here, but where was Kestra?

She must have survived long enough to bring me to this pool. I called her name and started from the water before I heard her voice behind me.

"You look better."

Startled, I splashed backward, then turned to see her.

Kestra stood in front of me, cleaned up from the mud from last night, but still looking more like an abandoned orphan than nobility of the Dominion. Her dress was stained with dirt and had been cut in jagged tears just below her knees. Her hair was tangled and hung loose on her shoulders. But her smile was genuine, and her natural beauty made the ruby necklace around her neck sparkle brighter. That necklace was her final link to the Dallisors.

"You're all right." I wasn't sure if it was a statement or a question.

She wrapped her arms around herself. "I'm cold, but I'm all right."

"It's warm in here." I grinned and held out a hand for her.

But she only shook her head. "I can't, Simon. You know why."

I remembered now. There was magic in these waters. There had to be, for nothing else could have healed me overnight. Something in her Endrean blood either couldn't, or shouldn't, access the magic.

"How'd you know about this place?" I asked.

"I didn't. I stumbled upon it, almost literally, last night. I thought I'd use the water for a drink and to clean us both up. But the magic started working on you almost immediately."

"And how are you alive . . . in here?"

"I don't know that either. I feel the spirits around me. They're curious, and divided on what to do with me. There's definitely an agitation from my presence, so if you're able to walk, I think I've tested their patience long enough."

Without a second's delay, I stood and left the water, to my surprise, drying off immediately. My clothes were burned in places and torn in others, but no worse than Kestra's. From here, I could see her shivering, unable to benefit from the water's power. Hopefully, walking would warm her, especially after we got out of the forest and into the sun. Here, the shadows ruled, memories of those who failed to get out.

I took Kestra's hand, lacing our fingers together, and hopefully sending the message that I wanted to stay with her, no matter the consequences. We faced some difficult choices ahead, and not only because she was Endrean. If everything I suspected was true, we had only touched the surface of the problems waiting for us.

She allowed me to hold her hand, but the walls she kept around herself had risen again, thick and formidable, as if she'd said too much last night and regretted it. Getting anything more from her would've been hopeless, except I had a plan. There was one thing she cared about more than her secrets.

Darrow.

I fine-tuned this idea for almost an hour of walking until we saw the first break in the trees through which we could leave the forest. By then, her shivering had stopped, and hopefully her defenses had softened. On our final step from the forest, I said, "I propose a game. I'll make a guess. If I'm correct, I get to make the next guess. As soon as I'm wrong, the game ends."

She glanced sideways at me, unimpressed. "Why should I play?"

"Because if I guess wrong, you win, and you'll want the reward." I squeezed her hand, knowing full well that losing this game would get me into serious trouble with the Coracks. "We have a chance to get to Silven before Tenger does. If you win, I'll release Darrow to you, without any further conditions."

Kestra stopped, tears welling in her eyes. "You'd do this for me?"

My smile widened. "*If* I lose. But I warn you, I'm a good player."

She nodded and took a deep breath. "All right, go ahead."

"Darrow is a Halderian."

She shrugged, obviously relieved that the first guess was relatively mild. "To have gotten close enough to pull off my rescue, Darrow must be part of their clan. I think he intended to explain everything at the inn, before we returned to Woodcourt. Darrow must've arranged for the Halderians to meet us there. They'd give me the key to the diary and then once we were at Woodcourt, Darrow could have sat with me to read it. But when you and Trina brought me to the inn instead, Thorne became suspicious. That's why they attacked."

That was my theory too, more or less. A harder guess now. "The Halderians kidnapped you because you're Endrean."

She stopped walking, weighing her answer. "I don't know that."

"You said they tried to kill you. No one would hate an Endrean more than the Halderians."

Her fingers stiffened in my hand, as if she was trying not to make this a fight. "Yes, they made their feelings perfectly clear. But they only told me I wasn't a Dallisor."

I tilted my head, trying to work that out. "You've known that for three years?"

"I didn't believe them! I thought they were trying to divide me from my family. When I asked Darrow about it, he became angry, and I never asked again. But what does it matter if they want to kill me for being a Dallisor, or for being Endrean? Either way, I get the same welcome party."

We began walking again, finally getting enough distance from the forest to see the first blades of grass. I no longer had her hand. This game would only get more difficult, for both of us. Knots were forming in my stomach, warning I was about to stumble upon a guess that would separate us forever.

"Guess number three: Darrow saved your life. Which is why it's important for you to save him now."

"That matters, of course." She looked over at me. "You must release Darrow."

"Why?"

She shook her head. "If you don't know, then—"

"What is Darrow's importance?" As soon as I spoke, the details came together in my mind. "Darrow is a Halderian. You think he might be able to claim the Olden Blade."

She smiled, looking almost pleased that I had guessed it. "He's strong, and he has honor and courage. He would be an ideal Infidante."

"But Tenger has the Blade. I know how cruel he was to you before, but I've fought alongside him many times. There's a reason he's our captain."

"And there's a reason Darrow was able to rescue me from the Halderians. I only ask that he be given the chance to claim the dagger before Tenger puts his choice forward."

"Tenger won't let you decide who becomes the Infidante." The instant I spoke the words, my heart thudded against my chest. Kestra was just as strong-willed as Tenger, maybe more. "No . . . it's just the opposite, isn't it? *You* won't let Tenger choose the Infidante."

"I can't control him."

"But for a few minutes, you did have control of the Olden Blade."

"In the pit? I gave the dagger away." Kestra's voice had risen in pitch. She was nervous. Agitated. I was close to something.

I continued, "I watched you search. You found the burlap sack almost immediately, but you hid it beneath your foot, only pretending to continue searching."

"Because I didn't want to give it to Tenger."

"That's not the point. You never looked in the sack. You just kept it beneath your foot. Why would you do that, unless you already knew what was inside?"

"Is that a question or a guess?"

"It's a fact." I felt bolder now. "You knew what was inside the sack because you put it there. That's why it looked new."

"Ridiculous! How could I get past the guards long enough to plant a dagger in the pit, then return to my room without a speck of mud on me?"

She walked faster. So did I. "Gerald planted it, then, on your orders. That's why he went down the wall first! But why would he go to all that trouble?" I suddenly stopped, certain I was correct. Wishing I wasn't. "The dagger in that burlap sack is a fake."

She stopped just ahead of me, but would not turn around. Her voice was commanding, unwavering. "The game is over, Simon."

Which one—hers or mine? My game had gone exactly as I'd intended, although it was nothing compared to the game she'd been playing against us. Everything that had felt like our discovery was a trick she must've been planning since the night we captured her carriage. It wasn't our idea to search the pit, it was hers. She'd wanted me to notice the burlap sack beneath her feet, to force her to hand it over, because that was more plausible than her offering it to us. Tenger's ambition, Trina's desperation . . . my emotions. She'd used all of it against us. Against me. Had anything been real?

My muscles tensed and I crossed in front of her. "You gave Tenger a fake dagger! What do you think he'll do when he figures that out?"

Her eyes became slits of anger. "Well, I don't know. Threaten me? Threaten my one true friend?" I flinched at her words, but she continued spitting them out. "There is nothing more he can do to me."

"There is always more he can do. Believe me, Kes, there is a reason the Coracks have survived this long. When Tenger figures out what you've done, he will make things worse. Killing Darrow will only be the beginning."

"And what if I hadn't given him something in that pit? Would I still be alive?"

No, she wouldn't. And if that was her only reason for giving Tenger a fake weapon, then I would have understood. But there was more, and it was worse.

I held out my hand to her. "Let me see your palm again, the one with the burn."

She glared at me, then did as I asked. I touched her palm, lightly brushing my finger along the edge of the burn. "Gerald went to the dungeons, not you. He planted the fake dagger in the pit, not you. This wasn't caused by a torch, like Trina thought." Now I looked up at her and saw a flash of panic in her eyes. "Where did this burn come from?"

"Asking questions is not how the game works."

"Then I'll say it: You found the real Olden Blade."

She bit her lip, keeping her attention on the ground. Looking anywhere but at me. Looking as if she wished the earth would split apart wide enough to swallow her up.

I felt a split of my own. To succeed, the rebellion had to find the Olden Blade. Getting it was my entire purpose for being here in the first place. I wanted to be right about my guess.

And I hoped I was wrong. If Kestra had found the Olden Blade, and passed a fake one on to Tenger, then she was in serious trouble. I would not be able to protect her from the consequences of that decision.

"Answer me, Kes."

Finally, she nodded.

The gesture was small, a slight tilt of her head that would've been imperceptible had I not been studying her so closely. Yet the revelation still hit me like a punch to the chest.

She had found the Olden Blade.

Which led to the larger question involving that burn on her hand, a question I barely dared to ask. Taking a deep breath, I whispered, "Did you claim it? Kes, are you the Infidante?"

· THIRTY-SEVEN ·

KESTRA

Simon repeated his question a second time, or maybe a third time before I heard him, the urgency rising in his voice.

I couldn't look at him, and not because I was afraid of what I'd see in his eyes, but for the truth he'd see in mine.

I started with the easiest end of the conversation: "I was not the only thing my mother—Lily Dallisor—saved from the dungeons."

Except for an arched eyebrow, he barely moved. "She smuggled out the very weapon her husband had been searching for?"

"According to the diary, Lily believed the dagger might save me one day, *from* her husband. She hid it in her room, the one place in Woodcourt that Henry Dallisor never allowed to be disturbed or searched, because of his love for her."

His eyes tightened on mine. "And you tried to claim it?"

"I thought maybe as an Endrean—" I swallowed hard, pushing down the frustration and feelings of failure, and the idea that at my best, I would never be anything more than an outcast. "I had to know."

"And?"

His voice was tender, seeming genuinely concerned for me. Which made this harder.

He might have forgotten he was holding my hand, or maybe

why he was holding it, but when I clenched the palm again, he glanced down at it, then back at me.

Fighting the worst of my emotions, I said, "If the dagger does not want you, it will let you know. This burn marks my attempt to claim it, and my failure."

He nodded, then folded his hand over the back of mine, drawing it closer to him. Drawing *me* closer to him, into his arms, where I could have remained forever. What emotions was I feeling from him? Relief? Hope? To him, this wasn't failure. It was deliverance.

The corner of his mouth lifted. "This is good, Kes. For us."

Us. I liked the sound of that and mirrored his smile. He was right. No one else had to know of my bloodlines. I could choose my own future.

I could choose him.

My eyes invited him closer, and his grin widened. His breath greeted my cheek, and my heart pounded. With a hint of a smile, my lips parted.

But as he moved toward me, I whispered, "Wait."

Somewhere on the road below, the sounds of an approaching wagon echoed. I ducked low in the weeds with Simon beside me.

It was an old wagon with an arched canvas cover, headed west on the road below. The driver was even older and probably wouldn't notice much around him, might not hear as well as he used to.

Might not realize he was about to carry extra cargo.

I looked over at Simon, feeling a spark of hope. "We could walk to Silven, or catch a ride."

He nodded, though the seriousness in him had returned. He

had one question left to ask, and I knew he would soon. But I was finished giving him answers. Our game could go no further.

We stayed low as we plowed through the grasses, hurrying toward the road. The driver was singing to himself, a rousing tune that would be grounds for his arrest if a Dominion soldier heard it. Music was important to Halderian traditions, so Endrick made any form of it illegal, except when it was performed in honor of his presence. As if any singers could swallow their fear of him enough to croak out a few notes.

When the wagon rode by, Simon and I bolted from the roadside and took up chase. Simon reached the back of the wagon first, grabbing the rear board and hefting his weight up on the body bar. He stretched out a hand for me, and I took it, letting him lift me up too. He helped me squeeze beneath the canvas first, then followed me inside. The wagon never slowed down. The driver didn't know.

There wasn't much back here. The wagon bed was about half full of hay, hence the reason for the canvas, to keep it dry in case of rain. Two wood trunks sat on either side of the wagon. A quick peek into each trunk only revealed clothes, one for men, and the other full of dresses. Food would have been better. On the wagon floor near the backboard was a tablet, similar to my father's. That meant our driver was either loyal to the Dominion, or a trader. Or both. A near-perfect image of my face was displayed on the tablet, with a message below it that read, "Kestra Dallisor, Reward for Return." Lovely. A reminder that the Dominion could, and would, follow me into any corner where I might try to hide. Worse still, a reminder of the trouble I was introducing to Simon's life, regardless of the Olden Blade.

I'd have crushed the slab if I had both a hammer and an indifference to whether the driver heard me, but since neither of those held true, I picked up the slab and dumped it out the back of the wagon.

Simon had been watching me with a pronounced frown. "You can't destroy every tablet, Kes. A lot of people will see that message."

"Outside Highwyn, most people don't have tablets." And for those who did, this was simply another problem I'd have to deal with.

But not right now. The hay beckoned me to rest, and Simon would benefit from sleep too. He removed his sword and laid it within reach. I patted down a place beside him, resting against his arm, though I was surprised he didn't pull me in any closer.

Tension was thick in his voice when he said, "We still need to talk about the dagger."

"Hush. We need this ride more. No talking."

Obviously, we needed to be quiet, but our aged driver was still singing, and between that and the crunch of the wagon wheels on the dirt road, he wasn't likely to hear us.

Simon kept pushing. "Where is the Olden Blade now?"

The final question I knew he'd ask.

My answer was ready. "It's safe, and my secret alone. There are no remaining clues to its whereabouts. When we get to Tenger, I'll tell him the terms of our agreement will change. If anything happens to me, that dagger will be lost forever."

He scoffed. "You're going to blackmail the Coracks?"

"They blackmailed me. I think it's fair."

"Tenger is not interested in fairness. He's interested in winning."

"So am I." With that, I rolled away from him, taking a few breaths in hopes of leveling my temper.

"Don't turn away. We have to settle this."

"It is settled, Simon. You just don't like the answer." He protested that, but I ignored him, determined to either sleep or pretend to.

Beside me, I felt his energy stirring like a boiling pot. It would frustrate him to wonder how close he had come to getting the Blade, and how far from it he was now. I knew he'd still try to get answers from me, but it wouldn't work. He'd learn nothing about the Blade, not until I was ready. With those thoughts swirling in my head, it was a long time before I fell asleep. When I awoke sometime later, he had fallen asleep too.

· THIRTY-EIGHT ·

KESTRA

Our driver was no longer singing, but a light rain pelted the canvas. If we were careful, the rainfall would mask any sound of our being in here.

I studied Simon, still asleep close beside me. A small scar lined one eyebrow. I'd never noticed that before. When he was awake, there was always a tension in his expression, even when he was smiling. But now, he looked younger, in need of tenderness rather than another fight. If I were anyone else, I could have been that person for him. I could have shared my heart with him and together, he and I would have faced whatever the future held.

If I were anyone else.

That single thought put an ache in the back of my throat, one that threatened to choke me if I couldn't distract myself. Then I remembered the trunk next to me, full of dresses. Perhaps this trunk offered a greater blessing than if it had been filled with coins. I pushed through the dresses until I found one that should fit me and that was slightly less hideous than the others. It was an off-shoulder pale green gown with a cream lace corset, one I could tie without help. No bead-work or sash seemed to belong to this gown, but the poor rarely wore those anyway. The dress possibly outdated Antora itself, and there was a tear in one seam of the arm, but who was I to judge? Last night, I'd cut off the entire bottom half of my skirts, which now dangled unevenly just below my knees. My overdress was stained with mud, its original color unrecognizable. And I was sure the fabric had picked up any number of odors from the dungeons, a smell I had no desire to remember.

I checked again to be sure Simon was asleep, then removed my overdress. Beneath it, the upper half of the shift was intact, and the green dress's long skirt would hide the ruined lower half anyway. I didn't find any cloaks in the trunk, but the sleeves of the dress were long and I had Simon to help warm me. This dress was an unforgiveable offense to fashion, but it was good enough for now. I'd just avoid looking down at it. Forever, if necessary.

As soon as I finished, I turned to see Simon lying on the hay with his hands behind his head, staring at me with a smile on his face.

I tilted my head, amused by the gleam in his eyes. "You were watching me?"

His grin widened, suddenly mischievous. "Only for the last few minutes . . . unfortunately."

Playfully, I swatted at his shoulder, but he caught my hand and pulled me down to him, face-to-face. The quiet laughter between us quickly became serious. Time itself seemed to slow. He was staring at me again but I knew he would not let me go. Nor did I want him to.

He leaned up on one arm, bringing his body closer to mine. His lips closer to mine. Our noses touched, and his breath was on my cheek, a reminder for me to exhale, if I could. Then his hand was on my waist, and I brushed my fingers across his shoulder. When he drew back again, enough that our eyes met, his gaze burrowed so deep into me that I felt myself letting go of the outside world. Letting go of my past and my worries and everything that stood between him and me. Letting go of my last secret.

No, not that one.

But it seemed he was going to try. Keeping his voice low, he said, "I'm going to make a guess. If I'm right, our game continues."

I groaned. "No, Simon—"

His knuckle followed my jawline. "You want us to be closer, but it frightens you."

Fear? No, it was bigger than that. Only three nights ago, he had proclaimed his hatred for me. Could that have changed so fast? He was still under oath to the Coracks, and sworn to kill anyone in my bloodline. Fear was the smallest description of what I felt.

His fingers reached my hair, pushing and twisting through the strands. He moved his thumb to trace across my cheek softly, dizzyingly. "You trust me, and you don't. You believe in my purpose, but not in my leader. You believe in me, but—"

"I do believe in you, Simon. I believe in your heart and your passion. I know who you are, and who you are meant to be, and I believe in you to become that person. But I need you to believe in me too."

Somehow, for as good as that had sounded in my head, it had been the wrong thing to say. His tone cooled as he whispered, "Where is the Olden Blade, Kes?"

I pressed my lips together, staring at him just as intently, but making my refusal clear.

"I'm not asking for Tenger's sake, or Trina's. This is just between you and me."

"And your oath to the Coracks. Correct?"

His eyes flashed and the warmth between us frosted. He said, "If it's the only way to save you, yes, I'll honor my oath. This secret is far too dangerous."

"I'll take that risk."

"Not alone, for your own sake. You need my help!"

"It's none of your concern what I do!"

"Maybe I want it to be my concern! I want *you* to be my concern!" He cursed and released me entirely, mumbling something beneath his breath.

To have been so near him and then so suddenly apart took the air from my lungs, a cruel suffocation. When I could, I whispered, "If you have something to say, then say it."

At first he wouldn't look at me, or couldn't bear to. But slowly his eyes met mine, exposing a pain in him that I hadn't seen before. Or reflecting something he saw in me. With our eyes locked, his breaths came faster and deeper. So did mine.

After what seemed like hours, he said, "You are ripping at my heart, Kes. Every time I reach out and you pull back. Every time you offer a smile to someone who's not me. When you doubt me, or mistrust me, or hide your secrets away, it's like a claw that shreds me from within. When we're together, I forget how to breathe, but when we're apart, I realize you've become my air. I want you to take a risk, but take it with me. Risk yourself with me."

"Simon, you know who I—"

"I do know, and I'm telling you that I don't care. If you can't cross this bridge between us, or you won't, then tell me now and let me tear you from my soul. But don't hold me in this awful middle place where I can't get closer and I can't get away from you."

His words pierced me. I *felt* them more than I heard them, like a shiver up my spine, or a pounding in my chest. When he went silent, all I could think was that my next move would change everything.

I touched a stray lock of his hair, folding it back into place, then slid a finger down the side of his face. My eyes met his again, communicating what I wanted. Immediately, his hands reached for me, wrapping around my back and pulling me to him, bringing his lips to mine. This wasn't the cautious, stale moment such as Basil had offered in his embrace. This first kiss with Simon was like a wave, compelled to reach land, each brush of his lips tumbling into the next, asking for more.

His kiss ignited emotions in me I'd never known could exist. Thoughts emptied from my mind until all that remained was the feel of his lips, the press of his hands, and the beat of my heart, pulsing for him, aching for more of him.

I held on to each second as if nothing so perfect could possibly continue, but then there was another kiss, another rise in the flood of my emotions, another surrender to him. With every touch, I belonged more to him, and him to me.

Our growing passion communicated everything he wanted. A land free of Endrick's rule, a place of peace where nothing existed but him and me. And a future for the two of us, together. He wanted that, and he believed getting the Olden Blade into the right hands was the way to achieve it. As I came toward him for another kiss, I realized that was all I wanted too.

It was . . . until it wasn't. Until I remembered Darrow and what would be necessary to gain his freedom. Until I remembered that there would have to come a time when Simon went one way, and I went the other. Until this moment had to end, far sooner than I wanted.

It took all my strength to force myself away from him, and when I did, he sat up as well, sensing that something was wrong.

"Kes . . ."

I shook my head. "If it were only my life at stake, then I would take the risk, but I will not obligate you to the same. That's not fair."

Simon took my hand in his. "Your life *is* in danger, more than ever before. If you'd tell me where—"

"—where the Olden Blade is?" My tone sharpened. "Is that why you kissed me? To weaken my defenses?"

"I kissed you because I'm falling so fast for you that I expect at any second to crash into a reality where you're not here. And you won't be, if you won't tell me where the dagger is. This secret could get you killed."

"This secret is my only chance to live!"

Silence collapsed the world between us. Our own Pit of Eternal Consequence where we might fall forever. I wanted to believe him, just as I wanted to believe *in* him, and that somewhere ahead was a tomorrow that belonged only to the two of us.

But we had gotten too close to the edge. I could not give away this secret, and he would not give in until he had what he wanted.

Our story was never going to end any other way.

I scooted back against the side of the wagon. Waiting for him to say something and knowing he wouldn't, because nothing he'd say *could* fix this. A pit had opened inside me, one that I doubted would ever be filled again.

So this was what it felt like when a heart shattered.

• THIRTY-NINE •

SIMON

If Tenger knew I'd kissed her, if he knew I'd kissed her like that, I'd be expelled from the Coracks. Tenger would say there was no way I could have such strong feelings for Kestra and still be loyal to his orders. Maybe that was true.

Further complicating things was the way our kiss had ended. Kestra was at the far side of the wagon now, staring at me as if I should have some brilliant solution to the hundreds of problems she had created. Maybe if I understood a fraction of the way her brain worked, I'd know what to say. Why did she have to complicate everything? Why did she have to *be* so complicated, a jumble of lines that intersected and diverged and encircled each other with no discernible reason?

She obviously felt confused, and I couldn't blame her for that. For her, every cubit of Antora had become a land mine. Everyone she met for the rest of her life would be treated with suspicion, because they all had a good reason to seek her out.

So did I, but for very different reasons. Kestra had become like fire to me. I needed her, I was drawn to her, but being this close was burning me. This must be why Gerald had warned me not to fall in love with her. But I doubted I had any choice. Not anymore.

Why did it have to be this way? Couldn't I love her and remain dedicated to the Coracks? Couldn't Kestra become part of the search for the Infidante?

No, not *part* of the search. Kestra had claimed that responsibility solely for herself. No one else knew where the Olden Blade was, a fact more dangerous than her bloodline. Surely she knew that the future of our entire country was at stake. Why was she doing this?

Suddenly, I began to understand that jumble of lines intersecting and twisting within her. I couldn't stretch them out straight enough to answer any of these knotted questions. I didn't even know where to start.

Across the wagon, Kestra still hadn't said a word. Finally, I whispered, "Talk to me, please."

Before she could speak, the wagon halted. I lifted a finger, warning her to remain silent. Then I listened, hoping to pick up any clue as to where we were or why we had stopped so abruptly.

It was probably nothing. Maybe the driver had simply arrived at his destination or was taking a break to stretch his legs. But it was strangely quiet outside, and my instincts warned me to be careful.

I parted the back flap of the canvas to look out but as soon as my hand was spotted, someone grabbed it and yanked me from the wagon, over the backboard, and dropped me on the ground like a hot coal.

Before I could warn Kestra to run, someone introduced his boot to my ribs, a younger man. At least it wasn't a Dominion soldier's iron-toed boot.

The older man who had been the driver snarled, "Stowing away in my wagon, you thief! You'd better hope there's something in here to pay me for the ride!" He put a boot on my chest, then bent down and pulled the satchel from my shoulder.

I shook my head. "Don't!" But the boot punched down on me again.

The driver stuck his finger through Garr's ring that had been in the bottom of the satchel and showed it to his companion. "Look at what I found! This should fetch a fine price at market."

"Remove that from your finger or I will cut it off!" Kestra yelled as she jumped from the wagon, holding my sword.

The younger man chuckled as he swaggered toward her. "Aren't you a pretty thing? Be careful, or you might hurt yourself."

Her grin darkened. "It won't be me who gets hurt." She lifted the sword with a confidence that would unnerve the bravest warrior and charged over to the man. The tip of it must have connected somewhere, because a second later, I heard him stifle a cry.

"That's a scratch." Kestra nodded at the driver, who had almost frozen in place since she emerged. "You'll get worse if you don't put that ring back inside the satchel and return it to my friend. Now!"

Instead of cooperating, the driver put his boot back on my chest. I didn't know why he bothered. They'd already done enough damage there.

"I've seen your face before," the driver said. "On my tablet, I think."

Kestra didn't blink. "That girl you saw on the tablet doesn't exist. But I do, and my sword is just as real. Let him go."

"Thieves and stowaways," he continued. "The rot of Antora. One day the Dominion will punish you all."

"As they'll punish you for singing?" Kestra asked. "If you were going to break the law, I wish, at least, you'd have stayed in tune."

Surprisingly, the driver chuckled. "A fair complaint, I suppose. Let's not fight here. You're far too pretty an opponent. Pay for the ride and we'll both be on our way."

"We're not thieves, and the Dominion is the rot, not the solution to it." Kestra lowered my sword. "Return his ring, and I will pay you for our travels with this."

I knew what it was, the ruby necklace from her mother, Lily. I mumbled a *no*, but I doubted that anyone heard me.

"Agreed." I heard the ring drop, and then the satchel dropped beside me. I clutched the handle, dragging it close to my side. Kestra immediately handed over her necklace, and the boot was removed from my chest.

She added, "In exchange for that necklace, you both must promise not to tell anyone you've seen us here."

The men gave a halfhearted agreement that they'd probably break after calculating what the Dominion would pay for the whereabouts of the girl on their tablet.

I rolled to my least injured side while both men returned to their wagon and drove on. Once they were gone, Kestra knelt beside me. "Healing pools are not as common as you seem to think, the way you go around getting yourself kicked."

"Nor are physicians common enough for you to go around stabbing everyone who crosses you."

She smiled. "Remember that, next time you think of crossing me. Are you all right?"

"I'm fine. They just knocked the wind out of me."

"Yes, and probably took a few of your ribs with it."

They had. But I hoped she wouldn't notice my grimace as I stood again. She returned my sword, but exchanged it for possession of my knife.

Once we began walking again, I said, "That necklace belonged to your mother."

"The ring belonged to your adopted father."

"And I can't repay you for protecting it. Thank you." I took her hand, grateful for a moment of peace between us. Maybe one of our last peaceful moments.

Her thoughts were already looking ahead. "Those men will report us, despite their agreement."

"Then let's get as far as possible before they do."

"Do you know where we are?" she asked.

Trees were scant here, and the grass was brittle and sparse. The salty sea wind that blew inland left much of this land too arid for farming.

"We're not far from Silven," I said. At our current pace, it'd be several hours' walk. I wondered if Tenger was already there.

"Silven!" Kestra stopped and groaned. "Why didn't I think of this before? Celia used to come to Silven to shop. She claimed that Silven had better markets than Grimlowe, which was closer to the Fields. She lied to me."

"It was the truth, in a way. But she came to the markets to sell, not to buy."

"She sold *me*." Kestra clicked her tongue in disgust. "I hope I went for a good price."

I didn't know Celia's price for betrayal, only that the Coracks would've paid almost anything for it. And I had no doubt Kestra would find out the full story before she let the matter rest.

A few miles later, I finally spotted the first homes on the outskirts of the city. Farm homes. Maybe someone inside would give us a ride into town, and perhaps have a bandage for my ribs.

"Where do the Coracks hide here?" she asked.

"We don't hide. That'd be too obvious. We don't appear different from other Antorans, and we don't act different, at least not in the open. If you could look at me and identify me as Corack, then I've made a mistake."

"Then where do we go after we get to Silven?"

"First, we find somewhere safe for you until I can get Darrow freed."

Her eyes moistened and she stopped walking long enough to release a slow breath. "You're still going to help me? After knowing my secrets?"

"It's because I know your secrets." I sighed, dreading the next few hours. With what I now knew, we shouldn't have come to Silven. Kestra couldn't possibly be prepared to meet Tenger, to stare him in the face and lie about a fake dagger. If the burden fell to me, would I lie to my own captain, a man I was dedicated to serving?

An idea suddenly lit inside my head. The solution to the one question she would not answer. It was equal parts dangerous and cautious, reckless and logical. Kestra wouldn't do things any other way.

I said, "I think I know where the Olden Blade is."

She released my hand and took a step back, her breaths suddenly coming in bursts. "You don't know. You're guessing, hoping I'll give the secret away."

"As we were leaving the dungeons, Gerald wanted to stay with you, but you ordered him to leave."

"Yes, to save his life."

"Or was it to save something else?" Gerald had not spent two decades as a spy at Woodcourt, waiting for Kestra to come of age, only to leave at her first request. "I think Gerald took two daggers into those dungeons. The first was the fake one he planted in the pit. But he also has the second dagger, the real one. On your orders, he escaped with it, right under Tenger's nose."

By then, she was calmer, although she had become silent, her eyes darting around as if searching for a way to convince me that I was wrong. When she failed to come up with a plausible excuse, she merely shrugged and said, "If that was my plan, then admit it's a good one. The Blade belongs to the Halderians, and no one else."

"You think that'll be good enough for Tenger? You think he'll laugh this off, what a good joke you've played on the Coracks, and now all is forgiven? You have no idea how badly you've complicated things!"

"I had to complicate things. Tenger is dangerous!"

"You are every bit as dangerous! If he is manipulating who the Infidante becomes, then so are you!"

"That dagger is ransom for the life of my friend. Do not equate my actions with his."

"What of Gerald's life? Don't you respect the danger he is in?"

Her voice became flat. "Do not lecture me on danger! I know exactly what I've done, and I'd do it again."

I cursed and started in with a retort, but heard a sound in the distance. Horses. I squinted in that direction, hoping it was anyone but Dominion soldiers. It probably wasn't them—they preferred the faster oropods. I then hoped it was anyone but Tenger.

Whoever was coming, my third hope was that Kestra wouldn't be careless enough to speak her Dallisor name. Silven wasn't exactly bursting with a Dominion-loving population.

"They're looking for us," Kestra mumbled. "Should we hide?"

Around us, gorse and heather fluttered in the evening breeze, along with vast patches of Corack weeds. A mouse would have trouble hiding here. Someone on horseback shouted, a voice I recognized.

"Do you know him?" Kestra asked.

"Gabe Willen," I mumbled. He was a year older than me, tall and muscular with coal-black hair that he kept tied back at the nape of his neck. All the girls had eyes for him, and he knew it.

He was also my friend. I raised a welcoming hand and kept my tone casual. "It's just me."

Gabe sauntered closer, his eyes settling on Kestra far too long before shifting my way. A smile widened across his face and he slid off his horse. "Simon Hatch! What stampede ran over you?"

"The other guy looks worse." He laughed when I said it. That was a good sign.

"I heard you were part of some secret plan. Was she part of that plan?" Gabe's eyes returned to Kestra, with a flirtatious smile I'd knock off his face once my ribs were healed. "Who's this?"

"A friend," I said. "Why are you out here?"

"A wagon driver pulled into town an hour ago, trying to sell a ruby necklace he claimed had been given to him by a couple of young people stowing aboard his wagon. Tenger ordered us to investigate."

"Tenger's here?"

Gabe motioned vaguely behind him. "Back there, on one of the other horses. We brought a cart, because that driver also mentioned someone was injured. You, obviously." Gabe put an arm around me, failing to notice my grunt of pain when he did. "Tenger thinks you're dead. We even made a toast to your loss last night. Guess I'll have to take back all those nice things I said."

I tilted my head toward Kestra. "If I'm still alive, then it's thanks to her. Listen, I need a place for her to stay. I'll wait here for Tenger."

"You're hiding her?" Gabe released me and let out a low whistle. "Things just got more interesting. Does she have a name?"

"Not yet."

Gabe circled Kestra, taking her in. He didn't seem to recognize her, and nothing in her appearance would give her away. Her dress was beneath what the poorest girls of Antora would wear. Her hair had been combed out with her fingers. It fell loose over her shoulders, which a Dallisor would have considered unacceptable. She also had my knife again, and was holding it in a tight grip.

But if Gabe knew any details of the mission, it wouldn't take him long to guess at who she was.

"I won't defy the captain," Gabe said. "Sorry, Simon. Not even for you."

"I'm not asking you to defy him." I shuffled forward, aware of the bruising on my ribs. "I'm only asking for time to talk to him. Please, Gabe."

He smiled at her again. "Is her name Alice? She looks like an Alice."

"Call her whatever you'd like. Just help me."

Gabe hesitated, and Kestra groaned, losing her patience. "He won't help. I'll find someplace to go on my own. All I want is the . . . item I came for. After that, I'll leave. Tell Tenger that."

"Tell him yourselves," Gabe said as Tenger's horse approached along with three other riders and one cart. Trina was on the captain's right flank, and the cart was pulled by the man Kestra had stabbed that first night, Pell. His glare was murderous, but it was nothing compared to Tenger's icy expression. In response, Kestra's knife twisted in her hand, ready for action.

Tenger's eyes barely brushed over me before they settled heavily on Kestra. "Take her," he ordered his men. "Our business with this girl is not finished."

· FORTY ·

KESTRA

I had thought I was prepared to face Captain Tenger, but something in the set of his jaw stopped my heart. My grip glove was on his right hand, which deepened the pit in my stomach. Beside me, Simon went tense too. He shouldn't have, not if he still considered himself a Corack. Did he? I tried reading Simon's stony expression, but failed. He wasn't giving up any secrets here. Neither would I.

Tenger's men jumped off their horses with disk bows in hand. Some of the disks they held were far more dangerous than the silvers, and illegal for anyone but Dominion soldiers. Simon probably wouldn't draw his sword against other Coracks, but I had a knife and a simpler morality about using it. If they started a fight, I would finish it.

"She came here to talk with you!" Simon called. "Not to be attacked."

"What attack?" Trina asked, still on her horse beside Tenger, and wearing her usual charming glare. "We just want to talk without her waving a knife at us. Drop it, Kestra."

"Kestra . . . Dallisor?" Gabe turned to Simon. "You brought a Dallisor here? Are you insane?"

Maybe he was. Or from everyone's reactions, I was beginning to wonder if I was the one who'd gone mad. Tenger's smug posture only irritated me further.

"You left Simon for dead." I raised the knife, mostly in defiance of Trina. "I saved him. I also gave you the Olden Blade, as we agreed. In exchange, I want my servants back."

"Ah yes, you want Celia and Darrow." Tenger looked around him with an amused expression. "Did we bury her driver yet? I can't remember."

"Is Darrow alive?" I knew how desperate I sounded, and that giving away my emotions weakened my leverage to negotiate. But I was desperate, and could never pretend otherwise. "Is he?"

"Barely." Tenger became serious again. "I doubt he's well enough to travel. Perhaps we can find you a comfortable place to stay until he gets better."

A comfortable place to stay? Was it comfortable behind Corack bars? Because I suspected that's what Tenger had in mind.

Keeping the knife where everyone could see it, I said, "Provide me with a wagon, and Darrow and I will leave tonight."

Tenger clicked his tongue. "What a pity. I'm afraid we've recently run out of wagons. But if you'll talk with me, answer my questions, then by the time we're finished, I may be able to locate something with wheels. Perhaps also some food and blankets for your journey . . . home."

That last word was meant to injure. Home was no longer an option for me, and he knew it.

"Let me speak to Darrow," I said. "After that, you and I can talk. It's that simple."

"That simple?" Trina raised a brow. "We don't trust you."

"But you do trust *me*." Simon shuffled forward. "I promise I will not let Kestra do any harm to the Coracks."

It was a carefully worded phrase. He hadn't promised to tell them who I really was, or even that he and I had become something more than . . . whatever we had been a few days ago. Simon had only made the promise he knew he could keep. Because I wasn't here to hurt the Coracks, or to add to my list of enemies. But I wouldn't leave without Darrow.

"You owe me this," Simon said to Tenger. "For what I sacrificed in the dungeons, you owe me your trust. I've proven my loyalty."

"Yes, but is that loyalty to us, or to her?" Tenger gave a grim smile. "All right, let's get these two back to Silven, as quietly as possible." He rode closer to me. "How should we address you now? I gather you've abandoned the reason to be called 'my lady.'"

"I'd be happiest if you don't address me at all. Take me to Darrow."

"We'll talk first, over supper," he said. "If I like your answers, then we'll try to locate your man."

"Darrow first," I started to say, but Simon put a hand on my arm.

"Let him win this one," he whispered. "You have bigger battles ahead."

Tenger cocked his head, enjoying his small victory. "Besides, I'm sure you're both hungry."

Neither of us had eaten in over a day. I wanted to see Darrow, but I also liked the idea of getting some food first. Maybe I could let him win this one.

"Give me that knife," Tenger said. "It wouldn't be a polite conversation otherwise." It wasn't a request. When I handed it over, he cocked his head toward his riders. "Get Simon onto the cart and check his injuries. Gabe, you'll escort our guest."

"No." I reached for Simon's arm but he had stepped farther away from me. "I'll ride on the cart, with Simon."

"If you do, you'll draw attention to us both." Simon barely met my eyes. "Go with Gabe. I'll see you in Silven."

It felt like he was pushing me away, now that he was with his own people again. Maybe it really was about avoiding attention—or maybe he would be different now, more like the coldhearted Simon who had intercepted my carriage three nights ago.

Another battle lost. Reminding myself again that I was here for Darrow and nothing more, I followed Gabe to his horse. He helped me up first and saddled in behind me, closer than I liked. I had hoped we would travel into town near Simon's cart, but Gabe took us on a wider route, away from the others.

"Kestra Dallisor." Gabe said my name slowly, savoring each syllable as if it were a dessert he wished to devour. "No wonder Simon didn't want me to know who you are. If I breathe the Dallisor name in the town square, we'll have a mob after you within minutes."

"Don't breathe in the town square, then."

"Spoken with ice!" Gabe chuckled. "You've got the spirit of a Dallisor."

"I'm not a Dallisor. Not anymore."

Not ever.

Up ahead, Gabe pointed out a small wooden box on the ground, stained nearly to the color of the soil. When I noticed it, I saw a line of them spreading out as wide as I could see.

"Proximity alarms," he explained. "Magnets that detect the iron inside Dominion soldiers' hearts. Any of them cross this line and the magnets will start snapping together, sending a signal into town. I designed them myself."

"Do they work?"

He chuckled. "Well, yes . . . in theory. You'll be safe here, Miss Not-a-Dallisor-Anymore."

The Dominion soldiers didn't worry me. Tenger did.

As we entered Silven, I better understood what Simon had meant about the Coracks blending in with the population. This was a simple town of wooden buildings and rutted dirt roads. Open shops lined the dirt road, though there weren't many people around. I supposed they were out working. It'd be hard enough just to put supper on the table each night, so it would be easy for them to miss certain oddities about their town, or, more likely, to ignore them.

I thought of other towns I had passed through in years past. Were they all infested with Coracks this way, blending in with the local population until the opportunity came to attack us?

To attack *them*. The Dallisors were *them* to me now, not *us*.

"Hello, Gabe!" A girl from the far end of the street saw him and gave a friendly wave. She must not have recognized me, but I definitely knew her.

Celia.

Just as I had done once with Simon, I slid off Gabe's horse and began running. Gabe called for me to wait, but he had to secure his horse first, giving me a good lead. At some point, he would realize I also had his knife.

As soon as Celia realized that it was me racing toward her, she panicked, looking in every direction for a place to run. Let her try.

She could scramble up the side of the nearest building and I would figure out a way to be on top by the time she got there.

Once I came within reach of her, Celia raised her hands, dropping the basket of bread she'd been carrying. "Kestra, I'm sorry!" Her eyes were on the knife, though I had yet to raise it. "They forced me—"

"Forced you to what? Wander freely about this town with enough money to buy a new dress and fresh bread? What torture you must have suffered here!"

"I didn't want to betray you."

I snorted. "And I didn't want to be betrayed. So we still have one thing in common."

Gabe had caught up to us now and stood beside us, ready to intervene if a fight broke out. It wasn't necessary. I would never hurt Celia. I only wanted to understand her. And maybe yell a little. Or a lot.

Celia sniffed with sadness. Which might've been genuine humility, but maybe not. When she had screamed out with pain the night my carriage was attacked, she'd obviously been faking because there wasn't a visible scratch on her, and she had just been openly flirting with Gabe.

She could say whatever she wanted. I no longer had any reason to believe her.

Still, she was trying. "I'd been coming to the market here in Silven for weeks before they figured out who I was. I never spoke your name to them before that. I never sought them out."

"So when they asked if you served me, that's when you told them?"

Tears fell onto Celia's cheeks. Also fake, I assumed. "Do

you know why I worked for the Dallisors, my lady? My mother was a handmaiden for your mother. She knew things about you, the truth about you, but she never spoke a word of it, except to me. After your mother died and my mother was dismissed, I went to the manager of your father's household—"

"Gerald."

Her hand flew to her throat, apparently surprised that I should know him. "Yes . . . Gerald. I demanded money or else I'd reveal your true history. Instead of paying me, he offered me a choice. Either to be sent to Woodcourt's dungeons, or serve you."

The corner of my mouth lifted. "What a terrible choice."

She missed the sarcasm. "It was, my lady. You have a reputation, of being—"

"Charming? Friendly?"

"Difficult." Celia's cheeks reddened. "But then I got to know you, the real you, and changed my mind. You can be nice, if no one tries to control you. And you can be fun, in a why-are-you-always-risking-my-life sort of way." She bit down on her lip, almost ashamed to look at me. "But I never forgot who you are, the kind of person you'll eventually become. So when the Coracks approached me, I listened."

She had intended to make me feel better, but her words stung my heart. "You never thought of me as just me. I was only an enemy waiting to happen."

"It wasn't like that. I told the Coracks where we'd be traveling, and when, but nothing more. They only wanted something retrieved from your home. I wrote the letter to your father, accepting the marriage arrangement, so that he would allow you to return. They swore not to harm you."

"They didn't make that same promise about Darrow." My knife lifted. "Where is he?"

Gabe cut between us. "Don't answer her, Celia. Tenger's orders."

"Celia, where is Darrow?"

She had forgotten how to speak, apparently, and I was running out of time. If she knew anything, I had to make her tell me.

Her mouth clamped shut, and it was a call on my bluff. I lowered the knife, handing it over to Gabe. "You continue to betray me. I might be difficult, but at least I'm loyal. I was your friend, Celia. You never were mine."

She called my name as I turned away, but I didn't look back. There was no point in it. She had betrayed a Dallisor girl who no longer existed. Which meant from now on, she was nothing to me.

· FORTY-ONE ·

SIMON

Tenger and I made it into Silven just in time to observe Kestra's confrontation with Celia. As he helped me from the cart, he asked, "Is she always like this?"

My grin widened. "Actually, she's quieter than usual today."

Tenger's stare shifted to me, heavy enough that I felt it. When I turned, he said, "I didn't think it would happen to you, Hatch. Not with a Dallisor."

"That what would happen?"

"You're compromised. You have feelings for that girl."

There was no point in denying it. A blind man would've detected a connection between us. "I'm not compromised, Captain. I still believe in the plan."

"Believe in the plan from a distance. After tonight, you'll be reassigned."

I'd known this was coming, but hadn't decided what to do about it. Disobedience meant expulsion from the Coracks. But if I left Kestra now, they'd swallow her whole.

My only choice was to make her tell Tenger where she had hidden the dagger. And then maybe, if I was lucky, I could persuade Tenger to let me find Gerald and retrieve it. Hopefully, before Endrick got to him.

Once it became clear that Kestra wasn't going to harm Celia, Tenger muttered that Celia had probably deserved worse and told me to bring Kestra to meet with him under the bookshop.

I wasn't sure what Kestra had said, but Celia was still standing when Kestra and Gabe walked away, so I took that as a good sign. Celia remained exactly where Kestra had left her, ashen-faced and frozen in place, which Kestra couldn't have seen, but I was sure she could sense it.

She reached my side and smiled. "I feel better."

"We need to talk, alone."

Her smile fell, and she cast a cautious eye at Gabe. He'd obviously been assigned to monitor us because he stayed on our heels, entering the same bookshop where Tenger had gone. The owner wasn't Corack, but he was sympathetic to our cause and could be trusted.

"Corack tunnels run beneath most of Silven," I explained to Kestra. "This bookshop accesses a secret room downstairs."

"Below a bookshop?" she coolly replied. "I didn't know Coracks could read."

"We can read. Or . . . most of us can. Careful with the insults, Kes, I'm a Corack too."

"Yes, you are." She stopped and this time her eyes turned on me like a whip. "And I am not."

Maybe she could be, if she'd just tell the truth about the dagger. It was a secret she was willfully keeping because no matter what her feelings were for Simon Hatch, the boy, she still did not trust Simon, the Corack.

I glanced at Gabe, who was standing closer to us than he needed to be. "Give us a minute alone."

"I'm supposed to bring you directly to Tenger."

I cocked my head. "Tell him I overpowered you on the way inside. There was nothing you could do to stop me."

Gabe chuckled. "Not even on your best day, Hatch." But he did leave.

When he'd gone, I led Kestra down a row of thick books that reminded me of the hedge path where Basil had spoken to her last night. From the spark in Kestra's eyes, she might've been drawing the same comparison. I wondered again what had happened between her and Basil. Was that something else standing between us?

She folded her arms against a rigid body, displaying stubbornness at the worst possible time. Tenger had led the Coracks for the seven years of our existence. Time after time, we had outsmarted the Dominion, outmatched forces with twenty times our numbers, and survived despite being targeted for annihilation. Credit for all of that went to the captain. Kestra would not win at this meeting.

"We don't have much time," I began. "You said you have a plan for the Olden Blade. I want to hear it."

"What I said is that the plan is my secret, and it will stay that way until Darrow is returned to me."

She was maddening, deliberately so. "You trusted Gerald with the plan, but not me?"

"Gerald only knows what little I had to tell him."

"Such as where to hide the most valuable weapon in Antora?"

"Hush!" She shifted her weight to the other foot, clearly irritated. "If you knew my plan, what would you do?"

"I would tell Tenger, so we could find Gerald and get that dagger back." Before she could object, I added, "The Dominion will already be after Gerald for escaping the dungeons. And now he's carrying the one object Endrick desires most. That's your doing, Kes."

She licked her lips and looked away. This was clearly something she had not considered.

"Talk to me." I was almost begging now. "Any Infidante is better than losing the dagger again."

"Now who's naïve?" she asked. "Do you think everyone who might claim the Blade is the same quality warrior? If we want to see Endrick defeated, the Infidante must be the strongest possible choice!"

"But it's not your choice. The dagger will choose who it wants, no matter who tries to claim it."

"What if it's Tenger?"

"If it is, I'll support him. I don't always agree with his methods, but the Dominion fights in the mud. If we intend to fight back, we have to get dirty."

The muscles on her face tightened. Through gritted teeth, she said, "That's why Darrow should bear the Blade. He won't compromise right and wrong to win."

What a convenient answer that was, to have the luxury of cheering for a battle from the sidelines. "Tell me this much. Do you know where Gerald is now?"

A beat passed. "I can't tell you that."

"Are you sure he can keep the Blade safe?"

"Are you sure Tenger could?"

Another minute of this and my brain would split apart. I took a deep breath. It didn't help. "If Tenger agrees to release Darrow, can you get the Olden Blade back again?"

Her eyes softened. "Stop asking questions you know I won't answer. Don't make me keep refusing you."

"Kes—"

"A few nights ago, Tenger threatened me. Now it's my turn. If Darrow isn't released tonight, there will be no Infidante. I'll disappear by morning and take my secrets with me."

"If you disappear tonight, it's because Tenger doesn't accept threats! You must know what he will do to you!"

"Then he'll lose any chance to get the Blade!"

Gabe poked his head around the corner. "Time to go." Kestra started forward, but he put out an arm to block her. "You made it hard for me to eavesdrop, Miss Dallisor, but I have some idea of what's going on. You should know that Coracks never play fair. Our only chance at winning is to cheat, and Tenger is a master at it."

She only stared forward until he gave up and told us to follow him downstairs. With my injured ribs and a pit in my stomach the size of a boulder, I lagged behind. By the time I got there, Kestra was seated at a large table across from Tenger and Trina. Gabe stood against the wall and caught my eye, subtly gesturing to the lever blade at his side. Tenger must have just given it to him. Surely Kestra noticed it too.

Once I took my seat, a meal was brought in, some flatbread and boiled rabbit and a sheep's milk cheese made in Silven. As was always true for us, the food was simple, nothing to draw any attention to itself, but I dug into the food with enthusiasm. Kestra was eating too, though with measured bites. She wouldn't give Tenger an edge by letting him think she needed anything.

We weren't far into the meal when Tenger reached beneath the table with the hand that wore the grip glove, and put the fake dagger on the table. He was sending Kestra two strong messages: This dagger could be touched, and there would be consequences if she couldn't explain where the real dagger was.

The first bead of sweat broke out on my brow.

"I'm curious," Tenger began. "How did you know this was the Olden Blade when you found it?"

I set down my fork. One sentence into the meal and Tenger had already killed my appetite.

Kestra mostly ignored the captain. She took a forkful of food as she said, "After seventeen years, any other blade would've rusted in that pit."

"True, *if* this one had been down there that long. But what if this had only been in that mud for a few minutes?"

Kestra remained calm, though I caught the flutter of her lashes. "I know why you're suspicious. You expected it to light up for you, or whatever fool you hoped would become the Infidante. Since it didn't, you accuse me of tricking you."

Tenger's smile darkened. I'd seen this expression on his face before, and it wasn't good.

"Perhaps you can explain this." Tenger turned the Blade over and pointed to the handle. "The name Dallisor is carved here, in very small print. A person could miss it if they were not studying every detail of the Blade as intently as I did."

Kestra didn't blink, though it was obvious she had made a serious error. "If Risha chose to honor her captors, who are we to question it?"

Tenger threw the dagger into the corner of the room, letting it clatter onto the ground. "Where is the Olden Blade?" It was a demand, not a question.

She responded just as fiercely. "Where is Darrow?"

"*If* she knew about the Blade, I'm sure she would tell us," I said meaningfully. When her only response was to take another bite of food, I added, "Kestra and I searched Risha's cell together. It wasn't there."

"Then you looked in the wrong place!" Tenger turned to Kestra. "You must go back to Woodcourt and search until it's found."

Now she dropped her fork. "You can't be serious. After all I've done, all you forced me to do, you know very well I can never return there!"

"You're a Dallisor. They'll take you in before admitting that one of their own blood could betray them."

"That's the whole point—" I began.

She quickly interrupted. "The point is that even if they do accept me, I was supposed to marry tonight. If I go home, those plans will immediately resume. I won't be at Woodcourt long enough to find the Blade."

"What are your choices?" Tenger asked. "You have no means to survive on your own, and no Antoran will accept you. I'm your only protection, and to get it, you'll do as I say."

She arched her neck in defiance. "Or I'll leave Antora."

Trina snorted. "What country would take you in, risking Endrick's wrath?"

No one would. Not for any price. Kestra knew this better than anyone.

But she didn't show it. Her brow was knit in concentration, as if trying to control her temper. "Wherever I go, it won't be in service to the Coracks."

"Then you failed to deliver on your agreement!" Tenger stood so quickly his chair fell to the floor behind him. His right hand widened, a quick test of the grip glove. "You know what that means!"

I knew. It would start with the grip glove and an absence of mercy. It would end with her death, or Darrow's. That explained Gabe's lever blade.

Beneath the table, my hand quietly shifted to my sword. Even if I had the strength to swing it, I still couldn't use it against my captain and friends. Nor could I let them harm Kestra. My heart pounded against what was left of my ribs, leaving my chest throbbing with pain.

"Kill me, and you'll lose your last chance to find the Olden Blade." Kestra raised her voice. "Heed my demands, and you might yet see it."

Tenger's tone darkened and he made a gesture toward Gabe, silently ordering him to pull out his weapon. "Heed *your* demands? No, my lady—"

"If you want the dagger, you will not threaten me."

"This is no idle threat, Kestra. This is real." Tenger flicked his eyes and Gabe stepped forward, the sharp tip of the lever blade facing her.

Tenger would say it was a shame, that he had given her the chance to save herself, that he'd had no other choice. He would say she was a necessary sacrifice. He would give the order.

I had to stop it.

"She didn't fail." I refused to look over at Kestra as I spoke. "She's hidden the Olden Blade out of reach of the Dallisors, and out of our reach if we harm her. Kestra knows where it is—only she knows."

Everyone turned to Kestra for a response. Except me. From the corner of my eye, I saw her hand on the table, clenching and unclenching.

"Is this true?" The fact that Tenger wasn't screaming was proof of miracles.

Kestra wasn't answering, and even if she tried, it'd likely be laced with curses at me. Let her be angry. I'd just saved her life.

Tenger quickly lost patience with her silence. With a snap of his fingers, Gabe disappeared through a different door in the room and returned a moment later half-carrying Darrow, who could not have stood otherwise. I gasped when I saw him. His cheeks were sunken in and his eyes, which bore evidence of laugh lines, had hollowed out. The wound had torn free from its cauterization and was covered in a bandage that had bled through. Why had they let him get this bad? Any respect Kestra might have had for the Coracks would be lost now.

"Kestra?" Darrow tried to say something more, but no sound escaped his lips. I doubted he had enough strength for it.

Her face tense with worry, Kestra started to get up, but I pulled her back into her chair, whispering, "Don't make this worse."

"You'd know all about making things worse," she snapped. Yet she remained in her seat, her eyes seeing nothing through her anger but Darrow.

A third person came through the door, our physician. Loelle had been with the Coracks since long before my time, and I knew almost nothing about her except that if you could get to her alive, no matter what condition you were in, she could probably heal you. Trina once told me that Loelle had some Endrean medicines, miraculous treatments that made cauterization powder seem like roadside dust. Now I wondered *why* she had these treatments. What if Kestra was not the only Endrean to have survived Endrick's wrath?

"This is Loelle," Tenger said to Kestra. "She's kept your servant alive until now, but what I order her to do next is entirely up to you. In Loelle's hand is the medicine Darrow needs to survive. If he gets it, by morning he will be healed and returned to your service, as promised. In Gabe's hand is a lever blade, capable of stopping Darrow's pain in an entirely different way. Who would you have me give orders to?"

Darrow shook his head at Kestra and mumbled, "Let me go. Don't trust them."

"Where is the Olden Blade?" Tenger asked. "Tell me before the count of three, or trust *me*, Darrow's fate will be decided. One—"

"Heal him first! Please!"

"Two—

"Don't do this!"

Tenger lifted his hand and pointed to Gabe, giving him the order. "You've disappointed me, my lady. Even worse, you disappointed Darrow here."

"I have disappointed him, but for different reasons than you think." Beneath the table, Kestra had already raised the skirts on one leg. She reached down and I heard the quiet snap of her garter against her thigh. Inwardly, I groaned. I'd forgotten about that.

She lifted an object wrapped in a thin cloth and set it on the table, unfolding the cloth enough to let everyone see what it was.

"The Olden Blade is here."

· FORTY-TWO ·

KESTRA

Everyone rose to their feet upon seeing the Olden Blade. It seemed a moment frozen in time, with no movement from anyone, other than turning to Tenger for further orders. I remained in my seat, drawing the rewrapped dagger closer to my body, preventing anyone from trying to take it. If I could touch it without being burned, I'd gladly introduce them to its point.

"Enough!" Tenger finally whispered, keeping his eye on the Blade. "Take your seats, all of you!"

I was still in my chair, but I was the only one. Gradually, everyone else returned to where they had been before, with one exception. Simon. When everyone else sat, he merely walked out the door, back up the stairs from where we had entered. I called his name, but the door had shut behind him. It was clear he wasn't coming back.

Well, maybe he shouldn't have revealed to Tenger that I knew where the Blade was. Tenger had been bluffing with the lever blade before, or . . . maybe he hadn't. Either way, Simon should have trusted me with my lie.

And maybe I should have trusted him with the truth.

For as far as he and I had come, nothing between us was so different from that night he attacked my carriage. He was a Corack.

I was his enemy.

"How long—" Trina's teeth were gritted together so tightly that I barely understood her. "How long have you had it?"

"I found it a few hours before we left Woodcourt, right before I was confined to my room."

"That's why you gave me the trousers to wear. You needed a dress."

"That's why a lot of things, Trina."

"You will give me that dagger," Tenger said.

"First you will give Darrow his medicine." When Tenger hesitated, I added, "You'll take the dagger from me anyway, so you have nothing to lose. But I do. Give him the medicine, I'll give you the weapon, and then you will all leave the room and let me talk to Darrow alone."

Tenger considered my offer with a raised brow, entertained by my boldness. After a long silence in which I was sure he would refuse me, he finally nodded permission at Loelle, who poured the vial of medicine into Darrow's mouth. I hoped what Tenger had said before was true, that this would heal Darrow by morning. Getting him back alive had always been most important. I had to remember that.

"Now the Olden Blade." Tenger held out his hand.

"One word of caution," I said. "If you try to touch it directly, it will burn the skin."

"I could do it," Trina said.

"If you wore gloves, maybe," Gabe put in.

"Yes, after pouring his life force into this dagger, I'm sure that Lord Endrick overlooked that tiny detail." I scowled. "Only a Halderian can touch the Blade, and only someone worthy of it can claim it."

Trina leaned forward. "Who would you consider worthy of the Blade? Someone like you? For a while, I thought we might become friends, that maybe you weren't the spoiled, selfish girl I had expected to meet. But I underestimated you. You are pure Dallisor, cold and calculating and with a soul more dead than the Ironhearts. You lied to us—you lied to *me*, despite knowing everything I risked to get that dagger! Never ask for my help again. Never ask me to care for you. Because if you do ask, I will turn my back and remember that you only think of yourself."

As recently as three days ago, I would have responded with every cruel thing I could think of to say, including an insult to her grandmother or a comment on the angle of her nose. Three days ago, I'd have made sure the last word was mine, as all Dallisors did.

Which was her point. My ears rang with her accusation, that I was pure Dallisor. I had been raised by them, my opinions and attitudes shaped by their prejudices and desire for power. Yet within my veins, I was Endrean, bearing the same blood as the wicked man to whom the Dallisors kneeled. Both in body and in spirit, I was irredeemable.

Which meant I could hardly deny Trina's accusations.

But Tenger felt differently. He stood, seeming to tower over her and intending it that way. "Kestra Dallisor is *not* our enemy, Trina. Obviously, there must be consequences for what she's done, but we want her on our side."

Trina might've missed her captain's meaning. "Consequences? I'll take that dagger from her, sir, and run her through with it!"

Which, I noted, was a fine reason *not* to give her the dagger.

I stood as well, putting the wrapped Blade behind me. To Tenger, I said, "You'd trust the Olden Blade to someone who hands out threats like sugared treats? This weapon will doom our country if mishandled. Do not trust this responsibility to her."

Tenger sighed, and nodded. At least we agreed on that. "Trina, you will leave us."

"But I—"

"You need rest. Now go."

Trina shot me a glare that could cut stone, and probably confirmed her accusations against me. I had gotten the last word, after all. With a pronounced frown at Tenger, she stomped up the stairs and left. A cold silence followed in her wake, none of us entirely sure what should happen next.

"Much of what she said about you was true," Tenger began.

"Much of what she said was not," I countered. "For example, I never wanted her for a friend."

A grin tugged at his mouth. "Join us, Kestra. It will take some time for us to trust each other, but you would be a valuable addition to the Coracks."

I looked over at Darrow, not at all subtly. "Let's make a bargain. Choose a Halderian who has the spirit and the skill to defeat Endrick. If it's someone I can support, then I will join the Coracks and help your Infidante succeed."

Tenger tilted his head. "My choice will succeed, I assure you. Give me the Blade."

His choice wasn't Darrow. Surely he meant himself. The thought that all of us might be forced to follow this man into battle turned my stomach.

"Darrow and I need a horse and wagon. Once he's in it and I'm in the driver's box, I will give you the Blade."

Tenger smiled and nodded at Gabe, who drew his lever blade again. "You must know you've lost any chance to set terms."

The exact reason for my anger with Simon. Before Gabe came any closer, I put the dagger down on the table, then pushed it across to Tenger. "The master of the Olden Blade bears a terrible responsibility. I hope you understand that. Now, Darrow and I need that wagon."

Tenger picked up the dagger inside its cloth, examined it, then when he was satisfied, he stood and said to Loelle, "Find Simon and tend to his injuries. Gabe, you wait outside the door to be sure she doesn't try escaping."

"No, I'm free to go!" I bit into the words. "You lied!"

"As did you, my dear." Tenger gave me a polite bow, an insult really, then followed Gabe out of the room. The instant he closed the door, I ran over to Darrow, falling on my knees beside him. Nothing in his appearance had changed from the last few minutes, but he did seem to be breathing easier. "The medicine, is it helping?"

"It will soon, Kestra. They haven't been unkind. At her request, Celia was assigned to watch over me, and to bring me anything I need. She should be here soon."

She probably would be, if I had not frightened her and accused her of so many foul things. I had a temper too.

"Why didn't you tell me, Darrow?" Tears welled in my eyes. "Why didn't you tell me I'm Endrean?"

A slight gasp escaped him, though this seemed to come from emotional rather than physical pain. His whole expression softened when he looked at me, an unspoken apology. "Tell you such a cruel thing? And describe how you'd be hated, and targeted by every clan in the country? How you'd be compared to Endrick as if you were anything like him? How could I do that?"

"What am I supposed to do now? I'll never kneel to Endrick again, but he's my blood, maybe the last of my blood. Do I help these people kill him?"

Darrow shook his head. "I must tell you—"

"Am I meant to develop magic? If so, is it true that it will corrupt me?"

"You must avoid magic at all costs." Darrow's eyes were open wide, and clearer than they had been before. "Endrick can sense magic. If he decides to come after you, no one will be able to protect you."

"Except the Infidante. I intend to help him go after Endrick instead. Darrow, I'll help you do that." He blinked hard, as if he'd heard me wrong. I touched his arm. "By tomorrow morning, you'll be well enough to travel. You must go back to the Halderians, to your people. Captain Tenger will offer them the Olden Blade. You need to claim it."

He shook his head. "I'm no one, Kestra. Only a servant."

"A servant who has more talent with a sword than anyone I've ever known. You have access to the Dallisors, and thus to Lord Endrick. And you have me. Once you become the Infidante, I will do everything I can to help you succeed. Please, Darrow, you must go to that ceremony."

Darrow closed his eyes. "For your sake, I will do it. But I must go alone. You are not safe among my people. Not unless—"

From out on the stairway where Gabe still waited, footsteps

pounded down toward us. Simon burst through the door, breathless and clutching his side. I guessed Loelle had started treating him, but she clearly hadn't finished. He crossed the room to me in three wide steps.

"That bump on the back of your neck, where Lord Endrick touched you. I need to see it."

I stood and pulled my hair over one shoulder. He whispered, "I'm sorry, this might hurt." And he pressed his thumb down on the bruise.

I gasped and reached up to my neck. He wasn't just pushing on the bruise, he was moving his thumb around it, each motion sending new sparks of pain through me.

"What are you doing to her?" Darrow attempted to sit up and failed. "Stop that."

Simon did stop, but his eyes were wild with fear. "We must leave immediately."

"Why? What's wrong?"

"Gabe's proximity alarms are going off." He grabbed my hand, taking me toward the doorway where Darrow had come in. Tunnels lay straight ahead but he was pulling me up a separate set of stairs, not even allowing me a chance to tell Darrow good-bye. "Do you trust me?"

"I'm furious with you!"

"Yes, but do you trust me?" He stopped on the stairs long enough to say, "The bruise on your neck is there because something is beneath the flesh, placed there by Lord Endrick. Tenger believes Lord Endrick has a kind of magic that allows him to track a person, to find them wherever they are."

"I'm being tracked?"

"If he finds you, he finds the heart of the rebellion. Tenger is getting as many people as he can out of Silven. We must get you out too. The Dominion armies are coming."

We weren't to the top of the stairs before an explosion outside shook the earth.

They were not *coming*. The Dominion armies were here.

· FORTY-THREE ·

KESTRA

I pulled against Simon's hand. "We have to go back for Darrow!"

He tugged in his direction. "As long as that tracker is in your neck, bringing Darrow with you is the worst thing we could do. Let's get as far from Silven as we can and hope to draw the armies away from him."

A cheerful thought. I would bring their armies to me.

We climbed a set of stairs, pushing up on a door built into the floor that took us into a humble family home with a cradle in the corner. Whoever lived here was probably on their way out of town already. Or, at least, I hoped they were. The Dominion would not spare them just because they had children.

We hurried out the door onto a road with hundreds of people who were already swarming southward. The armies must be coming from the north, where more explosions continued shaking the ground. Every boom surely represented deaths, of Coracks, their sympathizers, and far too many innocents who might never have guessed a rebellion was among them.

"I left a horse here." Simon looked up and down the road, his grip on my hand tightening. "It's gone. Wait here and hide."

"What about Darrow?"

"Someone else will come for him."

"I can help!"

He pushed me back into the gap between the home we had just come from and a neighboring building. "If you wanted to help, then you should have told me about the Olden Blade. Stay here and hide until I get back. Nothing gets easier if you're recognized."

I shook my head. "If you come back . . . with this tracker, if you're with me—"

Simon met my eyes. "I'm coming back, and we're getting out of here together. Wait here."

Before I could answer, he ran off, moving against the direction of the crowd. These people would never outrun the armies, not all of them. Not even most of them.

"They're getting closer!" a woman cried.

The screams of others not far ahead of the crowd confirmed that. To the north, more explosions rocked the town. The Coracks wouldn't plant ground mines here, so that was the Dominion armies at work. Black smoke rose in vast columns in the distance, thick and foul in its stench. I wondered if the Dominion was doing that as well, or if the Coracks had lit the fires to buy themselves extra time.

Where were the Coracks anyway? While growing up, I'd heard about their battles with Lord Endrick's forces. They weren't ones to run away, to hide.

They must be in the tunnels beneath the town.

As was Darrow. I had to give him time to escape.

My breaths came in bursts as I ran from the alley and climbed to the top of a broken wagon abandoned at the side of the road. I hesitated there, perfectly aware of the foolhardiness of calling attention my way. From here, I saw the chaos in the streets, heard the cries of the children being desperately hurried away, and choked on the bitter smell of smoke from the fires. Darrow never would have allowed me to take a risk like this. But he wasn't here to stop me, which was the point of climbing onto this wagon in the first place. I stood tall and shouted, "Don't run. There are more of us than them! Fight back!"

"And be slaughtered?" a woman shouted.

"If you are, then fall while facing your enemy, not cowering from him! If you can wield a weapon, whether it's a bow or sword, or a rock from beneath your feet, then wield it with pride. Fight!"

One such rock came hurtling through the air toward me, close enough that I had to duck to avoid it. "Then we fight against you, Kestra Dallisor!" someone yelled. "I know who you are. You would trick us into surrendering!"

Upon hearing my name, the crowd responded with stabbing glares, as if I had attacked the town. Or brought the attackers here. Did they know this was my fault?

I backed up, though on this wagon, there wasn't anywhere to go. "Will you be so foolish? To fight someone who has no weapon while those who do are bearing down upon you?"

"What weapon counters cannons and disk bows?" someone yelled. "What if they come on condor?"

If they did, Silven would be erased from Antora's map. I dreaded the thought of it.

Someone tossed a sword on the ground, near the wheels of the wagon. "If it's easy to challenge Lord Endrick, you do it!"

Challenging Lord Endrick. That was my role now. I was

Endrean, but not evil. A rebel, but not a Corack. Antoran, but a traitor. Whatever that made me, I intended to fight.

Hundreds of panicked people were filling the streets; it was so crowded that I had to push my way through them as I moved upstream with the sword in my hands. Less than a minute later, I encountered the first soldiers.

I knew how Endrick arranged his armies. He sent his weakest into battle first, expecting them to die but hoping they would force the enemy to reveal their strength. This first wave would all be Ironhearts, soldiers he considered expendable—tools more than living beings. They were dangerous because of their numbers, not their skills.

Darrow's training entered my mind. "Be aware of your surroundings, but focus only on the enemy closest to you."

So I did. I charged directly into the first soldier, a shorter boy who should've held a plow rather than a weapon, and stabbed him in the arm. He wasn't the first person I'd stabbed, or wanted to stab in the last few days. I would have to reevaluate my personal ethics on fighting . . . later. Directly behind me, a second soldier raised his arm, volunteering the weakest point of his uniform to my sword. A third man had initially passed me by, but returned when his companions fell. He was a bigger challenge, but everything Darrow had ever taught me came to my mind. Feint when they thrust. Parry every blow. Look for their pattern, because everyone fights with a pattern, and then use that against them. And if you want to be good, then be the exception and never fight with a pattern.

As soon as the third man fell, I waded farther upstream through the crowd, but now other Silvenians were fighting with me. The second group of soldiers we encountered was larger, and far more skilled. Some had the glazed look of Ironheart soldiers, but not all. Worse still, this group carried lever blades, larger and newer than Gabe's. I had to be careful.

So I attacked from behind, choosing my targets carefully. My biggest mistake cost me a scratch to one arm from a lever blade that its user separated too early. I answered with a stab wound of my own, one given with little mercy because the scratch was deep enough to scar, and I resented that. Two Silvenians beside me fell, dispatched by a large soldier who turned my way, only to be stabbed in the back by a Silvenian woman. These people were rallying to save their town, but where were the Coracks?

Coracks rarely fought in open battles. They didn't train that way, and the general belief was that they had neither the numbers nor the weapons to compete with Endrick if it came down to an open battle, as this one was.

But here, their homes and families were threatened, and, I assumed, the bulk of their weapons and storehouses. Surely they would not run and abandon all of that.

Simon wouldn't run, I knew that. But where was he?

And where was Darrow? Had he escaped that underground room? I needed to know for sure.

I began running back toward the bookshop, but as I did, a screech echoed overhead. Condors. By my count, at least ten of them.

The first bird flew low, creating a shadow that stretched as wide as the road. I shuddered, seeing a rider on its back, wearing Endrick's colors. Bringing Endrick's doom. As dangerous as the condors had been when Simon and I were forced to escape into the forest, it was their riders who had the power to destroy whole towns.

Condor riders placed small cannons onto the backs of their birds, capable of spitting out fire pellets like a hailstorm. Simon's sword could swat away the pellets that came from a revolver, but even a hundred swords couldn't counteract the scattershot from cannons. These cannons would have caused the explosion up the road, destroying buildings, flushing out all those in hiding. Killing those who could not leave.

Darrow.

If I had not yelled at Celia, she would have been with Darrow. She could have helped him escape. Why had I been so foul to her?

Another explosion shook the earth behind me. "Take cover!" I yelled to anyone within reach of my cry.

In addition to the cannons, each rider held a disk bow. To my horror, they were firing down black disks like flower petals at a wedding. Each disk greeted its victim with slashing wounds that left screams all around me, including one man who had been running at my side. That disk could have been meant for me.

Silver disks would have been bad enough. They had injured Darrow and killed the garrison who had been escorting me out of the Lava Fields. Silver disks were dangerous, but they weren't magic.

Dominion soldiers carried disks created by Lord Endrick, ones that showcased his cruelty. There were disks of many different colors, but black disks were among the worst. They brought instant death, no matter where the victim was hit. The other colors' effects had never been explained to me, and I didn't want to find out.

Suddenly, an explosion above sliced through the air and I

instinctively ducked, covering my head with my arms. Pieces of the wooden buildings flew apart, their planks bursting from within. The flying shrapnel hit at least one condor, felling it. Its rider was instantly attacked and his blades stolen by the Silvenians. When it was safer, I stood again, keeping my sword ready with one hand, but with the other, shielding my eyes to better see what had happened.

The explosion revealed an enormous series of small cannons on rotating platforms and at varying heights. Their operators, almost certainly Coracks, began firing at the condors, hoping to chase them away. The condors tried fighting back, but were repelled by the cannons. Never in my life had I seen such a thing, or even conceived of it.

The Coracks might prove effective against Endrick after all.

Then from the distance the sound of barking dogs could be heard, running toward us. More dogs than I could count ran into the battle, immediately attacking the legs of the soldiers, bringing them down and dragging them away. They left everyone else entirely alone.

About fifty or sixty Silvenians had joined me this far into battle, all of them standing by, watching the dogs, as I was doing. It was better to let the Coracks take over now.

I ran again, pushing through the crowd, retracing my steps toward the bookshop. The condors hadn't gotten this far south yet, and I hoped the Coracks would keep them busy where they were.

The fallen wagon where I had stood was just ahead, though someone had moved it to act as a sort of barricade where a group of children were hiding. No, that wouldn't be good enough.

"Run!" I called to them. "You must leave town."

The older ones took the younger children by the hand or in their arms. "Don't stop running until it's quiet," I told them. "Be brave."

And then I gave myself the same advice. The bookshop was just ahead. I harbored all my courage, or what was left of it, and tightened my grip on the sword. I had to get in and out before any condors came.

But as I ran, I heard a single screech overhead, piercing the air and sending a spike of fear through me. *Run faster*, I told myself. *Get to Darrow.*

I put a hand on the bookshop door, but as I did, a boom from cannon fire filled the air above me. Before I opened the door, the bookshop itself exploded. The blast threw me backward, almost to the middle of the road, the air bursting from my lungs.

Even as I lay there, reeling from disorientation, one thought broke through.

Darrow.

I screamed and flew to my feet, dizzy from shock and with my ears ringing like steeple bells. I wasn't steady, but at least I was moving.

The bookshop was gone, nothing more than strewn pieces of brick, long splinters of broken wood, and shards of glass. What didn't explode outward had collapsed into a deep hole in the ground where there had once been tunnels and a meeting room.

Where Darrow had been.

I stood there, suddenly frozen, incapable of movement, or rational thought, or of conceiving the faintest idea of what to do next. Should I wait here, or run? Or dig through the wreckage? Maybe Darrow was still alive.

But he couldn't be. Not unless he had already gotten out on his own. Like everyone else, he would've gone south.

The same rider that had just leveled the bookshop released another round of fire pellets farther down the road, exploding a second building there. Darrow couldn't have gone far enough on his own to escape this devastation.

I smelled fire. Smoke began rising from the bookshop, its immense heat licking my face and forcing me back. The flames seemed to be coming from below the wreckage. Fire was inside the tunnels, any that had not already collapsed.

And giant shadows crossed above me. More condors.

They had killed Darrow.

I couldn't breathe.

Silvenians ran past me, some of them urging me along with them, but I didn't move. I didn't care enough to try.

I had made myself a traitor. Abandoned my family name, and with it, every comfort, every security I'd ever known. All to save Darrow.

Somewhere behind me, a horse charged through the crowd. I squinted up and saw Simon there, offering me his hand. I only stared back at it. "Darrow's dead."

Another explosion behind us shook the earth, momentarily throwing me off balance. Simon's eyes flicked to what little remained of the bookshop, then he held out his hand again. "We've got to go, Kes."

"Did you hear me?" I screamed. "Darrow is dead!"

He dismounted, grabbed me by the waist, and pushed me onto the horse. When he climbed back into the saddle behind me, he put one arm around my waist and said, "I'm sorry, I really am. But if we don't leave, others will be mourning for us."

Somehow I held myself together as we rode alongside the fleeing Silvenians. Tears streamed down my face, and my chest filled with more pain than I'd thought any person could contain. I didn't understand how I was still able to breathe, and barely cared if I did. Through all of that, we kept riding.

Less than a mile later, Simon turned left at a crossroad, taking us toward some hills on the outskirts of the town.

Waiting for us there, also on horseback, were Tenger and Gabe. Trina was with them, but had an oropod with yellow-green markings that she must have taken from one of the Dominion soldiers. I was surprised that she knew how to approach such a creature without getting bitten, much less to ride one. I certainly didn't. Gabe had a deep cut on one arm, much worse than mine, but Trina and Tenger seemed to have escaped the worst of the battle. Were they good at fighting, I wondered, or better at hiding while their townspeople fought? While Darrow died.

"Let's take care of this," Tenger said, eyeing me. "Before she leads the armies to us as well."

Trina raised a knife. "She won't do that." A wicked gleam brightened her eyes. "Let's see if you trust me now."

· FORTY-FOUR ·

KESTRA

We rode into the hills until we were far enough from town that the battle noises became little more than an echo. How many deaths did each explosion represent? I couldn't help but wonder, and couldn't bear to think of the answer. A part of me remained in Silven, on that road in front of the bookshop. I never should've joined the fight. How arrogant that had been, to think I would make any difference. I should have gone directly into the bookshop to get Darrow.

Still behind me, Simon had a hand on my arm. I barely felt it. "Maybe he escaped."

Maybe. But it hurt too much to have hope.

The hills we were entering contained mostly grassland, dotted with trees as we rode higher. We dismounted behind the hills, where we'd have some privacy, at least until Endrick tracked me again.

"What'll happen to the people back in Silven?" Gabe asked Tenger.

The captain only shrugged. "I hope the Coracks we left behind can do enough damage to save as many people as possible. But it won't be pretty. That was a slaughter."

"It's her fault." Trina flung an accusing finger in my direction. "She brought them to us."

"She didn't know!" Simon said, crossing in front of me. "And she lost someone too."

Everyone in the group stopped to look at me, which I hated. In a gentle tone that actually sounded sincere, Trina said, "I'm sorry, Kestra. I really am."

Tenger added, "That was never the plan."

I didn't look at him, couldn't force myself to. Did it matter that Darrow's death was not in the plan?

Then Tenger continued, "We'll discuss this later, but for now, that tracker must come out. Trina, get your knife ready."

"No!" I grabbed Simon's wrist, holding it with an iron grip. I knew little about medicine, but Trina's knife was filthy. Using that to cut into my flesh couldn't be good. Of course, keeping the tracker in my neck was worse.

Tenger's voice was matter-of-fact. "If you won't cooperate, our alternative is to tie you to this tree and all ride away."

"Let us do this, please." Simon put his hand over mine, hoping I would trust his words. "There's no other choice. They'll already be tracking you to this spot. Tracking all of us."

This time, there was no demand in his eyes, only a pleading for me to listen to him, to believe him. I wiped my clammy hands on my skirts, mumbling, "Just do it!" The less time I had to think about it, the better.

We were near a large poplar tree that had partially fallen, its trunk suspended from the ground by other trees that blocked its path. Tenger directed me to kneel beside it and then to lean my forehead against the trunk so that my neck would be angled upward. Simon knelt on the opposite side of the tree and took my hands firmly in his. "I'll be with you the whole time," he said. "You'll get through this."

"Not if Trina does it," I said. "And not with that knife."

Gabe pulled another knife from his vest and held it out to Trina. I didn't know if it was cleaner than hers, but I was certain it could not be dirtier.

"Trina's the only one with any medical training," Simon said, keeping firm hold on my hands. "It has to be her."

"I'm cutting near the spine." At least Trina seemed to be taking this seriously, though that was hardly enough to give me confidence in her. "Hold still, Kestra, because one wrong move and you're either paralyzed or dead."

"Have you ever done this before?"

"I've seen it done."

"Are you serious?" I shook my head at Simon and tried pulling away. "This is madness!"

"Having a tracker in your neck is madness," Tenger said. "Now put your head down."

Gabe placed a stick between my teeth, and Tenger dumped something that smelled like alcohol over the back of my neck. My dress soaked up the extra liquid, leaving me with a cold chill that caused me to shiver. No, it wasn't the alcohol. I was too terrified to breathe.

"It's all right." Simon's voice was calm but his eyes spoke otherwise. "I'm here."

No part of this was all right. None of this was right at all. I felt the edge of the knife against my skin. It was sharp, but Trina's grip was sure. Whatever it meant for me, she knew exactly where she would start.

"Hold still," Trina said.

I screamed from the first cut, biting down on the stick to mute it, and Simon squeezed my hands tighter. A second cut followed, even deeper. Nausea enveloped me as lights flashed inside my tightly closed eyes.

"I see it!" Trina said. "It's the same ball used for Ironheart soldiers."

Gabe handed her something that she used to retrieve the tracker. That part was far more painful than the cut had been. My nails dug into Simon's hands and I couldn't feel him squeezing back anymore, though he must have been. Tenger poured more alcohol into the wound, which nearly made me leap from my skin. Gabe knelt beside me to steady my body's shaking.

Trina leaned down to show me the tracker, which I looked at but didn't really see. It struck me as similar to a small marble, but I wasn't focusing anymore.

"It's out," Trina said. "I've got to seal the wound."

"Gabe, go destroy the tracker." Tenger was already fading from my view. Everything was fading, nothing but gray corners moving inward. "I'll help with this."

I'd never know exactly what happened after that. Before I passed out, the last thing I heard was Simon telling me everything would be fine. Did I trust that?

I had to.

When I awoke, I was lying on some cut pine boughs, which I supposed were meant to be a sort of cushion while I slept. A cloak was spread out over me, one I'd never seen before. I vaguely wondered how long I'd been here. The sun had risen, and yet it didn't feel as if any time had passed.

Simon, Tenger, Trina, and Gabe weren't far off, but they were huddled close together in quiet conversation. With an unsteady hand, I felt around for the sword I had found in Silven. It was gone, which was no surprise. One of them would have taken it while I slept. Next, I felt the back of my neck. I had expected the bandage would encircle my neck entirely, but they had sealed it against my skin with some wax. Trina was the first to notice my movement.

"That's a Corack technique." Her smirk was triumphant. "As long as we keep the wound clean, if we seal it afterward, there's almost never any infection."

Then I remembered Darrow. And suddenly, I didn't much care whether I got an infection or not.

Simon walked toward me. "From what we can tell, most of Silven was destroyed, but the battle has ended. The soldiers have left. We're safe, for now."

"Where's the tracker?"

Gabe smiled, obviously proud of himself. "I couldn't break it, so I fixed it to a branch and sent it down river. The armies will be following that stick for miles."

Simon crouched beside me. "How do you feel?"

Even shrugging hurt. "Like someone who hates me just mined the back of my neck."

"You're welcome," Trina said. "If I wanted to kill you, I would have done it then. Remember that."

I remembered very little from last night, and far too much from before that. She and I would never be friends. "What happens now?"

"We took a heavy loss last night." Tenger had been tending to his golden leg, readjusting the strap where it was attached to his thigh. But he looked up. "I hate to say it, but the Coracks may need to join forces with the Halderians. We'll need their numbers to give our Infidante a chance of getting close to Endrick."

"The Halderians have been content to sit back while we fight the Dominion," Gabe said. "Why would they join us now?"

Tenger smiled at me, before I turned away in disgust. "Because we have the Olden Blade. We'll go down to the Hiplands today."

The Dominion knew that's where most of the Halderians had gone, but Endrick had been forced to ignore the Hiplands, in order to deal with the Coracks.

Simon said, "Gabe and Trina will go north and try to find any surviving Coracks to begin regrouping." His fingers interlocked with mine. "You and I will go with Tenger to the Hiplands."

"To the Halderians?" Irritated, I pulled my hand away. "Why not push me off a cliff now and save them the trouble?"

"Then you'll go north, as Trina's ransom against further Dominion attacks," Tenger said.

Another great plan. Tenger had treated me as ransom last night. How well had that worked out for him?

Simon nodded at the cloak covering me. "Trina grabbed that on her way out of Silven. When we reach the Halderians, keep the hood up. No one should notice you."

I hoped he was right. I didn't want to think of the Halderians as enemies—they were Darrow's people, and Gerald's. But I doubted they'd afford me the same courtesy. I would go to the Halderians long enough to see the new Infidante. Depending on who it was, I'd stay and fight, or get as far from this country as possible.

I briefly wondered if Simon would consider leaving Antora with me. Would his feelings be enough to make him turn his back on his oaths, on his future? Could he ever love me, without condition, without second-guessing the wisdom of giving his heart to an Endrean?

I wanted to ask, but if I did, I couldn't bear to hear him tell me no. So I wouldn't ask. I wouldn't allow myself to hope. If I left Antora, I'd go alone.

Gabe had found a few wild bilberries, which he shared with all of us, though there weren't nearly enough to go around. I wasn't hungry, but Simon forced me to eat them anyway, insisting I take his as well.

Tenger carried the Olden Blade wrapped in a cloth and tucked in his belt. I had already casually checked his palm for a burn, wondering if he had tried to claim the Blade, like me. There was no sign of a burn, so he must be waiting until the ceremony to make an official claim. If he had successfully claimed it, he would have told us.

Before mounting his horse, Tenger pulled me aside. His attitude seemed different than his usual arrogance. He made no attempt to intimidate or frighten me, yet he still carried the authority of the man in charge. "There are some things you must accept, Kestra. Thousands of Antorans have died since Endrick took power. Darrow's death is a cruel one to accept, but there will be more before we succeed."

"Could he have survived?"

After years involved with the rebellion, Tenger had probably hardened beyond such foolish hopes. "Believe it, if that helps you. But now that you're with us, you're going to see the true effects of war."

"I'm not with you." Did he really think I'd ever fall in line behind him? "I'll fight on my own, or leave on my own."

"Then you'll die on your own. I know you think of us as enemies. I'd think the very same way if our positions were reversed. And maybe we were enemies when this all began, but I hope that will change in time."

I snorted, privately wondering how much time would have to pass before it was safe to tell him about my Endrean mother. A thousand years, maybe more?

He continued, "If you are committed to bringing Lord Endrick down, as I am, then can we start there, as friends?"

"I agree that Endrick cannot be allowed to remain on the throne. But that does not make us friends."

"I'm sorry to hear it," he said, looking almost sincere. "Perhaps one day."

Perhaps when it rained oxen. Not a moment before.

When I didn't respond, Tenger took the reins of his horse and swung into the saddle. We bid farewell to Gabe and Trina, and then Simon helped me into the saddle of his horse. I sat sidesaddle until I could find more appropriate travel clothes. Simon's arms went around me to hold the reins, but really, he was holding me, not so different from when he'd comforted me in the dungeons.

Tenger took note of it, but said nothing, and I was grateful for the silence. I couldn't fight everything. It was enough to remember to keep breathing.

Tenger set out ahead of us, taking us down the rugged coastline, high above the foamy seawater and deeper into the rolling hills. Their luster of the warmer months had faded, but spring would brighten them again. I thought of the loss of Darrow and hoped better times would come again for me too.

"How long until we reach the Halderians?" I asked.

"It's another two hours until we reach the Mistriver," Tenger said. "We'll follow that south and hopefully get there by nightfall. I don't like the idea of us out in the open overnight."

I didn't like that idea either. Near the Hiplands, few settlements existed where we might beg for food or lodging. Even if there were, we all had the look of vagabonds. We'd just have to push on and hope the Halderians welcomed us in.

Simon and Tenger would be greeted warmly, considering the gift they were bringing. I'd be grateful for anything kinder than open knives in the hands of those who reached out to welcome me.

Simon gradually put more distance between us and Tenger. When we were out of earshot, and he drew in a breath to speak, I jumped in first. An argument was coming. I intended to settle it in my favor.

"I told you I'd hidden the Olden Blade. It shouldn't matter where I hid it."

"You know it matters."

"Keeping that secret had nothing to do with my trust in you."

He scoffed. "Didn't it?"

"If you knew that I had the Blade, you'd tell Tenger. Not to hurt me, but to protect me." He started to answer, and I quickly added, "You proved me right on that. Last night, you revealed everything I'd told you about the dagger."

"Which saved your life!"

"That's my point!"

"What point? That you'd be better off dead?" He snorted with anger. "Because that was going to happen." A long silence passed before he spoke again. "Is there anything else you aren't telling me? Any secret, even if it's small?"

I countered, "Is there anything *you* haven't told me?"

A beat passed. "No."

"That's not true, Simon."

Every part of his face fell. "I'm going to be reassigned. The only reason I'm still here is because we lost so many Coracks last night. After we give the Blade to the Halderians, I'm supposed to join the Coracks up north . . . without you."

A pit formed in my stomach. "Tenger's separating us?"

"He knows why I want to be with you, and that it has nothing to do with the Olden Blade."

More silence followed. I understood those reasons, I shared in them. But that wasn't his secret.

"Are you going to obey Tenger?" I asked. "Go north?"

"What do you want me to do, Kes? Because I genuinely don't know." He shrugged, hopeless and empty. "Should I beg you to stay? Threaten you again?" He drew in a deeper breath, one that seemed to cause him pain. "Or let you go?"

"None of that." I lifted my hand to his cheek, borrowing his attention from the road ahead. "I want to see my reflection in your eyes again. I want you to fight with me when I'm wrong, and give in when I'm right. I want your courage, your compassion. Your smile." I took one of his hands that held the reins and wove my fingers in with his. "And I want a chance to end that kiss differently."

A shy smile tugged at his mouth. His lips brushed against the side of my neck, leaving a memory there. Now his smile widened, as if nothing existed in the world but us. His arm curled tighter around my waist, and I let myself fold into him. A chilly morning breeze washed over us, but I barely felt it. I was with Simon. I had all the warmth I needed.

"If you ride any slower, we won't be there until winter!" Tenger called. "Hurry!"

Simon chuckled and nudged the horse until it picked up the pace. Tenger had stopped to wait for us, but when he saw us coming again, he returned to the trail.

We passed no other travelers on the way to the Halderians, and any homes we came across had long been abandoned, now little more than shells of forgotten lives. I wondered about the families who had lived here, and what chased them away. Was this the consequence of war, or its aftermath under Endrick's reign?

"What are your plans?" Simon asked as if reading my thoughts. "Still leaving Antora?"

"I'll go to the Halderians, for now."

He said nothing, but a smile brightened his eyes when he looked at me. He believed I was staying because of him, and maybe I was, but there was more to it.

After being part of the Dominion for so long, stained by their spoils of war, I owed something more to my country than simply abandoning it. Repairing some of the damage could become my redemption. And maybe proof of the goodness of at least one Endrean.

Not far ahead of us, Tenger steered us off the road toward the Hiplands. He looked back long enough to assure himself we were still following, and politely nodded at me before turning around again.

What if I accepted Tenger's invitation to join the Coracks? Despite her bloodlines, Trina had joined. Would it be any worse for me?

I laughed to myself. That'd be like asking if a blizzard was worse than a single snowflake. I was Endrean. I was the enemy.

"The Halderians will offer a feast in gratitude for bringing the Olden Blade," Tenger said. "But I'll insist we go directly to the ceremony."

"The Blade can't be claimed until the ceremony?" Simon asked.

Tenger shrugged. "According to Halderian beliefs, that's when the Infidante becomes official. And after it's over, then we'll tell them what we're offering."

"Do you really think they'll unite with the Coracks?" I asked.

"They will, if they believe it's a chance to return to power. The Olden Blade will be claimed tonight." Tenger grinned over at me. "Maybe by a Halderian from their clan, or maybe the Coracks have a Halderian among us."

I changed my mind. Again. I could never take orders from Tenger.

Simon continued, "Whoever it is, we must agree to support them, because without that dagger, we will all fail."

"We need an Infidante to win," I said, "but it's no guarantee either. There are still a thousand ways we can lose."

Tenger patted the wrapped Olden Blade at his side. "Whatever happens, tonight we will change the course of Antora's future. After tonight, the real rebellion will begin."

Yes, that was exactly my worry.

· FORTY-FIVE ·

KESTRA

The Dominion knew the Halderians had begun to gather in the southern Hiplands, but Endrick still believed this was a broken clan, never to rise again. Life in the Hiplands was considered unsustainable due to the acidic soils, salty waters, and inedible vegetation. From what I'd overheard of Sir Henry's conversations on the matter, they figured the Halderians had either all died out by now, or soon would.

How wrong they were.

Earlier on the trail, Tenger had told us the Halderians called their village Nessel, and had warned us not to expect much. He was wrong too. The instant we passed through the town gates, a blossom unfolded before us. This was no mere village. The Halderians were doing more than gathering. They were resurrecting themselves.

"I heard they were trying to set up trade agreements with Reddengrad," Tenger mused. "They must have succeeded."

"I'll say." Simon poked my arm. "Maybe you should've married Sir Basil. He's probably very wealthy."

"As he told me, several times," I replied.

Though Basil must have been sincere, because if Reddengrad

had this much to offer Nessel, I could imagine what the country itself was like. In a brief survey of the town, we saw finely woven curtains hanging in every window. Shops full of goods lined the small market square, and at the sides of the road, wagons were ready to be loaded, I assumed for more trading in the coming days.

"Was this where they brought you when you were kidnapped?" Simon quietly asked me.

"I never made it this far south. The place they took me was a temporary camp. A lot of tents." Still, I raised the hood on my cloak, and for the first time became grateful for the shabby dress from the wagon. No one would look twice at me.

"Why is it so quiet?" Tenger sat at full attention in his saddle. "Where is everyone?"

"Listen." Simon stopped our horse. Off in the distance, a voice could be heard, though we were too far to hear any words.

"A meeting?" That's what it sounded like. A swell of worry rose in my chest, remembering every minute of my time with the Halderians before. Why had I thought it was safe to come here? As if they'd forget what they'd done to me, how they'd failed? Simon sensed my fear, and wrapped an arm tighter around my waist, a reassurance I very much needed.

"They must have known we were coming." Tenger untied the satchel holding the Olden Blade and we all dismounted. "They're expecting us."

The meeting was being held at the edge of town, in a field surrounded by a waist-high stone wall, and dug down at a gentle angle to create an amphitheater. The townspeople sat hip-to-hip on the hillside grass, facing the staging area at the bottom. I recognized the voice of the speaker. It was Thorne, the man who had been involved in my kidnapping, and the attack at the inn.

Darrow trusted him, I reminded myself, and hoped Darrow had not been hallucinating with pain at the time he told me so.

"My friends," Thorne was saying, "we have gathered you from throughout Antora because there is strength in numbers. There is no better time to act, to claim the heritage of power. The Halderians have never been cowards, never ones to hide and accept our fate. Our time to rule Antora has come again!"

Enthusiastic cheers rose from the audience. Several people here surely remembered the glory of ruling from the Scarlet Throne, when they were the beacon of Antora. They had hidden in the shadows long enough.

"Before we commence, let's have a song. The Halderian anthem."

It began as a somber, serious tune, one I'd never heard before. Of course, it was rare to hear any music at all in Antora, so I wasn't sure how to react. But I liked it. I longed to be part of it.

As the anthem rose in spirit, we felt ourselves pulled in closer, until Simon and I were standing behind the stone wall, with Tenger keeping watch a little farther off. Several other Halderians were crowded in front of us, making it impossible to see.

"What are you doing?" Simon asked.

I put a hand on his shoulder, using him as a brace for balance as I climbed the stone wall and stood on the top of it. Now I could see. Or be seen. I had to be careful.

Thorne was alone on the stage, and as I studied the intentness with which the other Halderians were following his lead, I realized they held him in great esteem. If only they had cared this much when he tried to tell them I was not to be harmed or threatened. Things might have turned out very differently.

The anthem ended with cheers and applause. As it did, Thorne's eyes grazed over the crowd, ending with me. Even with my hood on, he nodded in recognition and started to speak again, but all I heard was a thud behind me and a body falling to the ground.

I turned to see Simon collapsed on the ground, unconscious. Kneeling beside him was Tenger, though he had a cut over one eye. What had happened?

Tenger pointed to his left, where a large crowd of townspeople were in a densely packed clump. "The attacker ran that way!"

"Who was it?"

"I don't know—a spy maybe? Someone grabbed me from behind, trying to get the Blade. Simon stopped him but took a hit."

Tenger reached for his knife to give chase, but I shook my head. If Tenger and I started a fight with one Halderian, we'd soon be fighting all of them. "Help me get Simon somewhere safe! Then we'll figure out what to do next." I pointed to a building across the road with a sign identifying it as a cobbler's shop. It would have to do.

Tenger tucked the wrapped Olden Blade in his belt and picked up Simon's arms while I took his legs. A fat lump was already forming on the side of his head. Someone clearly didn't like the idea of us arriving here with that dagger.

The cobbler's door was open and his shop was dark save only for the waning sunlight filtering in through a front window. The small room smelled strongly of leather, which was to be expected considering the number of shoes we saw.

"Let's lean him against the workbench." Tenger cocked his head toward the back of the room. "That'll make it easier to tend to his wound."

I agreed, and we set him down as gently as we could. While Tenger removed Simon's sword so he could sit comfortably, I tore the bottom of my skirts to get enough fabric to wrap his head. I set to work at that, listening to Tenger explore the rest of the shop, ensuring we were alone.

I wrapped the wound and tied the knot to the side of his head. "That should help, but there must be a physician in town who can examine him."

"We'll find one, after the ceremony is over."

I shook my head, brushing my fingers across Simon's cheek. "No, let's do it now. I'll go, if you stay and watch him."

Something sharp pressed against my back, possibly one of the cobbler's tools for cutting the leather for the shoes. It was there as a threat, confirmed by the coldness of Tenger's voice. "You made this too easy, my lady, coming in here."

I didn't move. "Simon is hurt!" Then I drew in a breath. "And you hurt him! Why?"

Tenger was his captain. Simon had sworn loyalty to Tenger and had followed every order he'd ever been given. In return, the captain had brought a rock down on his head.

"He'll be fine. Simon needed some sleep, and you need to get out of my way." Tenger tossed me some leather cord. "Tie his hands." He poked me in the back with the tool, prompting me to obey.

"You have the Olden Blade," I said. "Why is any of this necessary? Just claim it!"

Tenger chuckled. "I'm not one of them, my lady. If I were, trust me, this dagger would already be mine."

And if *I* were one, I'd have claimed it first. The burn on my palm proved the truth of that.

As I continued working on Simon's knots, he said, "None of this would've been necessary if you had joined the Coracks when I asked you to earlier."

I snorted. "Pledge loyalty to someone who attacks one of his own and then threatens my life?"

"Pledge loyalty to the group that will bring forth the Infidante! It isn't too late, Kestra. Swear fealty to us and you'll walk beside me to that ceremony."

"What about Simon?"

He shrugged. "Until I have your loyalty, I don't really have his. Your oath can save him too."

"My oath to whom?" I looked back at Tenger. "Who do you want to claim the dagger?"

He checked my knots. "Tighten them. I'm not stupid."

"Aren't you?" I asked, though I began tightening the knots anyway.

"The Infidante could only ever be one person," Tenger said. "The natural heir to Risha's dagger." When I finished with Simon's knots, he pulled out another length of leather cord. "Now, you lean against the workbench, right next to Simon. Put your hands around the bench leg. Do it, Kestra."

I did as he said, and when he began tying my wrists, I muttered, "Then who is Risha's heir?"

"Trina told me that you found the prophecy carved on the wall of cell number four."

"One to Vanquish, One to Rule, One to Fall, But All to Fool," I mumbled. "No doubt the last line is a reference to what a fool you are."

"You're half-correct." He smiled, entirely pleased with himself. "The last line does reference me, and how I've successfully fooled everyone. For I have secretly put the Olden Blade into the hands of Risha Halderian's daughter."

I froze. "Risha had a daughter?" I tried to pretend that I didn't care about the answer, and failed at that too. Because no matter how I wished otherwise, I already knew it. "Trina?"

"She is the natural heir to the Olden Blade." Tenger finished tying my hands. "There is no question of how the ceremony will end tonight."

Trina? The girl who had threatened me with nearly every breath she drew? The girl who raged at the loss of a meal, hid her emotions with all the subtlety of the noonday sun, and who listed as her chief personal concern the desire for acceptance? This was who he wanted to entrust with bringing down the Dominion? At her best, it might take Endrick a full minute to devour her.

He continued, "We rode slowly to give her time to arrive without your interference. The ceremony will begin as soon as I pass the Olden Blade to her. It will end with the precious dagger in the hands of a Corack."

I barely heard his words. If Trina was Risha's daughter, then she probably did have the greatest claim upon the Olden Blade. She would become the Infidante, the *One to Vanquish.*

"I know you don't like or trust her," Tenger said. "I know she has flaws, but as the child of Risha Halderian, she has a unique destiny. After tonight, she alone will have the ability to kill Lord Endrick."

Or to be killed by him. They might as well save time and give the Olden Blade to Endrick now.

"Others may come forward," I said. "The dagger may yet accept someone else as its master."

"No," Tenger said. "It will be Trina, or no one. That's my job."

"Is that your only job? What about the second line of the prophecy?"

He grinned, so arrogant I felt my fists curling. *"One to Rule?* Yes, that will be fulfilled tonight as well." With that, he picked up his knife again, a weapon I now understood he would use against any other Halderian who tried to claim the dagger, or the throne. He sheathed it, then added, "It's not too late to pledge loyalty to the Coracks . . . and to your future king."

By now, my temper was boiling. "Bow to a man whose leadership casts such an insignificant shadow? You insult the true king."

His smile turned false. "The true king is whoever Trina names tonight. And if you try to stop us, you will lose."

The last I saw of him was a stern frown that he must have hoped would make me cower, or beg for him to accept me. I kept my gaze at him steady, hoping he would see nothing in my expression.

Because if he did, he would probably do worse than tie me to this post. My heart was in turmoil, yet I was determined to keep fighting. This no longer had anything to do with the defeat of Lord Endrick. To save Antora, I had only one choice left. I had to stop the person meant to save Antora.

· FORTY-SIX ·

SIMON

"Simon!"

My eyes fluttered at the sound of my name, though I wished I hadn't heard. My head pounded fiercely, worse than when the Dominion soldiers had treated my body like a kickball. What had happened?

Through the fog that was currently serving as my memory, I vaguely recalled Tenger raising a rock. Was it to attack me, or protect me from an attack?

Someone jostled my leg and called my name again. That was Kestra.

"Ow," I moaned. "Really, you're kicking me?"

"I'm sorry. Tenger—"

"So it was him. But why?"

"Your captain is protecting his choice for the Blade: Risha's daughter."

That thought took some time to process, but once it did, my breath caught in my throat. "Tell me it's not—"

"Trina. When she said she wanted to get the dagger for Tenger, she meant it literally."

"And if she becomes the Infidante, she'll put Tenger on the Scarlet Throne."

"That can't happen, Simon. Trina has to be stopped before that ceremony begins."

Was someone playing drums with my head? It felt that way. "You tried to touch the Blade and it rejected you. Maybe the same thing will happen to her."

"I'm Endrean. She's Risha's daughter. Trina has a better chance than anyone in that crowd."

I'd already been working at my knots, and so had Kestra, but neither of us were making any progress. I looked around for anything within reach that might cut the leather cord, but my sword was far out of reach, and we had the unfortunate luck of being in the cleanest cobbler's shop in all of Antora. That figured.

"Were there any tools left out on the workbench?" I asked. "Anything sharp?"

"I don't know. I wasn't paying attention to the bench."

I twisted my body around until I could fold my legs beneath me, and then hunched my back to bump the bench up in the air. It barely rose, but came down heavy enough that a few tools bumped with it. Nothing dropped to the floor.

"That . . . wasn't fun." Something in my chest had just snapped, I was sure of it. Whatever Loelle had healed inside me was probably undone.

"Can you do it again? But keep it raised a little longer?"

"Do you know how heavy this bench is?"

"I'm not asking you to twirl it. Just keep it raised for three seconds."

I sighed. "I'll give you two."

By then, Kestra had scooted her hands as low to the ground as possible. When I raised the bench, she needed to swipe the leather cord beneath the bench leg. Two seconds. That was all I could do.

I drew in a deep breath, raised my legs higher than before, then lifted the bench with my back. It barely came off the ground, and even then I struggled with the weight.

"I got the cord beneath the leg, but it's pinched there," she said. "Higher!"

"You do it, then!" I grunted. But with one last effort, I raised it just enough that she could pull the cord free. I let the bench drop and then leaned back against the table leg, exhausted.

Somehow, my head hurt worse than before. The pounding had become an incessant rhythm at the base of my skull. I figured if I slept again now, I might never wake up.

Kestra stood and found a small round knife, one that might cut boot leather. She twisted it to the right angle behind her back to slice at the leather cord. Seconds later, she was free.

She knelt beside me and freed my arms, but I didn't move. "I can't go out there with you," I mumbled. "I'll slow you down."

"Will you be all right? I don't want to leave—"

"You have to stop them. I'll be fine. Just you . . . be careful."

She smiled and leaned in for a quick kiss, then stood again and ran out the door. She wasn't gone more than five seconds before I cursed and forced myself to stand. Of every girl in Antora, why did I have to be falling so hard for *her*? I could've found a nice farm girl who'd spend her days making meat pies and milking our cows. I could've even chosen a Corack, someone who'd fight beside me—not against me. Of anyone, why Kestra?

Once I stumbled outside, I started toward the amphitheater. The crowd there was growing, and I couldn't see Kestra anywhere.

Down on the stage, Thorne was finishing up his explanation for the ceremony's procedure. It wasn't complicated. Anyone who wanted a chance to claim the dagger would be invited forward. They would introduce themselves to the audience, prove their blood as a Halderian, and then Thorne would decide the order in which people could attempt to claim it.

"As you know, my friends, the Olden Blade has a will of its own," Thorne said. "I do not choose the Infidante, nor can the Infidante select himself. The Blade will reject or choose its master on its own, and we must all follow that choice into battle. If you cannot accept these terms, I ask you to remove yourself from this gathering."

Thorne waited, and I watched for anyone to leave, but no one did. They might later regret that decision if Trina became the Infidante.

Thorne cleared his throat, then continued, "Since the Halderians have no living ruler, the first duty of the Infidante will be to select our king or queen. The heavens will honor their choice!"

I fingered the sword at my side. Trina would choose Tenger as king. Was I prepared to attack my own captain, a man I still believed was the right person to lead the rebellion? I would have to, if it came to that.

"All who wish to be tested, prepare yourselves!"

The audience cheered and a couple of larger men in the audience loudly boasted that they would claim the dagger. I tried to spot Trina or Tenger, but couldn't see either of them. Wherever they were, I knew Trina would be biding her time. She believed she was the Infidante, and maybe she was.

And where was Kestra? I couldn't see her either and hoped she had avoided finding trouble in the few steps between the amphitheater and the cobbler's shop. Knowing her, that was unlikely.

Murmurs began to spread in the audience as various people pointed out their candidates. Thorne waved his arms for silence, then continued, "Tonight we raise our hopes in honor of the Infidante, and bend our knees to a ruler. Who will it be?"

Now I found Trina. She was seated in the front row with the wrapped Blade on her lap, sitting as tall as if she were already the Infidante. She was skilled with a dagger and had great courage, even if it was sometimes misplaced. If she was successful tonight, I would have to honor that choice. Kestra would feel differently.

Finally, Thorne said, "This much is certain: Once the Olden Blade has chosen, it will light up, identifying the Infidante. At that point, there will be no doubt that we have Risha's successor, and the person tasked with the responsibility of killing Lord Endrick. Before any candidates put yourselves forward, I ask you to consider the weight of what you must do. Holding the Olden Blade is no guarantee you will survive Lord Endrick or his cruelty—for all her courage and strength, Risha didn't. The Blade will not keep you from hardships and trials; if anything, that dagger will bring them to you. You will take up the dagger, not to gain glory and honor for yourself, for you will likely receive neither. Despite all this, you must carry forward. For if you do not succeed, no one else will."

Thorne waited for his words to sink in before his command rang through the air: "Bring forth the Olden Blade."

On that cue, Trina finally emerged from the center of the crowd. Standing tall and proud, she walked onto the stage, holding the wrapped Blade in sacred fashion. Sudden movement in the upper part of the audience caught my eye. Kestra, without her hood on. She was pushing forward to get to Trina, but it was too late. Yet I noticed the determined expression on her face. This wasn't over.

Thorne set the wrapped Blade on a small table, then gently unfolded the cloth. He crouched down to study the Blade, his brow furrowing as he studied every detail of it. He stretched out a hand, letting it hover over the weapon, and closed his eyes as if attempting to feel any heat coming from it.

When he was satisfied, Thorne stood and announced to the crowd, "This is the Olden Blade!"

Trina stepped in front of him. "And I will claim it!"

I immediately began pushing my way into the crowd. Trina could be allowed her chance at the dagger, along with the other candidates. But the Halderians had to believe this was a fair process. They'd never join us otherwise.

"She has brought us the Olden Blade." Thorne's smile was forced and nervous, and anyone could detect the reluctance in his voice. "This girl took the risk of bringing it here. We will give her the first chance to claim it."

I had become lost in a crowd of Halderians pressing closer to the stage. For that reason, I only caught occasional glimpses of Trina, though I did hear her clearly announce, "You should all know me. I was born in a Halderian camp shortly before my mother's arrest, and grew up among some of you. My name is—"

"You are Trina!" a woman shouted from the crowd. "You were

exiled from our people because of your Dominion father—he fought for Endrick!"

"Your father betrayed us!" a man shouted. "How dare a traitor's daughter attempt to claim that dagger?"

Trina's voice rose in pitch. "Because a traitor's wife first claimed it! Risha Halderian is my mother. In her honor, I have trained as a warrior; I understand the Endreans' dark powers and strategies. I will kill Lord Endrick, the last of the Endreans!"

Boos erupted from the audience, and someone threw a handful of rocks onto the stage. Trina dodged them and moved back, deeper onto the stage.

"You're a Corack," another man said. "You want to steal the throne that rightfully belongs to us!"

"I am a proud Corack," Trina said. "I've risked my life fighting Lord Endrick while you all hid away in the safety of this place. But I have never forgotten my Halderian blood."

"What of your Dominion blood?" another person shouted. "You can't be trusted any more than a Dallisor."

"A Dallisor is here tonight!" I followed the sound of Tenger's voice until I saw him in the audience with Kestra in his grip, her face pinched in anger. If Tenger tried something, I had no chance to get to her in time. A fine protector I was.

Tenger pushed Kestra forward through the audience, many of whom were already murmuring Kestra's name. She wasn't fighting him, and kept a clear focus on Trina. I understood now. She had wanted to be captured. She wanted to be taken to that stage, where she had access to Trina.

But her plan was going to backfire.

"That girl is no Dallisor!" a woman yelled. "I know the truth about her. This girl bears the blood of our enemy. She is Endrean!"

That clearly wasn't common knowledge. The initial uproar threatened to become a mob, with most people on their feet and directing their anger at either Kestra or Trina. She was standing tall, biting on one lip and looking around in case anyone tried to rush the stage.

Tenger stared at Kestra with his mouth hanging open, his face hardened with sudden coldness. Obviously, he had not known who Kestra was, but now that he knew, he must have been thinking of the Corack oath regarding Endreans.

"Kill the Endrean!" someone cried.

"No!" Thorne stepped to the center of the stage, waving his arms and trying to get their attention. "I tried to warn you three years ago. This girl will help us, as no one else can! We need her!"

But his voice was drowned out in the anger of the crowd. Tenger put a knife to Kestra's throat, weighing the choice of whether to heed the crowd's wishes before the ceremony or after.

Their chants rose in the air, until it was all I could hear. "Kill the Endrean. Kill the Endrean."

· FORTY-SEVEN ·

KESTRA

I t didn't matter how high I arched my neck, Tenger's blade dug in deeper with every move I made. His grip on my arm was so tight he had cut off any feeling there. I doubted he truly wanted to kill me, but he might, if the Halderians kept this up. For them, my very existence was an injustice that should have been corrected three years ago. If Tenger did as they wanted, he would cement the bond between these two groups. He knew that better than anyone.

Thorne wasn't far away, but he couldn't help me now any more than he did three years ago. Besides, he had a bigger problem: Trina and the Olden Blade.

She stood in front of the dagger, clearly furious at having the attention turned away from her. But she was going to change that.

"Wait, Captain," she said. "First let me claim the Olden Blade. Then I'll take care of Kestra, proving my loyalty to the Halderians."

Tenger's knife lightened against my throat, though he pushed me to my knees and pinched a hand onto my shoulder. "If I'd known who you are, Endrean, you never would have made it this far," he muttered.

Well, this was a relief. Trina would kill me instead, immediately after claiming the Blade, which she was unqualified to wield. At least

I wouldn't have to be around to see the havoc she would wreak on my country.

Antora was still my country, and I was amazed by the sudden realization that I wanted it to remain that way. Had I betrayed it? Or had my country betrayed me? Would I die here as an enemy of Antora, or a martyr for it?

Above the continuing chants for my death, Thorne tried again. "My people, stop this madness! Kestra is our last hope! She—"

"No, *I* am your hope!" Trina shouted. "I am the daughter of Risha Halderian, heir to the Olden Blade, and your Infidante! This is my moment!"

With Tenger's nod of approval, Trina returned her attention to the dagger. The unruly audience shifted their attention to her, eager to see her reach for it.

Before she touched it, Thorne shouted, "Wait!"

Trina froze, but did not lower her hand. "Why?"

"Something is wrong," he said. "In the presence of so many Halderians, the Blade should have a faint glow about it, in anticipation of being claimed."

Now Trina pulled her hand away. "This is the true Olden Blade; I swear it is."

"I believe you," Thorne said to Trina. "This fits the description of the Olden Blade, and its nicks and scratches match those that were on Risha's dagger when we last saw it. However, we are certain it should glow for the Infidante."

Tenger leaned forward, staring at the dagger as if silently commanding it to glow. I doubted he could stare hard enough for a blade of magic to care what he thought.

"Maybe she broke it," I mumbled.

"This girl is a fraud!" a woman shouted. "Trina Halderian is not worthy of the Olden Blade!"

"No!" she shouted. "I am the Infidante! I will prove it to you!"

She put her hand onto the dagger's handle, and although she pulled away at first, she gripped it again and her face immediately twisted into a grimace. I knew exactly how much it was hurting her, but she refused to let go. It was a warning: Release the handle or it would kill her.

"This is mine!" she shouted. She tried to lift the dagger, to hold it aloft as a victor might do, but the dagger refused to move from its place on the table. I brushed my fingers across my palm. The burn had faded a little but would never go away entirely.

And now the Blade was burning her too. It was rejecting her. How could she *not* be the Infidante, I wondered, considering who her mother was?

"Her traitor blood is killing her!" someone called from the audience.

"I claim this dagger!" Somehow still able to speak, Trina had fallen to her knees and lines of pain were etched across her face. "I thought . . . I don't understand . . ."

Simon leapt onto the stage, and gave me only a passing glance before turning his attention to Trina. "Let go!"

Behind me, Tenger said, "It might take time, Trina. Stay strong."

"It's working!" she cried. "I will succeed here!"

No, she would die here. Her face was becoming gray and the flesh sinking inward. Why wouldn't she just let go?

One to Fall.

Back in the dungeons, we had believed the third line of the prophecy represented Endrick, but that was wrong. It was speaking of Trina. If she didn't let go soon, she would die.

The crowd was becoming more alarmed—and furious—that she was refusing to release a weapon that clearly had rejected her. Down in the audience, I saw more than one sword come out.

Although, to be fair, those swords might've been for me. I was the enemy here, far more than she was.

Simon grabbed Trina from behind, but she squirmed free, preventing him from getting control of the Blade. He had to be careful, or the Blade would hurt him too. I doubted his body could take much more punishment.

Forgetting about me, Tenger dove into the fray between Simon and Trina. I immediately reached for a knife hidden against my thigh, one I'd stolen from a distracted man in the crowd before allowing Tenger to capture me. As soon as the knife was in my hand, I grabbed Tenger's good leg, stabbing him in the calf.

When Tenger rolled away, his hand on the injury, Simon wrapped his arm around Trina's shoulders. "Drop the Olden Blade!" he yelled. "Trina, for your own sake, drop it, or I will stop you!"

If she had been any stronger, I was sure she would have kept hold of the Blade, but by now, she couldn't help but release it. The instant she did, she fell to the ground, unconscious.

The Olden Blade clattered to the stage floor. Simon was behind it, near Trina. Thorne was beside them, and Tenger was on the far edge of the stage. Slowly, I rose to my feet. The audience had gone entirely silent. None of us knew what to do next.

One to Vanquish.

Trina and Tenger both believed those words had been carved into the dungeon wall by Risha, speaking about Trina. But they weren't.

Suddenly, everything made sense. My mother, the last fugitive Endrean, who had betrayed Lord Endrick and stolen the Olden Blade, had carved those words.

Anaya had not been Risha Halderian's servant. It was the other way around.

My mother had claimed the Olden Blade.

My mother had been the Infidante.

And when she had carved those words into the walls, it was never about her. She knew her fate. What if she had described the one person she would have thought about endlessly in her final days?

Her infant daughter.

Me.

This was impossible.

Above the roar of the audience, Thorne whispered in my ear, "There's a reason the Olden Blade didn't glow before. It's already been claimed."

I tried to protest, but immediately felt uncomfortable beneath Thorne's steady gaze. "It wasn't me. There was no glow when I touched it."

"But you did touch it?"

"It burned my hand. It rejected me."

Thorne took my hand, softly rubbing his thumb over the burn. "If the Olden Blade had rejected you, my lady, you'd be dead now. You claimed it."

"No. I'm Endrean. My mother—"

"Yes, child, but who's your father?"

In a rush, the answer came to me, filling me with instant warmth and understanding . . . and pain. Where Henry Dallisor had always resented me, threatened me, and tried to push me away, someone else had taught me, trained me, and kept me safe. Someone else had loved me as a father should, telling me exactly who he was without ever saying the words.

"Darrow," I whispered.

"You have a Halderian father, and an Endrean mother who gave her life to steal the Blade away from Lord Endrick. Why do you think I tried to bring you here three years ago? The Infidante never could have been anyone but you."

I shook my head, still unsure of what to say. "I don't want this."

"But will you accept it?"

Would I? Someone had to bring Lord Endrick down. Someone had to end the Dominion's harsh reign over Antora. I'd lost so much already just to get to this moment. What more would I lose before completing the heavy quest that lay ahead?

Everything. Before this was over, I risked losing everything. But that didn't mean I could walk away either.

I looked down at my palm, squeezed a tight fist, and then walked forward to pick up the Olden Blade. I grabbed it with confidence. This time, it would not reject me.

The Blade itself lit up like a sun, so bright that it hurt my eyes. There was no sting, no burn, only warmth that passed from the Blade into my arm, fusing itself into my very soul. Everything had gone silent around me—I was aware of that although I couldn't see anything but the Blade.

My Blade.

The Olden Blade was mine. I had claimed it.

With that awareness, I held the dagger high, clasping it with both hands. And I kept it there until the glow finally faded. Once it did, and my eyes adjusted so that I could see the townspeople again, I realized that every person in the area had risen to their feet, their right arms folded against their chest in my honor.

"You are the Infidante," Thorne whispered.

One to Vanquish, my mother had written. Not speaking of herself, for she would never return from the dungeons. Not speaking of Risha, who would go to the same doom. Not even Risha's daughter, no matter how much she desired this. Those were Anaya's words, carved into a dungeon wall, beneath a home that bowed to Lord Endrick himself. From the bowels of Antora's enemy would come the Infidante, destined to end the enemy's rule.

She meant me.

· FORTY-EIGHT ·

SIMON

I couldn't believe what I'd just seen, or didn't want to. As the glow faded, Kestra lowered the Olden Blade. Her eyes remained determinedly forward, her jaw set square and strong in defiance. Yet I'd seen her look afraid before, and no matter how hard she tried to hide it, she was. The Halderians stared back at her, equally uncertain. Moments ago, they had chanted for her death. Now she was the one person who might save them, who might return their people to power.

Her people.

Just as Lord Endrick and the Endreans were her people. Her own blood was about to go to war with itself.

Thorne walked forward. "You know your first duty, my lady. The people would have you select our next ruler."

One to Rule.

Near me, Tenger was nursing his wounds. He glared fiercely at Kestra, but she didn't seem to notice.

Trina was sprawled on the ground beside Tenger, unconscious. The surprise she'd have upon waking almost felt cruel.

Kestra turned back to me. I'd become disheveled in the fight, with one missing boot, and with my tunic untucked and covering the handle of my sword. In response to her silent question, I shook my head, as serious as I'd ever been. With a curt nod, she faced forward again.

"I will give my selection for the throne in my own time," she said.

"Very well, my lady." Thorne took her hand with the Blade and raised it high, then called out, "My people, heed your Infidante, chosen to save the kingdom of Antora and restore the Halderians to the Scarlet Throne."

The cheer that rose from the crowd was muted and cautious. Kestra might hold the blade, but they had not forgotten who she was. I started toward her, hoping that after the crowd settled, I could speak with her, explain myself.

But it was not to be. Thorne cut between us, deliberately. "My lady, you must come with me. I have a safe place where you can spend the night."

"A *safe* place?" I asked. This was the man responsible for her kidnapping, and we were supposed to trust him now? "If she's the Infidante—"

"She is, while she lives," Thorne said. "But my people will not trust an Endrean girl raised as a Dallisor. Some will believe that if they kill her, they can obtain the Olden Blade for themselves." He gestured to the audience, which was already murmuring her name, all of it unfriendly. "They will accept her in time, but not tonight."

"Not ever." Kestra bit her lip, raising barricades around herself again. At least this time, I understood. I couldn't imagine how it must feel to be given the quest of killing the last of your blood, to save a people who wanted you dead.

"Wherever she goes, I go." I pushed toward her, but again, Thorne held me back.

"We will take care of her," he said. "Kestra is no longer your responsibility."

And that was it. She didn't have the chance to say good-bye before she was whisked away, and then Tenger was at my side, ordering me to help get Trina to safety. I obeyed, but for Trina's sake, not the captain's. Even as I lifted Trina into my arms, my mind remained with Kestra, wondering what was happening to her. Holding on to Kestra felt like keeping a handful of smoke, almost impossible. But I had to try.

In only four days, she had gone from being the spoiled daughter of my enemy to being the sole hope of a clan we were forced into trusting. Worse still, she had taken on the task of killing an immortal ruler. How could she possibly succeed?

———

It was very early in the morning before I found her again. Kestra was saddling up a horse the Halderians must have given her, a brown courser with a thick black mane and strong build. It would serve her well.

Kestra was dressed differently now, with her hair washed and braided, and in much finer clothes than the rags she'd arrived in. She had riding breeches that fit her perfectly, worn with a thick and parted overskirt to keep her warm, with or without a cloak. It lacked the bright colors or patterns of the Dallisors, but the muted style seemed more in keeping with her sacred quest. A low-hanging belt on her waist provided a sheath for a simple sword on one side, and the Olden Blade on the other.

I barely dared to greet her again. She was the same girl who had captured my heart and occupied my mind. And yet, she was a sudden stranger. I didn't know what to do, or say, or what to expect.

She turned before I had to say anything, but her smile was cautious. "No bandage for your head?"

"I'm fine."

She parted my hair to see where Tenger had hit me with the rock, then lowered her hand, looking as awkward as I felt.

"I was worried," she whispered.

It wouldn't be anything compared to the way I was worried for her. How could I tell her that? Make her understand that I hadn't slept a minute last night, not knowing if she was safe.

Kestra brushed a hand over her horse's mane. "His name is Shadow. He's the best they have."

"Good." Talking to her was like swimming through mud. "Good, I suppose."

She smiled. "The Halderians are training tigers as replacements for their horses. They believe it's the best way to combat the Dominion's oropods in battle."

That got my interest. "Tigers? Seriously?"

"They're hoping this latest breed doesn't try eating their riders . . . again. I was offered one, but I told them I'd take a horse until they get the details worked out."

My grin widened, then quickly faded. "Darrow would be proud of you, Kes. Your *father* would be proud."

Her eyes darted, though they were clearer now. "Why didn't he say something? He had hundreds of chances."

I understood Darrow's reasons, though I doubted she ever

would. If Darrow had told her the truth, he would have obligated her to become the Infidante. He was trying to save her from . . . this.

She shrugged away her sorrow, for now. "How is Trina?"

"Tenger is taking her back to the Coracks. We hope that Loelle can prevent any permanent damage. Trina wants to talk to you."

"No, absolutely not."

"My lady?" Tenger had come up behind us, with Trina at his side. His calf was bandaged where Kestra had cut him last night. Trina's hands were bandaged too, and her face was ashen. But the biggest change about both was subtler. They seemed . . . humbled.

Kestra's eyes roved from Tenger to Trina without registering any particular expression on her face, and she remained silent.

Tenger took a cautious step forward. "If I had known who you were—who you are—I would have helped you claim the Blade."

Would he? I wasn't sure, and Kestra still hadn't responded.

Tenger continued, "I won't apologize for how things happened last night, but I am sorry again about your father. It was never our intention that Darrow should die."

In all my time with the Coracks, I'd never heard Tenger apologize for anything. He considered apologies a weakness, intolerable from a Corack. So if he was saying these things, then it was part of his calculation to get Kestra on his side. Which he absolutely needed now.

"But it was your intention to kill me." Kestra's tone was flat, as unemotional as her expression had been. "Both of you."

"Not me," Trina said. "I asked Captain Tenger to let me do it because my plan was to spare you."

Kestra didn't react to that, though I did believe Trina. If she had wanted to hurt Kestra, she'd had plenty of chances before last night.

Finally, Tenger bowed his head to her silence. "The Coracks are at your service, my lady. We remain devoted to the cause of ending Lord Endrick's reign. Simon, if you ever want to come back, we will have you." He gave me a meaningful look, then he and Trina left. At least he had meant what he'd always said, that he would serve the Infidante, no matter who it was.

Kestra immediately turned to me. "What did he mean, if you want to come back?"

"I left the Coracks." I kicked at the ground, a habit that was starting to wear holes in the toes of my boot. "I can't continue to follow Tenger, not after last night."

"What will you do now?"

"Help you, of course."

Her eyes softened. "That's not your role, Simon. We both know that."

I shook my head in anticipation of her accusation. "Whatever you're thinking—"

"Last night when you came onto the stage, your tunic covered the handle of your sword."

"It came untucked."

"Your wrapping around the sword's handle came loose too. Your tunic covered it . . . deliberately. Why did you cover it?"

I didn't want to discuss this, not now. Maybe not ever. "I'm not—"

"There are three people who are forever connected to the dungeons. All are referenced in the dungeon prophecy."

"One to Vanquish." Reaching out, I tucked a loose strand of hair

behind Kestra's ear. "That's you, born into the dungeons. The third line, *One to Fall*, was fulfilled by Trina last night when she failed to claim the Olden Blade. She lost her mother to the dungeons."

"And you were the first to escape them," she said. "*One to Rule*. Simon, that's you."

Worry seeped into my chest. "Don't choose me, Kes."

"I don't have to. You've already been chosen."

I refused to look at her, but couldn't suppress the stiff rise and fall of my shoulders. She wasn't guessing. Somehow she knew.

She continued, "The exiled ruler of the Halderians was King Gareth. After you escaped from the dungeons, a man you called Garr took you in, even adopted you as his own son. Before his death, he gave you everything he had: his home . . . his sword." Her eyes met mine, perfectly calm, fully in control. "His legacy."

"No, he didn't mean—"

"His ring is in your satchel—why else would I have traded away my mother's necklace for it? And that's why you have his sword, and why you hid it last night. Why don't you want the Halderians to know he anointed you as king?"

"I'm no king. Nor do I have a drop of Halderian blood!"

"And I am an Infidante with the blood of their enemy. When I complete my quest against Lord Endrick, I will name you king. You have some time to get ready, but not much. I intend to complete this as soon as possible."

Shaking off her threats to have me crowned, I stepped closer to her, cupping her cheek in my hand and wishing it could remain there forever. How could she not understand how little I cared for the throne, and how much I cared for her? She leaned into my touch, placing her own hand over mine. I said, "If you have a plan, let me help."

"I want that," she whispered, and her other hand wrapped around the back of my neck. "It's all I want. But I have to go alone."

My brows pressed together. "Go where?"

"If it works, this won't be as hard as anyone thinks."

I looked at her horse again, and then with a thud against my chest, I understood. I released her and backed away. "You're returning to the Dallisors? Tell me you're not!"

"Tenger was right! That's the only way to get close to Endrick."

"The last time you were close to him, he nearly killed you with a simple touch of his hand. And he inserted a tracker into your neck!"

"But I know about that . . . now."

"He has other powers. Powers you can't protect yourself from because you don't know what they are!"

"And he doesn't know who I am. I can still get close to him."

"And then what? That dagger will not protect you."

"No, but my wits can. The last they saw of me was when you led me out of the dungeons with a knife at my neck. I'll tell them you took me to the rebel camp."

"A camp where you attacked their soldiers."

"None of whom lived to report what I did. They don't know I have the Blade, or that I've been here. I'll be admitted back to Woodcourt again."

I huffed, feeling angrier than before. "Where you'll immediately be married off to that twit, Sir Basil!"

"I won't! I'm going to defy Henry Dallisor: disobey his

command to marry, and refuse to speak to anyone about it . . . except Lord Endrick himself."

I shook my head, wishing it were enough to make her understand how much she was risking. "No, Kes, don't do it this way. Even if you succeed, how would you escape Woodcourt again, all alone this time?"

"I've been alone there for my whole life. At least I know the truth now, which will help me get through this. And—"

"And if something goes wrong, I'll have no way of saving you." I lowered my voice, hoping she would hear the worry in it and at least pay attention to that. "I won't even know it's gone wrong until it's too late."

She closed the remaining gap between us. It wouldn't work. I wouldn't be distracted. "Then I'll have to make sure nothing goes wrong." Her fingers pushed through my hair and remained there, drawing me nearer to her.

I was suddenly very much distracted. My eyes flitted down to her smiling mouth, and there was practically no air between us. "Please don't go. Not alone."

"Find me when this is over," she whispered. "Promise that you will find me."

I leaned in and kissed her, letting the press of my hands on her back, the beat of my heart against hers, speak the words I lacked the courage to say. The second touch of our lips was deeper, so that I almost believed our souls had connected. Her kiss emptied me of all thoughts but a wish for the world around us to stop turning, for a miracle to let this moment last forever. Or even for a single minute.

Couldn't I have just one more minute with her in my arms? Because she was already fading away, and I couldn't hold her tight enough to change the inevitable.

Our final kiss ended too soon. Like a song cut off mid-note, a breath drawn in but not released. It was a start without a finish, but I would finish it . . . soon.

We parted with reluctance, and I whispered, "Come back soon. I am a protector with no one to protect."

"I'm going to save Antora," she said. "And then you will rule it."

"Only if you are at my side." I handed her the horse's reins. "I will see you again soon." And think of her unceasingly until then.

She climbed into Shadow's saddle, patted his neck, and said, "I will return, Simon."

Kestra rode away so suddenly that she couldn't have heard my final words. "No, my lady. I will follow."

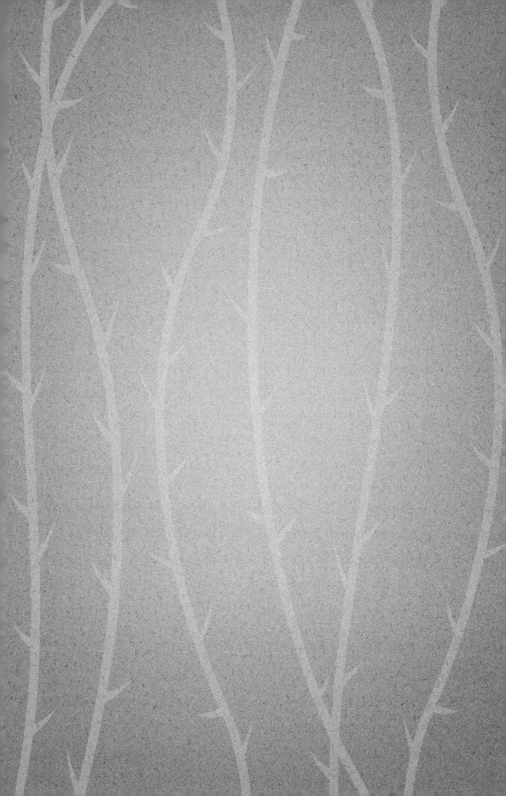

· ACKNOWLEDGMENTS ·

This book would never have been possible without the very significant contributions of my editor, Lisa Sandell, and agent, Ammi-Joan Paquette. From the early conceptual stages through the final edit, there is hardly a sentence that did not improve thanks to their attention, talent, and, most importantly, their dedication.

Thank you, Joan, for believing in me and encouraging me to take risks and to push myself. Lisa, thank you for seeing beyond who I am and finding ways to help me move closer to the writer I want to become.

I am also lucky to have a family who supports me through this crazy ride we're on. I could not do this without your support, your input, and your faith in me. To Jeff, thanks for understanding when it's four a.m. and a scene won't leave me alone. For filling in when I can't break away. And for enabling me with Mountain Dew. That is true love. To my children, nothing I'll ever accomplish as a writer could be greater than who each of you has become.

My gratitude extends to all those in the various divisions at Scholastic who have worked tirelessly to help this book go into the world. I cannot imagine a finer group of people with more passion for putting great books into the hands of young readers. It is an honor to associate with each of you.

Final thanks go to you, the reader. A character begins as an idea in the author's head, and is developed on the written page, but the character is not given life until you open the pages and walk into their story. As long as you are a reader, I will continue writing. Thank you, always and forever.

· ABOUT THE AUTHOR ·

JENNIFER A. NIELSEN is the acclaimed author of the *New York Times* and *USA Today* bestselling Ascendance Trilogy: *The False Prince, The Runaway King,* and *The Shadow Throne.* She also wrote the *New York Times* bestselling Mark of the Thief trilogy: *Mark of the Thief, Rise of the Wolf,* and *Wrath of the Storm;* the stand-alone fantasy *The Scourge;* the historical thriller *A Night Divided;* Book Two in the Horizon series, *Deadzone;* and Book Six of the Infinity Ring series, *Behind Enemy Lines.*

Jennifer collects old books, loves good theater, and thinks that a quiet afternoon in the mountains makes for a nearly perfect moment. She lives in northern Utah with her husband, their three children, and a perpetually muddy dog. You can visit her online at www.jennielsen.com.